GREEN LANTERN
Legacy

GREEN
Leg

LANTERN
acy

Minh Lê Author
Andie Tong Illustrator
Sarah Stern Colorist
Ariana Maher Letterer

JIM CHADWICK • LAUREN BISOM	Editors
STEVE COOK	Design Director – Books
MONIQUE NARBONETA	Publication Design

| BOB HARRAS | Senior VP – Editor-in-Chief, DC Comics |
| MICHELE R. WELLS | VP & Executive Editor, Young Reader |

DAN DiDIO	Publisher
JIM LEE	Publisher & Chief Creative Officer
BOBBIE CHASE	VP – New Publishing Initiatives & Talent Development
DON FALLETTI	VP – Manufacturing Operations & Workflow Management
LAWRENCE GANEM	VP – Talent Services
ALISON GILL	Senior VP – Manufacturing & Operations
HANK KANALZ	Senior VP – Publishing Strategy & Support Services
DAN MIRON	VP – Publishing Operations
NICK J. NAPOLITANO	VP – Manufacturing Administration & Design
NANCY SPEARS	VP – Sales

GREEN LANTERN: LEGACY

DC Comics, 2900 West Alameda Ave., Burbank, CA 91505
Printed by LSC Communications, Crawfordsville, IN, USA. 12/13/19. First printing.
ISBN: 978-1-4012-8355-1 • Junior Library Guild Edition ISBN: 978-1-77950-367-1

Library of Congress Cataloging-in-Publication Data

Names: Lê, Minh, 1979- author. | Tong, Andie, illustrator. | Stern, Sarah
(Colorist), colourist. | Maher, Ariana, letterer.
Title: Green Lantern : legacy / by Minh Lê ; illustrated by Andie Tong ;
colors by Sarah Stern ; letters by Ariana Maher.
Description: Burbank, CA : DC Zoom, [2020] | Audience: Ages 8-12 |
Audience: Grades 4-6 | Summary: When thirteen-year-old Tai Pham inherits
his grandmother's jade ring, he soon finds out he has been inducted into
a group of space cops knows as the Green Lanterns.
Identifiers: LCCN 2019040277 (print) | LCCN 2019040278 (ebook) | ISBN
9781401283551 (paperback)
Subjects: LCSH: Graphic novels. | CYAC: Graphic novels. | Inheritance and
succession--Fiction. | Superheroes--Fiction. | Ability--Fiction.
Classification: LCC PN6728.G74 L4 2020 (print) | LCC PN6728.G74 (ebook) |
DDC 741.5/973--dc23
LC record available at https://lccn.loc.gov/2019040277
LC ebook record available at https://lccn.loc.gov/2019040278

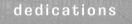

dedications

For my grandmothers and all the other real
superheroes in our lives.
—Minh Lê

For Zoe, Joshua, and Steph: couldn't have
done it without you guys. For being so wise,
reminding me every day to exercise. :]
Love youse.
—Andie Tong

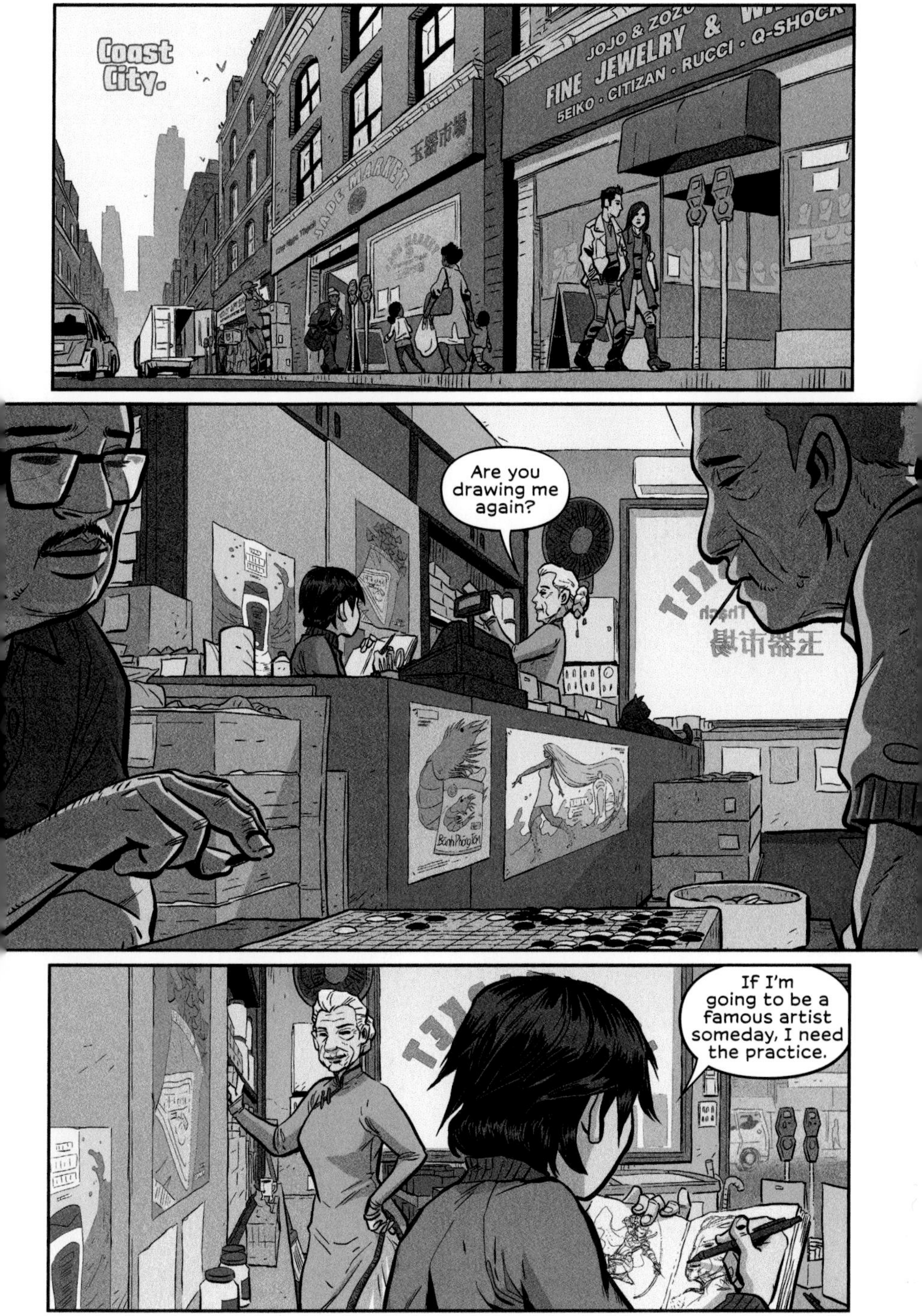
Coast City.
JOJO & ZOZO
FINE JEWELRY &
5EIKO · CITIZAN · RUCCI · Q-SHOCK
JADE MARKET
玉器市場
Are you drawing me again?
If I'm going to be a famous artist someday, I need the practice.

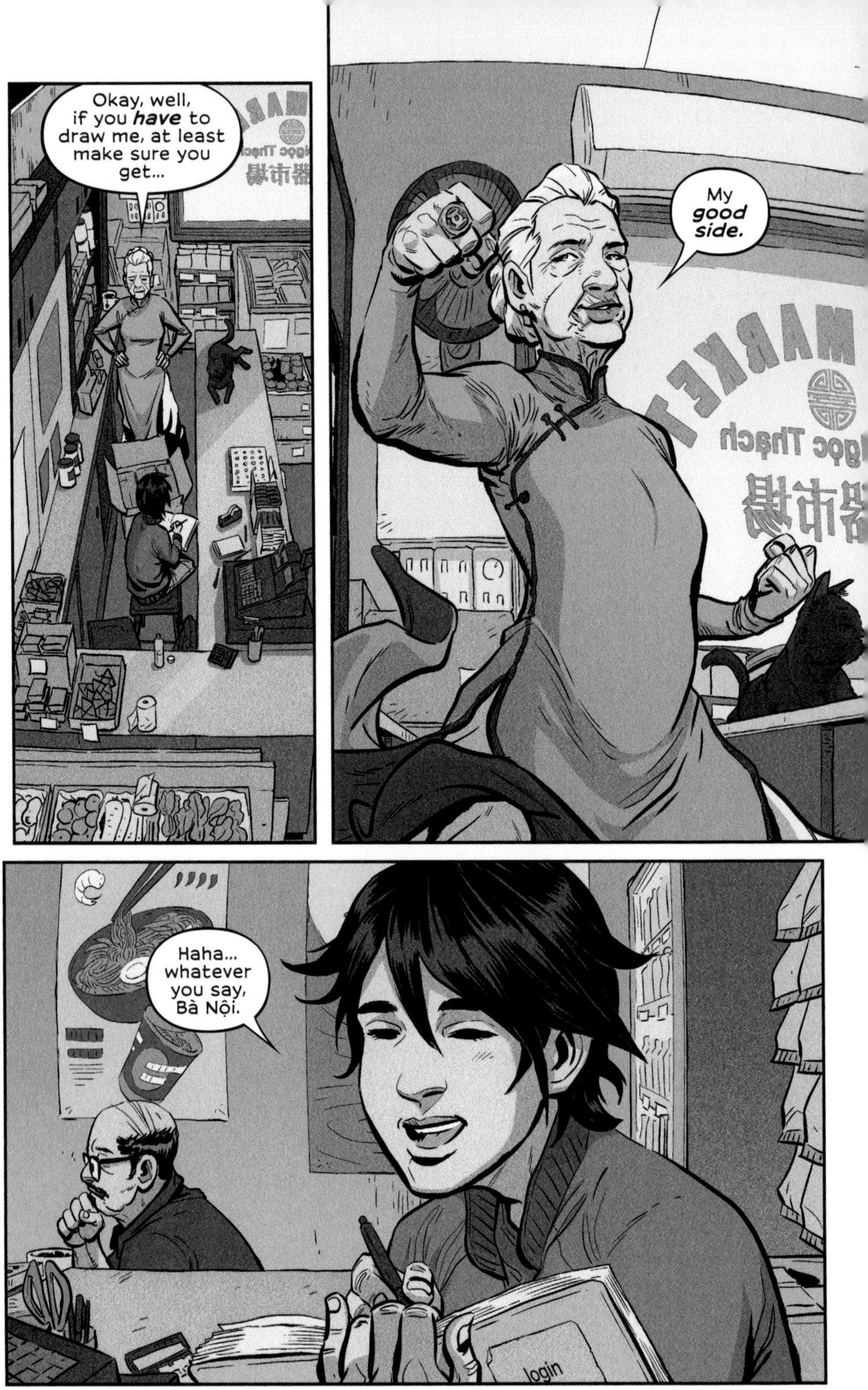
Okay, well, if you have to draw me, at least make sure you get...
My good side.
Haha... whatever you say, Bà Nội.
login

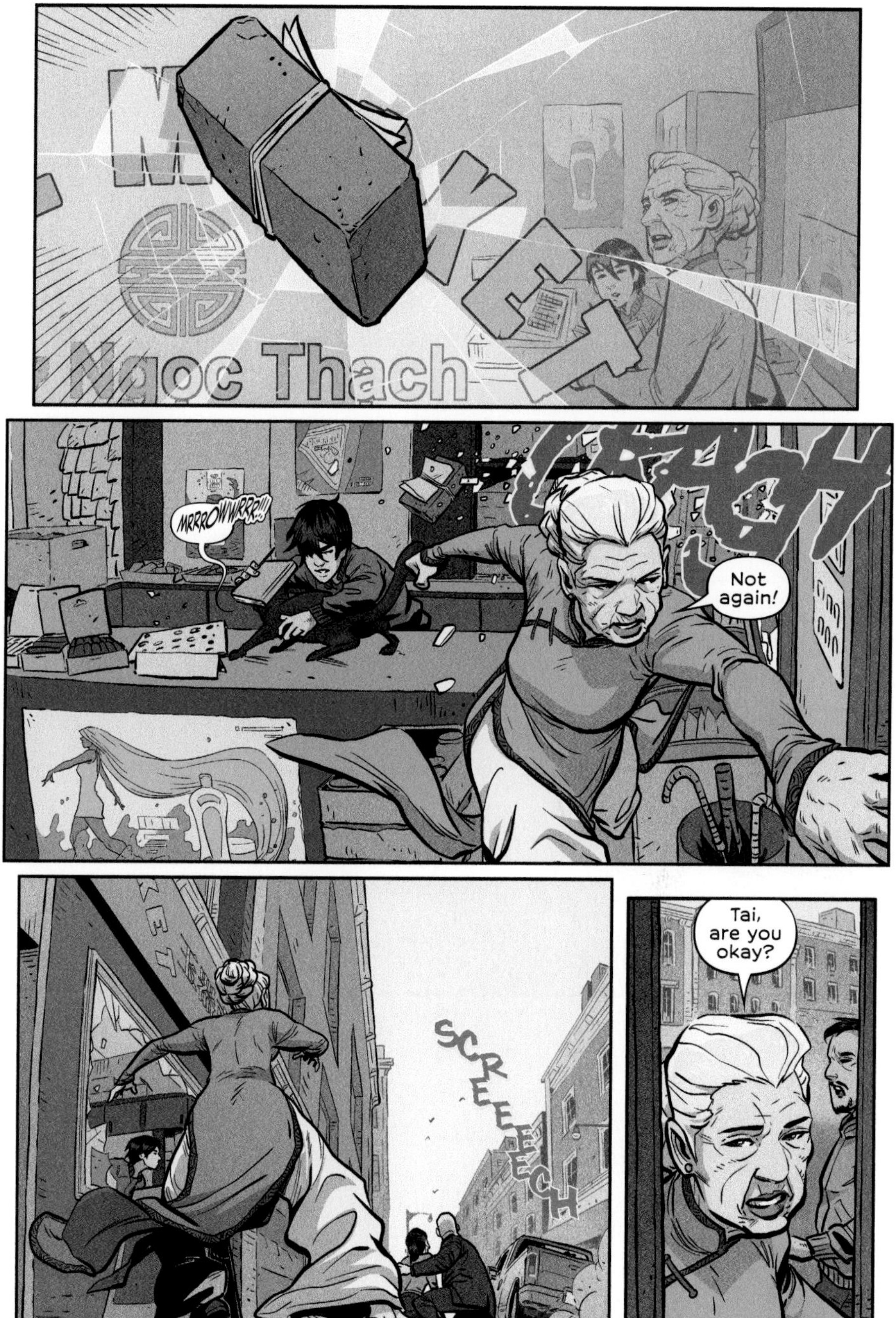
Ngoc Thach
MRRROWWRRR!!!
Not again!
SCREEECH
Tai, are you okay?

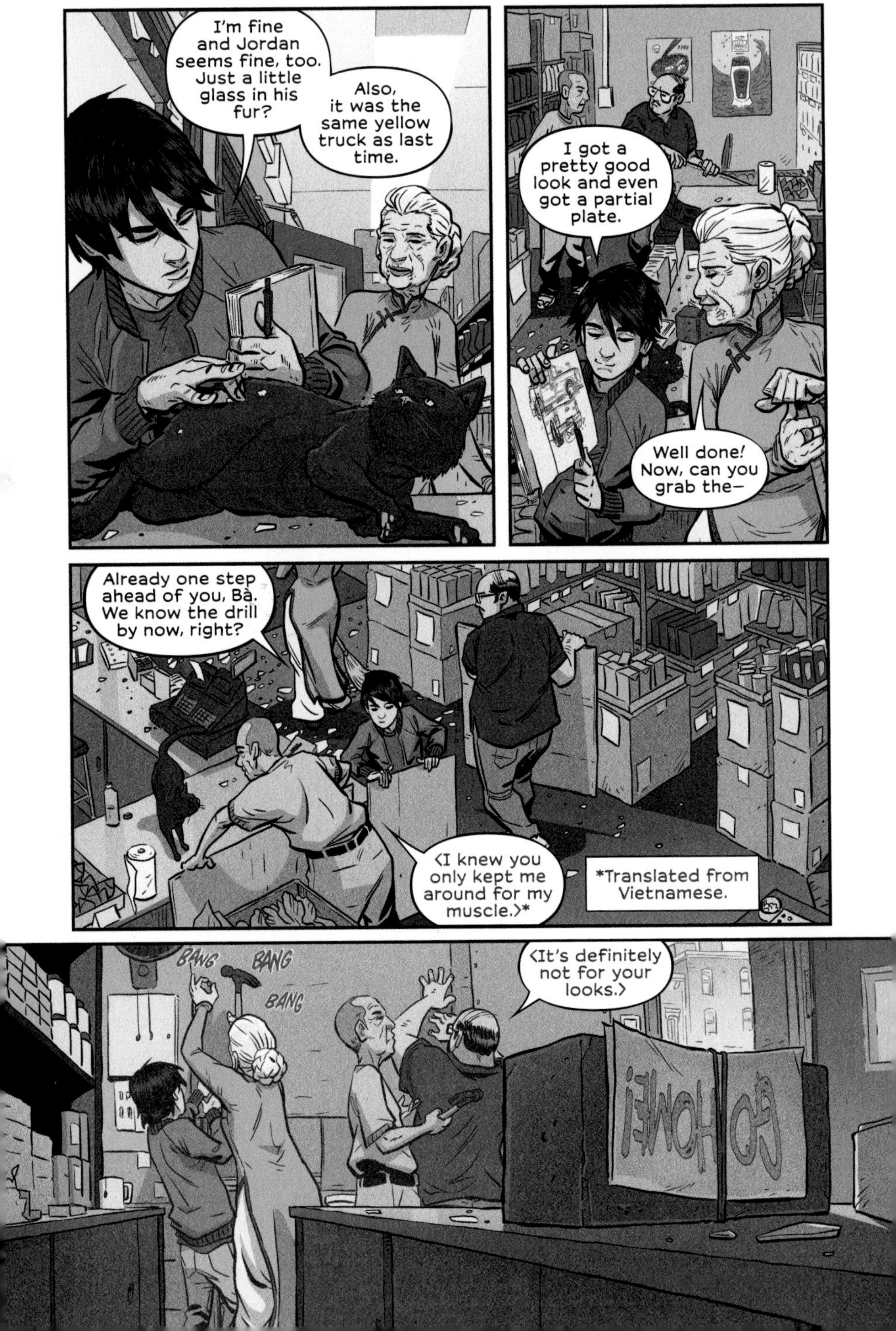
I'm fine and Jordan seems fine, too. Just a little glass in his fur?
Also, it was the same yellow truck as last time.
I got a pretty good look and even got a partial plate.
Well done! Now, can you grab the–
Already one step ahead of you, Bà. We know the drill by now, right?
<I knew you only kept me around for my muscle.>*
*Translated from Vietnamese.
BANG
BANG
BANG
<It's definitely not for your looks.>
GO HOME!

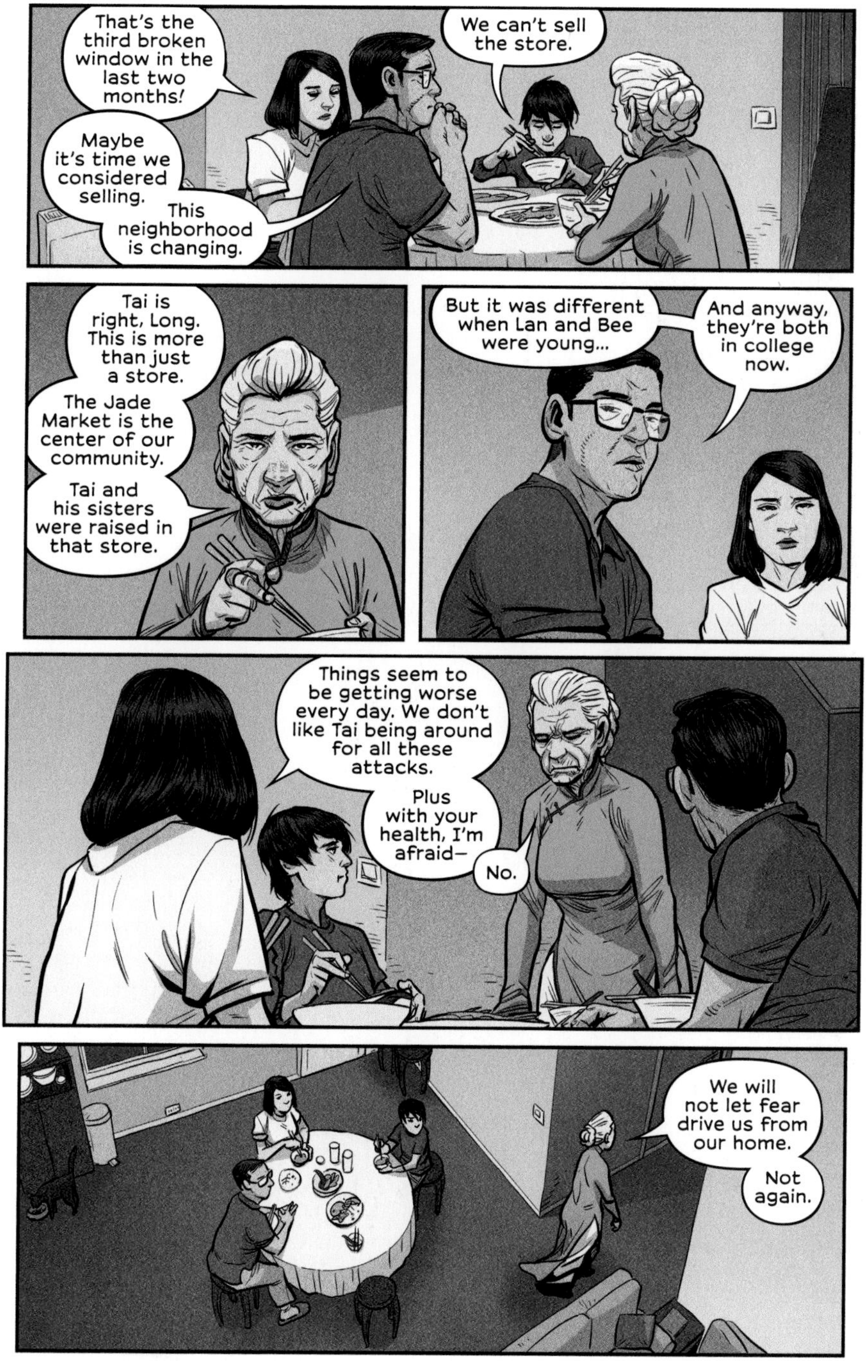
That's the third broken window in the last two months!
We can't sell the store.
Maybe it's time we considered selling.
This neighborhood is changing.
Tai is right, Long. This is more than just a store.
The Jade Market is the center of our community.
Tai and his sisters were raised in that store.
But it was different when Lan and Bee were young...
And anyway, they're both in college now.
Things seem to be getting worse every day. We don't like Tai being around for all these attacks.
Plus with your health, I'm afraid—
No.
We will not let fear drive us from our home.
Not again.

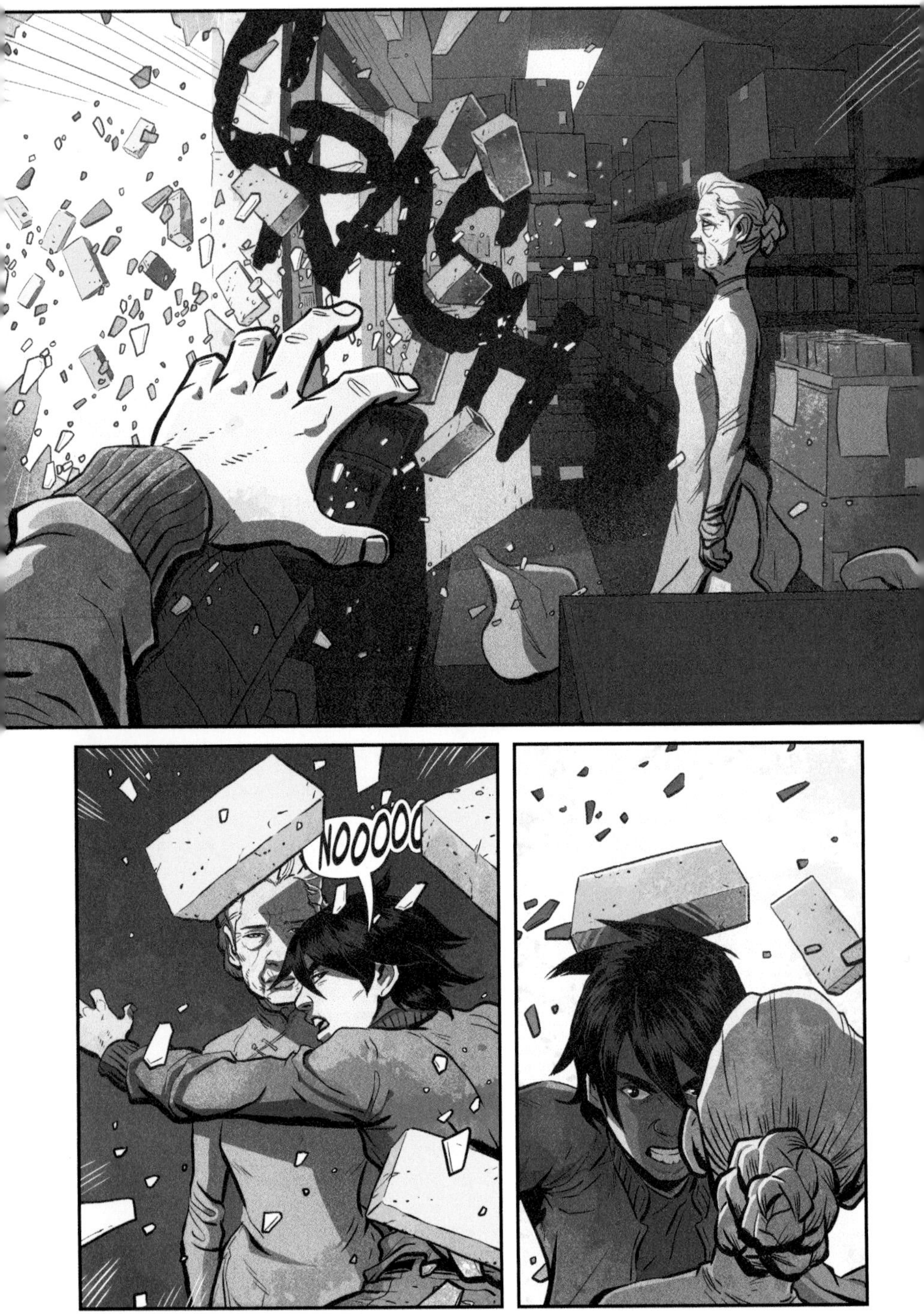
NOOOOO

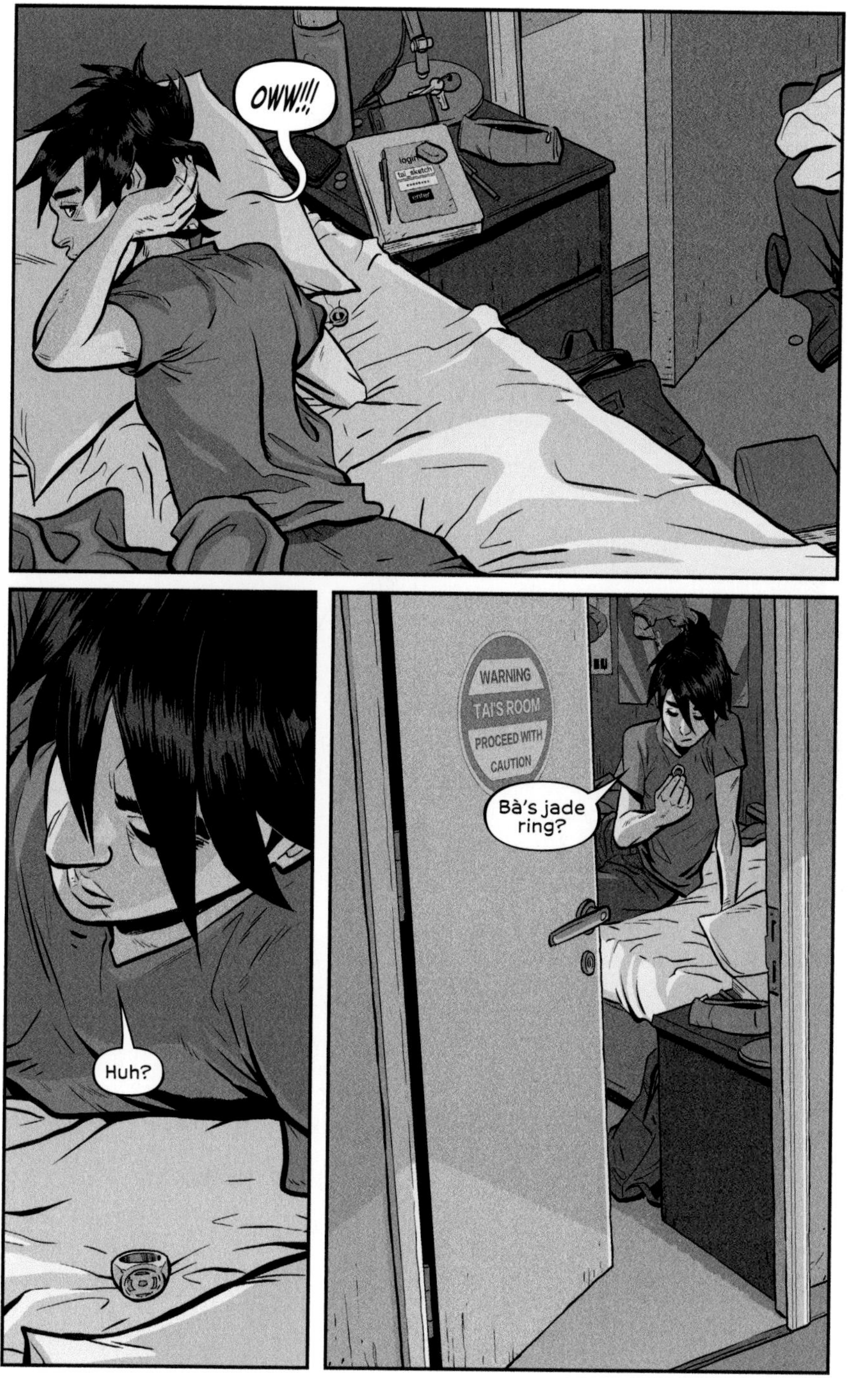
OWW!!!
Huh?
WARNING
TAI'S ROOM
PROCEED WITH
CAUTION
Bà's jade ring?

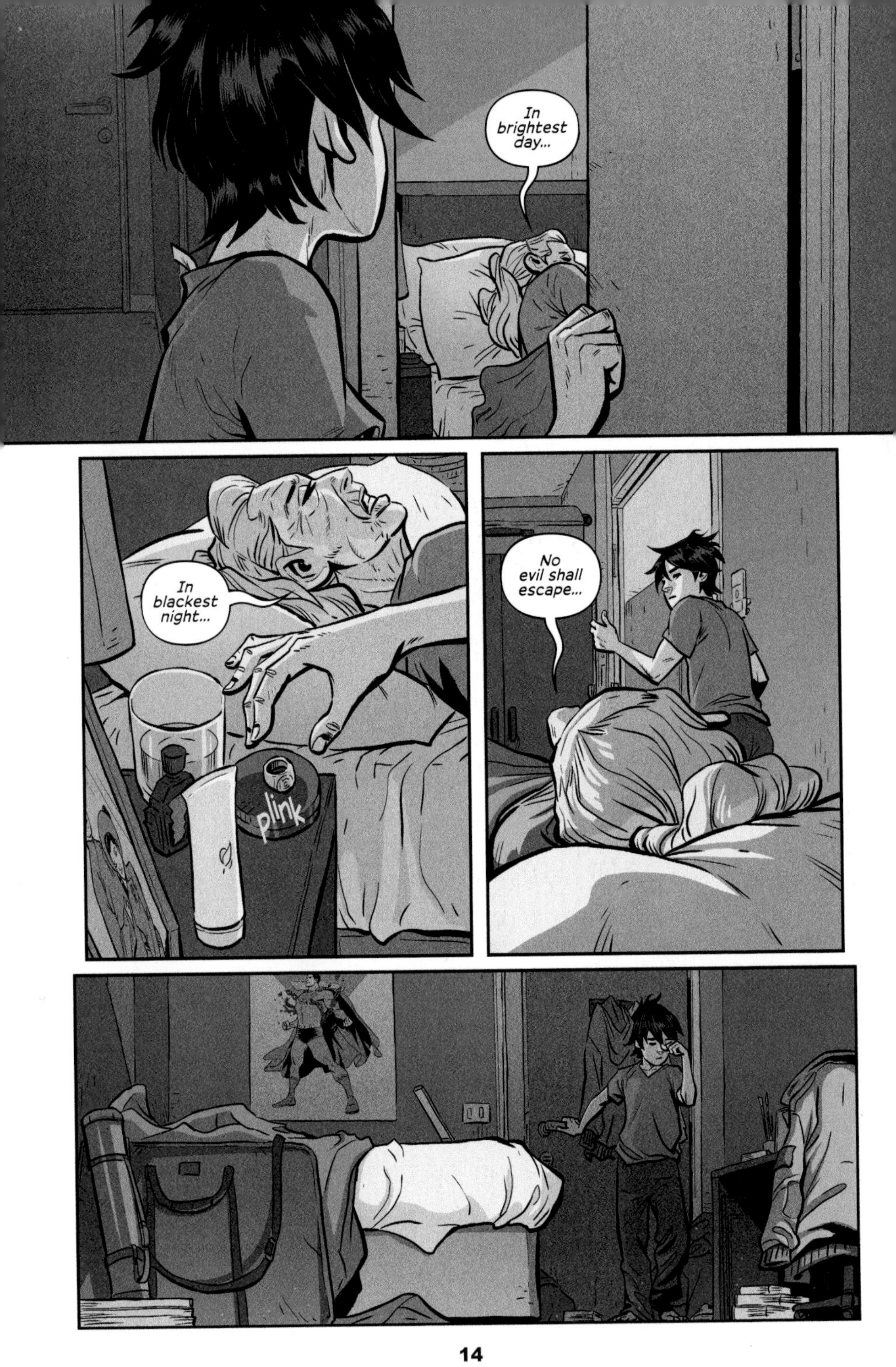
In brightest day...
In blackest night...
plink
No evil shall escape...

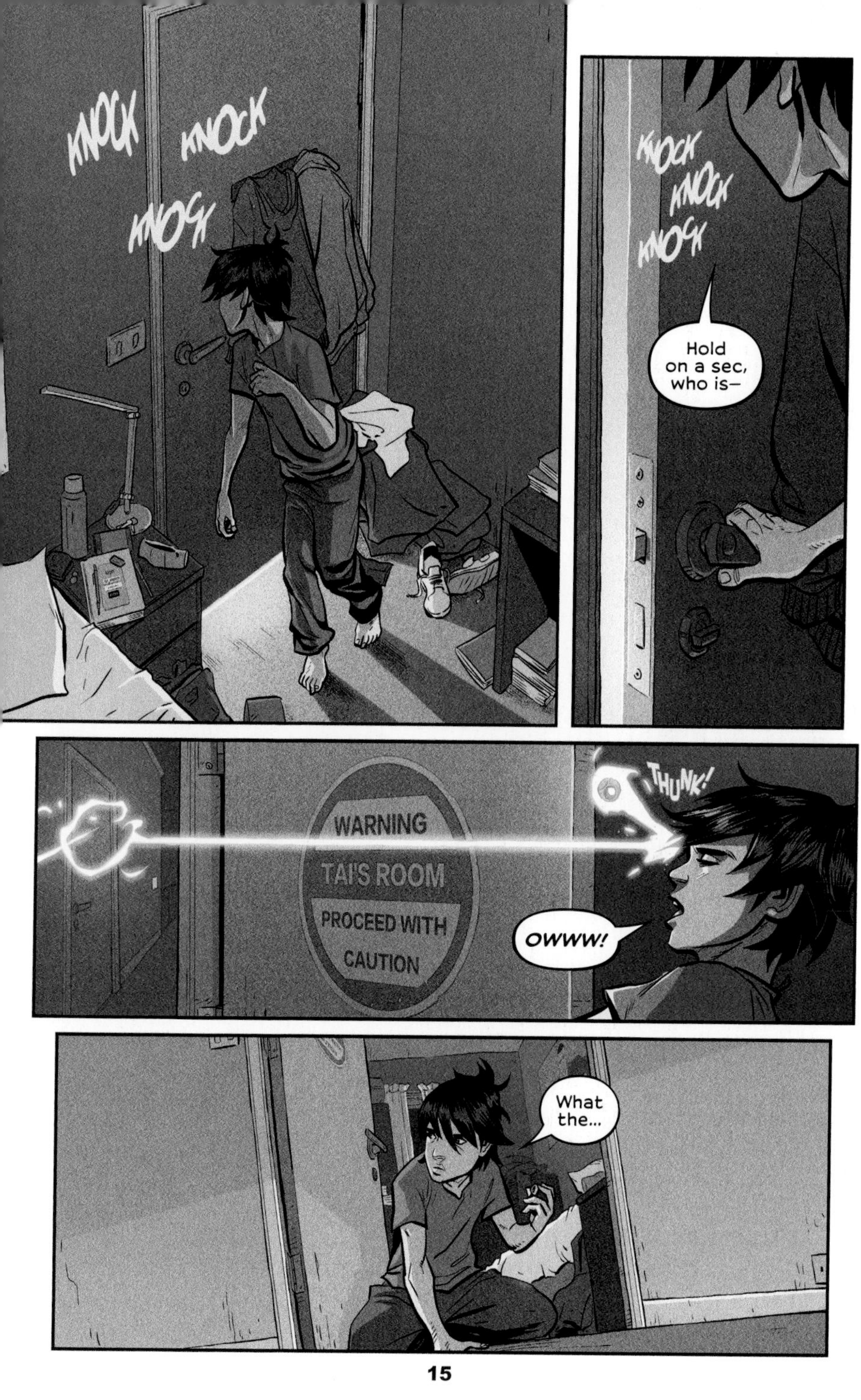
KNOCK
KNOCK
KNOCK
KNOCK
KNOCK
KNOCK
Hold on a sec, who is—
WARNING
TAI'S ROOM
PROCEED WITH CAUTION
THUNK!
OWWW!
What the...

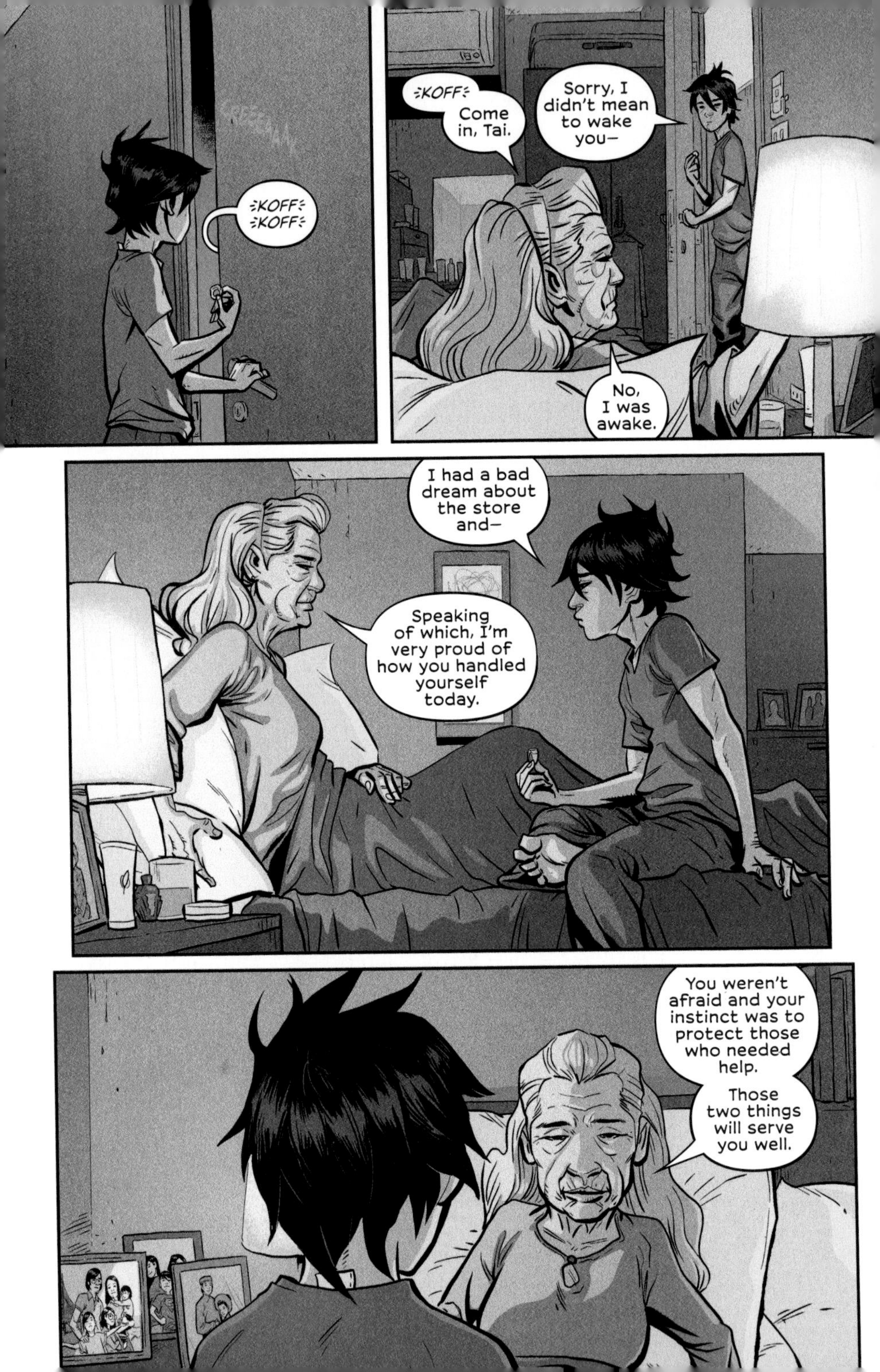

KOFF KOFF
KOFF
Come in, Tai.
Sorry, I didn't mean to wake you—
No, I was awake.
I had a bad dream about the store and—
Speaking of which, I'm very proud of how you handled yourself today.
You weren't afraid and your instinct was to protect those who needed help.
Those two things will serve you well.

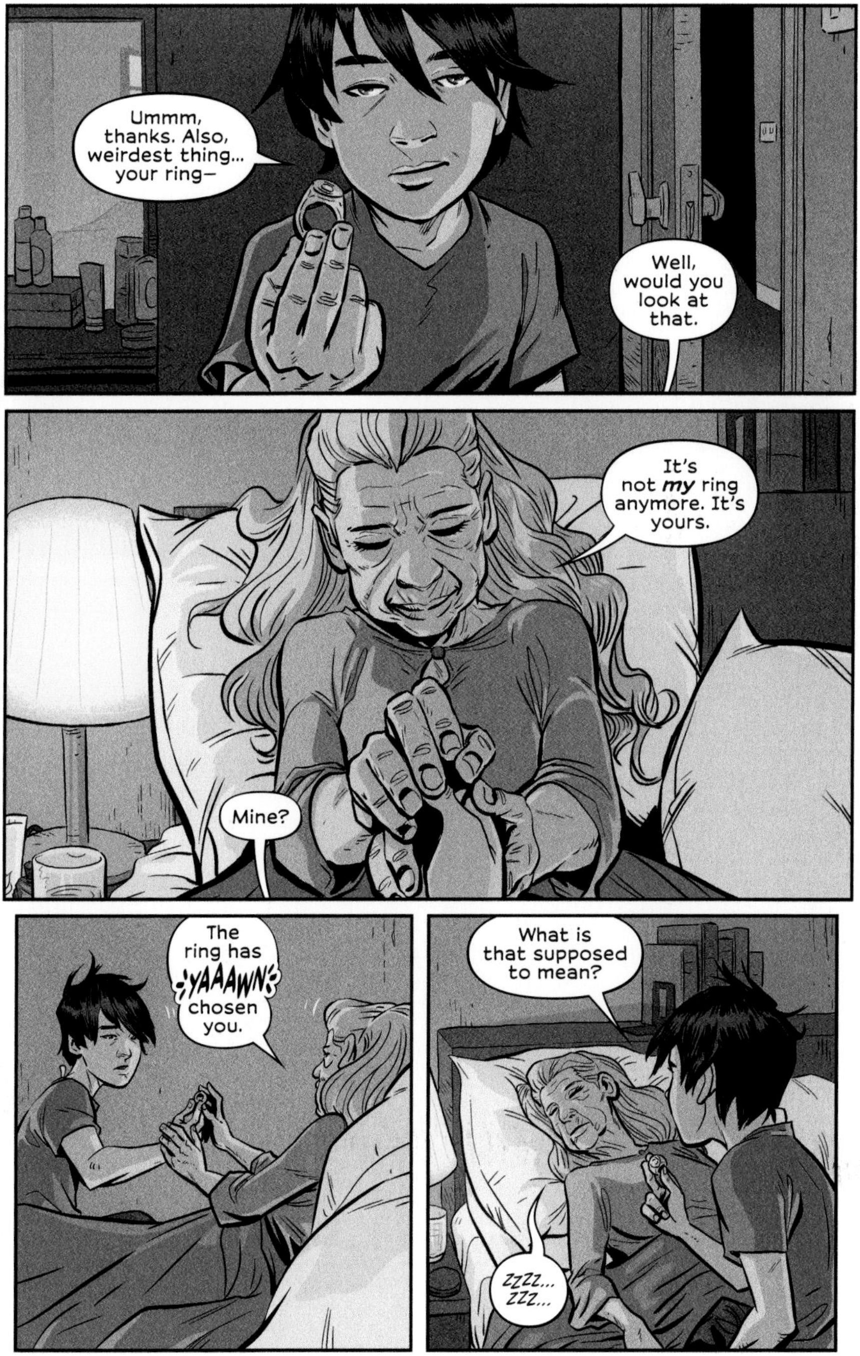
Ummm, thanks. Also, weirdest thing... your ring—
Well, would you look at that.
It's not *my* ring anymore. It's yours.
Mine?
The ring has YAAAWN chosen you.
What is that supposed to mean?
ZZZZ... ZZZ...

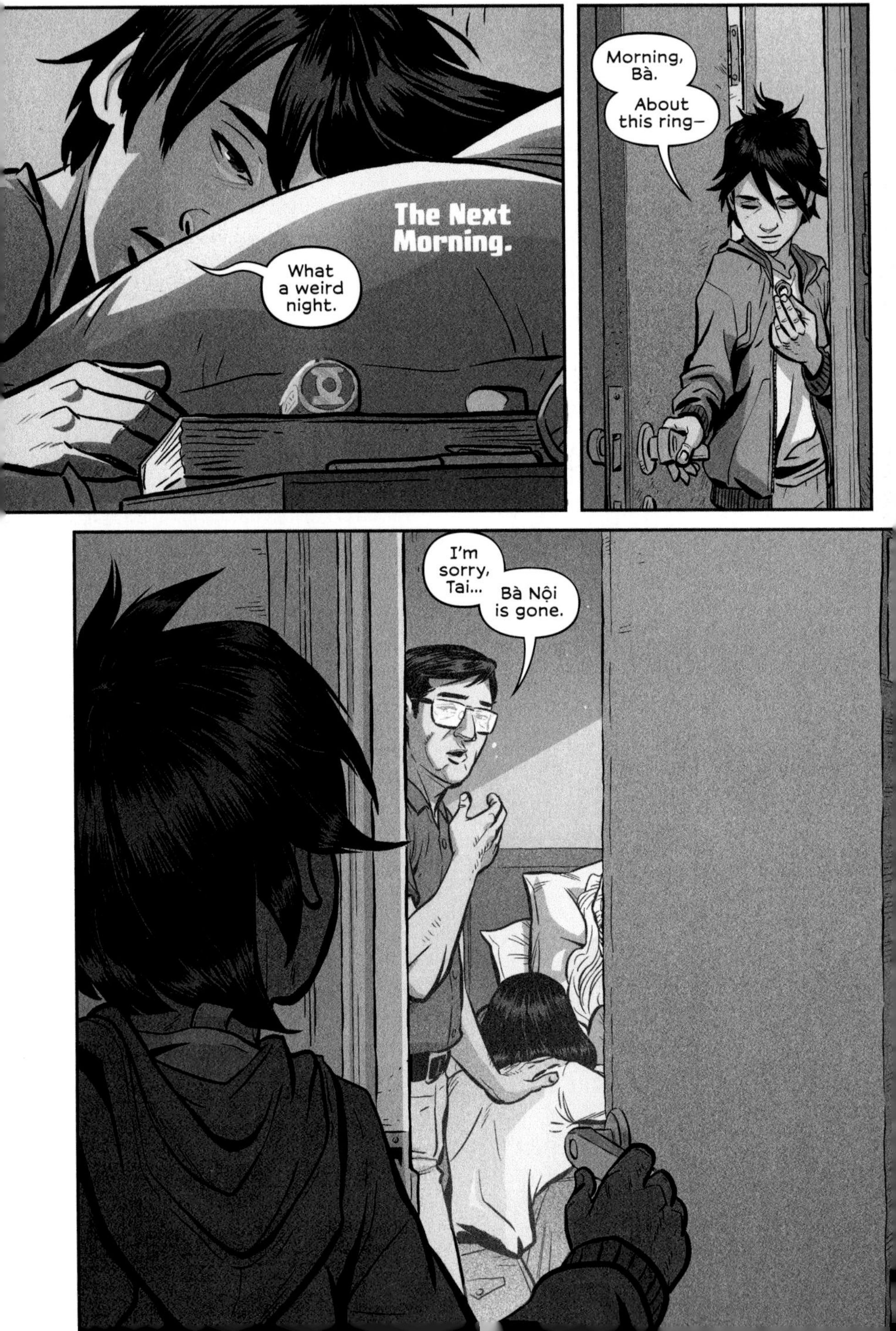
The Next Morning.
What a weird night.
Morning, Bà.
About this ring—
I'm sorry, Tai...
Bà Nội is gone.

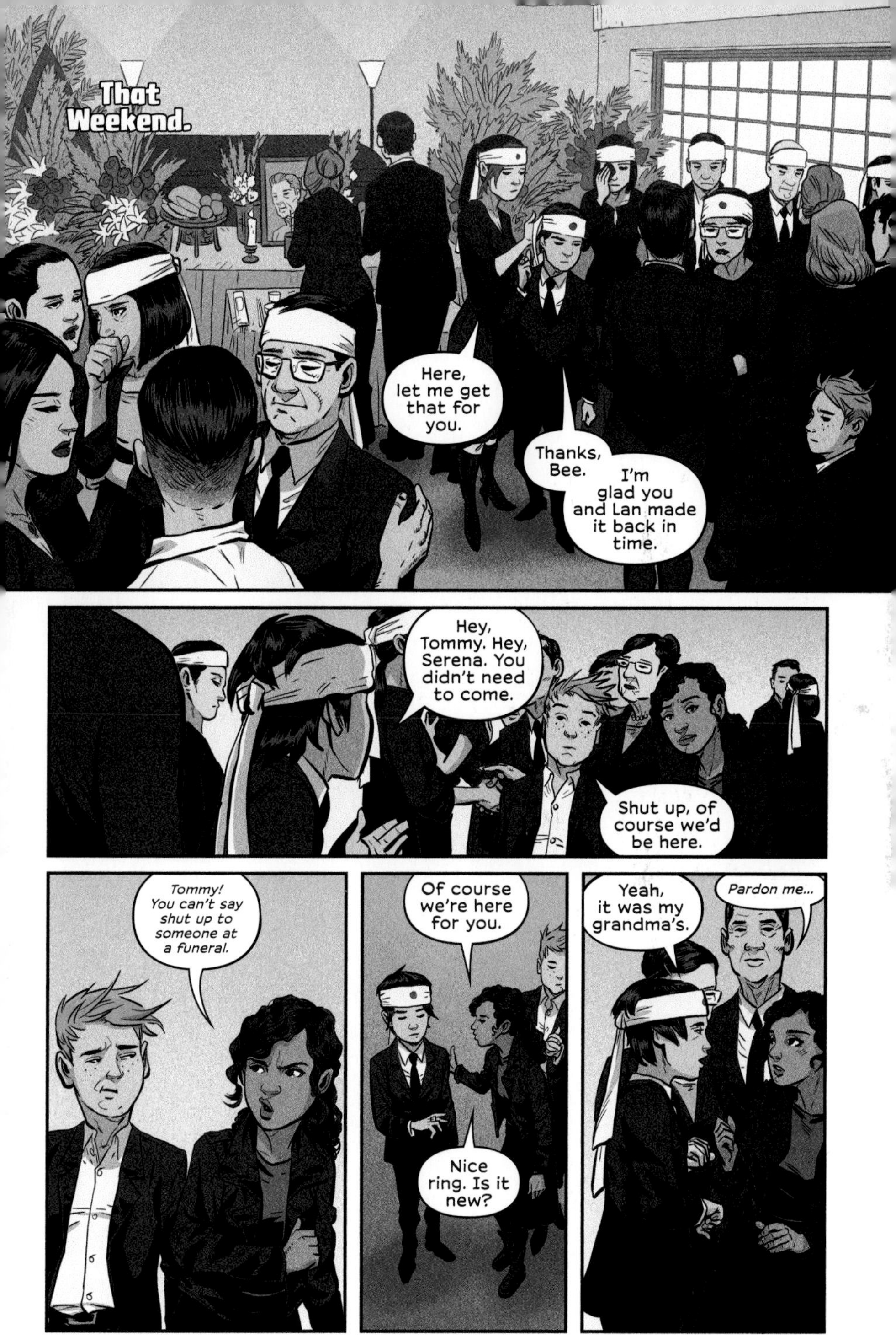
That Weekend.
Here, let me get that for you.
Thanks, Bee.
I'm glad you and Lan made it back in time.
Hey, Tommy. Hey, Serena. You didn't need to come.
Shut up, of course we'd be here.
Tommy! You can't say shut up to someone at a funeral.
Of course we're here for you.
Nice ring. Is it new?
Yeah, it was my grandma's.
Pardon me...

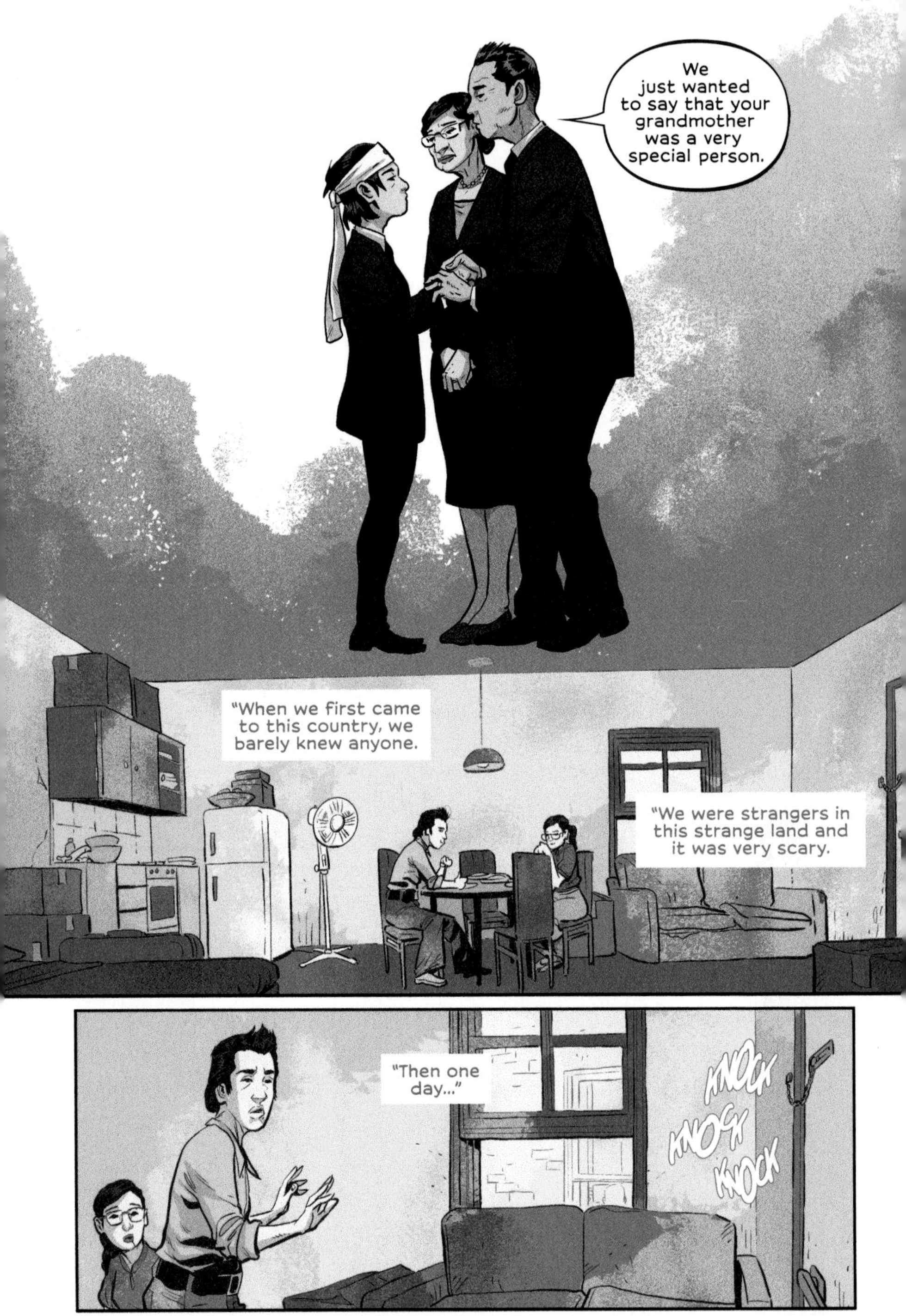
We just wanted to say that your grandmother was a very special person.
"When we first came to this country, we barely knew anyone.
"We were strangers in this strange land and it was very scary.
"Then one day..."
KNOCK
KNOCK
KNOCK

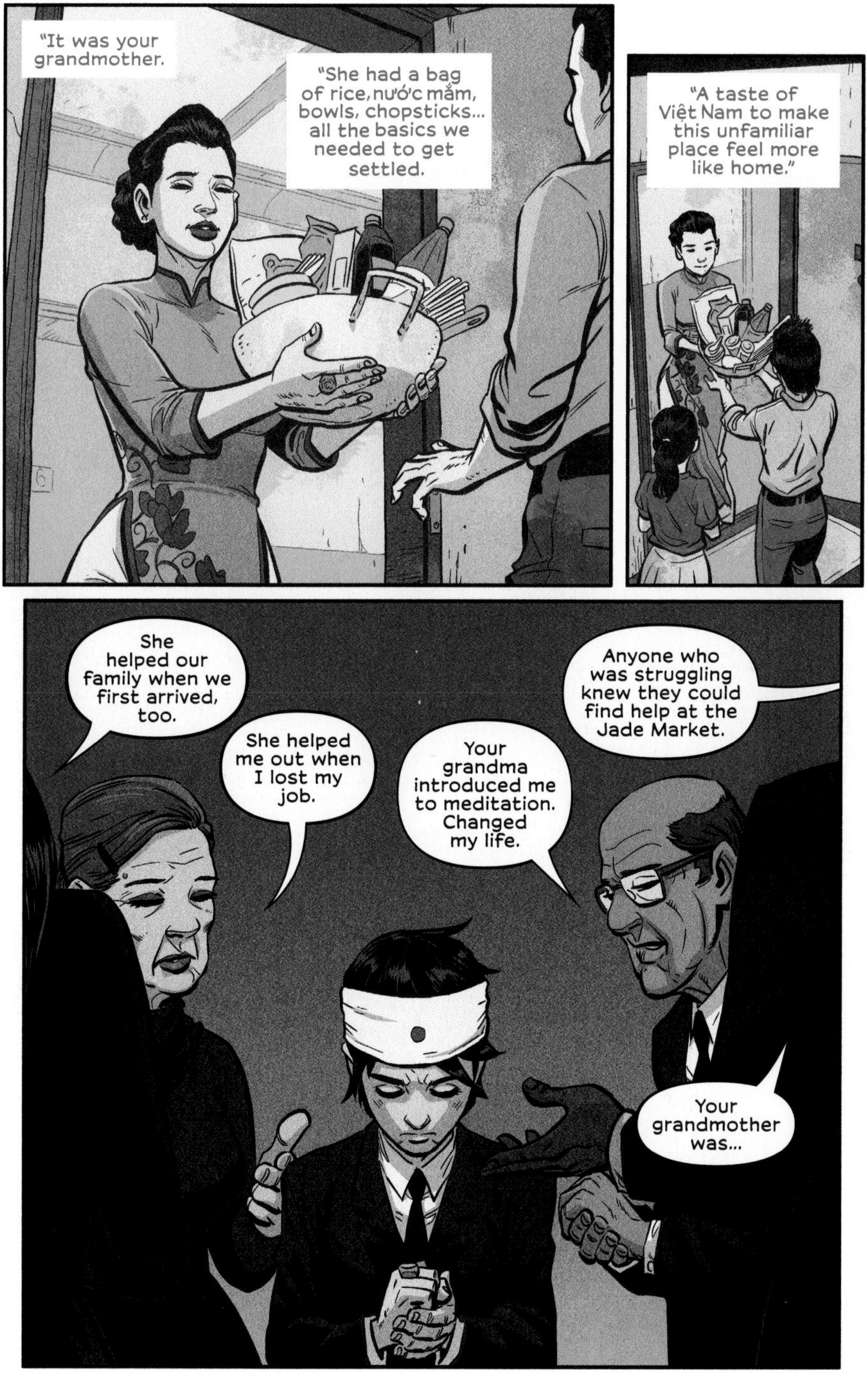
"It was your grandmother.
"She had a bag of rice, nước mắm, bowls, chopsticks... all the basics we needed to get settled.
"A taste of Việt Nam to make this unfamiliar place feel more like home."
She helped our family when we first arrived, too.
She helped me out when I lost my job.
Your grandma introduced me to meditation. Changed my life.
Anyone who was struggling knew they could find help at the Jade Market.
Your grandmother was...

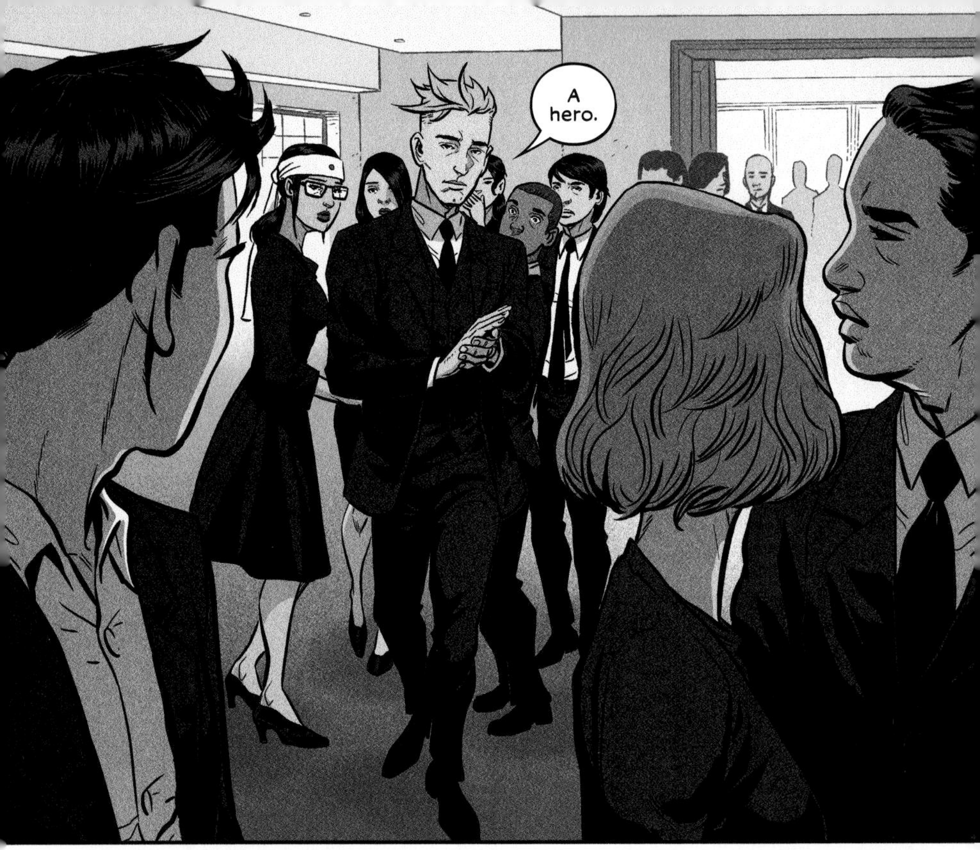
A hero.

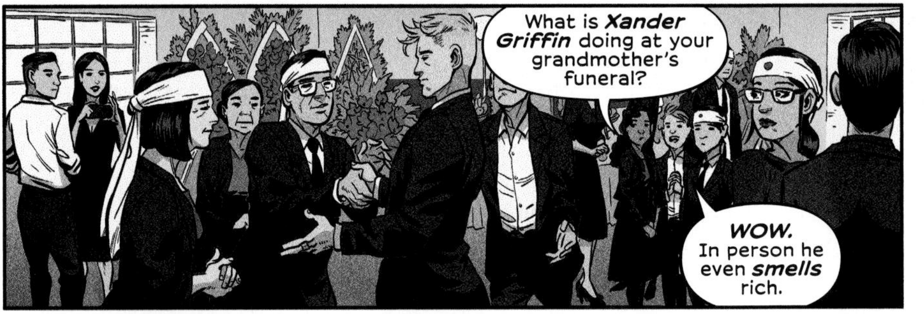
What is *Xander Griffin* doing at your grandmother's funeral?
WOW. In person he even ***smells*** rich.

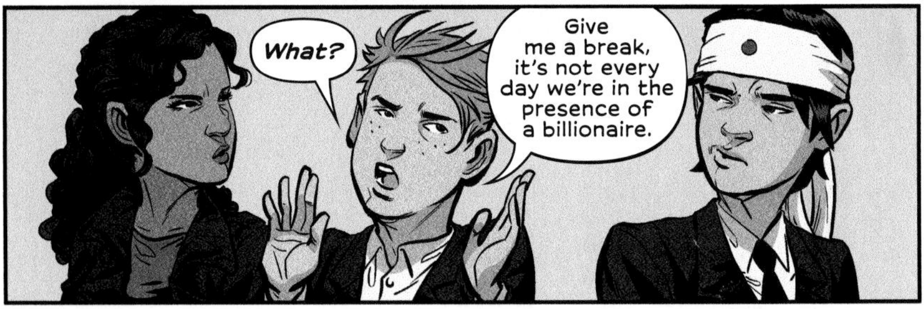
What?
Give me a break, it's not every day we're in the presence of a billionaire.

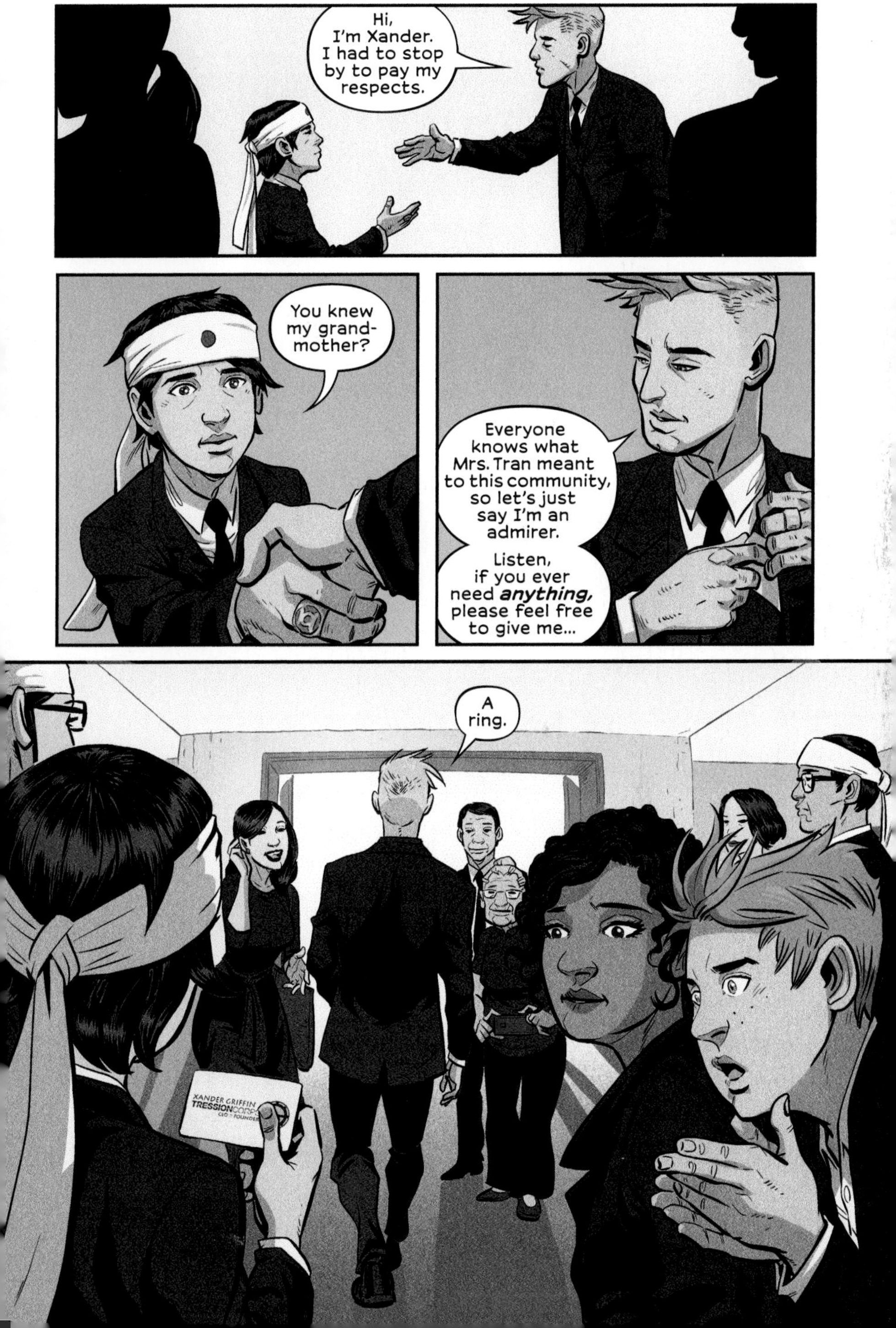
Hi, I'm Xander. I had to stop by to pay my respects.
You knew my grand-mother?
Everyone knows what Mrs. Tran meant to this community, so let's just say I'm an admirer.
Listen, if you ever need ***anything,*** please feel free to give me...
A ring.
XANDER GRIFFIN
FOUNDER

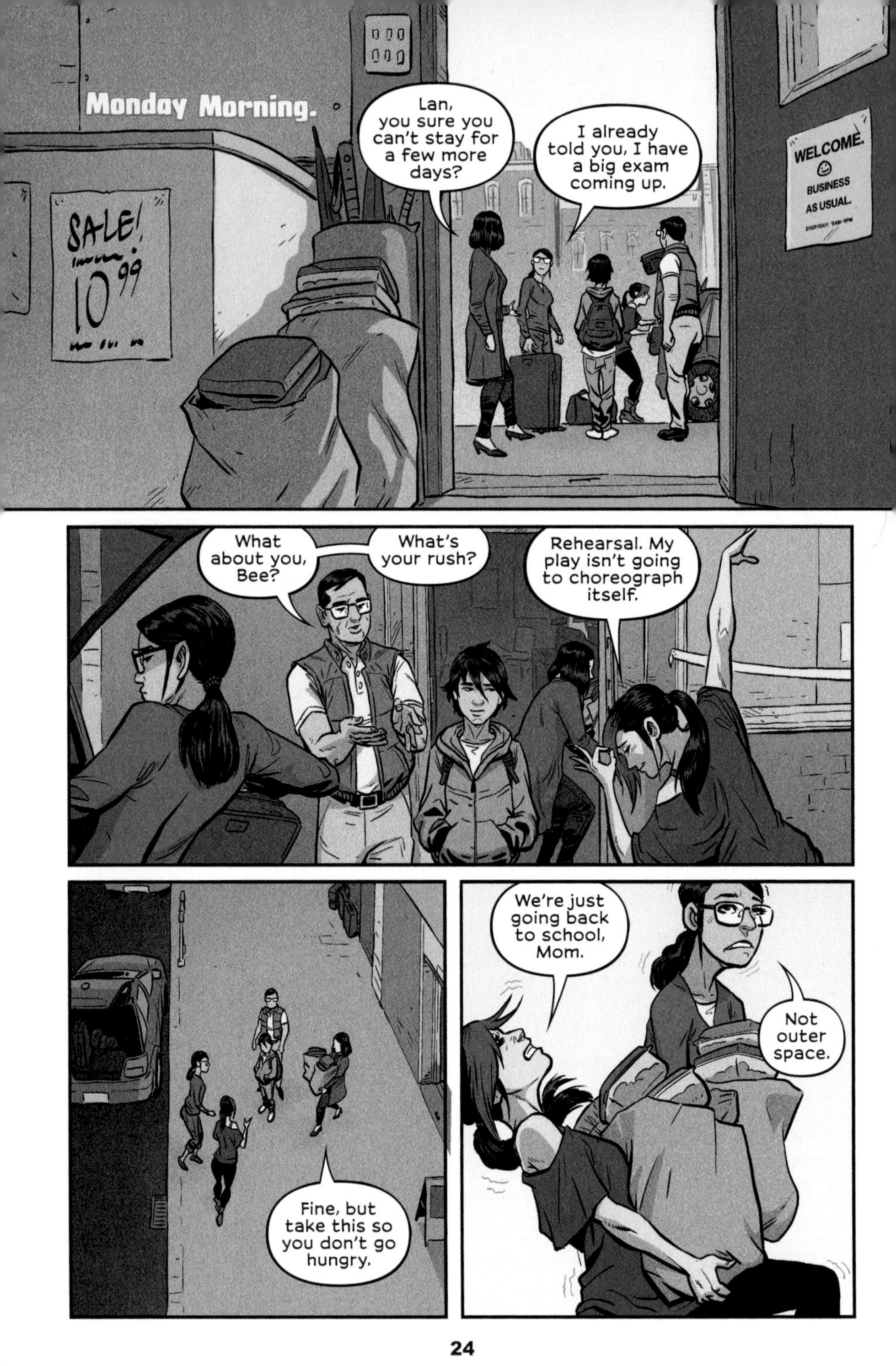
Monday Morning.
SALE! 10.99
Lan, you sure you can't stay for a few more days?
I already told you, I have a big exam coming up.
WELCOME. BUSINESS AS USUAL.
What about you, Bee?
What's your rush?
Rehearsal. My play isn't going to choreograph itself.
Fine, but take this so you don't go hungry.
We're just going back to school, Mom.
Not outer space.

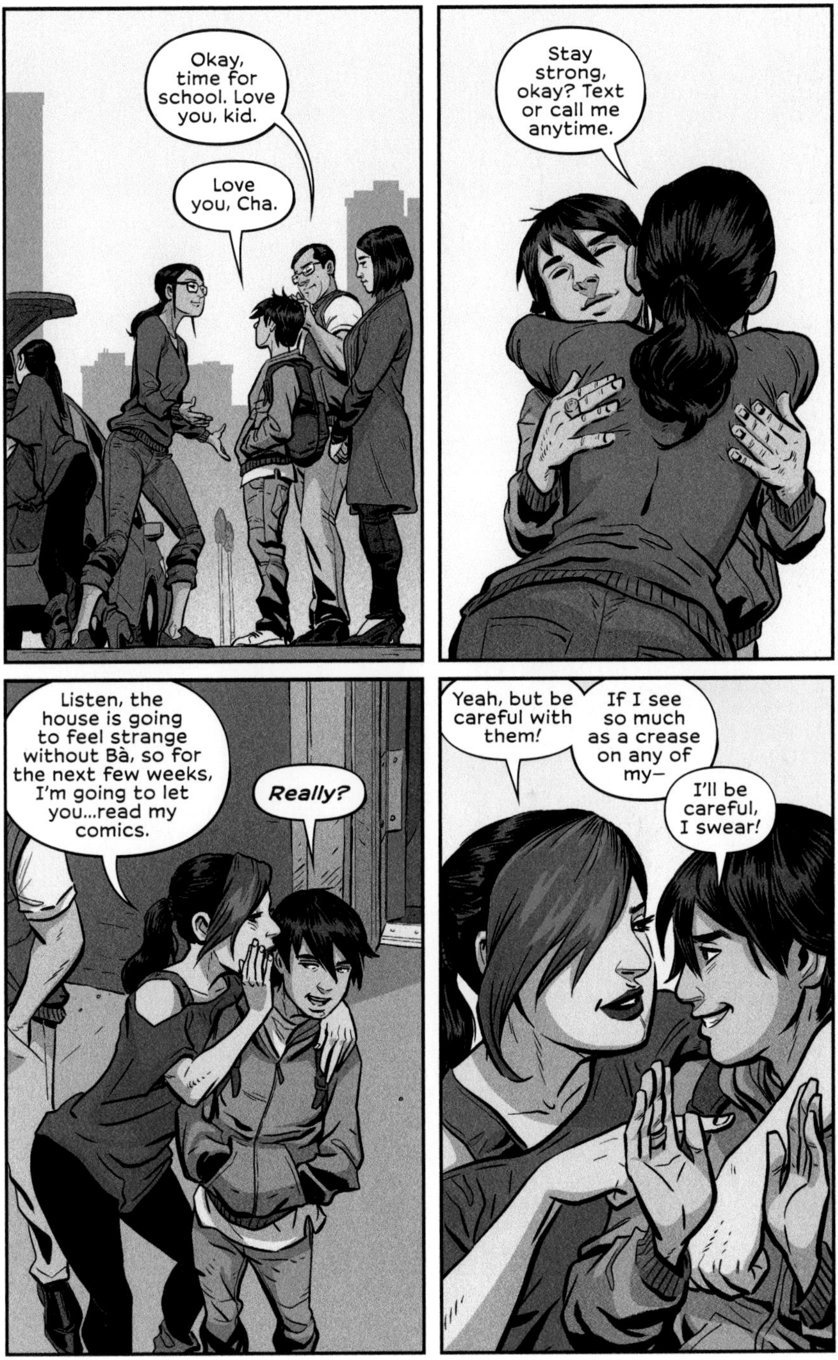
Okay, time for school. Love you, kid.
Love you, Cha.
Stay strong, okay? Text or call me anytime.
Listen, the house is going to feel strange without Bà, so for the next few weeks, I'm going to let you...read my comics.
Really?
Yeah, but be careful with them!
If I see so much as a crease on any of my—
I'll be careful, I swear!

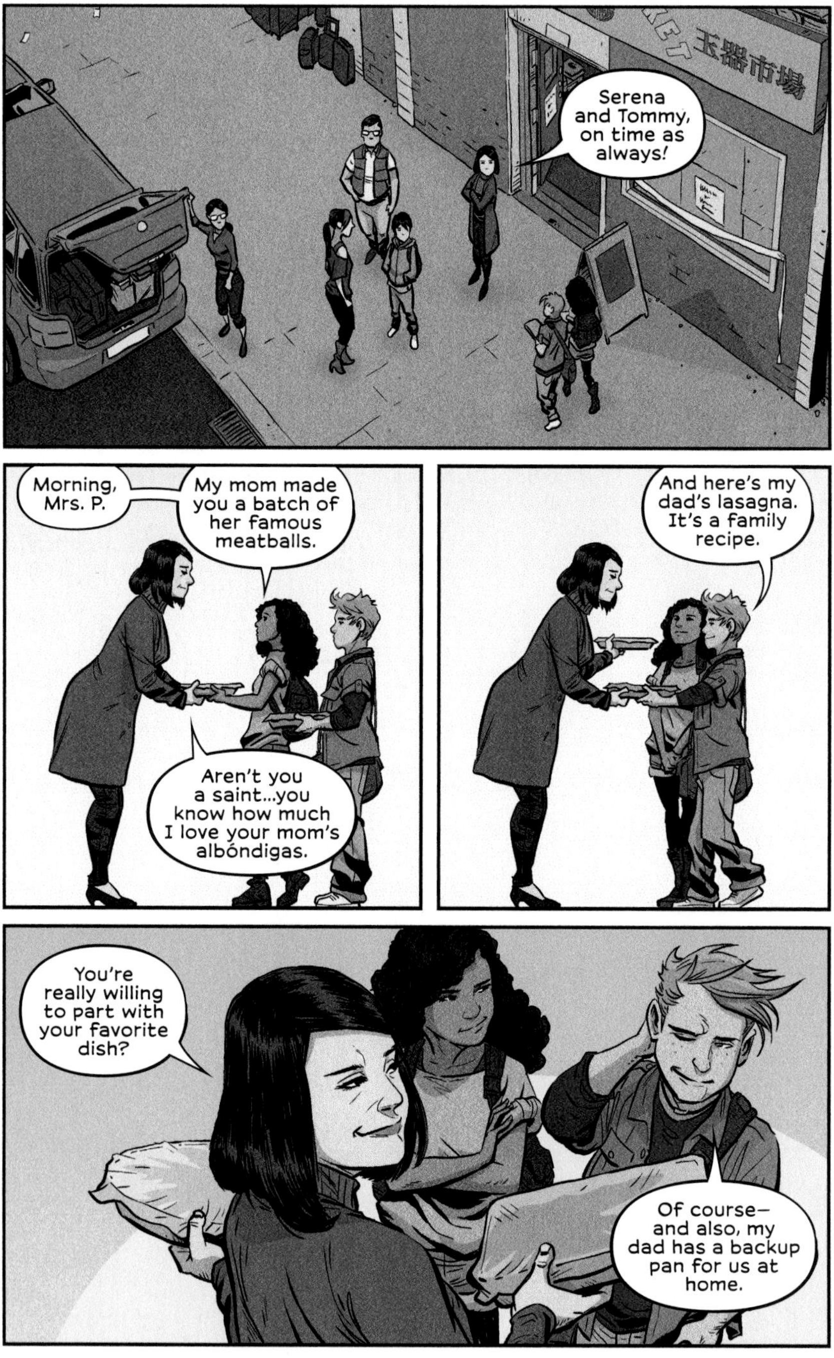

玉器市場
Serena and Tommy, on time as always!
Morning, Mrs. P.
My mom made you a batch of her famous meatballs.
Aren't you a saint...you know how much I love your mom's albóndigas.
And here's my dad's lasagna. It's a family recipe.
You're really willing to part with your favorite dish?
Of course— and also, my dad has a backup pan for us at home.

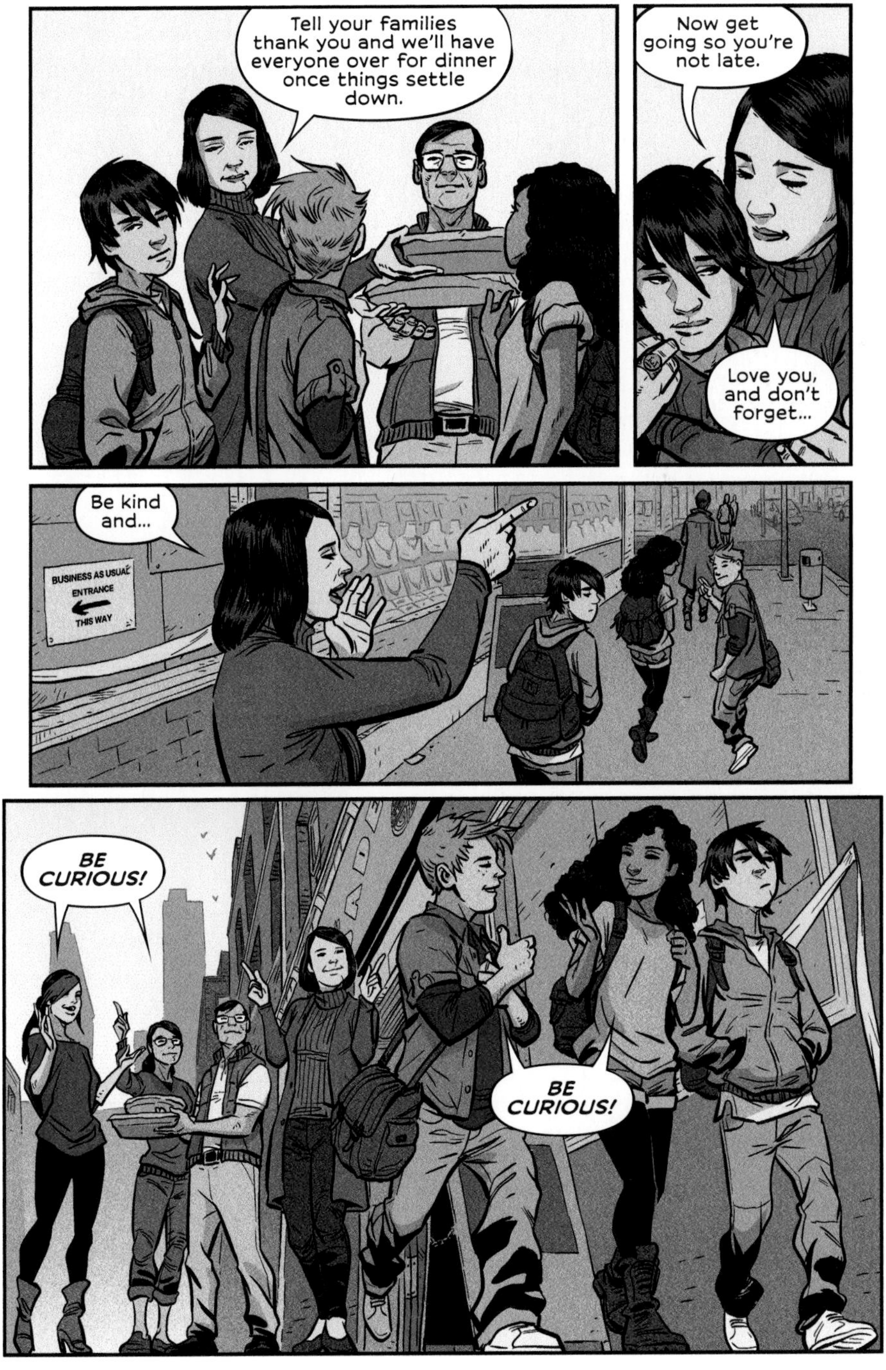
Tell your families thank you and we'll have everyone over for dinner once things settle down.
Now get going so you're not late.
Love you, and don't forget...
Be kind and...
BUSINESS AS USUAL
ENTRANCE
THIS WAY
BE CURIOUS!
BE CURIOUS!

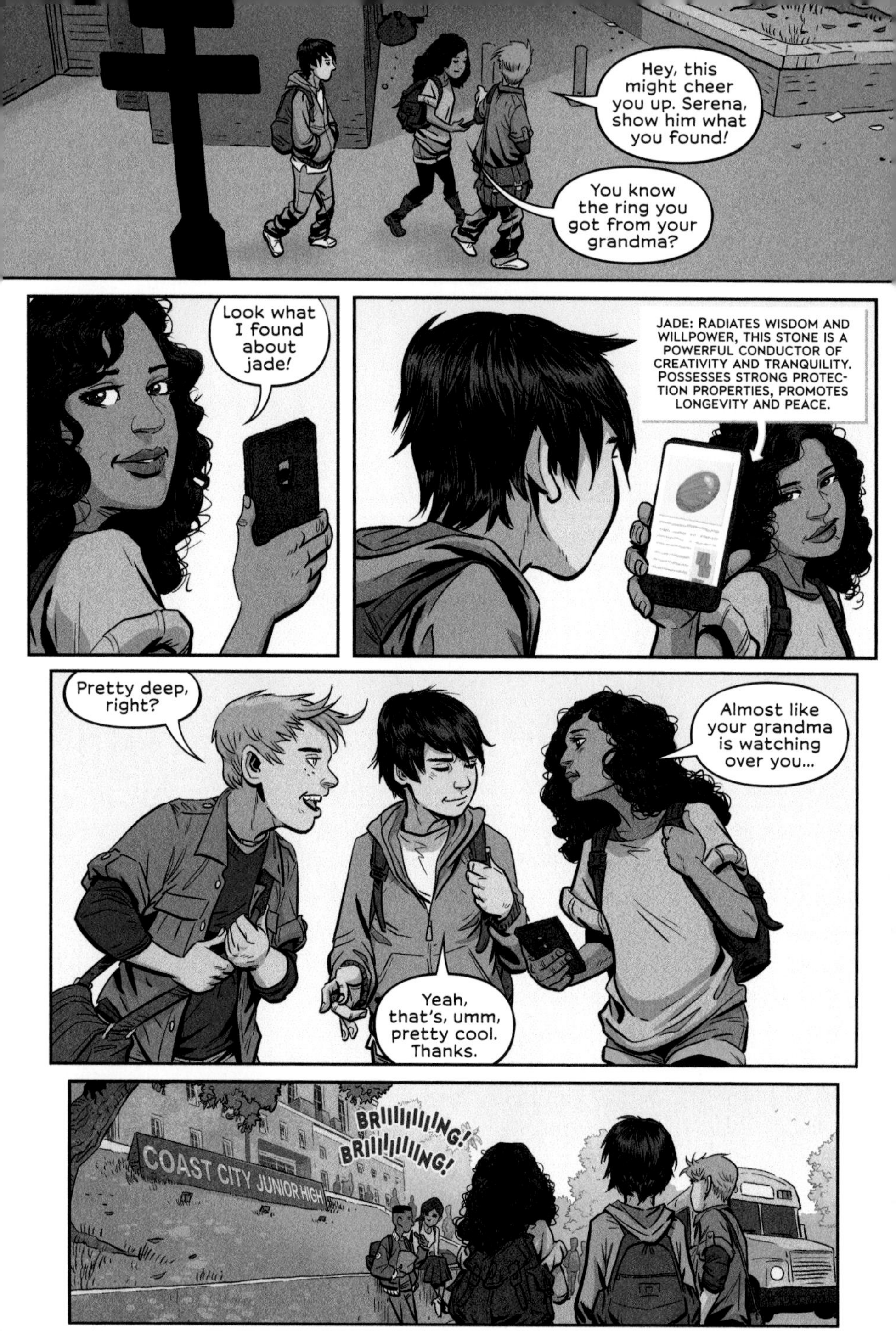

Hey, this might cheer you up. Serena, show him what you found!
You know the ring you got from your grandma?
Look what I found about jade!
JADE: RADIATES WISDOM AND WILLPOWER, THIS STONE IS A POWERFUL CONDUCTOR OF CREATIVITY AND TRANQUILITY. POSSESSES STRONG PROTECTION PROPERTIES, PROMOTES LONGEVITY AND PEACE.
Pretty deep, right?
Almost like your grandma is watching over you...
Yeah, that's, umm, pretty cool. Thanks.
COAST CITY JUNIOR HIGH
BRIIIIIIING!
BRIIIIIIING!

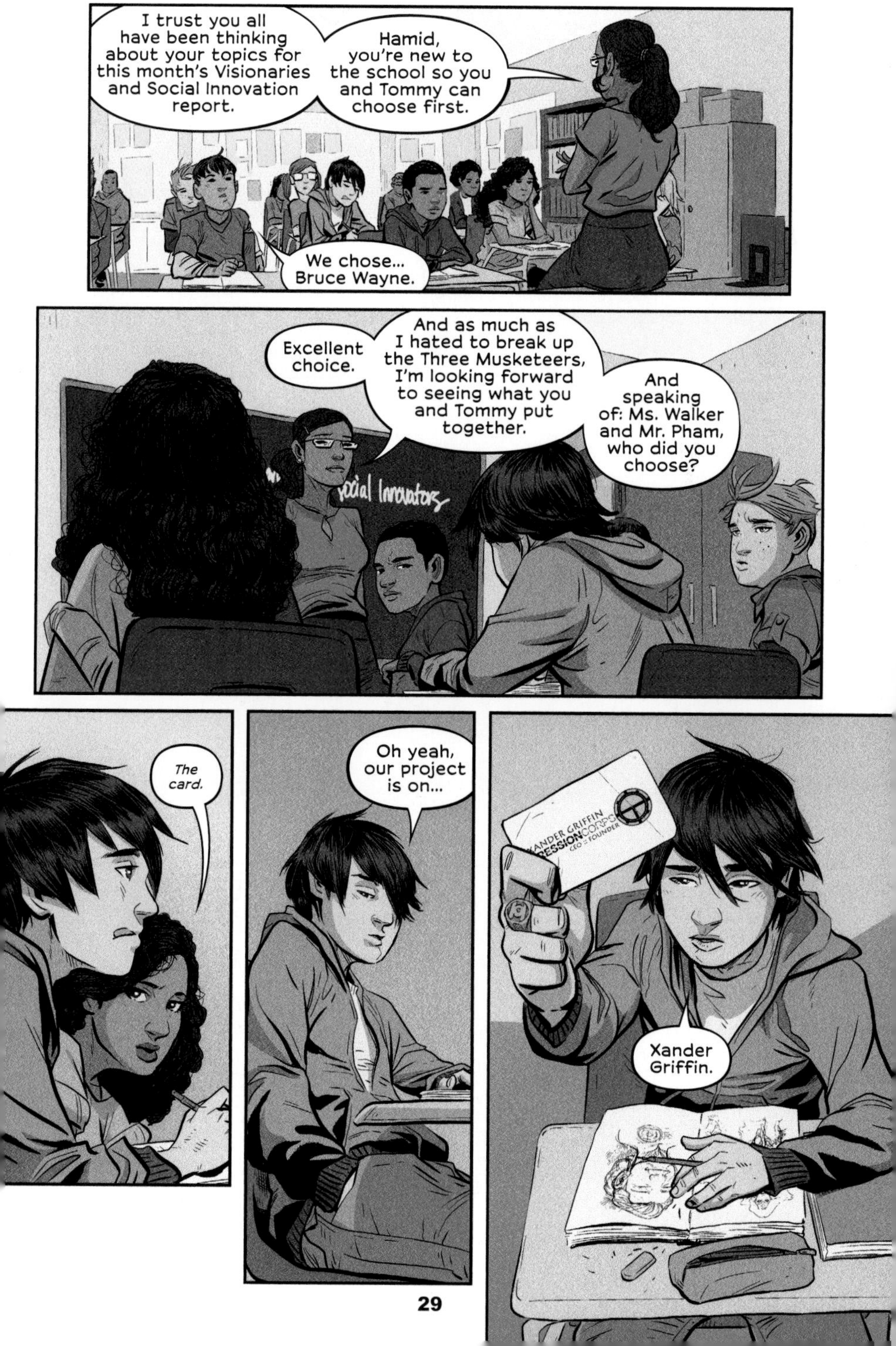
I trust you all have been thinking about your topics for this month's Visionaries and Social Innovation report.
Hamid, you're new to the school so you and Tommy can choose first.
We chose... Bruce Wayne.
Excellent choice.
And as much as I hated to break up the Three Musketeers, I'm looking forward to seeing what you and Tommy put together.
And speaking of: Ms. Walker and Mr. Pham, who did you choose?
The card.
Oh yeah, our project is on...
XANDER GRIFFIN
Xander Griffin.

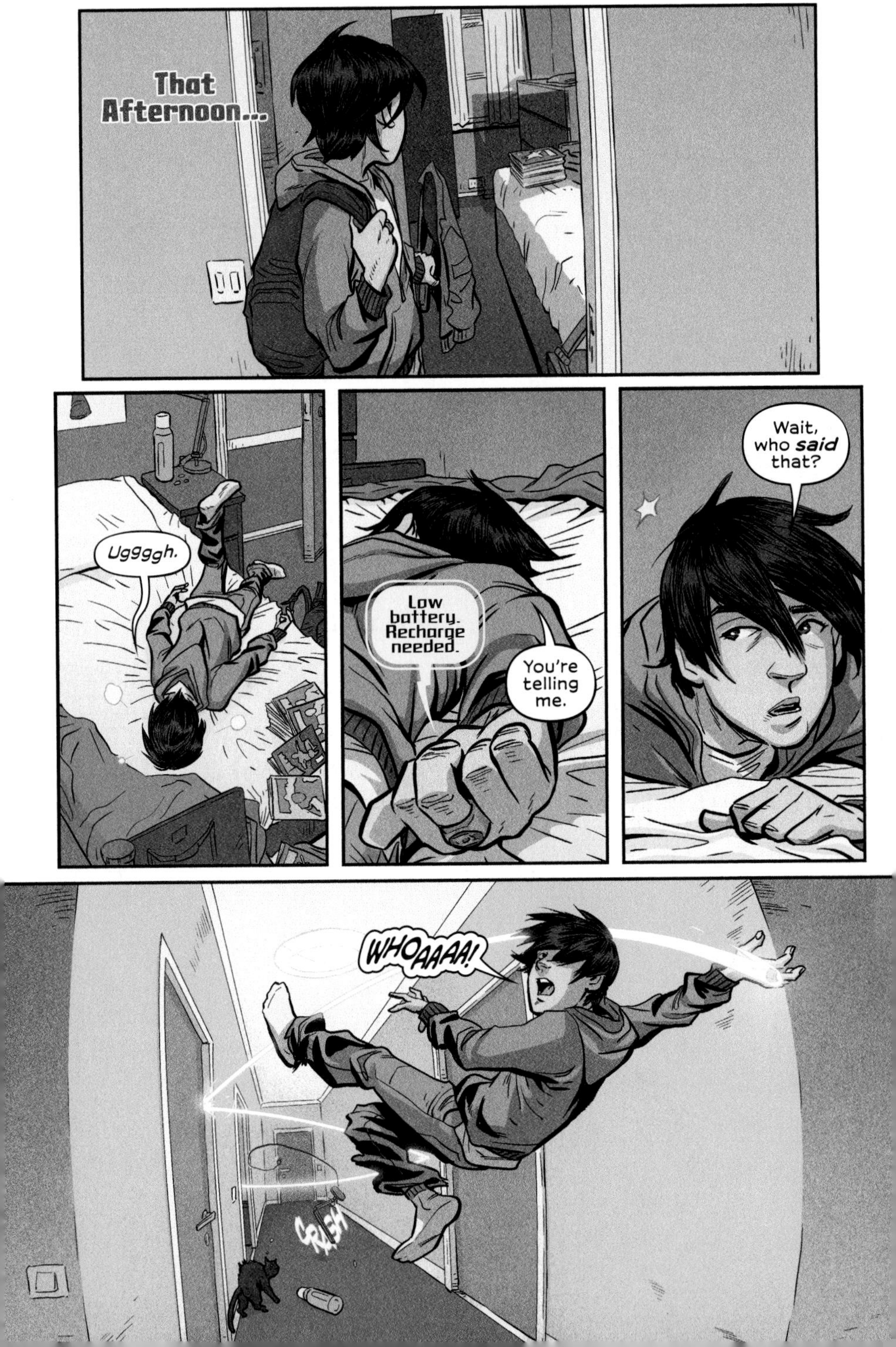
That Afternoon...
Uggggh.
Low battery. Recharge needed.
You're telling me.
Wait, who *said* that?
WHOAAAA!
CRASH

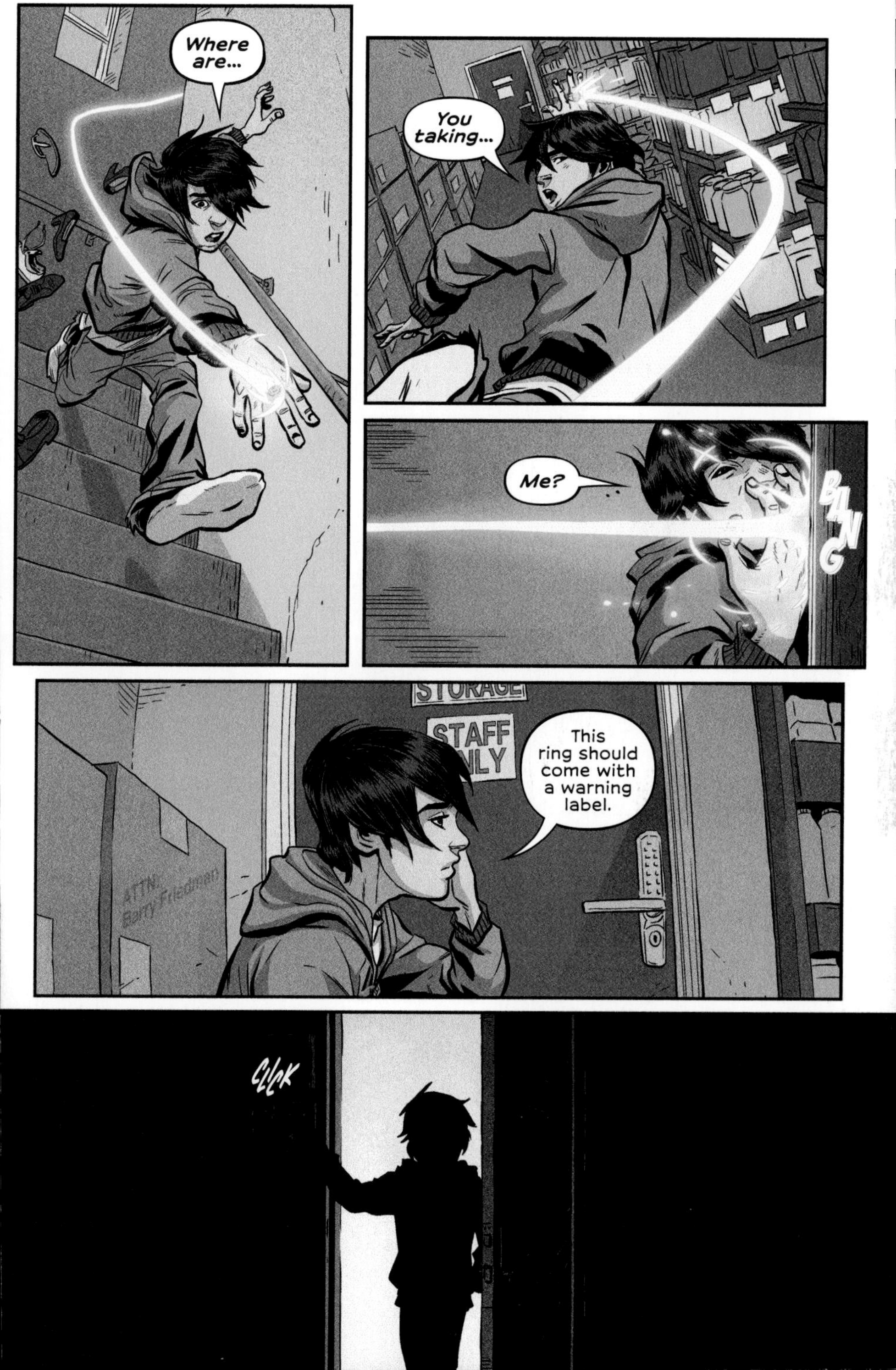
Where are...
You taking...
Me?
BANG
STORAGE
STAFF ONLY
This ring should come with a warning label.
ATTN: Barry Friedman
CLICK

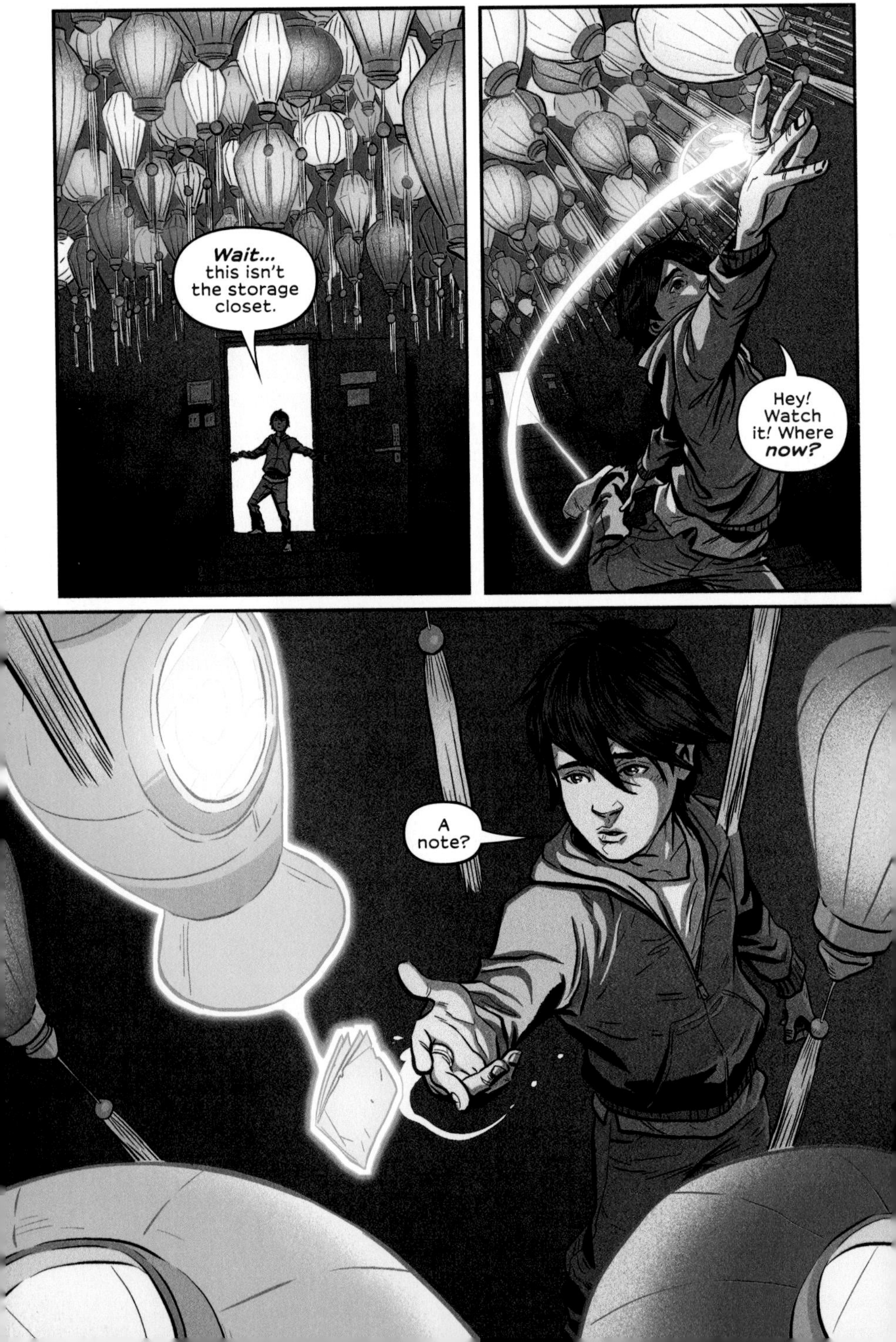
Wait... this isn't the storage closet.
Hey! Watch it! Where now?
A note?

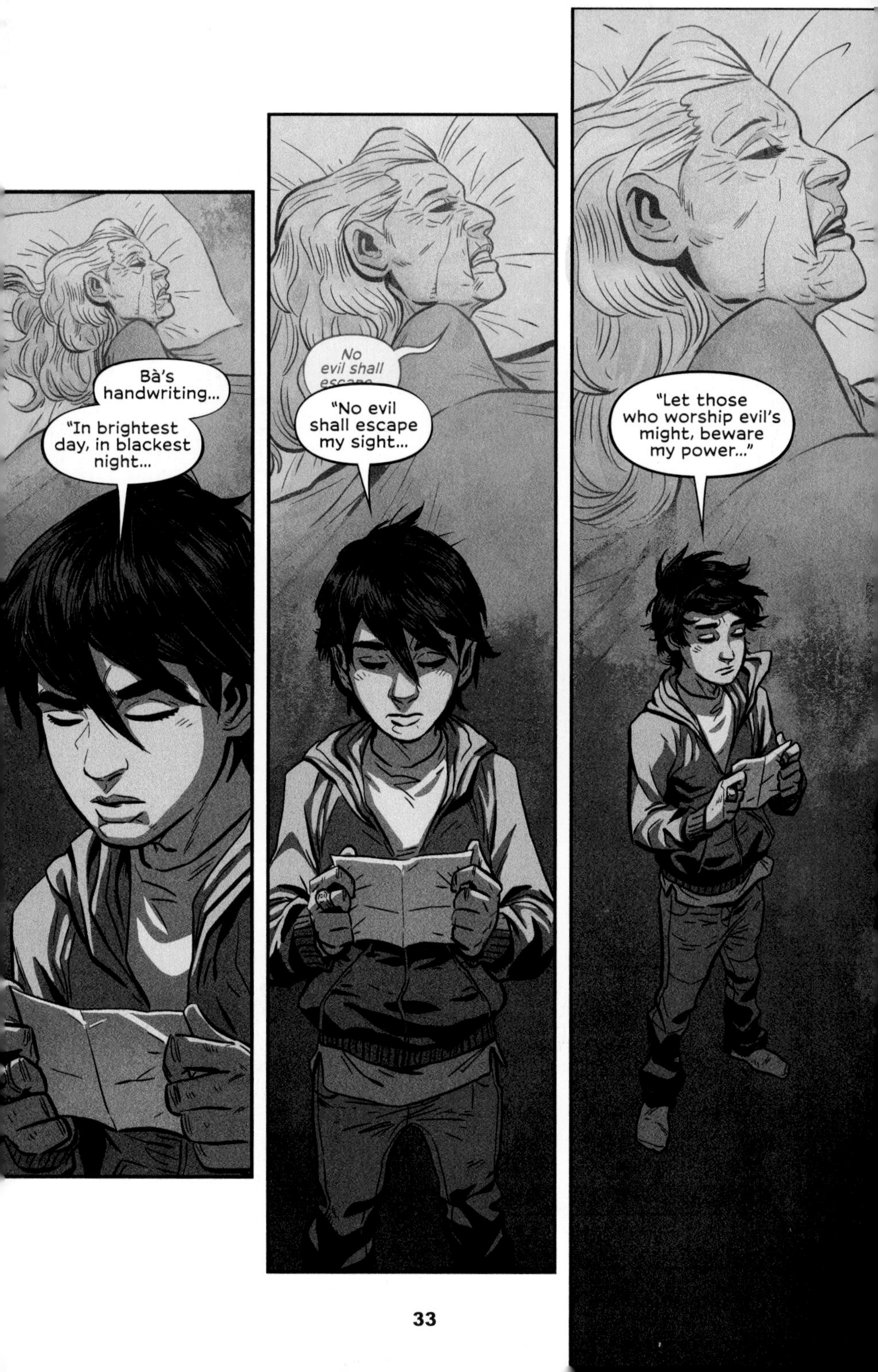
Bà's handwriting...
"In brightest day, in blackest night...
No evil shall escape
"No evil shall escape my sight...
"Let those who worship evil's might, beware my power..."

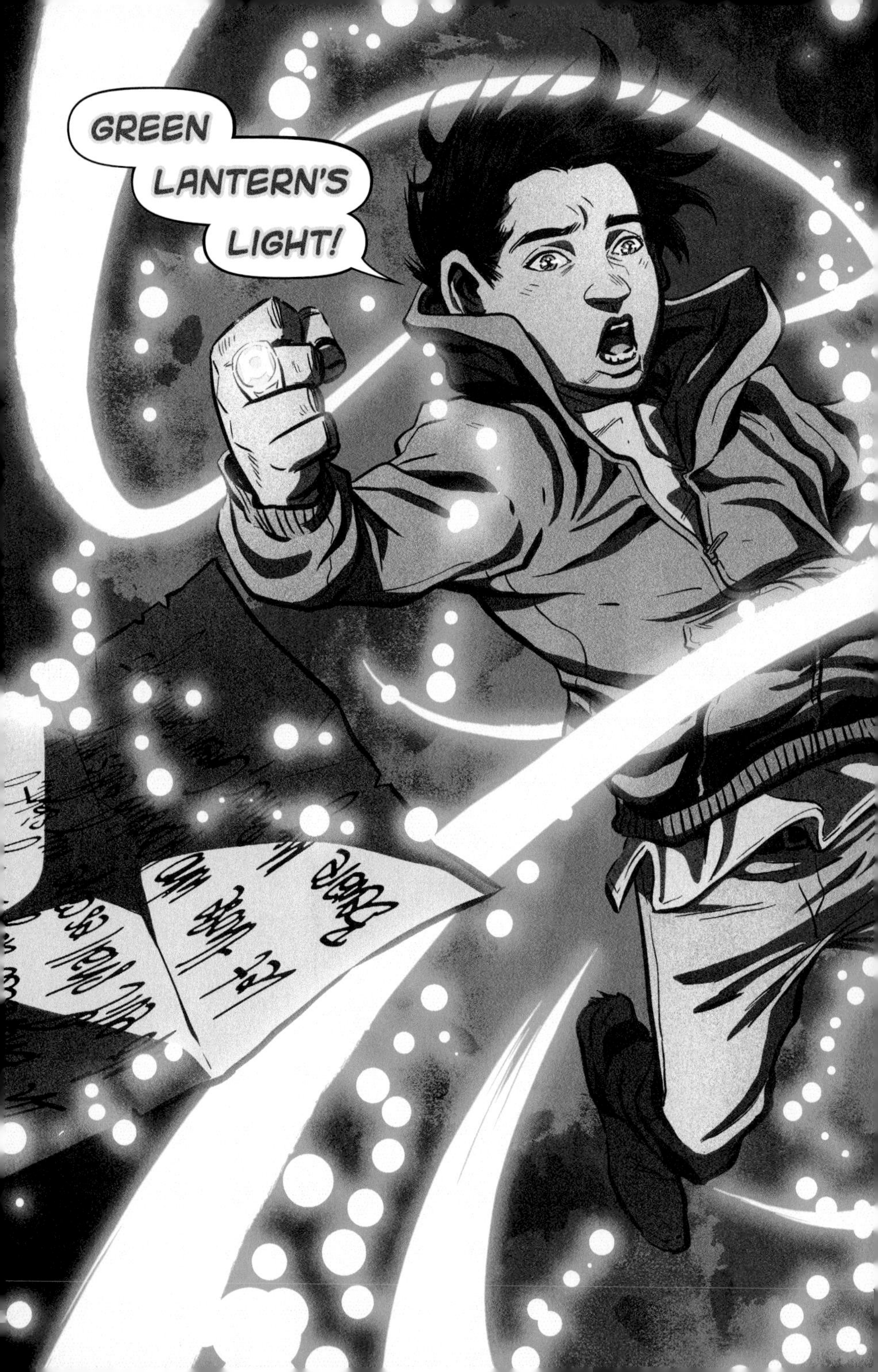
GREEN LANTERN'S LIGHT!

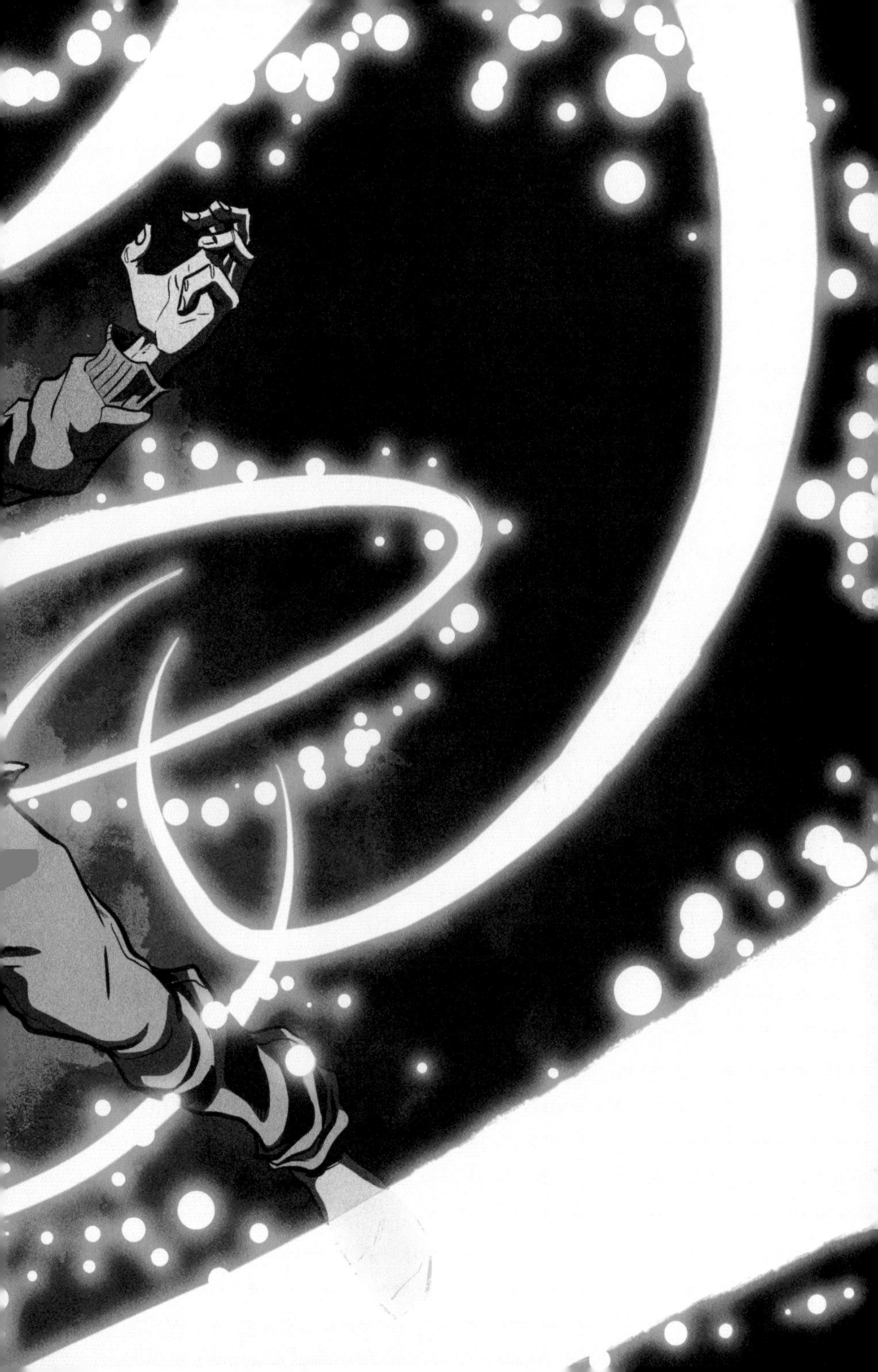

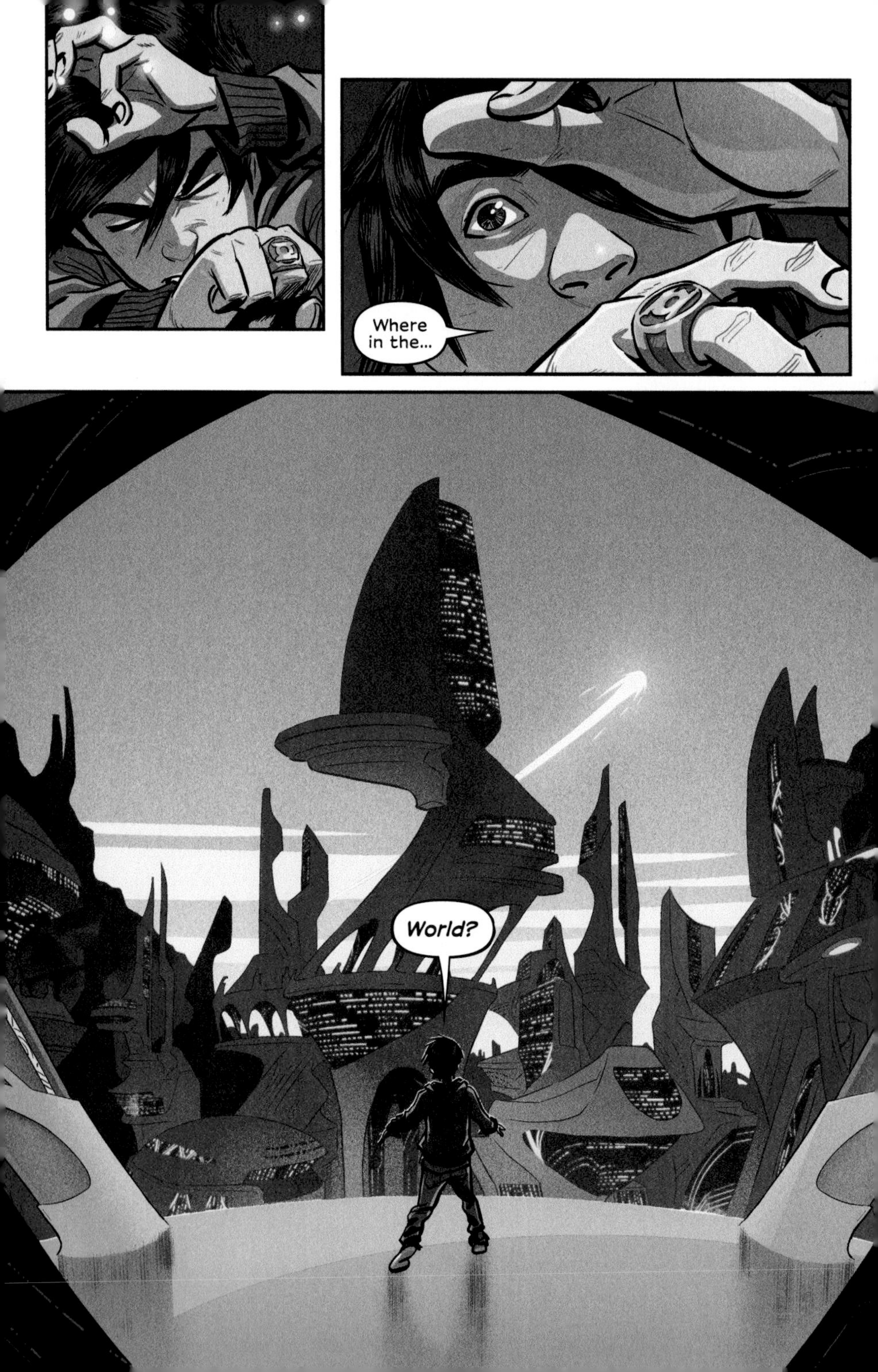
Where in the...
World?

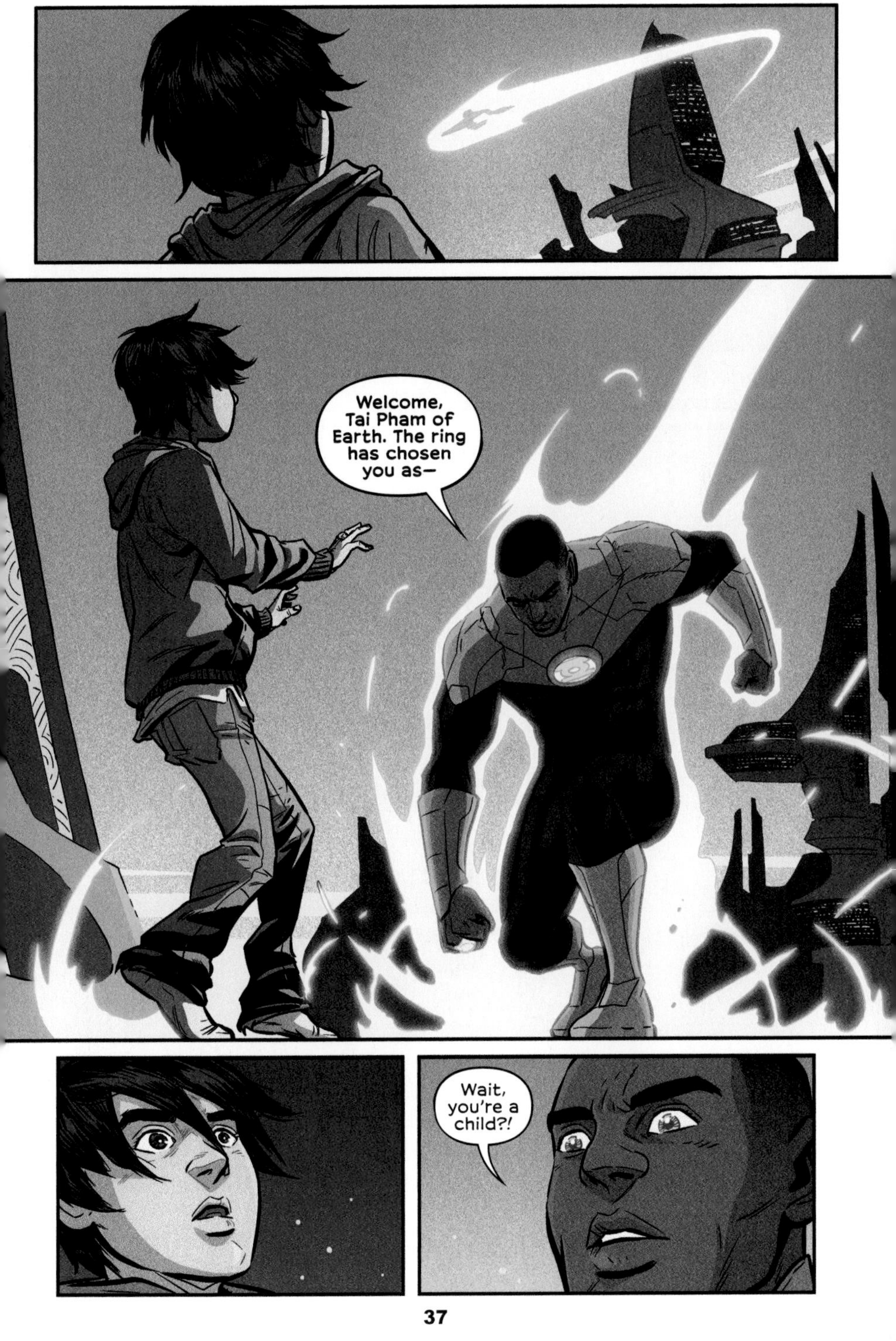
Welcome, Tai Pham of Earth. The ring has chosen you as—
Wait, you're a child?!

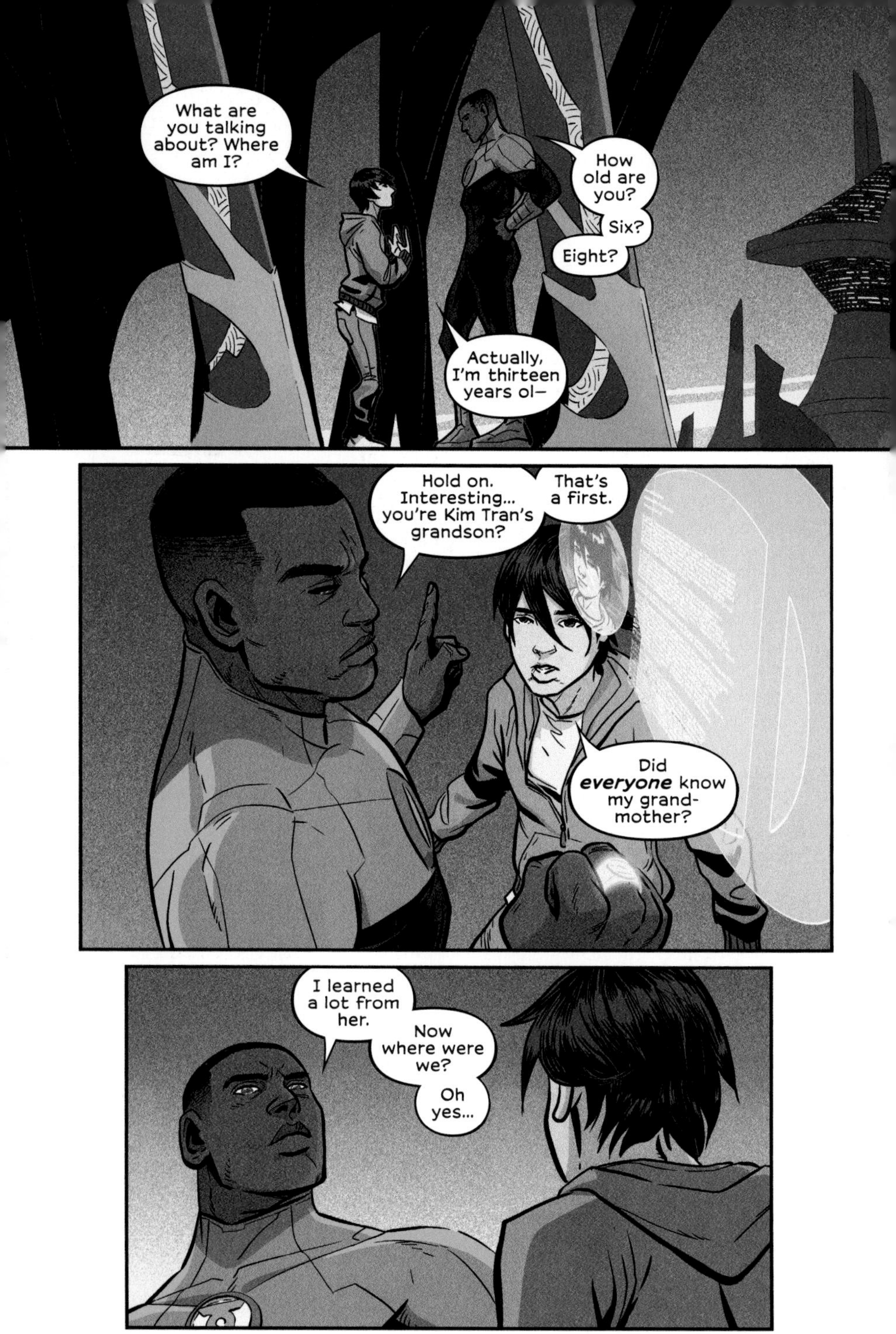
What are you talking about? Where am I?
How old are you?
Six?
Eight?
Actually, I'm thirteen years ol—
Hold on. Interesting... you're Kim Tran's grandson?
That's a first.
Did ***everyone*** know my grand-mother?
I learned a lot from her.
Now where were we?
Oh yes...

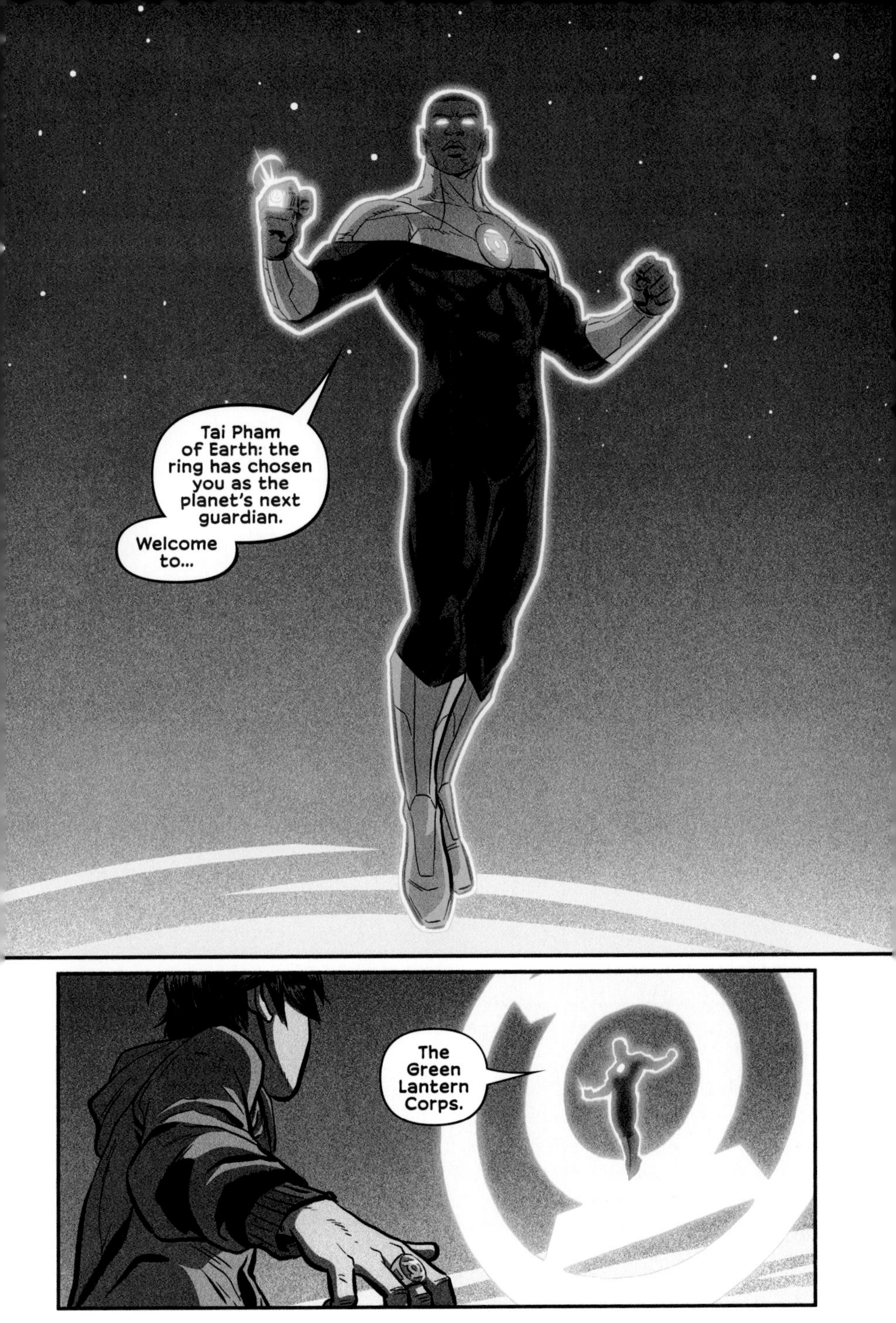
Tai Pham of Earth: the ring has chosen you as the planet's next guardian.
Welcome to...
The Green Lantern Corps.

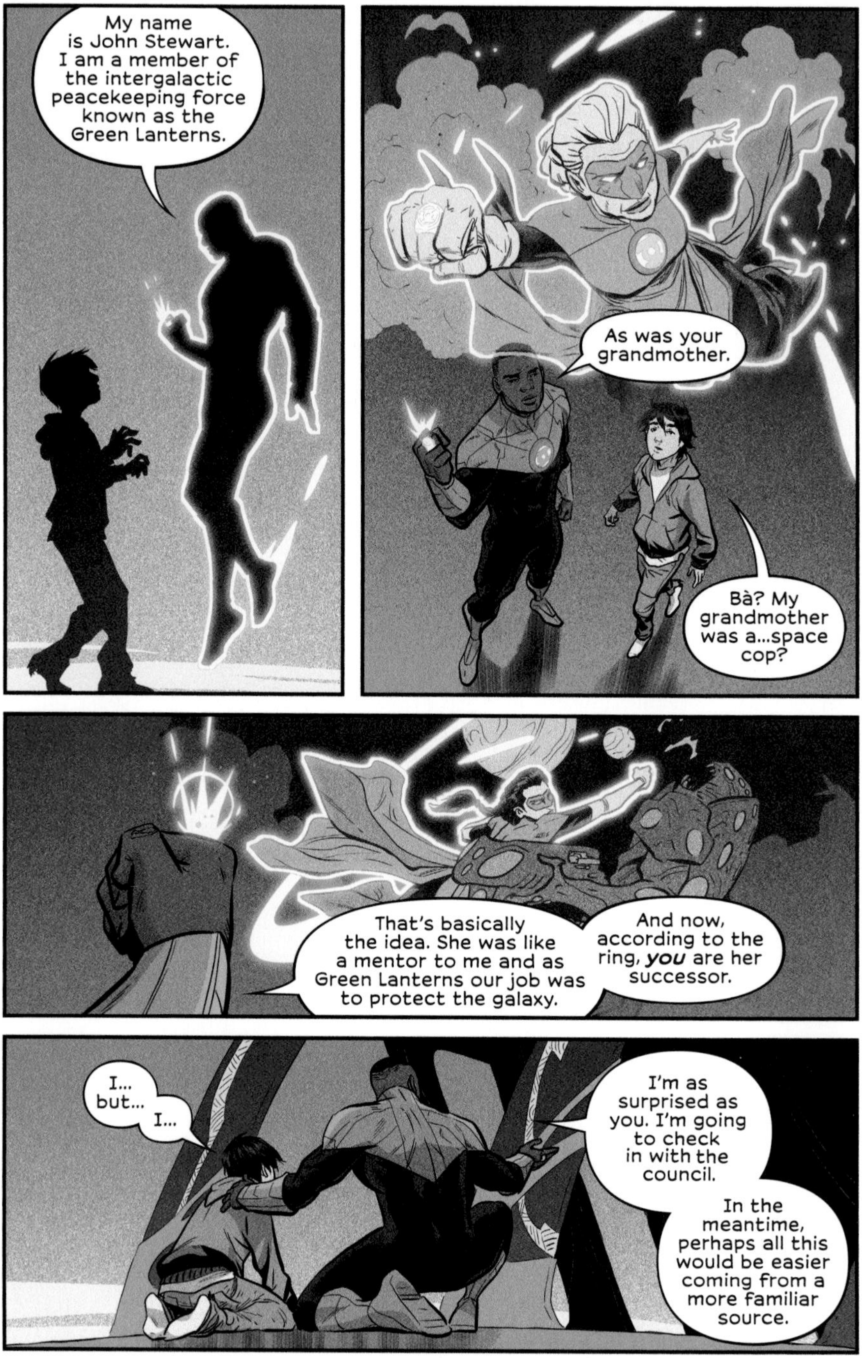
My name is John Stewart. I am a member of the intergalactic peacekeeping force known as the Green Lanterns.
As was your grandmother.
Bà? My grandmother was a...space cop?
That's basically the idea. She was like a mentor to me and as Green Lanterns our job was to protect the galaxy.
And now, according to the ring, ***you*** are her successor.
I... but... I...
I'm as surprised as you. I'm going to check in with the council.
In the meantime, perhaps all this would be easier coming from a more familiar source.

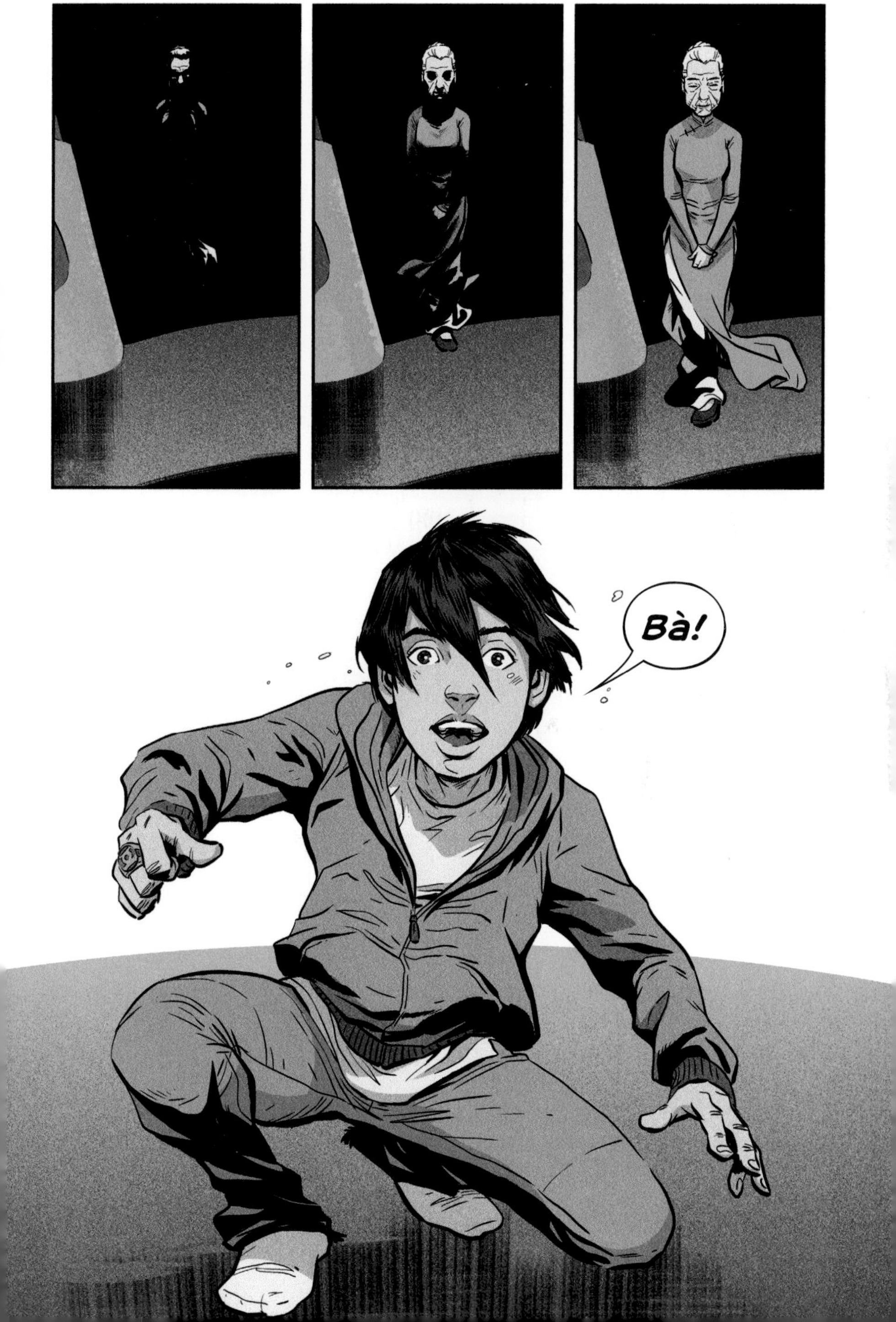
Bà!

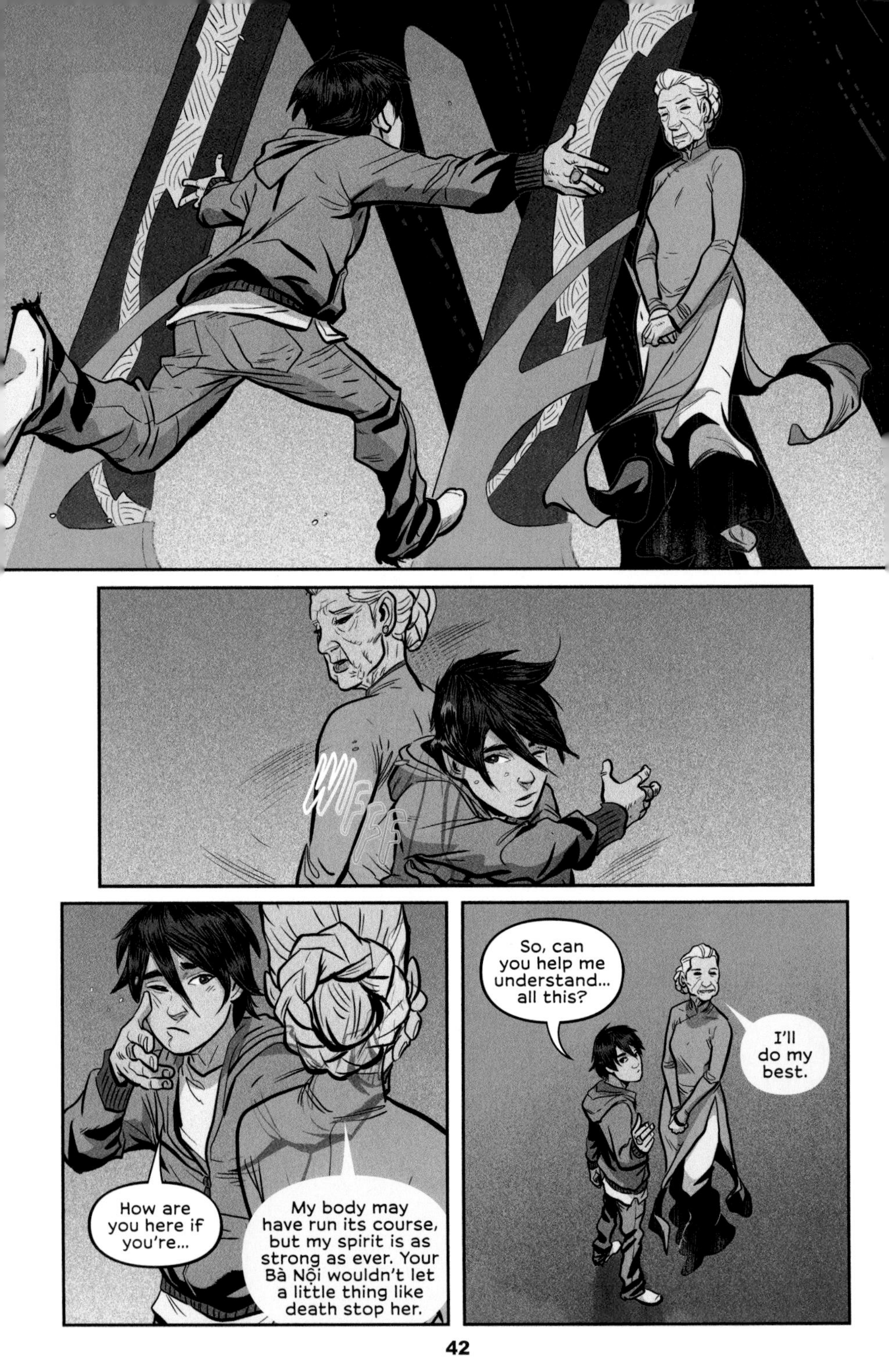
How are you here if you're...
My body may have run its course, but my spirit is as strong as ever. Your Bà Nội wouldn't let a little thing like death stop her.
So, can you help me understand... all this?
I'll do my best.

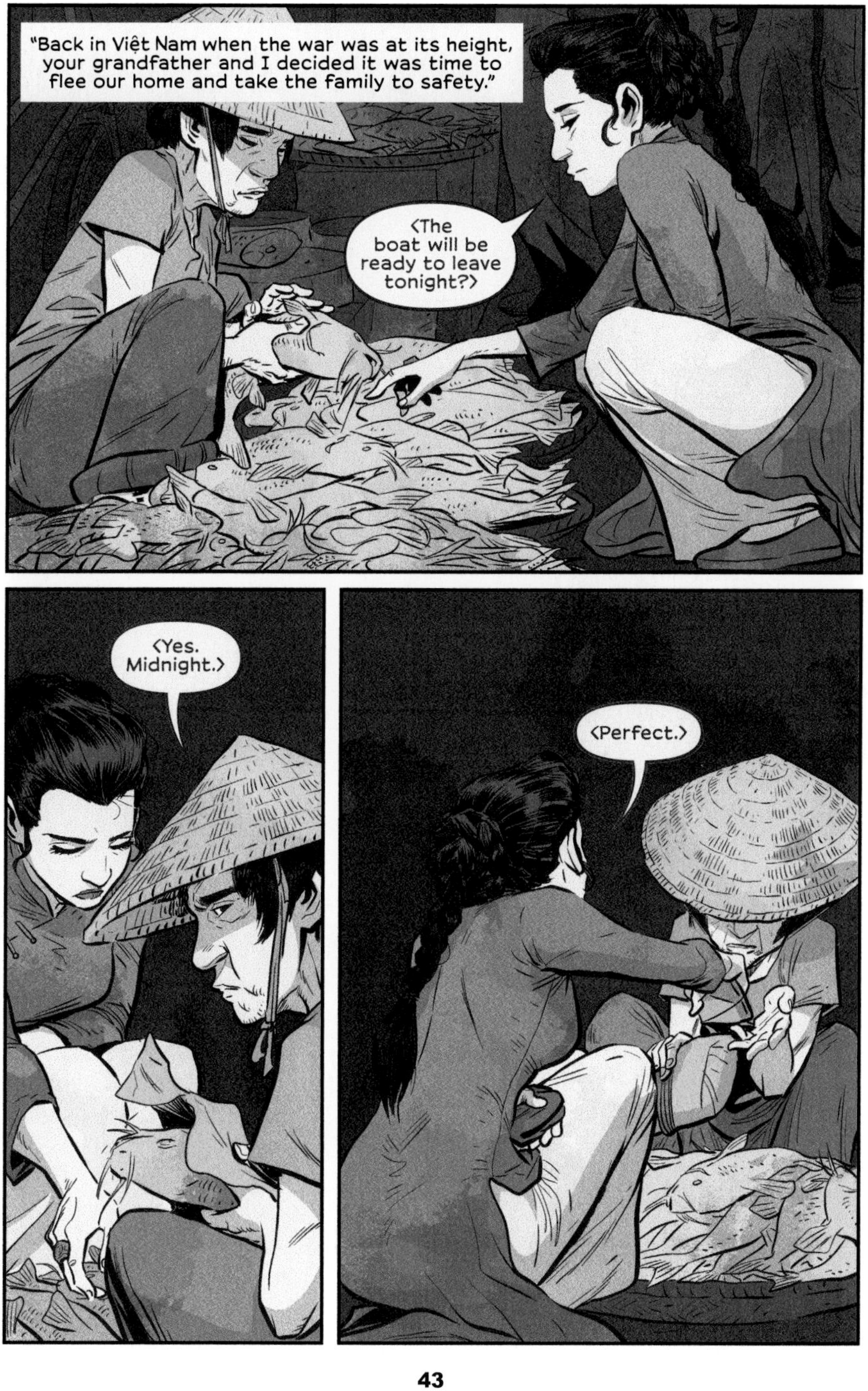
"Back in Việt Nam when the war was at its height, your grandfather and I decided it was time to flee our home and take the family to safety."
<The boat will be ready to leave tonight?>
<Yes. Midnight.>
<Perfect.>

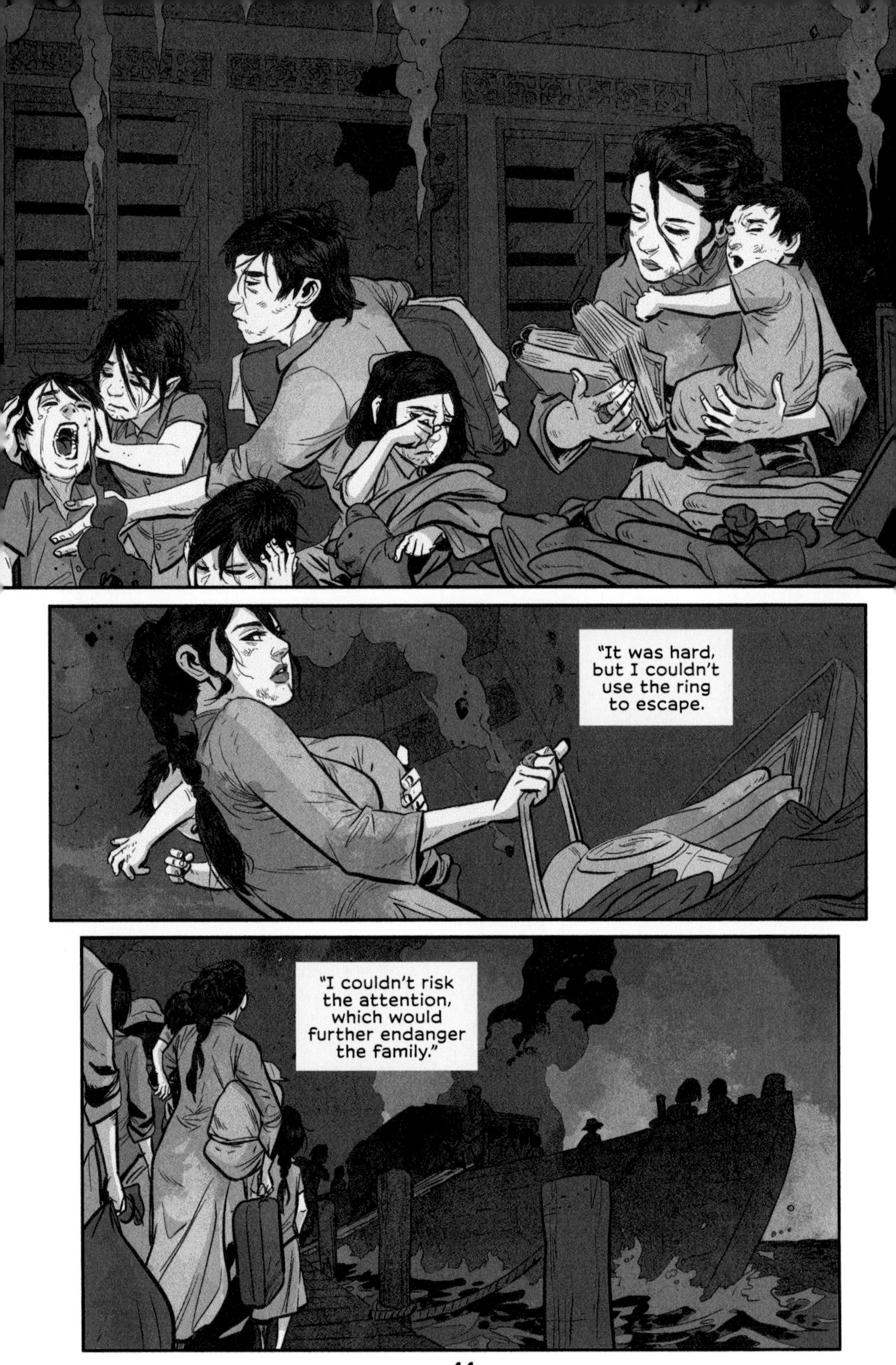
"It was hard, but I couldn't use the ring to escape.
"I couldn't risk the attention, which would further endanger the family."

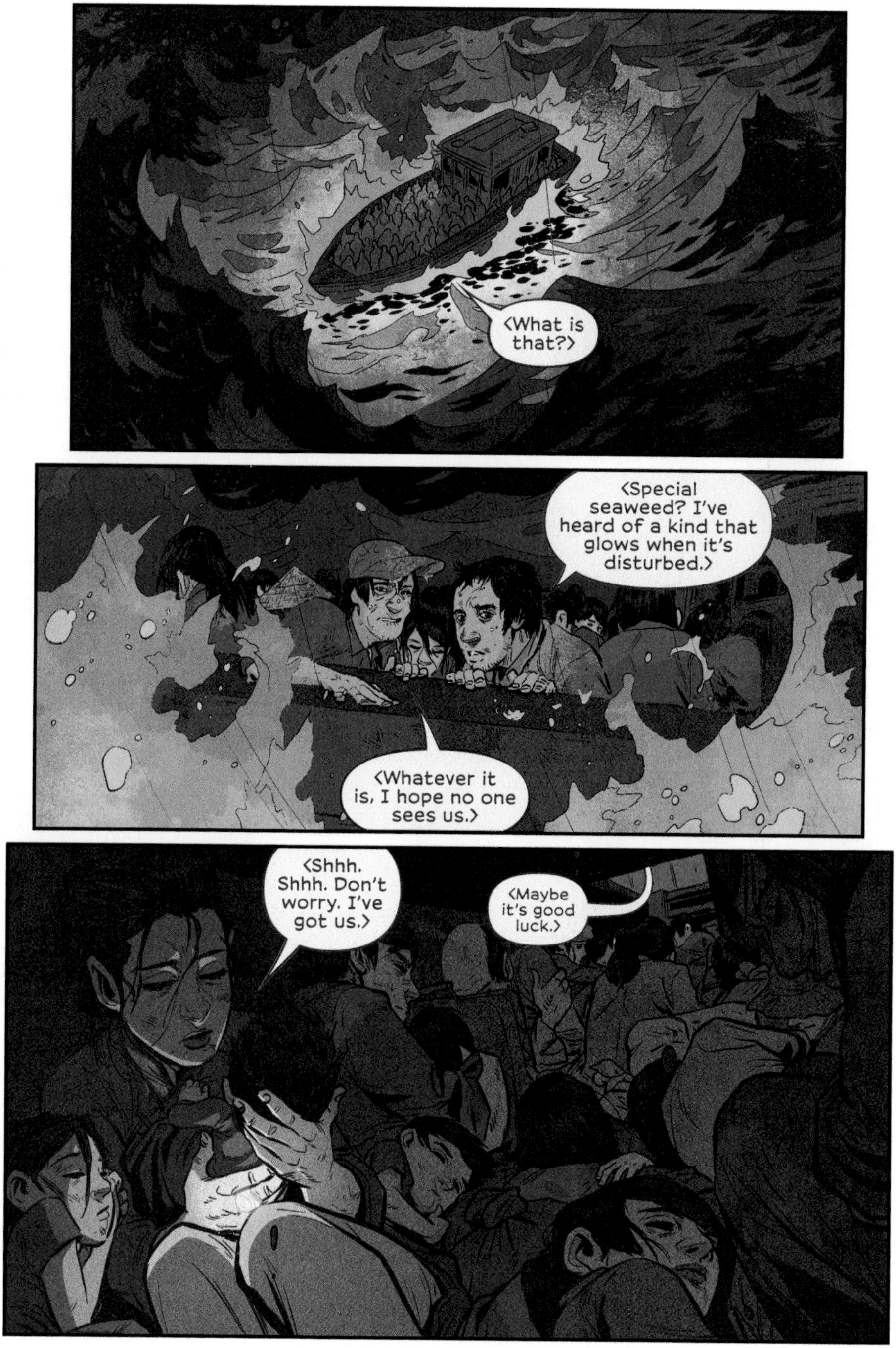

<What is that?>
<Special seaweed? I've heard of a kind that glows when it's disturbed.>
<Whatever it is, I hope no one sees us.>
<Shhh. Shhh. Don't worry. I've got us.>
<Maybe it's good luck.>

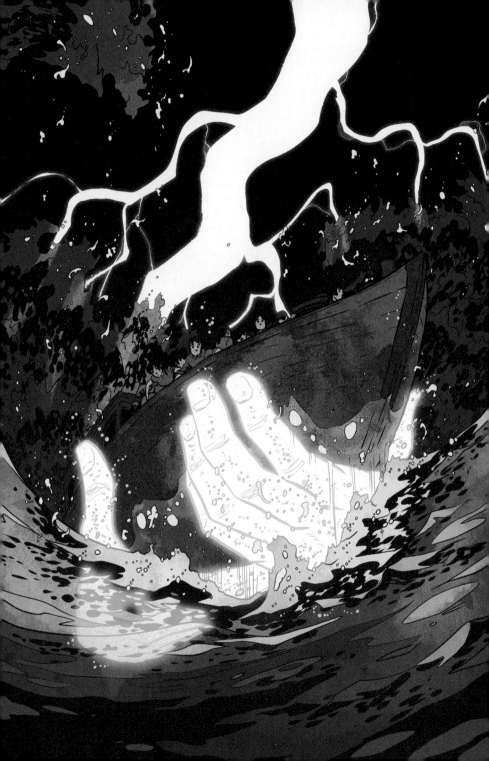

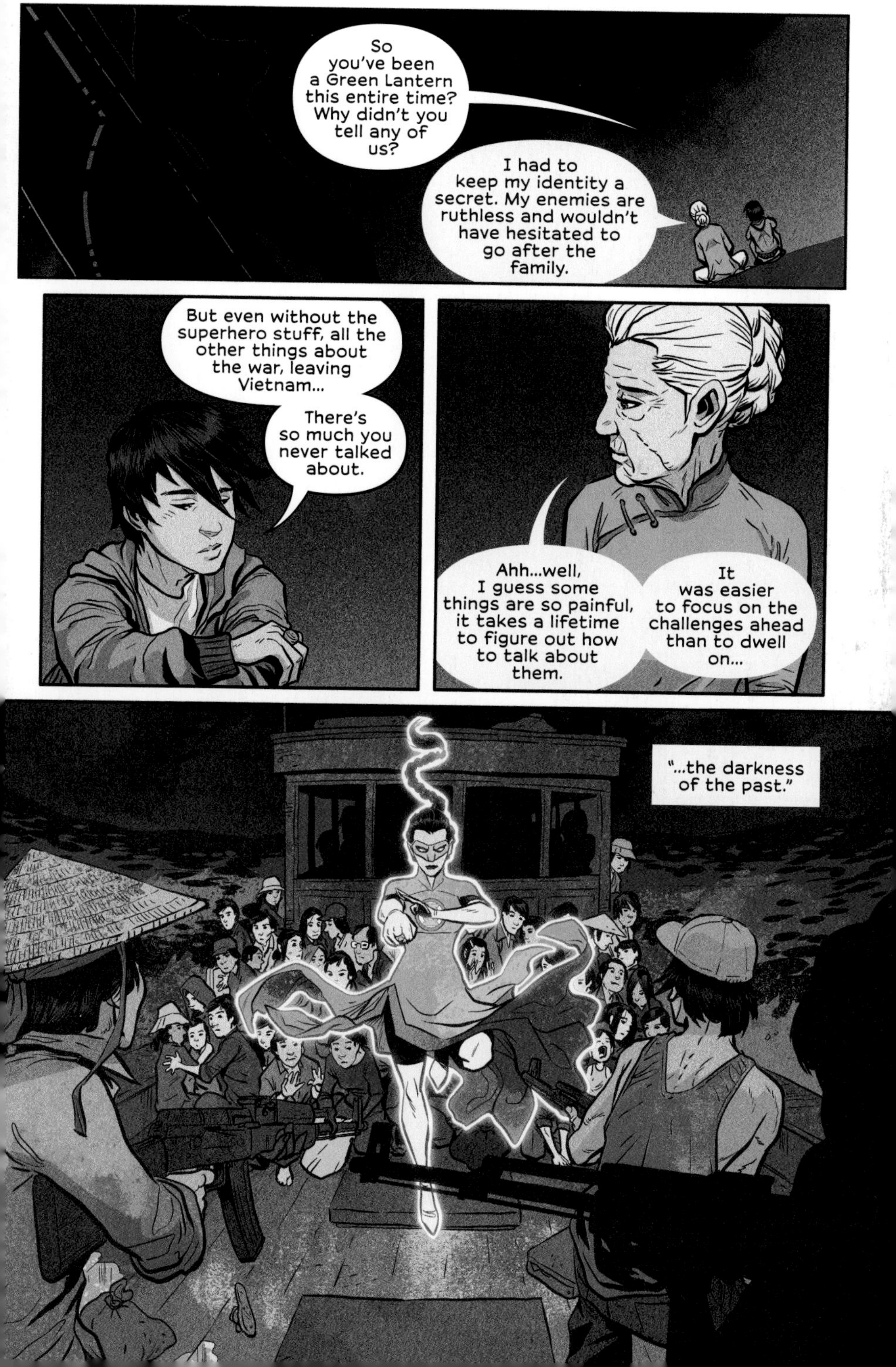
So you've been a Green Lantern this entire time? Why didn't you tell any of us?
I had to keep my identity a secret. My enemies are ruthless and wouldn't have hesitated to go after the family.
But even without the superhero stuff, all the other things about the war, leaving Vietnam...
There's so much you never talked about.
Ahh...well, I guess some things are so painful, it takes a lifetime to figure out how to talk about them.
It was easier to focus on the challenges ahead than to dwell on...
"...the darkness of the past."

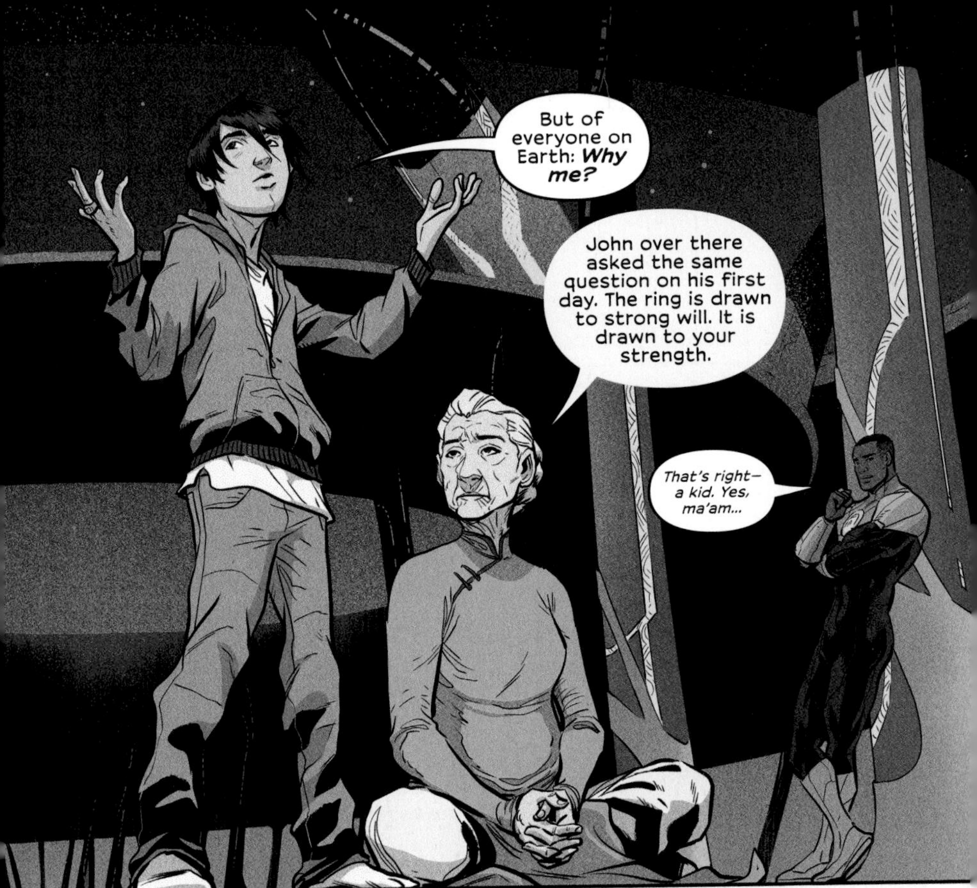
But of everyone on Earth: ***Why me?***
John over there asked the same question on his first day. The ring is drawn to strong will. It is drawn to your strength.
That's right— a kid. Yes, ma'am...

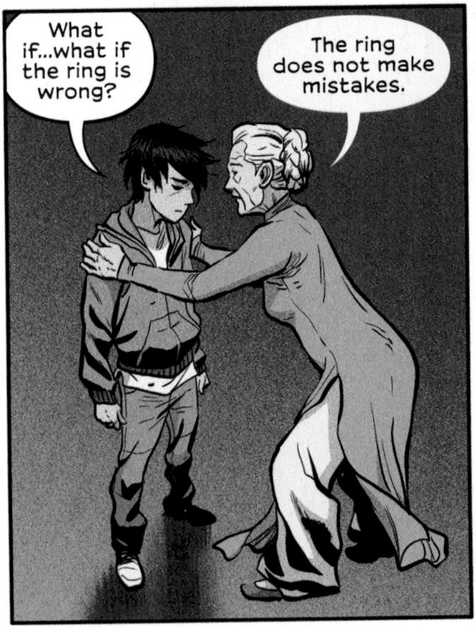
What if...what if the ring is wrong?
The ring does not make mistakes.

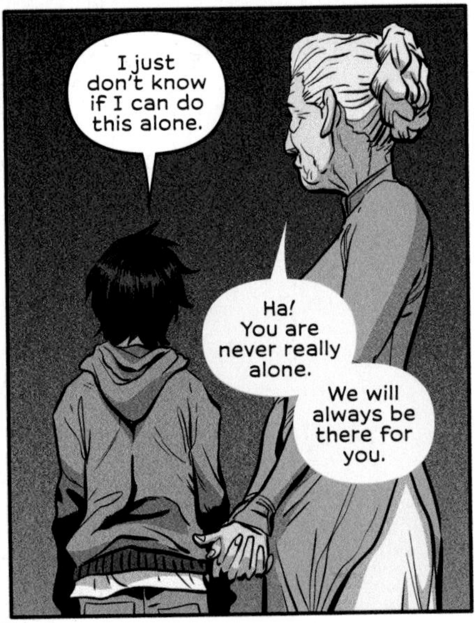
I just don't know if I can do this alone.
Ha! You are never really alone.
We will always be there for you.

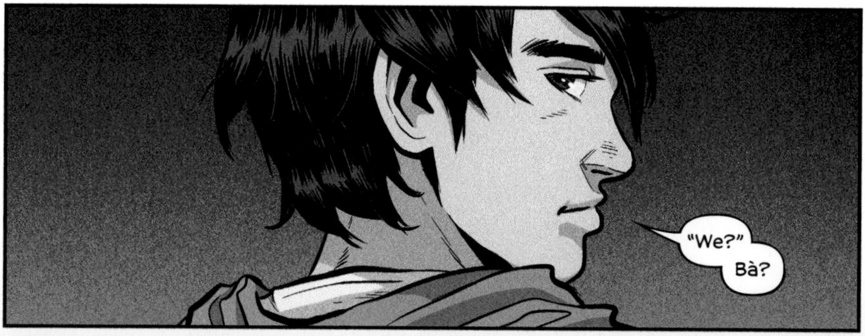
"We?"
Bà?

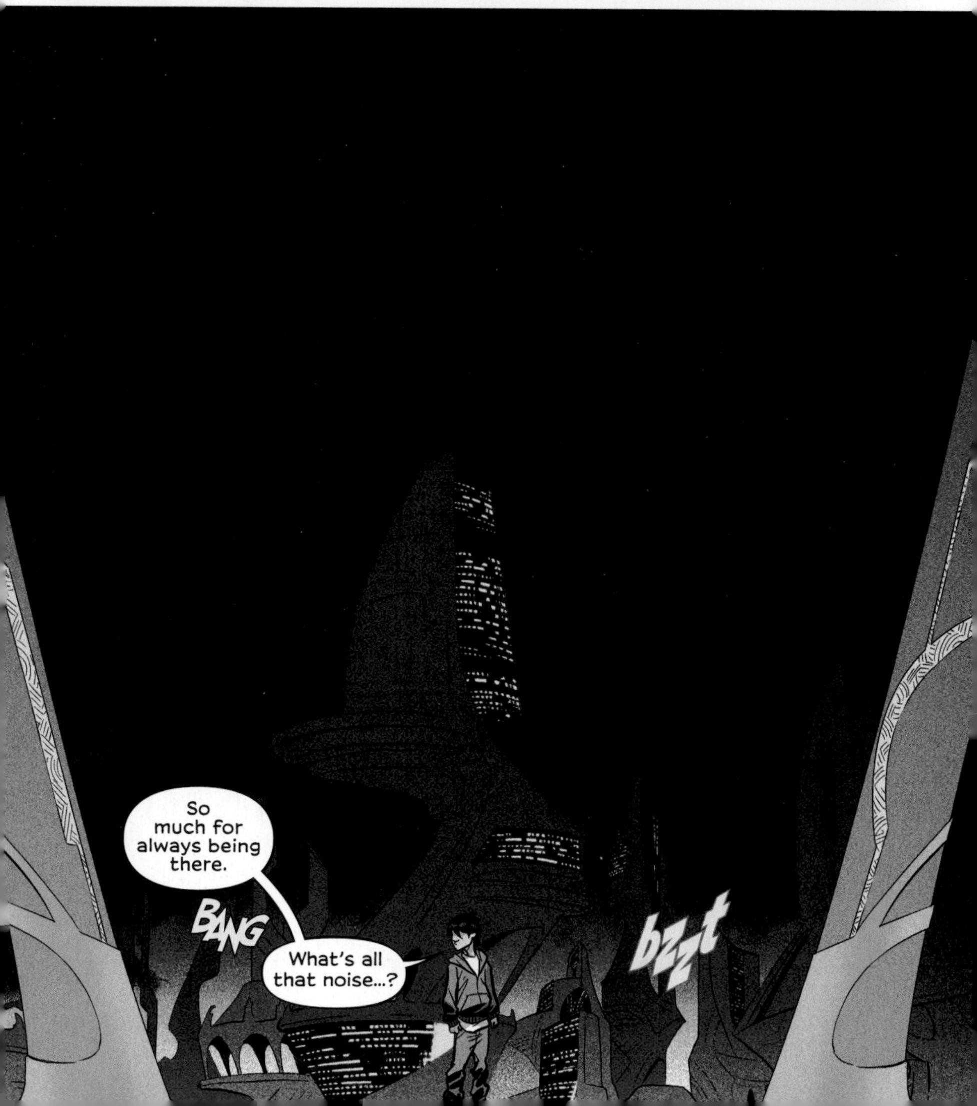
So much for always being there.
BANG
What's all that noise...?
bzzt

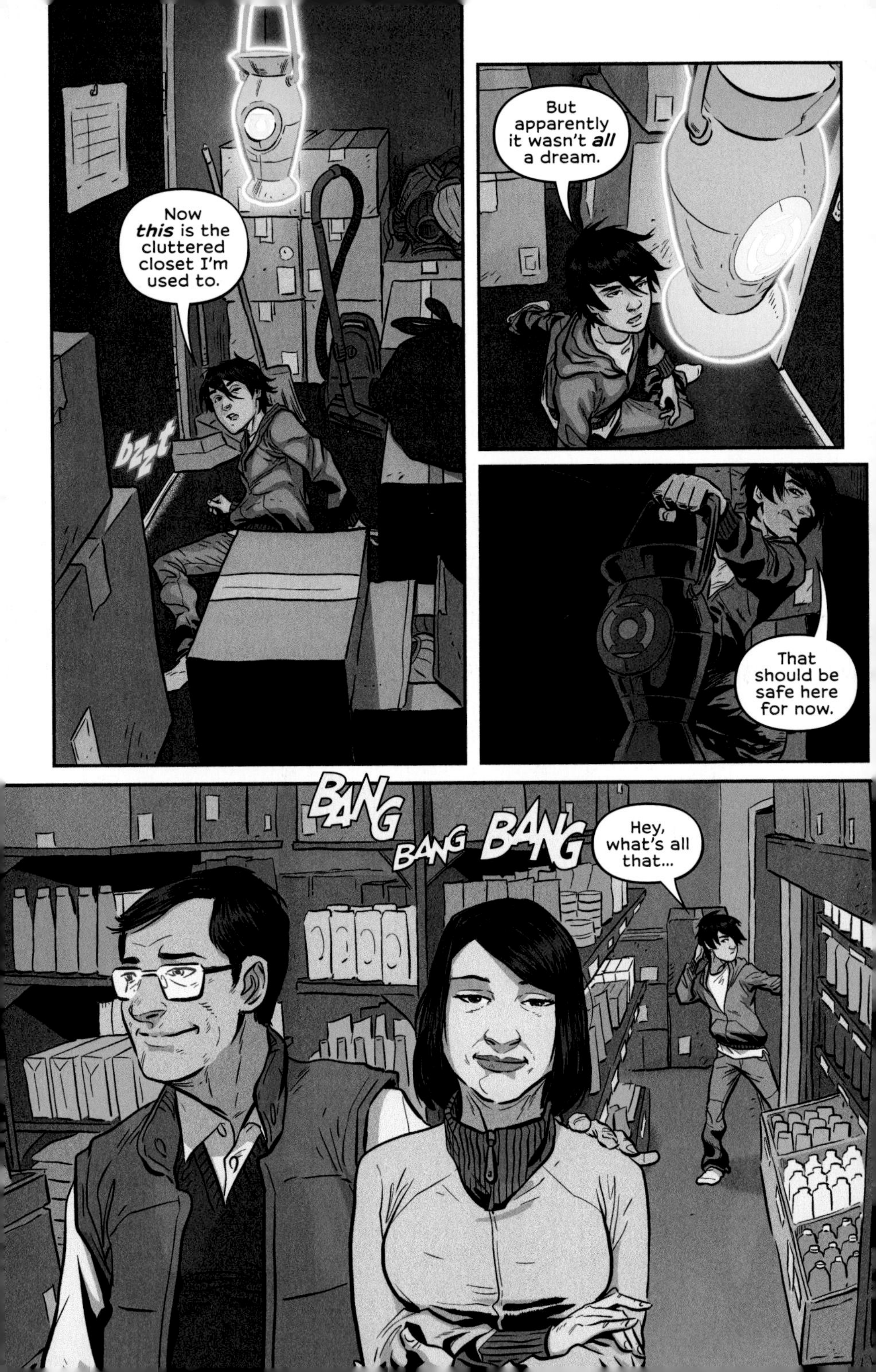
Now *this* is the cluttered closet I'm used to.
bzz-t
But apparently it wasn't ***all*** a dream.
That should be safe here for now.
BANG
BANG
BANG
Hey, what's all that...

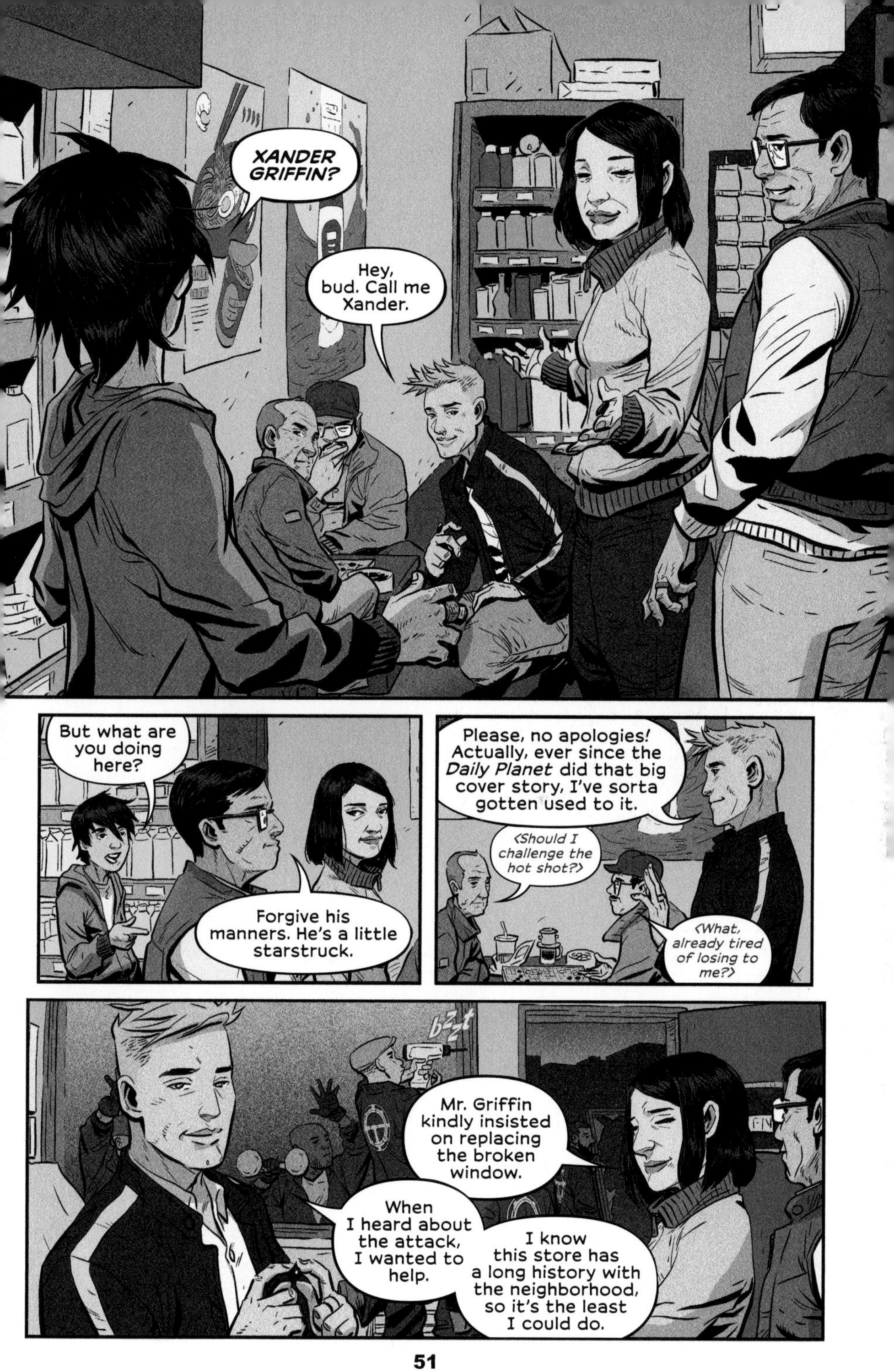
XANDER GRIFFIN?
Hey, bud. Call me Xander.
But what are you doing here?
Forgive his manners. He's a little starstruck.
Please, no apologies! Actually, ever since the *Daily Planet* did that big cover story, I've sorta gotten used to it.
‹Should I challenge the hot shot?›
‹What, already tired of losing to me?›
bzzzt
Mr. Griffin kindly insisted on replacing the broken window.
When I heard about the attack, I wanted to help.
I know this store has a long history with the neighborhood, so it's the least I could do.

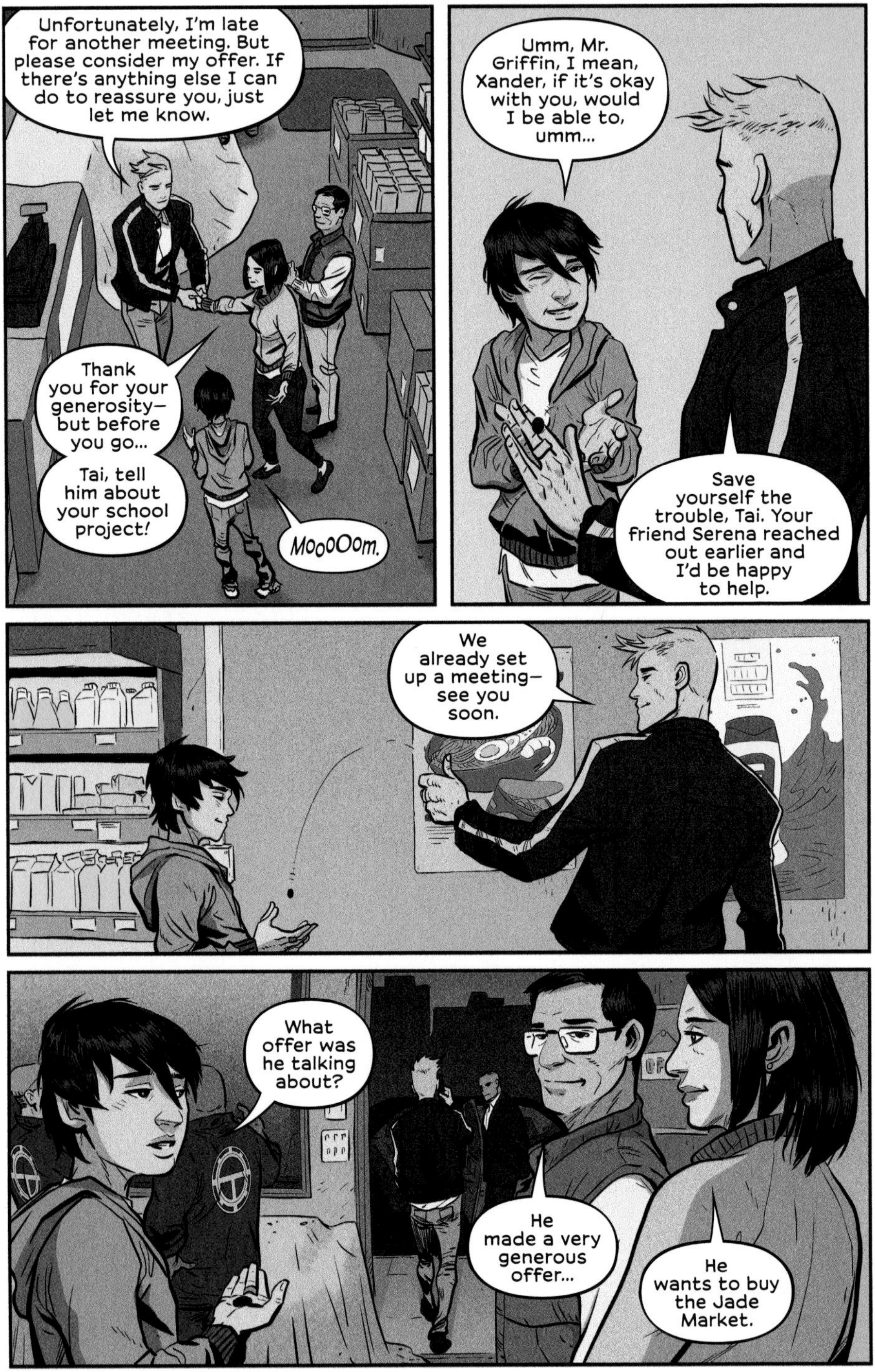
Unfortunately, I'm late for another meeting. But please consider my offer. If there's anything else I can do to reassure you, just let me know.
Thank you for your generosity—but before you go...
Tai, tell him about your school project!
MoooOom.
Umm, Mr. Griffin, I mean, Xander, if it's okay with you, would I be able to, umm...
Save yourself the trouble, Tai. Your friend Serena reached out earlier and I'd be happy to help.
We already set up a meeting—see you soon.
What offer was he talking about?
He made a very generous offer...
He wants to buy the Jade Market.

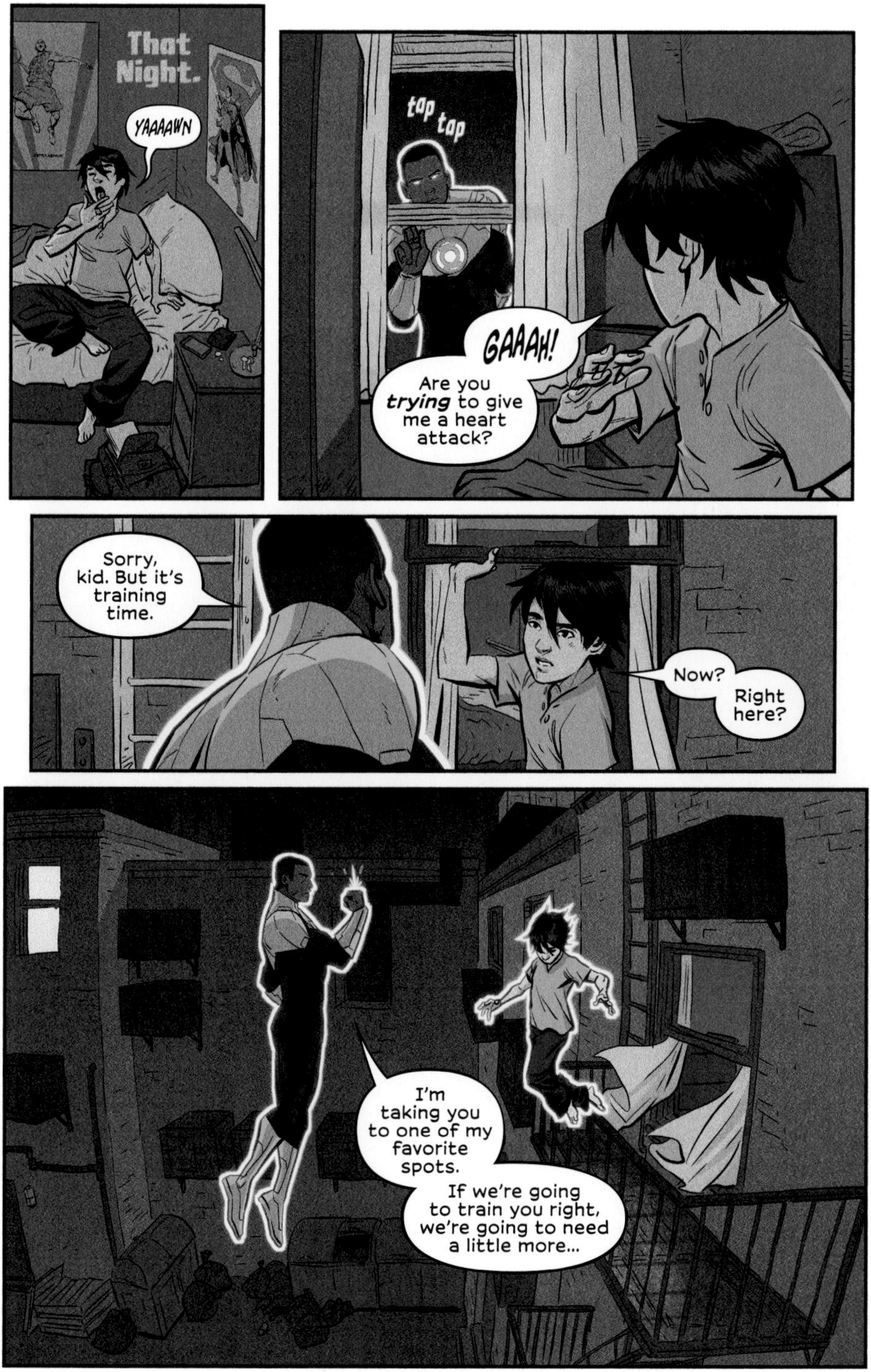
That Night.
YAAAAWN
tap tap
GAAAH!
Are you *trying* to give me a heart attack?
Sorry, kid. But it's training time.
Now?
Right here?
I'm taking you to one of my favorite spots.
If we're going to train you right, we're going to need a little more...

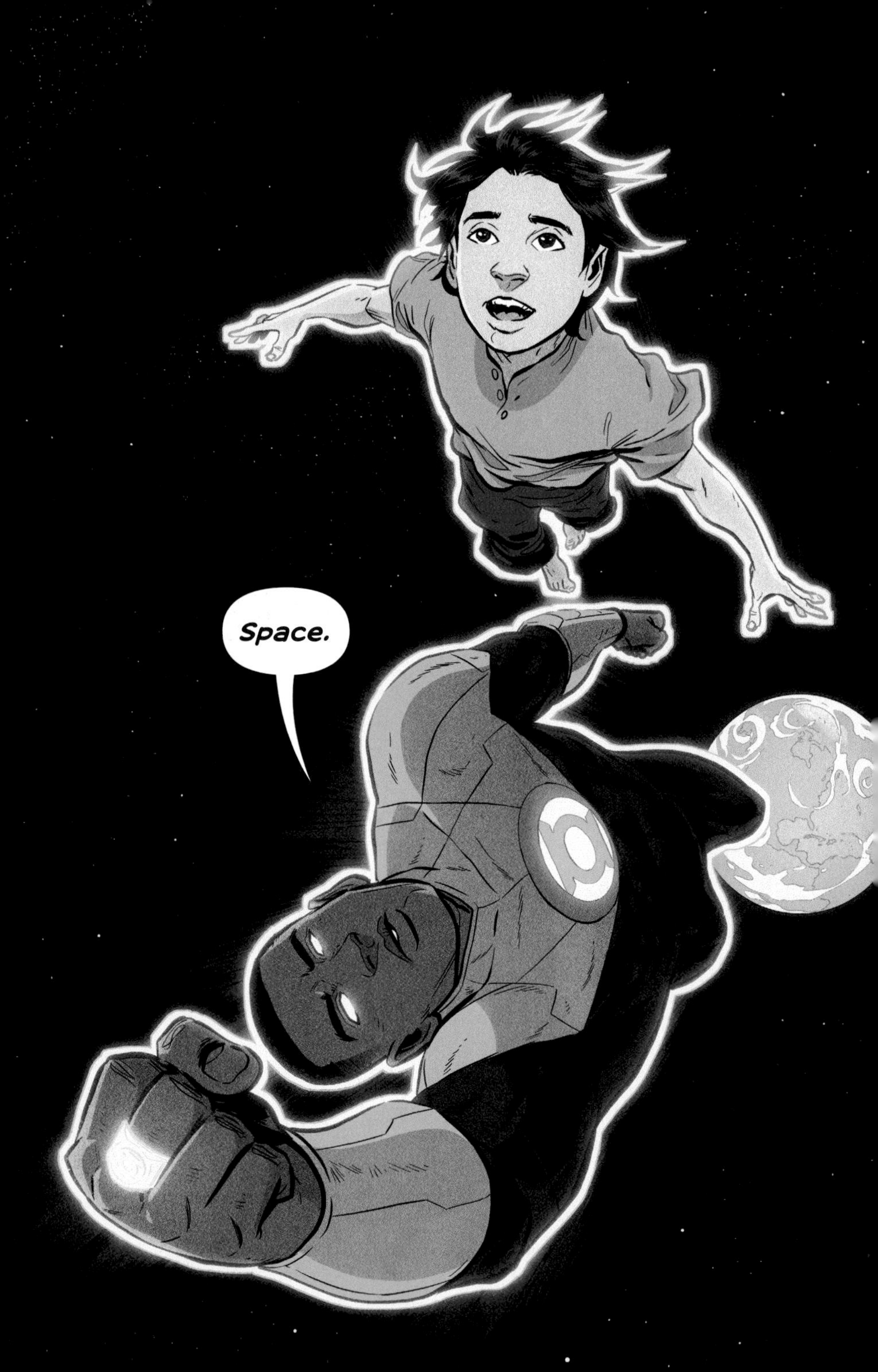
Space.

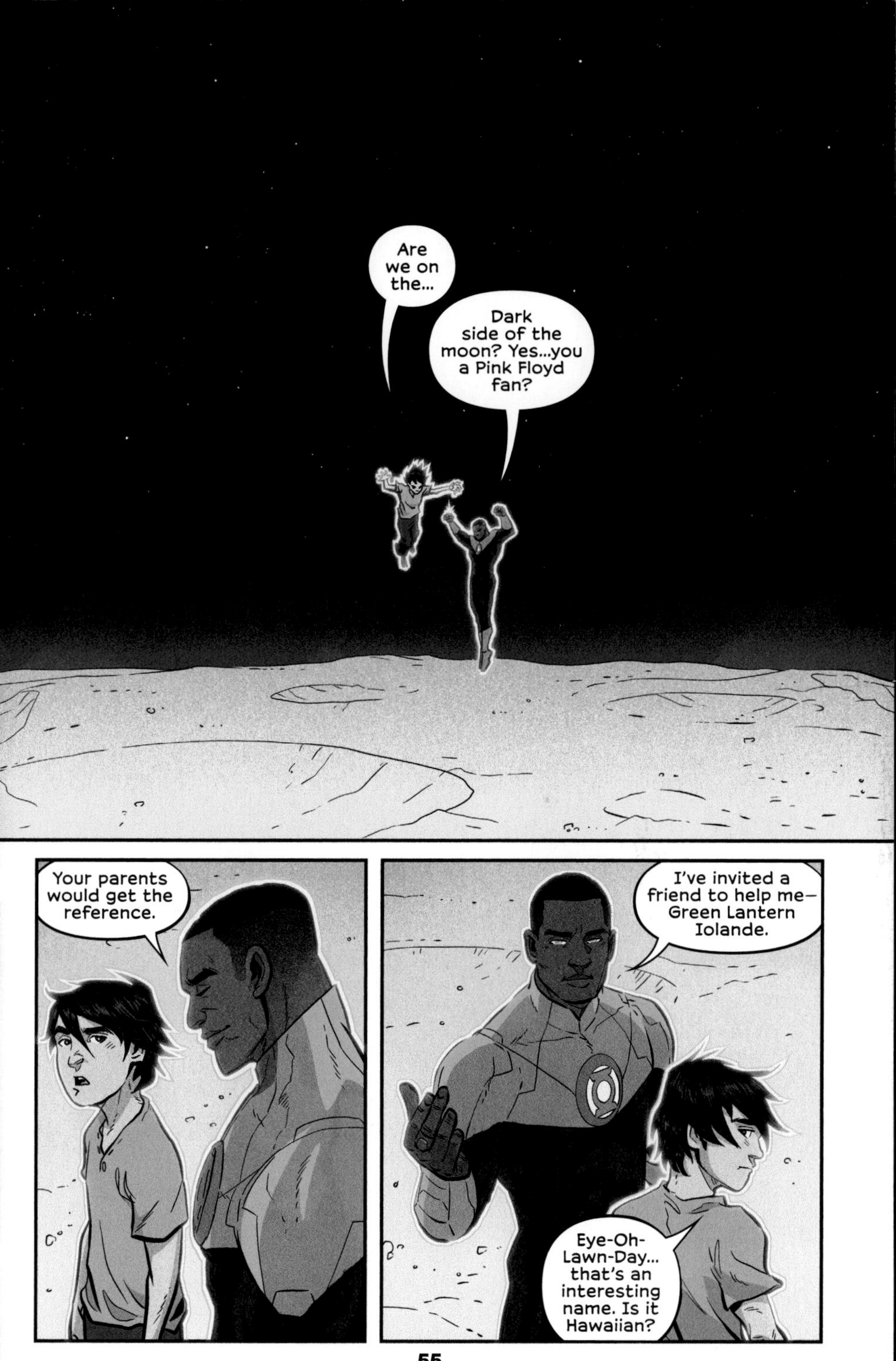
Are we on the...
Dark side of the moon? Yes...you a Pink Floyd fan?
Your parents would get the reference.
I've invited a friend to help me— Green Lantern Iolande.
Eye-Oh-Lawn-Day... that's an interesting name. Is it Hawaiian?

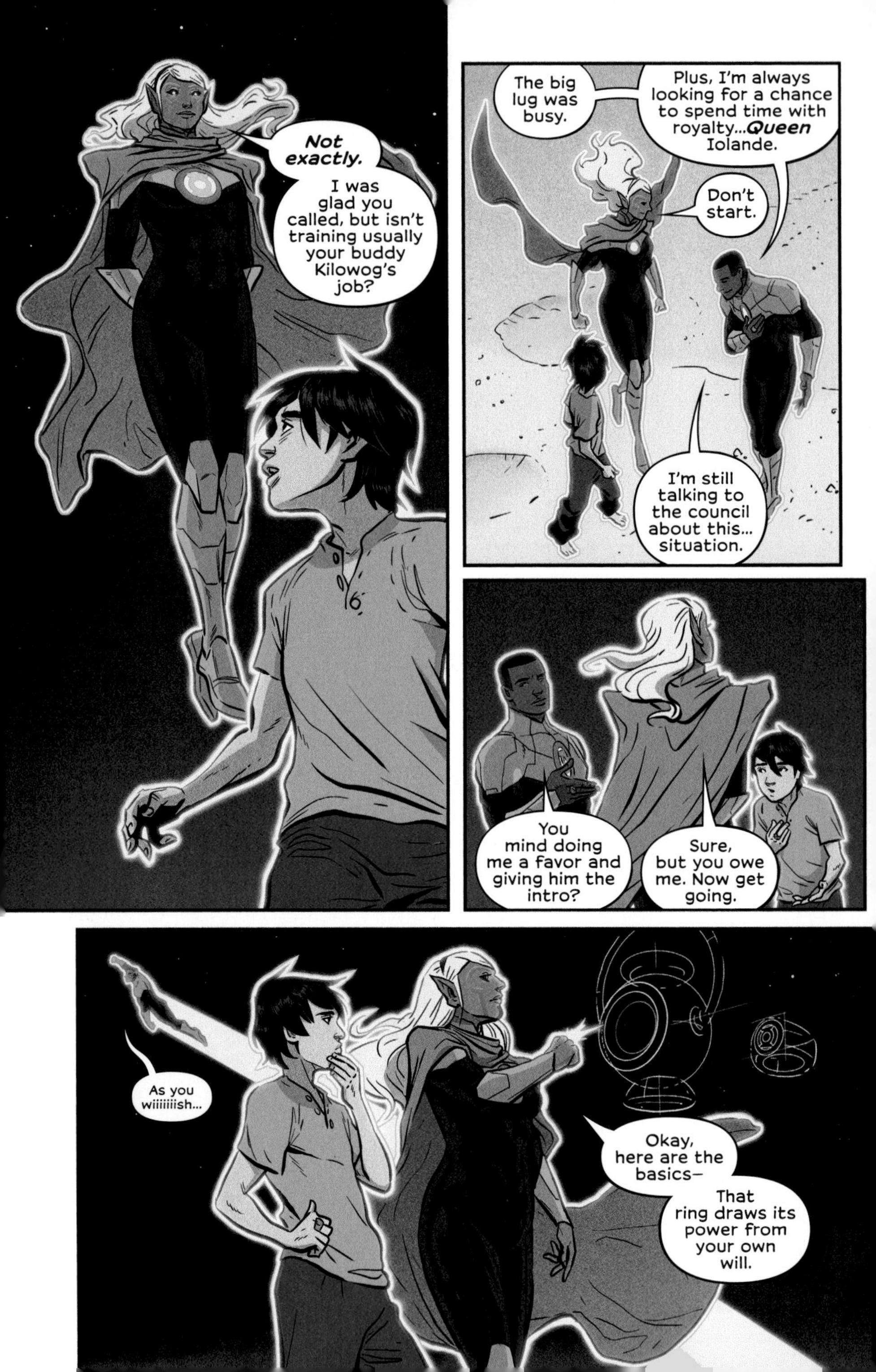

Not exactly.
I was glad you called, but isn't training usually your buddy Kilowog's job?
The big lug was busy.
Plus, I'm always looking for a chance to spend time with royalty...Queen Iolande.
Don't start.
I'm still talking to the council about this... situation.
You mind doing me a favor and giving him the intro?
Sure, but you owe me. Now get going.
As you wiiiiiiish...
Okay, here are the basics—
That ring draws its power from your own will.

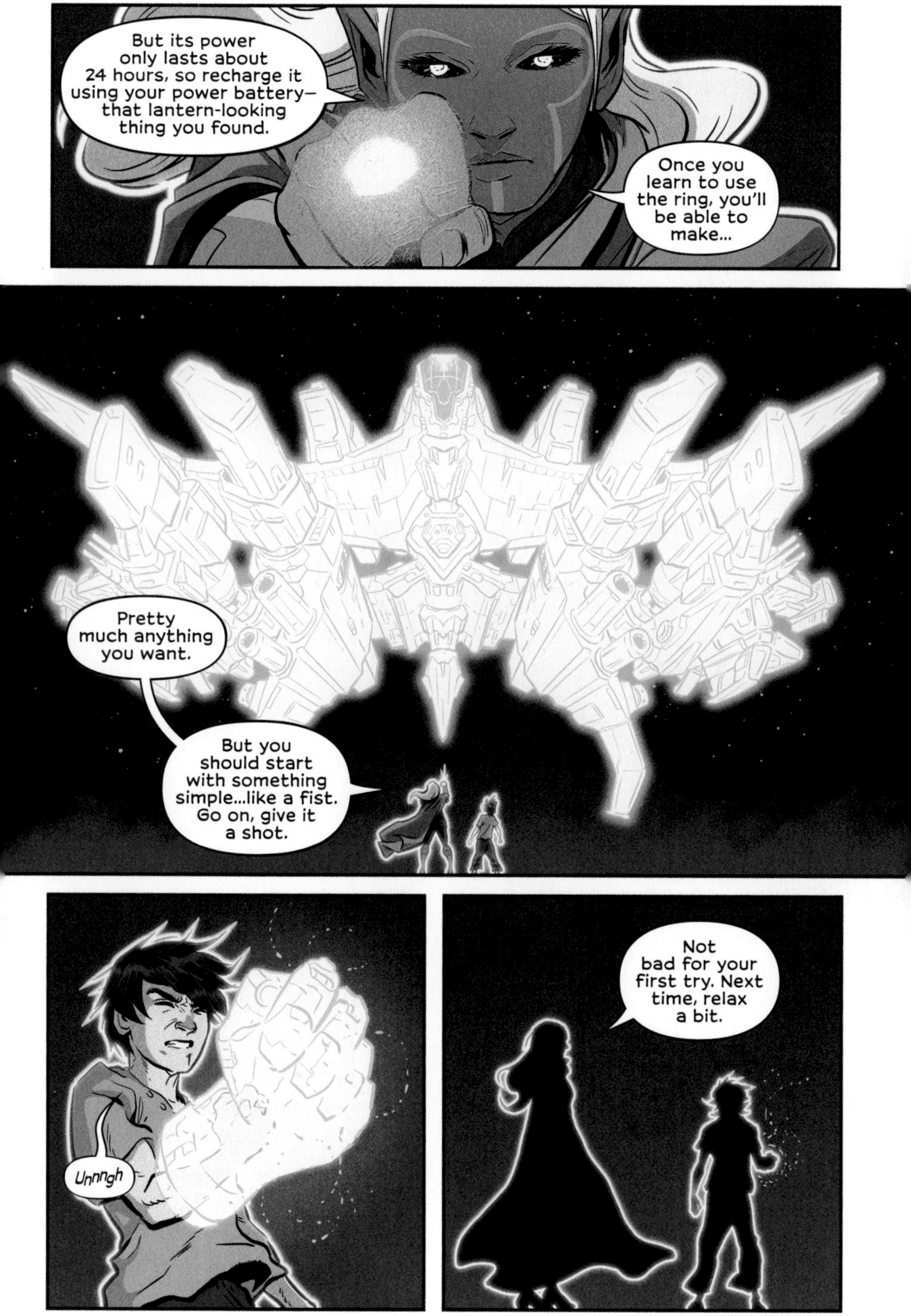
But its power only lasts about 24 hours, so recharge it using your power battery— that lantern-looking thing you found.
Once you learn to use the ring, you'll be able to make...
Pretty much anything you want.
But you should start with something simple...like a fist. Go on, give it a shot.
Unnngh
Not bad for your first try. Next time, relax a bit.

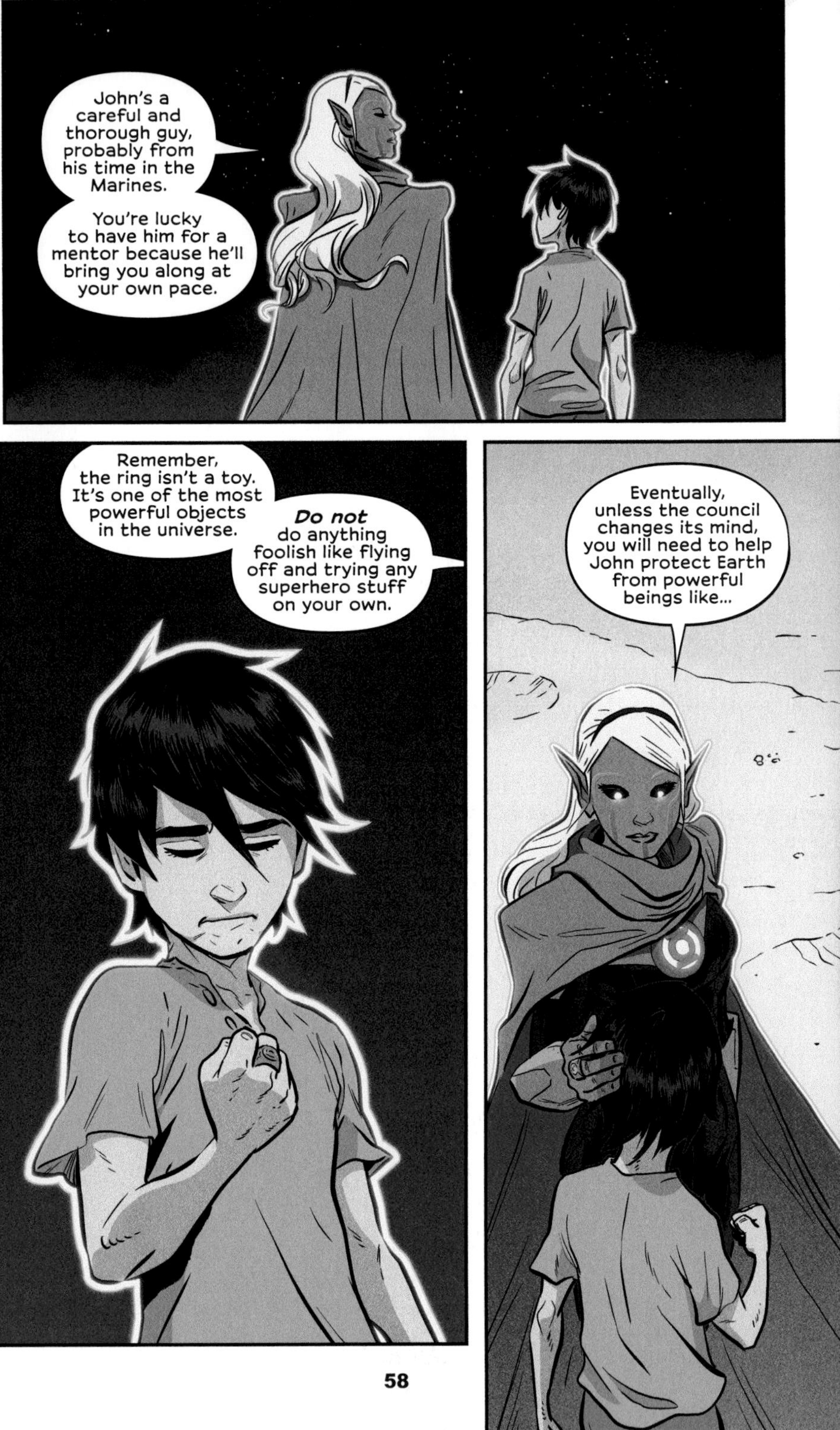

John's a careful and thorough guy, probably from his time in the Marines.
You're lucky to have him for a mentor because he'll bring you along at your own pace.
Remember, the ring isn't a toy. It's one of the most powerful objects in the universe.
Do not do anything foolish like flying off and trying any superhero stuff on your own.
Eventually, unless the council changes its mind, you will need to help John protect Earth from powerful beings like...

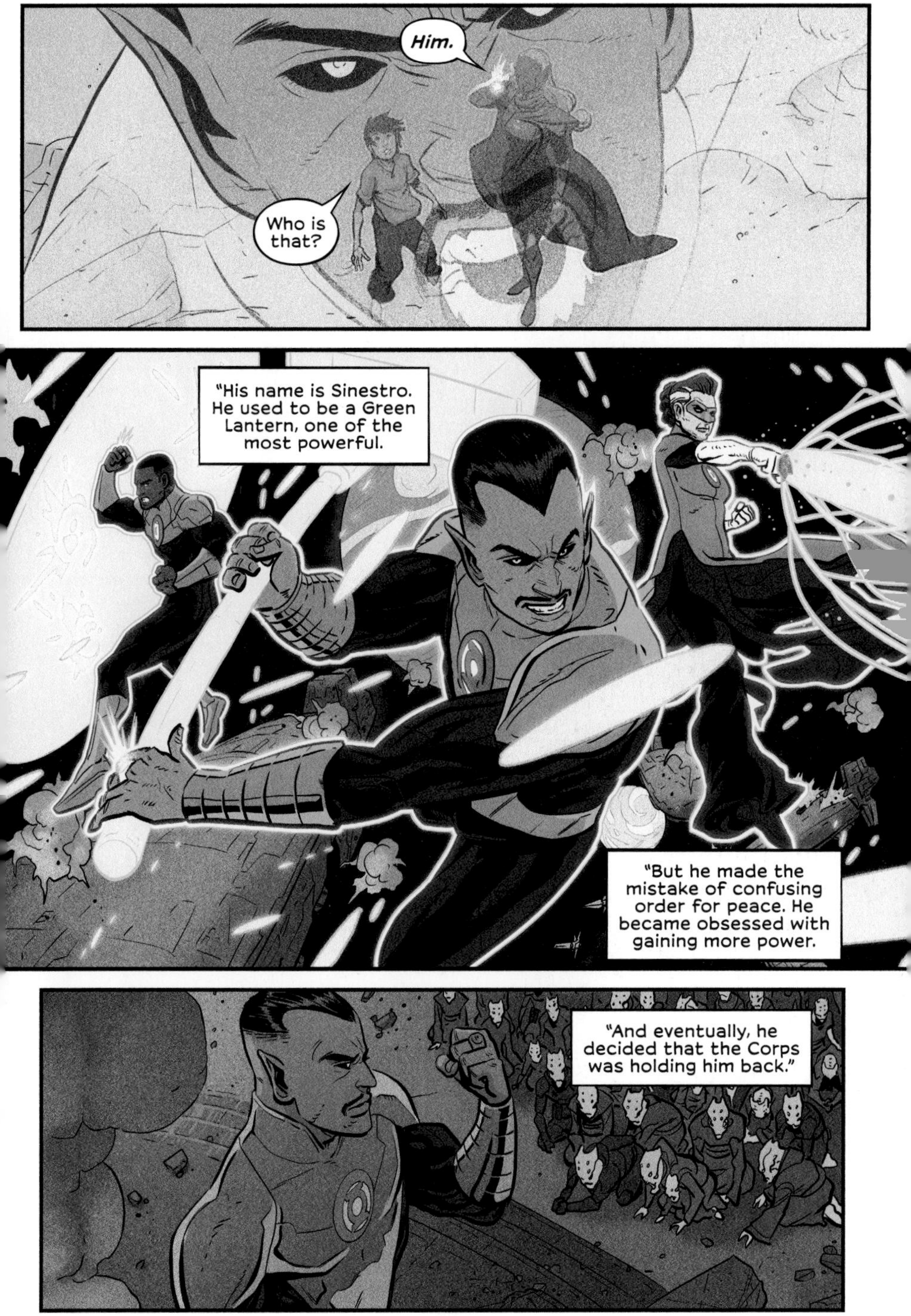
Him.
Who is that?
"His name is Sinestro. He used to be a Green Lantern, one of the most powerful.
"But he made the mistake of confusing order for peace. He became obsessed with gaining more power.
"And eventually, he decided that the Corps was holding him back."

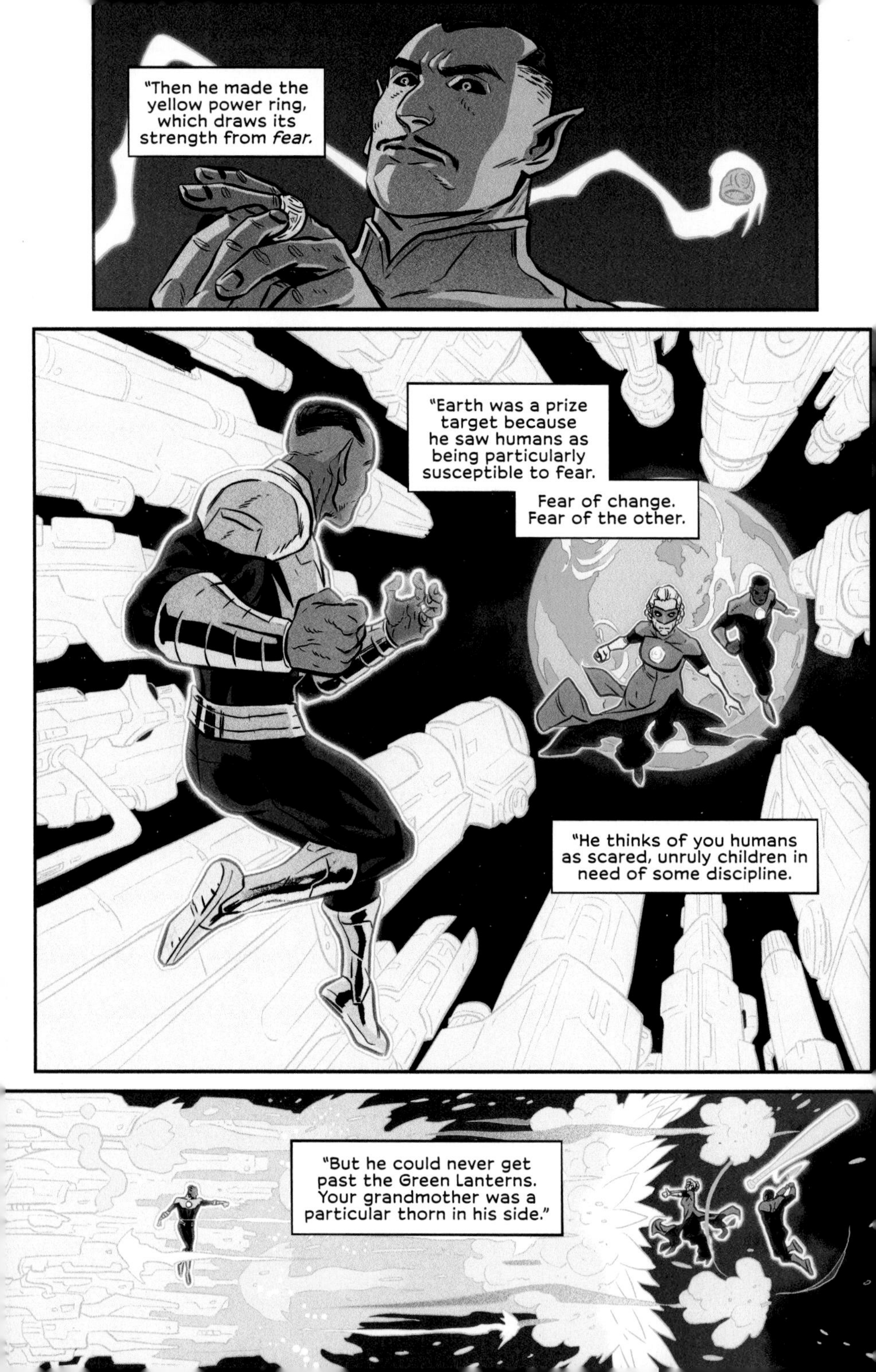
"Then he made the yellow power ring, which draws its strength from *fear.*
"Earth was a prize target because he saw humans as being particularly susceptible to fear.
Fear of change. Fear of the other.
"He thinks of you humans as scared, unruly children in need of some discipline.
"But he could never get past the Green Lanterns. Your grandmother was a particular thorn in his side."

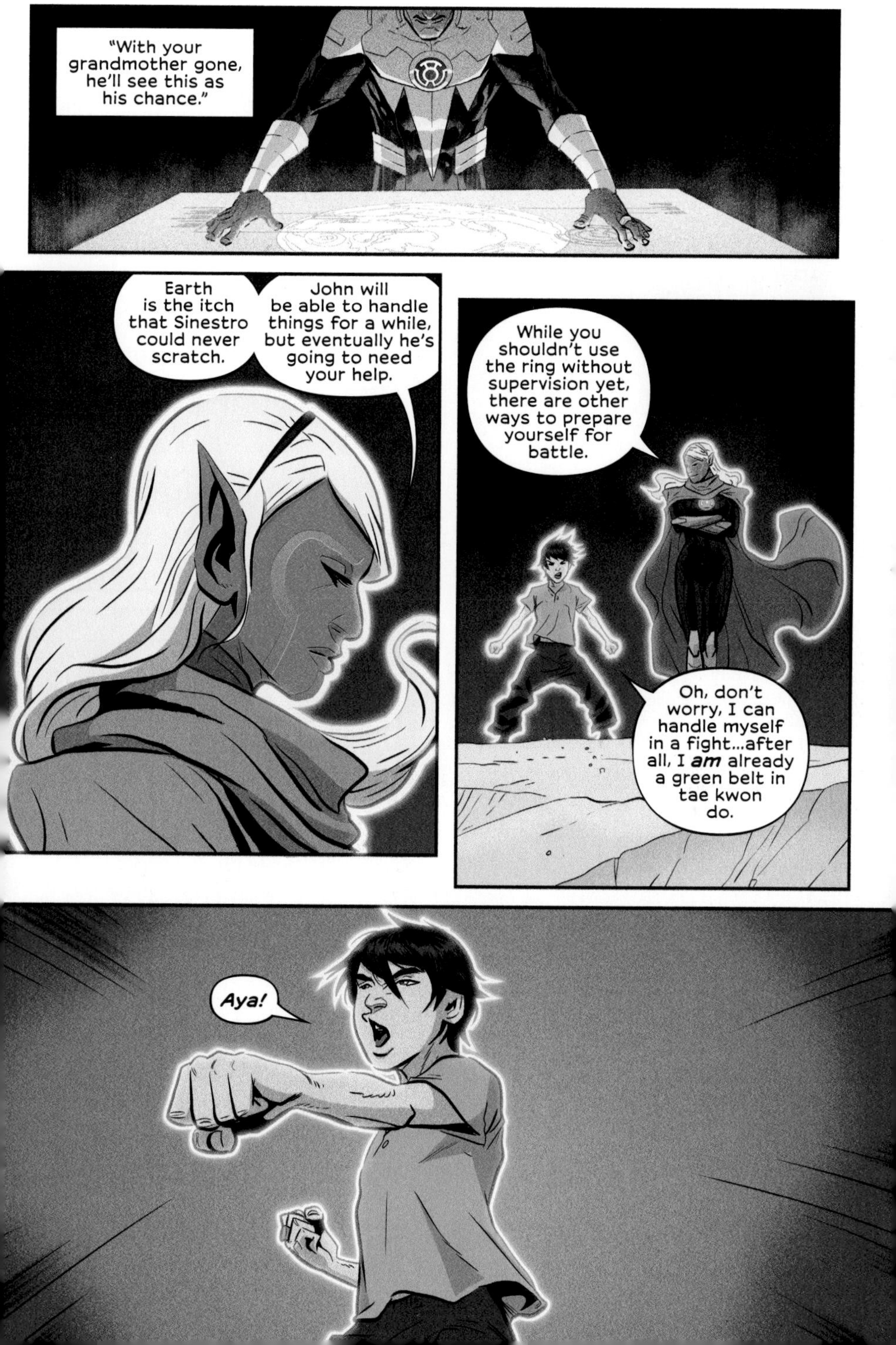
"With your grandmother gone, he'll see this as his chance."
Earth is the itch that Sinestro could never scratch.
John will be able to handle things for a while, but eventually he's going to need your help.
While you shouldn't use the ring without supervision yet, there are other ways to prepare yourself for battle.
Oh, don't worry, I can handle myself in a fight...after all, I *am* already a green belt in tae kwon do.
Aya!

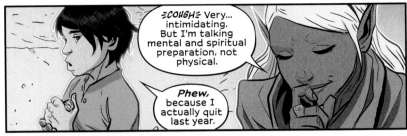

ξ*COUGH*ξ Very... intimidating. But I'm talking mental and spiritual preparation, not physical.

Phew, because I actually quit last year.

Your grandmother was especially strong because she developed her willpower through meditation.

But you're her grandson, so you must meditate, right?

Well, I try, but my legs get tired when I sit too long...

The time for excuses is over. Starting tomorrow, you meditate *every day.*

Yes, ma'am.

That's *your majesty* to you, newbie.

Oh, I didn't mean any—

I'm just messing with you.

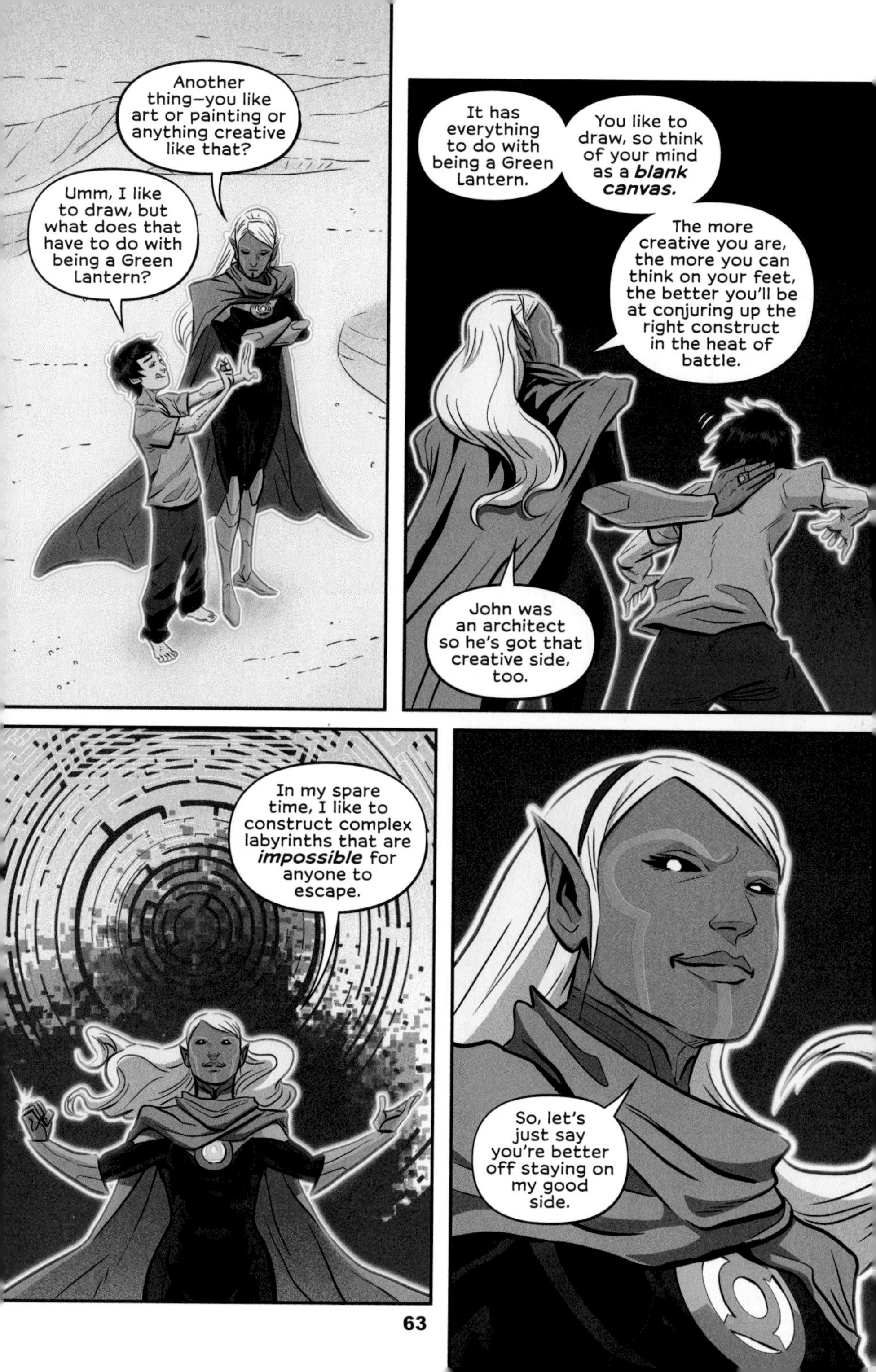
Another thing—you like art or painting or anything creative like that?
Umm, I like to draw, but what does that have to do with being a Green Lantern?
It has everything to do with being a Green Lantern.
You like to draw, so think of your mind as a ***blank canvas.***
The more creative you are, the more you can think on your feet, the better you'll be at conjuring up the right construct in the heat of battle.
John was an architect so he's got that creative side, too.
In my spare time, I like to construct complex labyrinths that are ***impossible*** for anyone to escape.
So, let's just say you're better off staying on my good side.

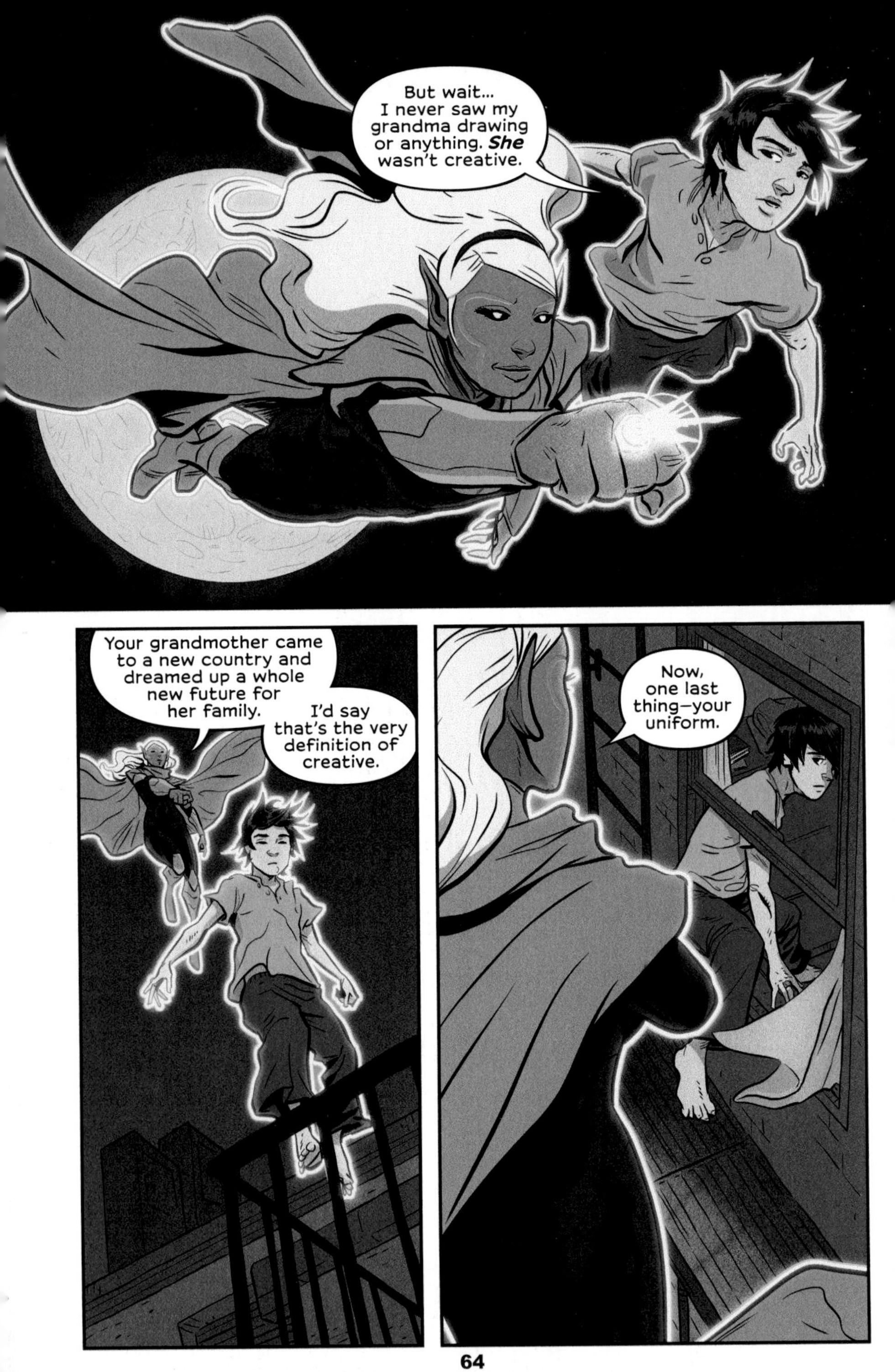
But wait... I never saw my grandma drawing or anything. ***She*** wasn't creative.
Your grandmother came to a new country and dreamed up a whole new future for her family.
I'd say that's the very definition of creative.
Now, one last thing—your uniform.

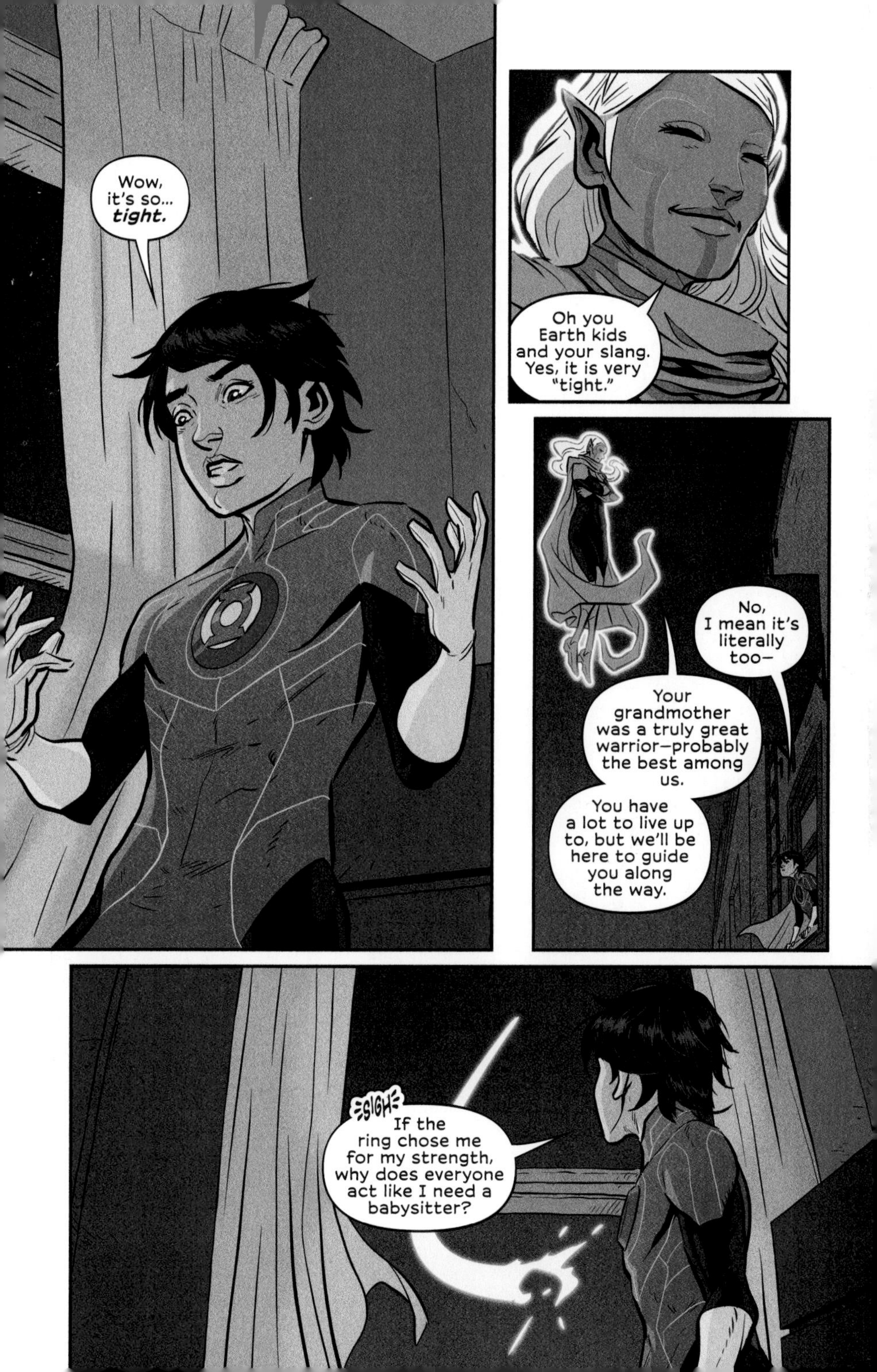
Wow, it's so... ***tight.***
Oh you Earth kids and your slang. Yes, it is very "tight."
No, I mean it's literally too—
Your grandmother was a truly great warrior—probably the best among us.
You have a lot to live up to, but we'll be here to guide you along the way.
SIGH
If the ring chose me for my strength, why does everyone act like I need a babysitter?

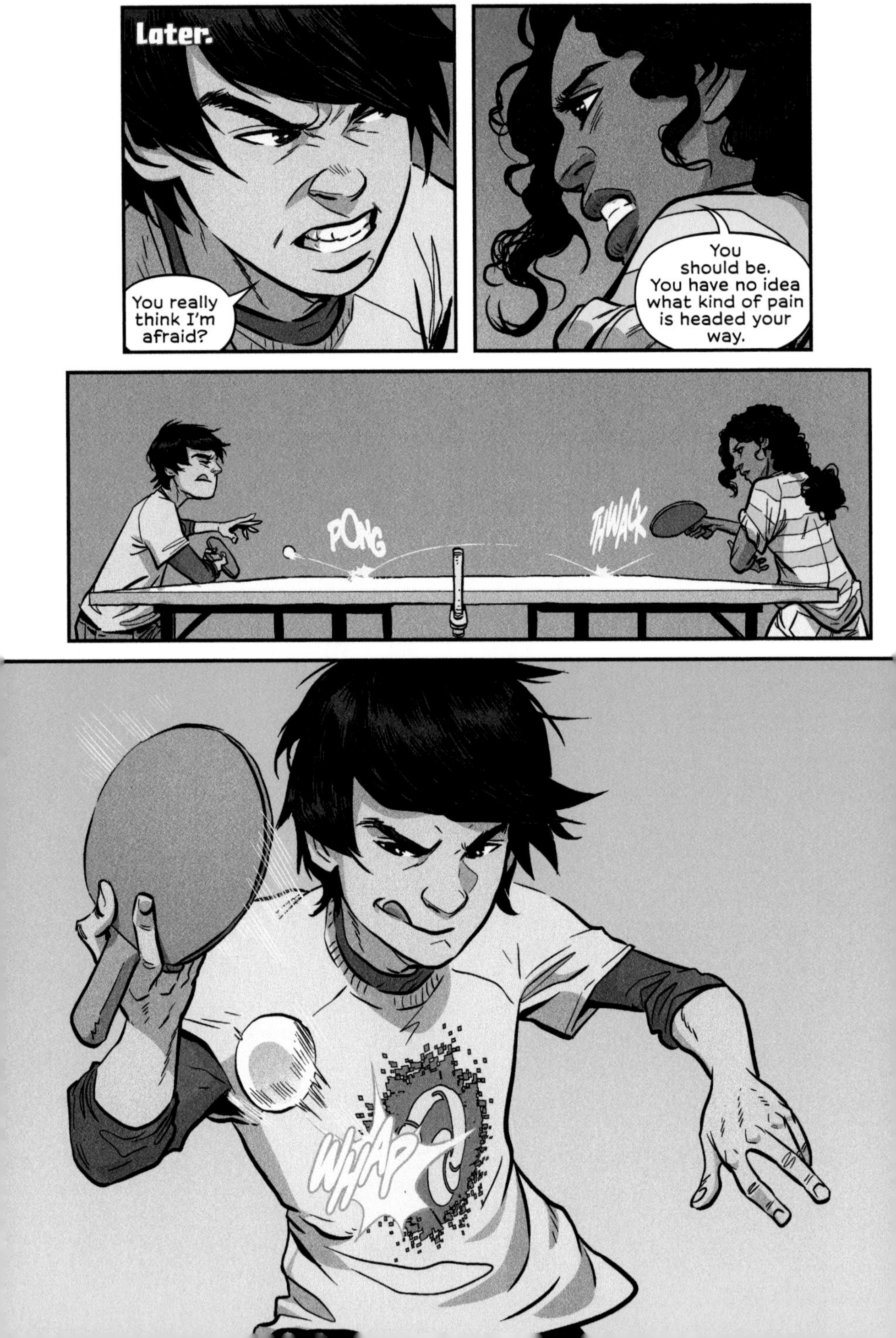
Later.
You really think I'm afraid?
You should be. You have no idea what kind of pain is headed your way.
PONG
THWACK
WHAP

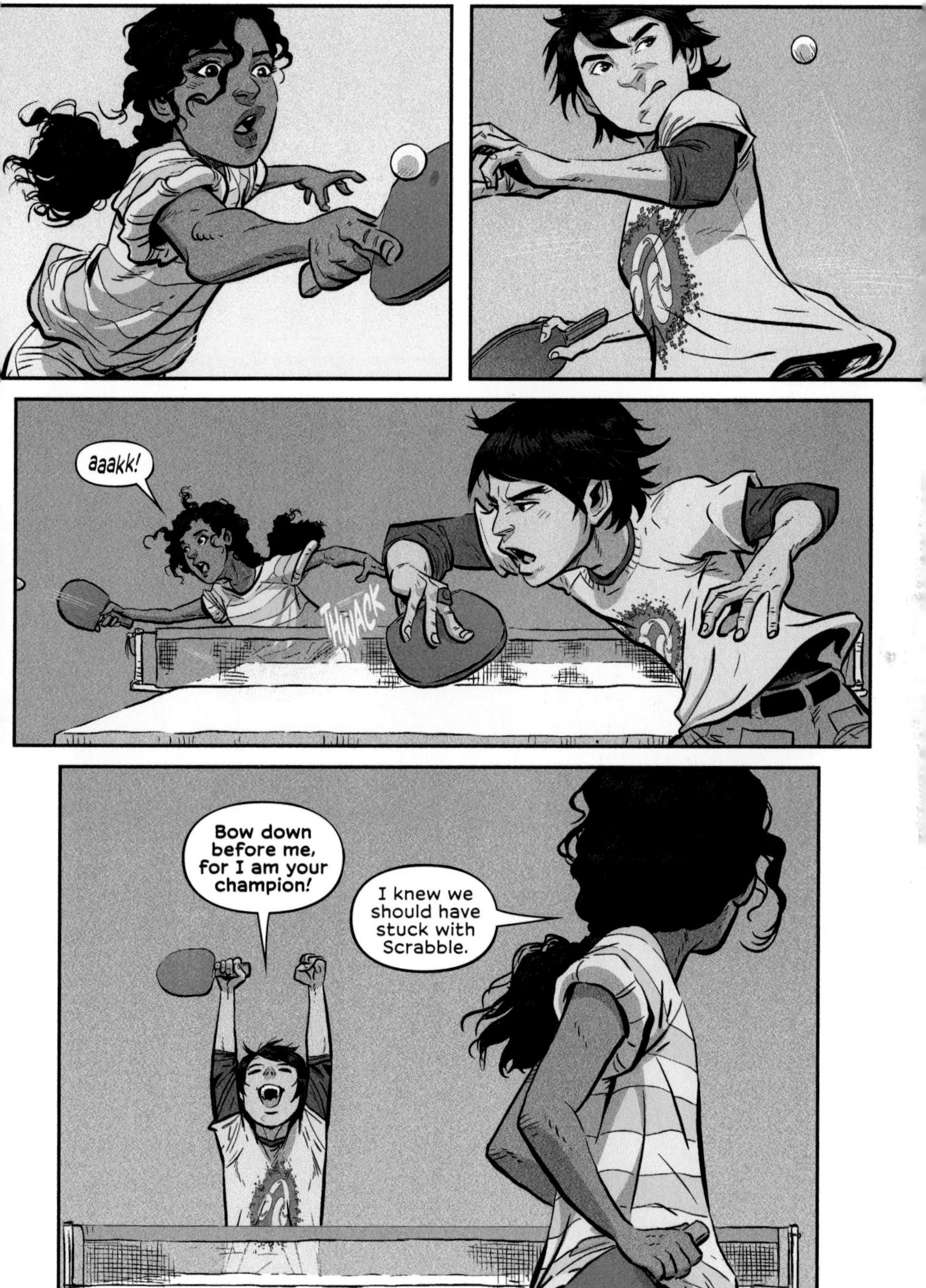
aaakk!
THWACK
Bow down before me, for I am your champion!
I knew we should have stuck with Scrabble.

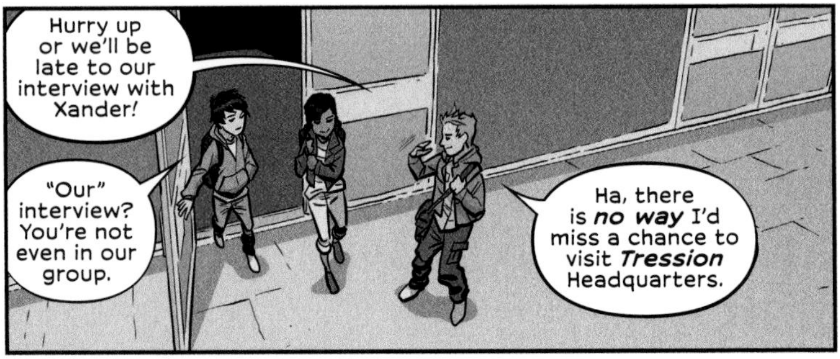
Hurry up or we'll be late to our interview with Xander!
"Our" interview? You're not even in our group.
Ha, there is ***no way*** I'd miss a chance to visit ***Tression*** Headquarters.

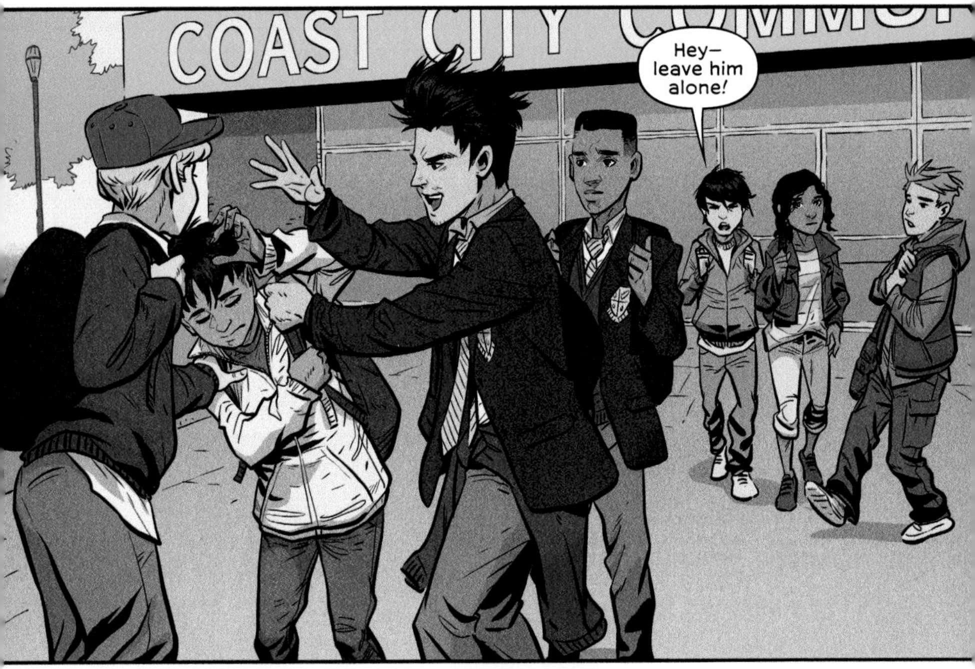
COAST CITY
Hey—leave him alone!

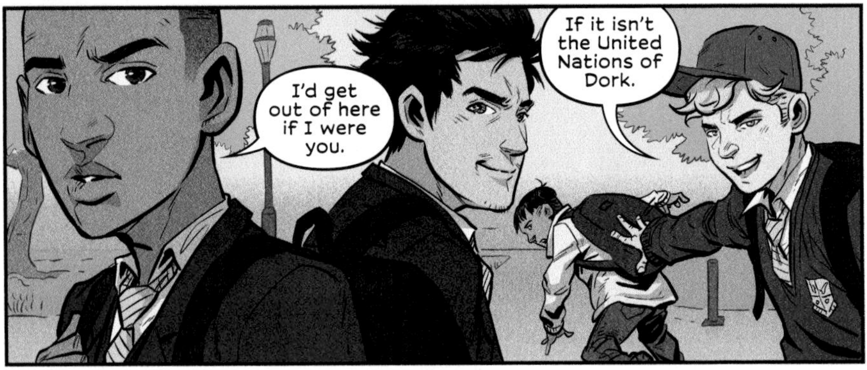
If it isn't the United Nations of Dork.
I'd get out of here if I were you.

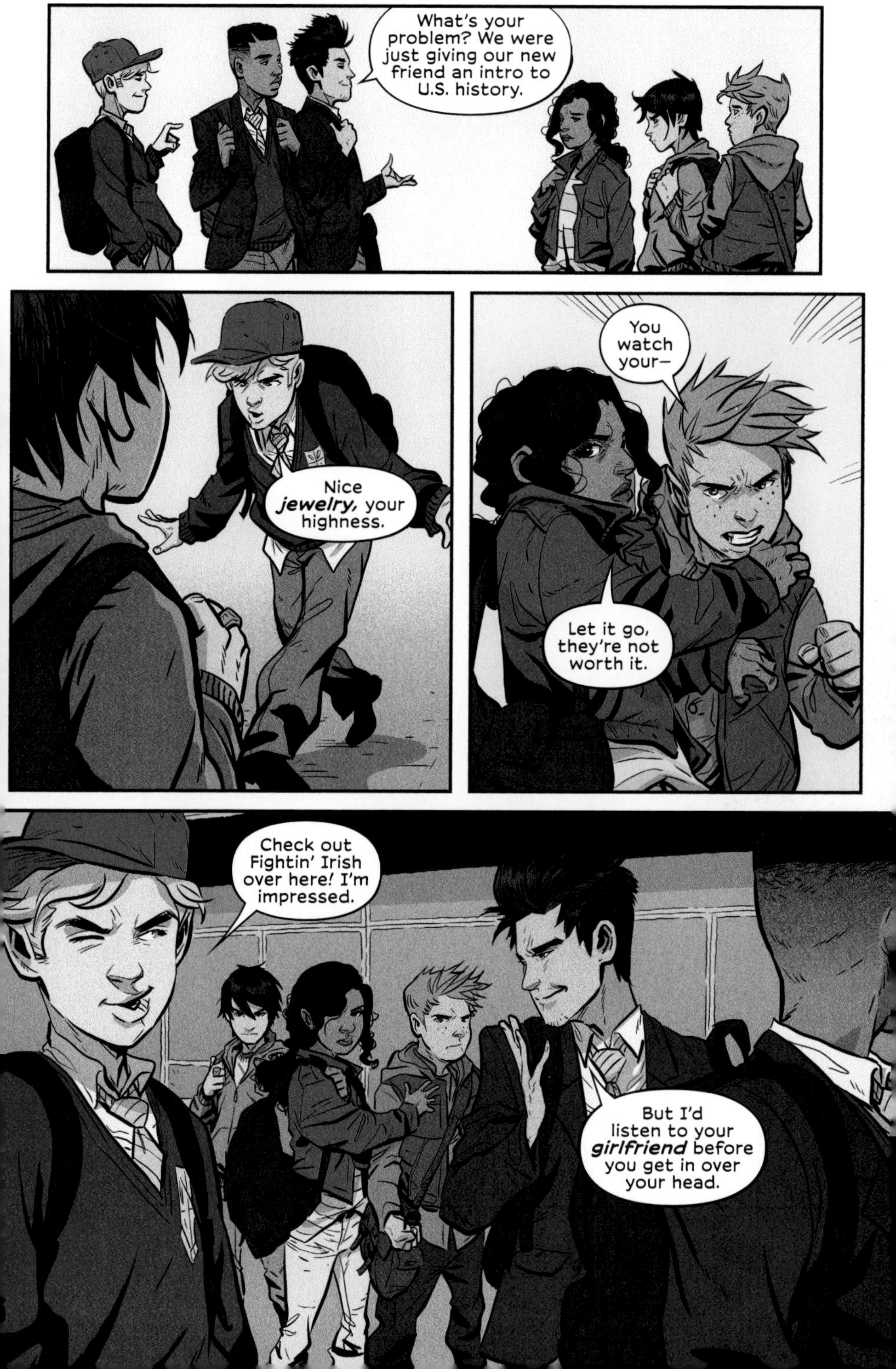
What's your problem? We were just giving our new friend an intro to U.S. history.
Nice *jewelry,* your highness.
You watch your—
Let it go, they're not worth it.
Check out Fightin' Irish over here! I'm impressed.
But I'd listen to your *girlfriend* before you get in over your head.

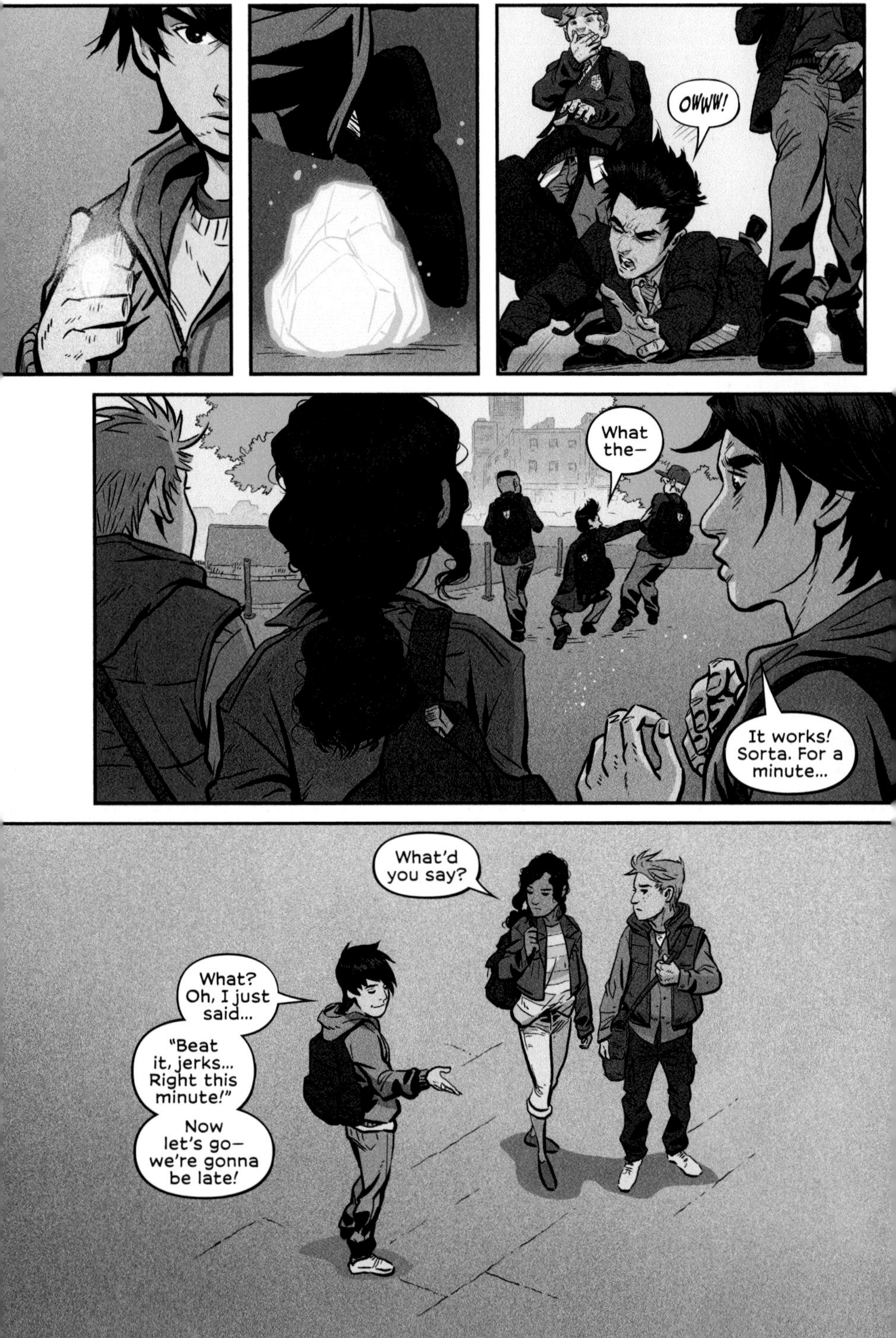
OWWW!
What the—
It works! Sorta. For a minute...
What'd you say?
What? Oh, I just said...
"Beat it, jerks... Right this minute!"
Now let's go—we're gonna be late!

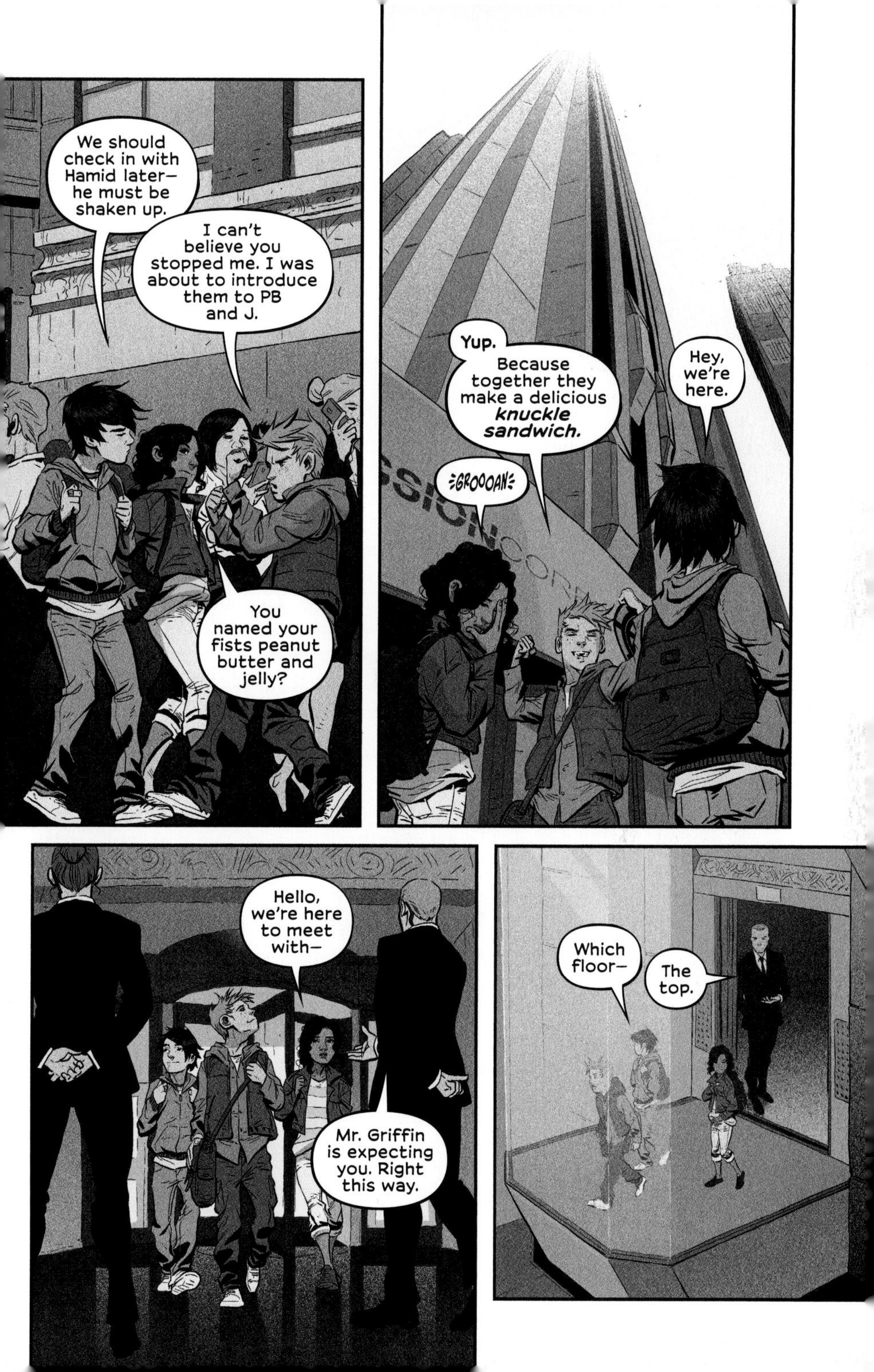

We should check in with Hamid later— he must be shaken up.
I can't believe you stopped me. I was about to introduce them to PB and J.
You named your fists peanut butter and jelly?
Yup.
Because together they make a delicious *knuckle sandwich.*
GROOOAN
Hey, we're here.
Hello, we're here to meet with—
Mr. Griffin is expecting you. Right this way.
Which floor—
The top.

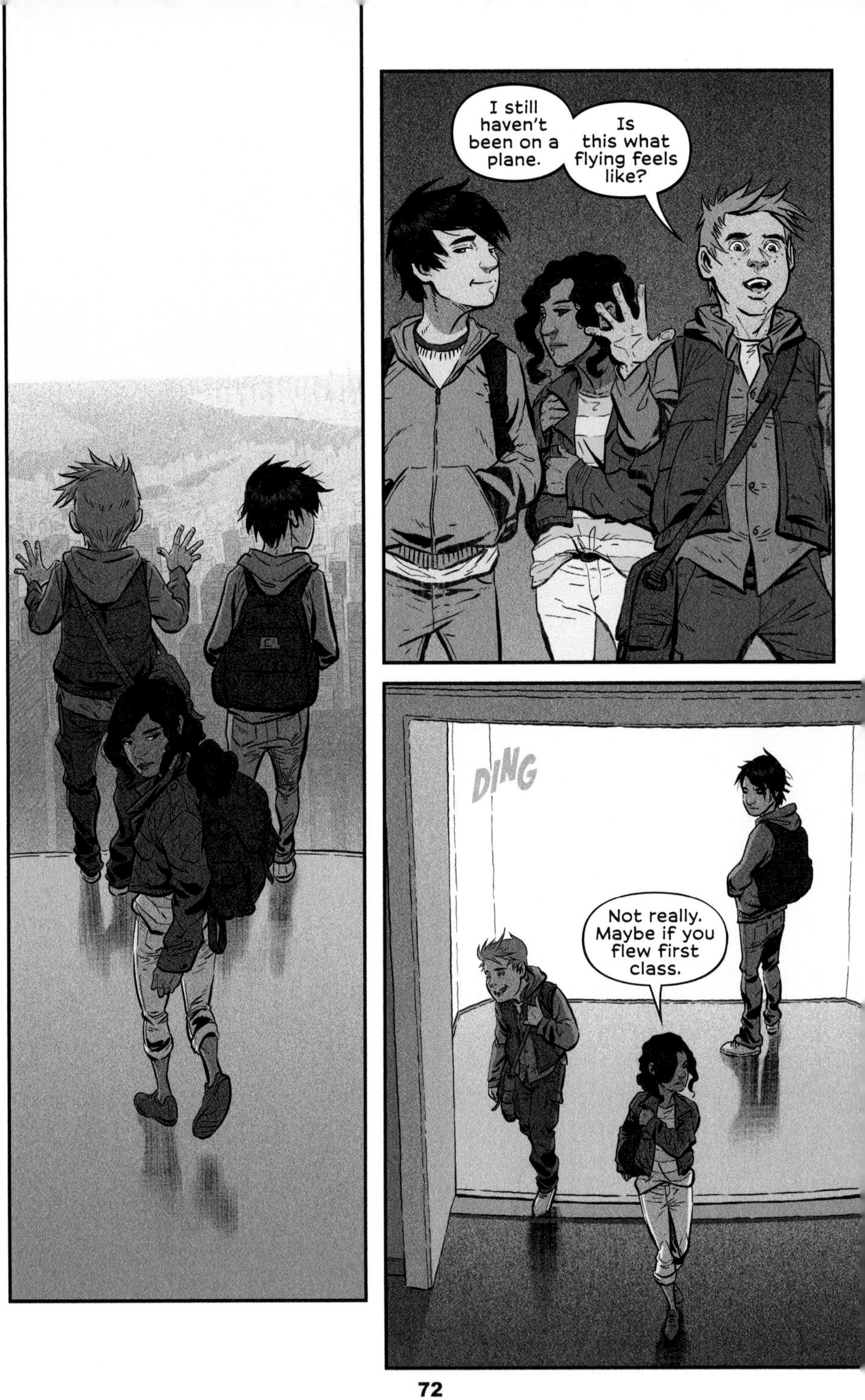
I still haven't been on a plane.
Is this what flying feels like?
DING
Not really. Maybe if you flew first class.

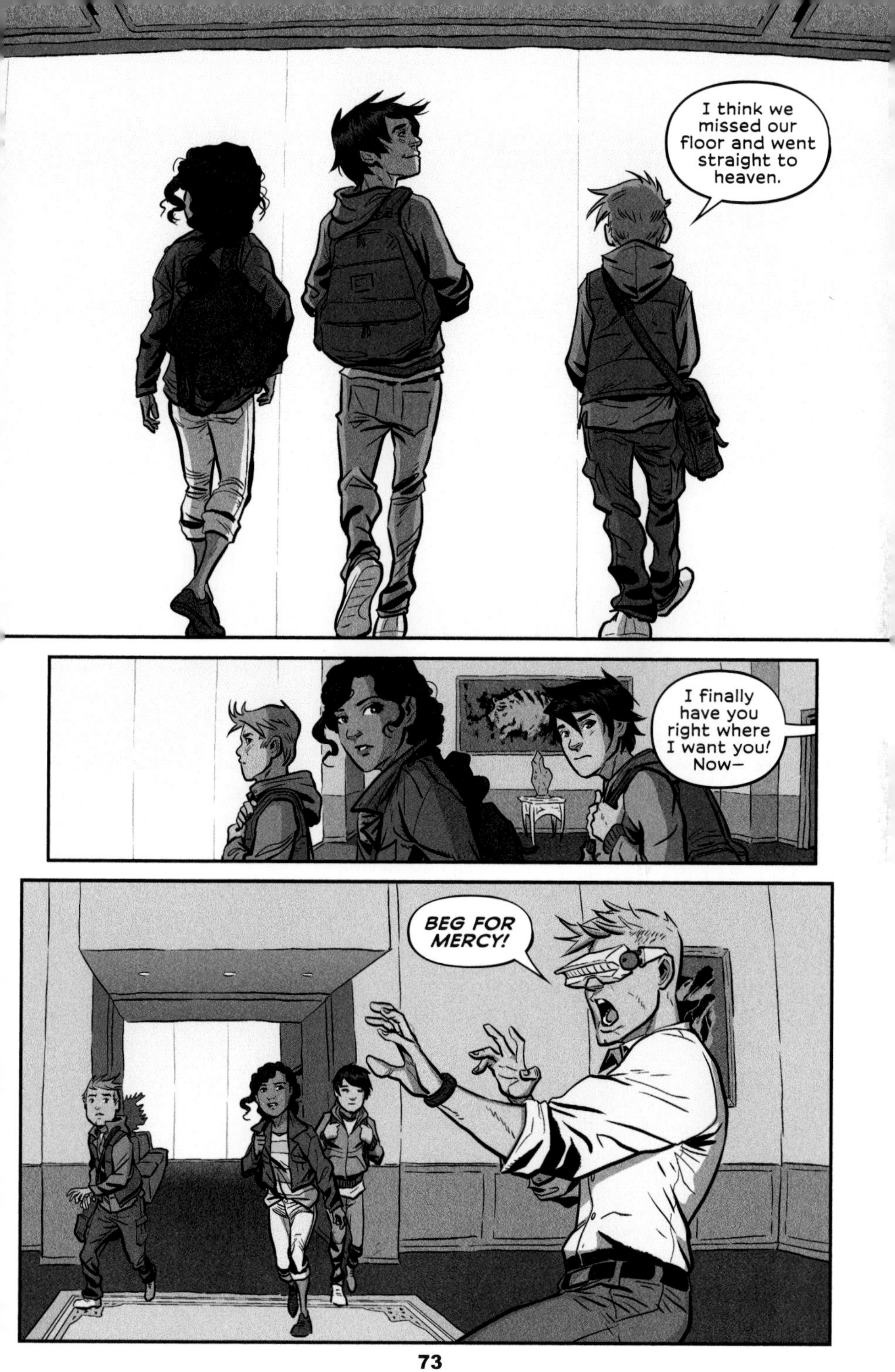
I think we missed our floor and went straight to heaven.
I finally have you right where I want you! Now–
BEG FOR MERCY!

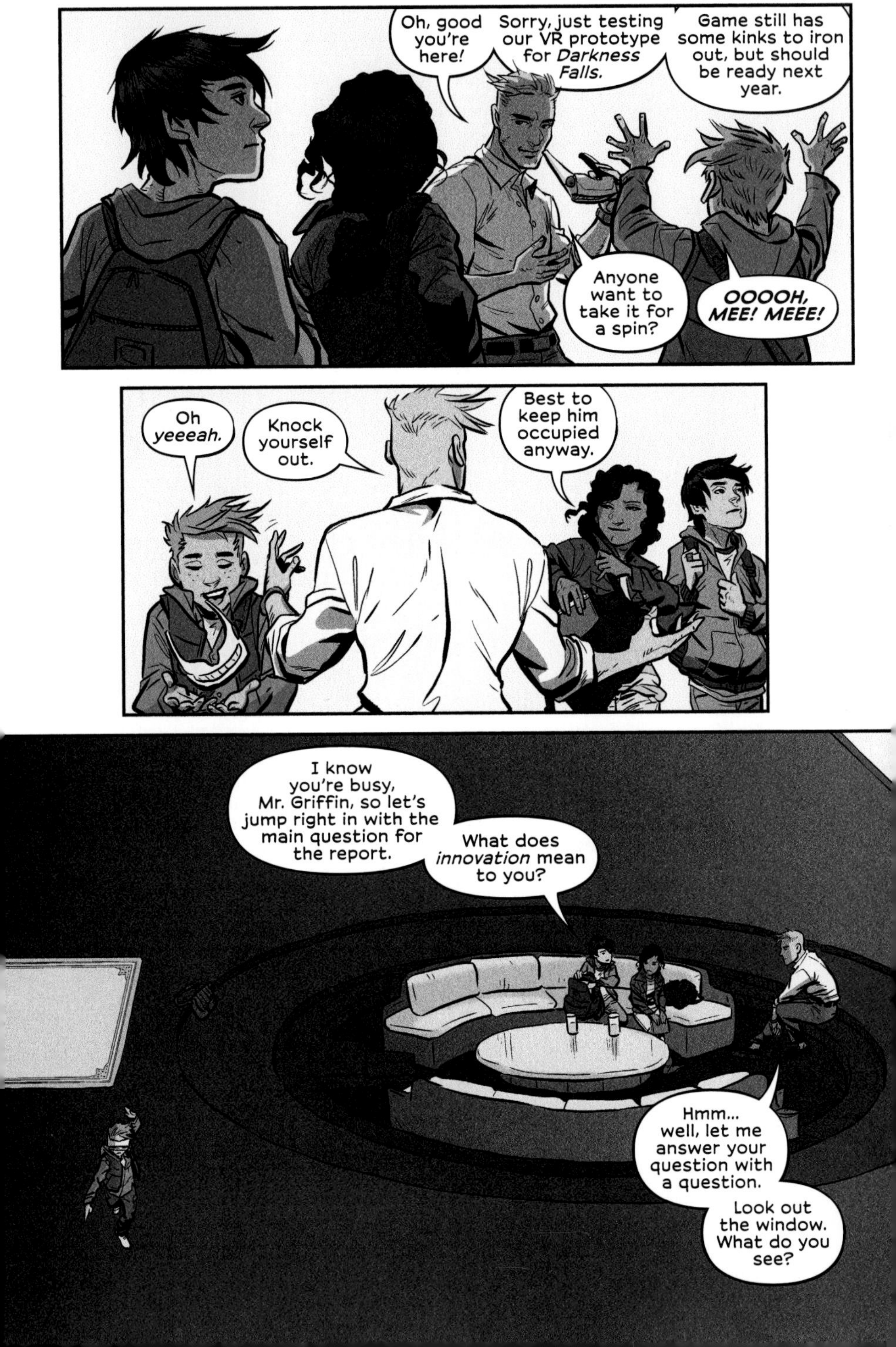

Oh, good you're here!
Sorry, just testing our VR prototype for *Darkness Falls.*
Game still has some kinks to iron out, but should be ready next year.
Anyone want to take it for a spin?
OOOOH, MEE! MEEE!
Oh *yeeeah.*
Knock yourself out.
Best to keep him occupied anyway.
I know you're busy, Mr. Griffin, so let's jump right in with the main question for the report.
What does *innovation* mean to you?
Hmm... well, let me answer your question with a question.
Look out the window. What do you see?

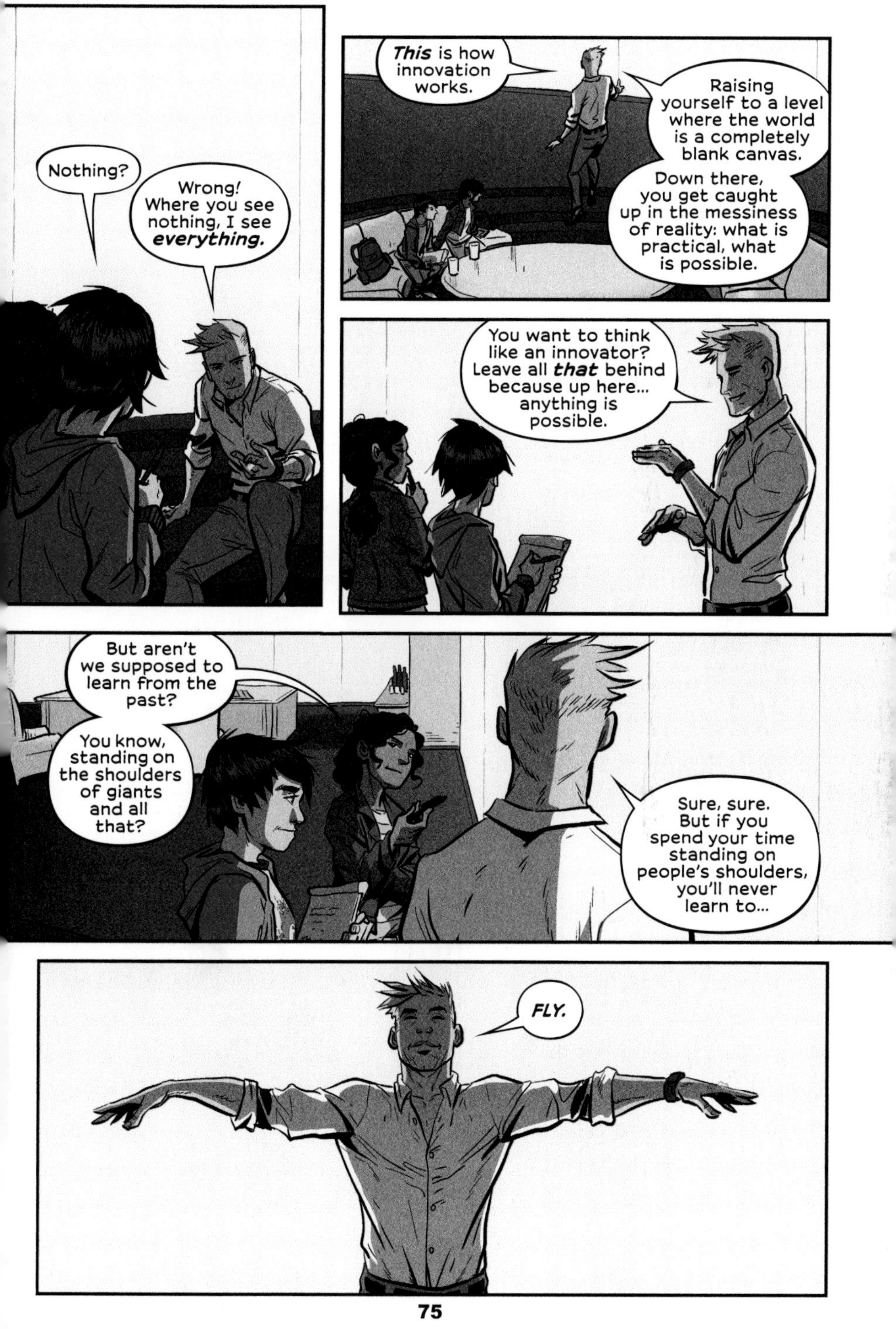
Nothing?
Wrong! Where you see nothing, I see *everything.*
This is how innovation works.
Raising yourself to a level where the world is a completely blank canvas.
Down there, you get caught up in the messiness of reality: what is practical, what is possible.
You want to think like an innovator? Leave all *that* behind because up here... anything is possible.
But aren't we supposed to learn from the past?
You know, standing on the shoulders of giants and all that?
Sure, sure. But if you spend your time standing on people's shoulders, you'll never learn to...
FLY.

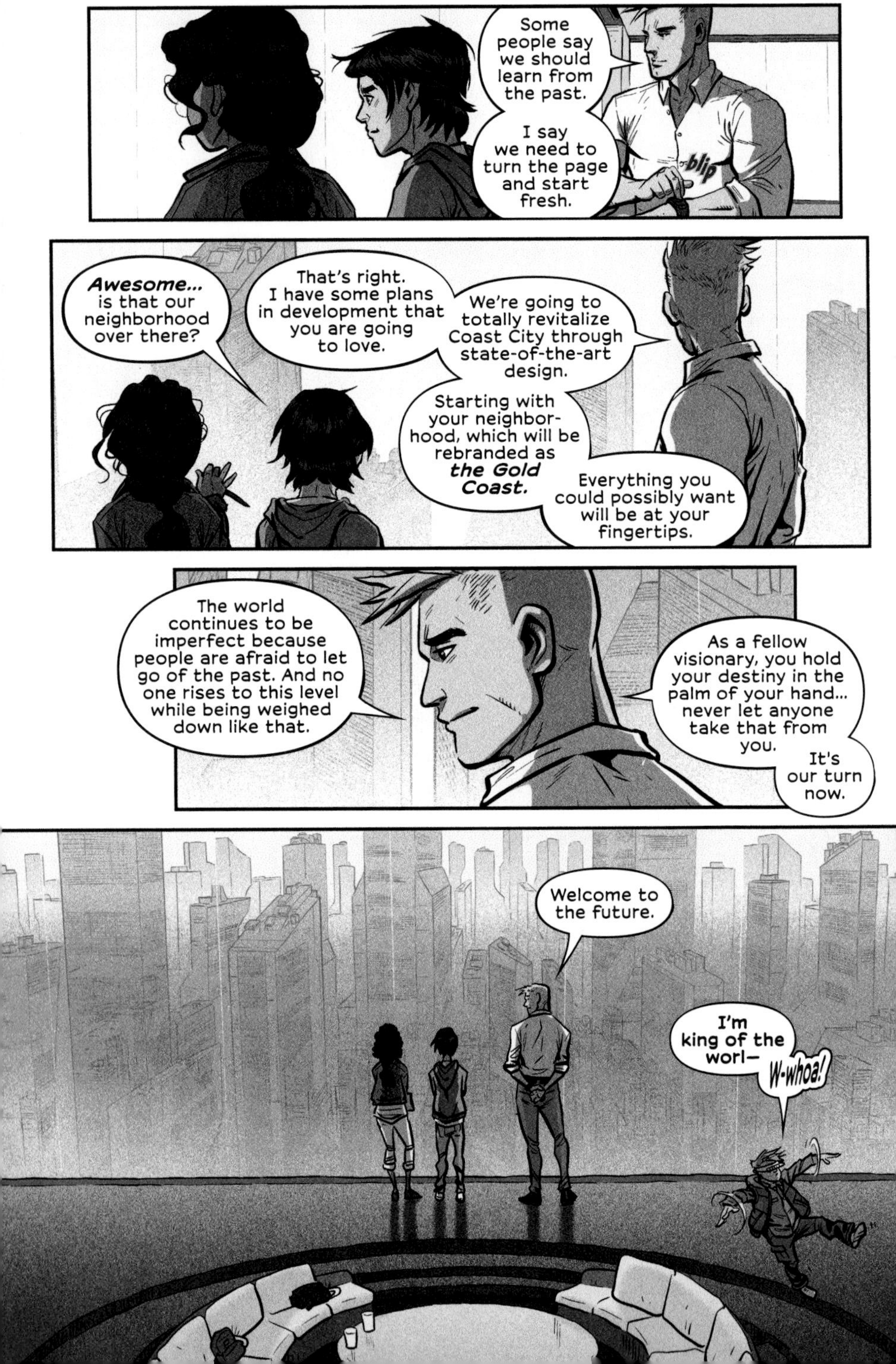
Some people say we should learn from the past.
I say we need to turn the page and start fresh.
blip
Awesome... is that our neighborhood over there?
That's right. I have some plans in development that you are going to love.
We're going to totally revitalize Coast City through state-of-the-art design.
Starting with your neighbor-hood, which will be rebranded as *the Gold Coast.*
Everything you could possibly want will be at your fingertips.
The world continues to be imperfect because people are afraid to let go of the past. And no one rises to this level while being weighed down like that.
As a fellow visionary, you hold your destiny in the palm of your hand... never let anyone take that from you.
It's our turn now.
Welcome to the future.
I'm king of the worl—
W-whoa!

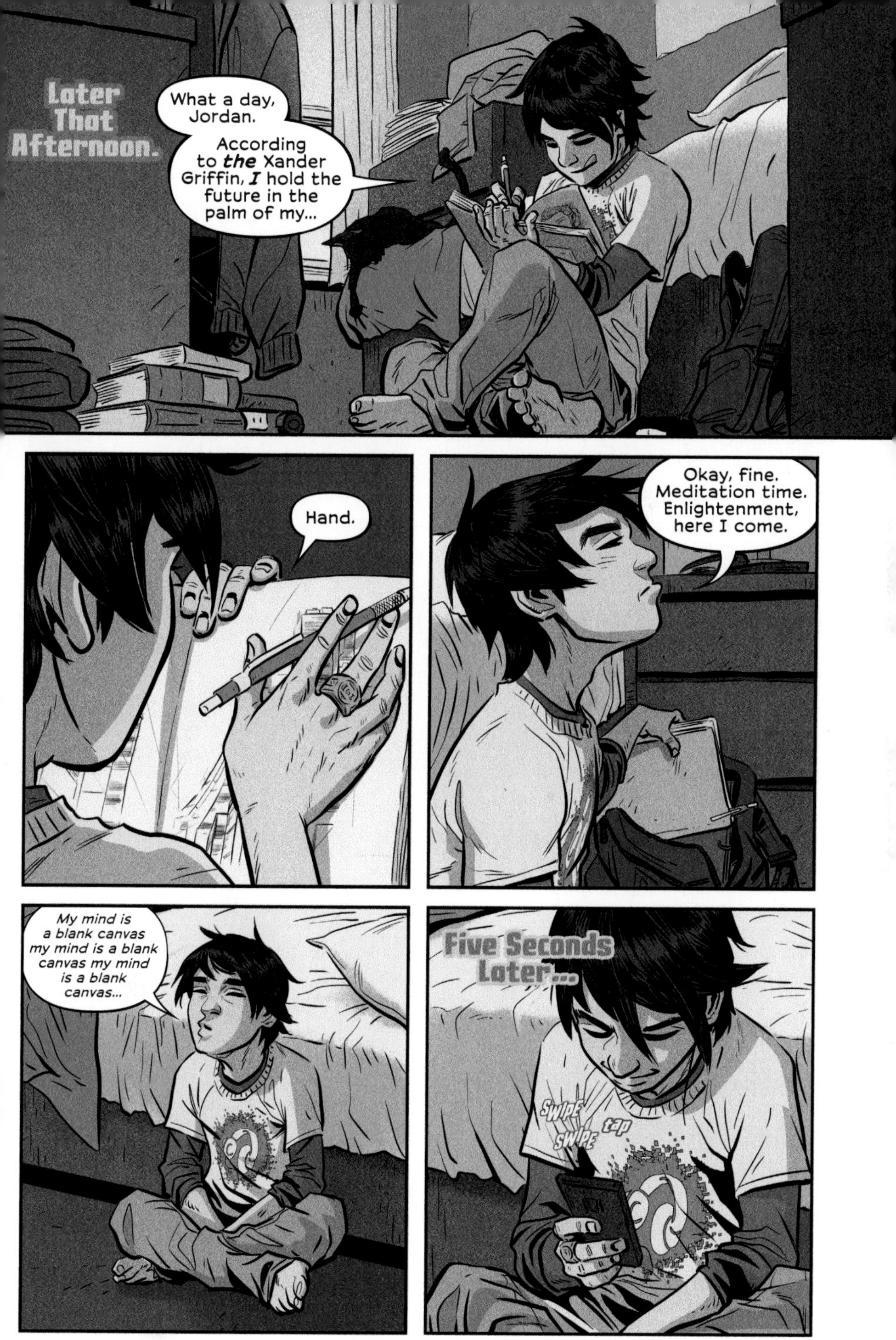
Later That Afternoon.
What a day, Jordan.
According to *the* Xander Griffin, *I* hold the future in the palm of my...
Hand.
Okay, fine. Meditation time. Enlightenment, here I come.
My mind is a blank canvas my mind is a blank canvas my mind is a blank canvas...
Five Seconds Later...
SWIPE
tap
SWIPE

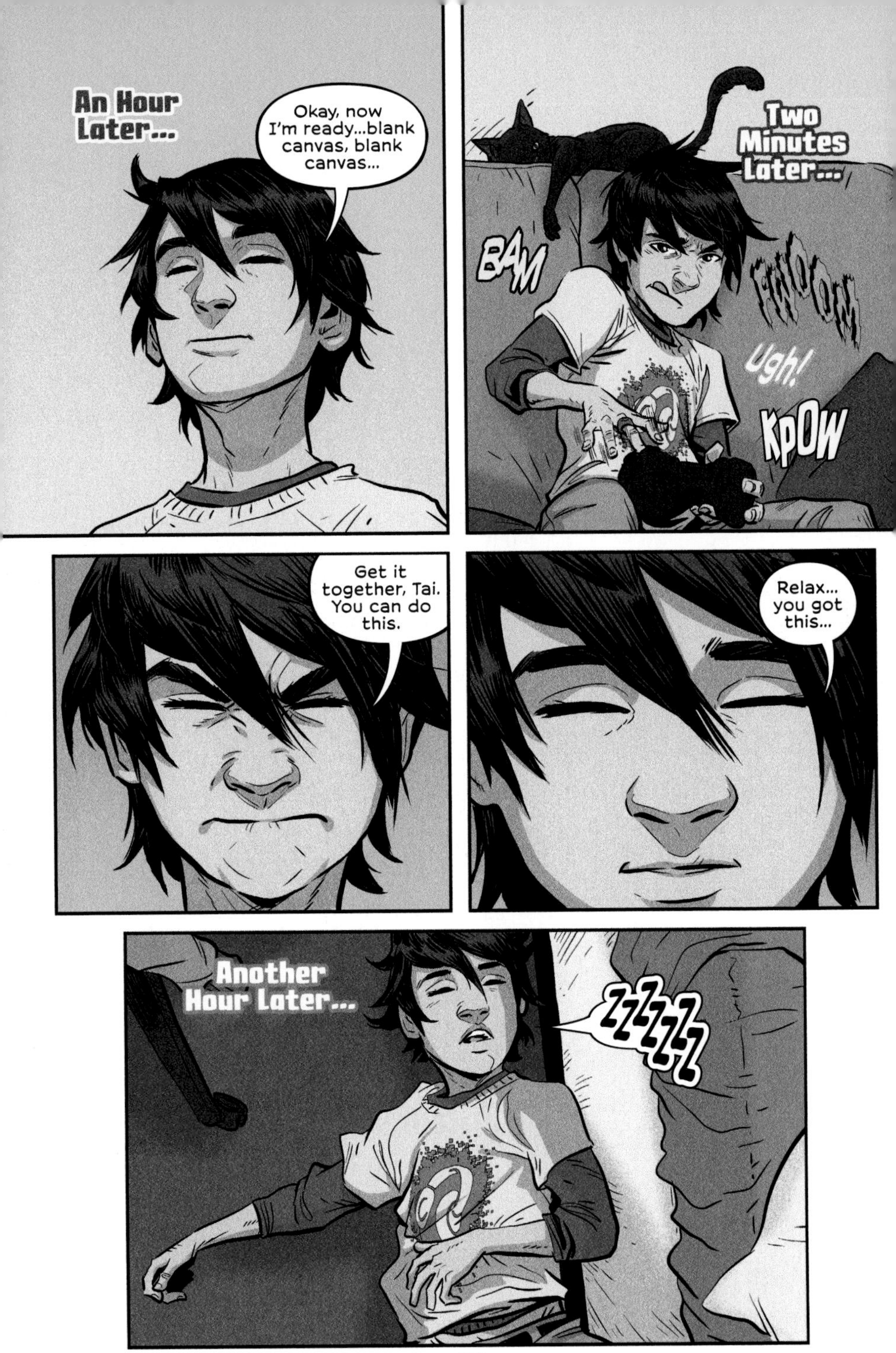
An Hour Later...
Okay, now I'm ready...blank canvas, blank canvas...
Two Minutes Later...
BAM
FWOOM
Ugh!
KPOW
Get it together, Tai. You can do this.
Relax... you got this...
Another Hour Later...
ZZZZZZ

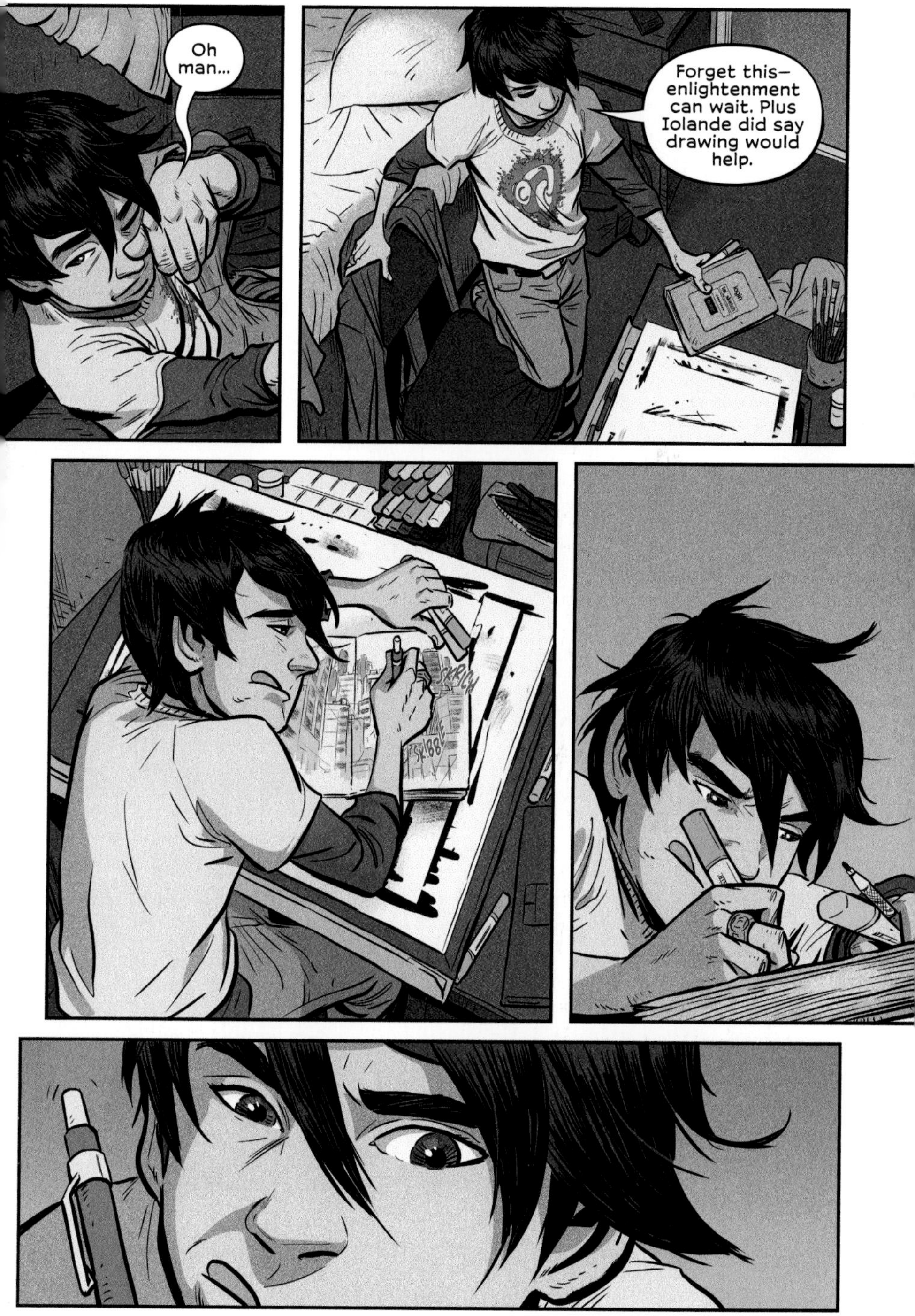
Oh man...
Forget this—enlightenment can wait. Plus Iolande did say drawing would help.

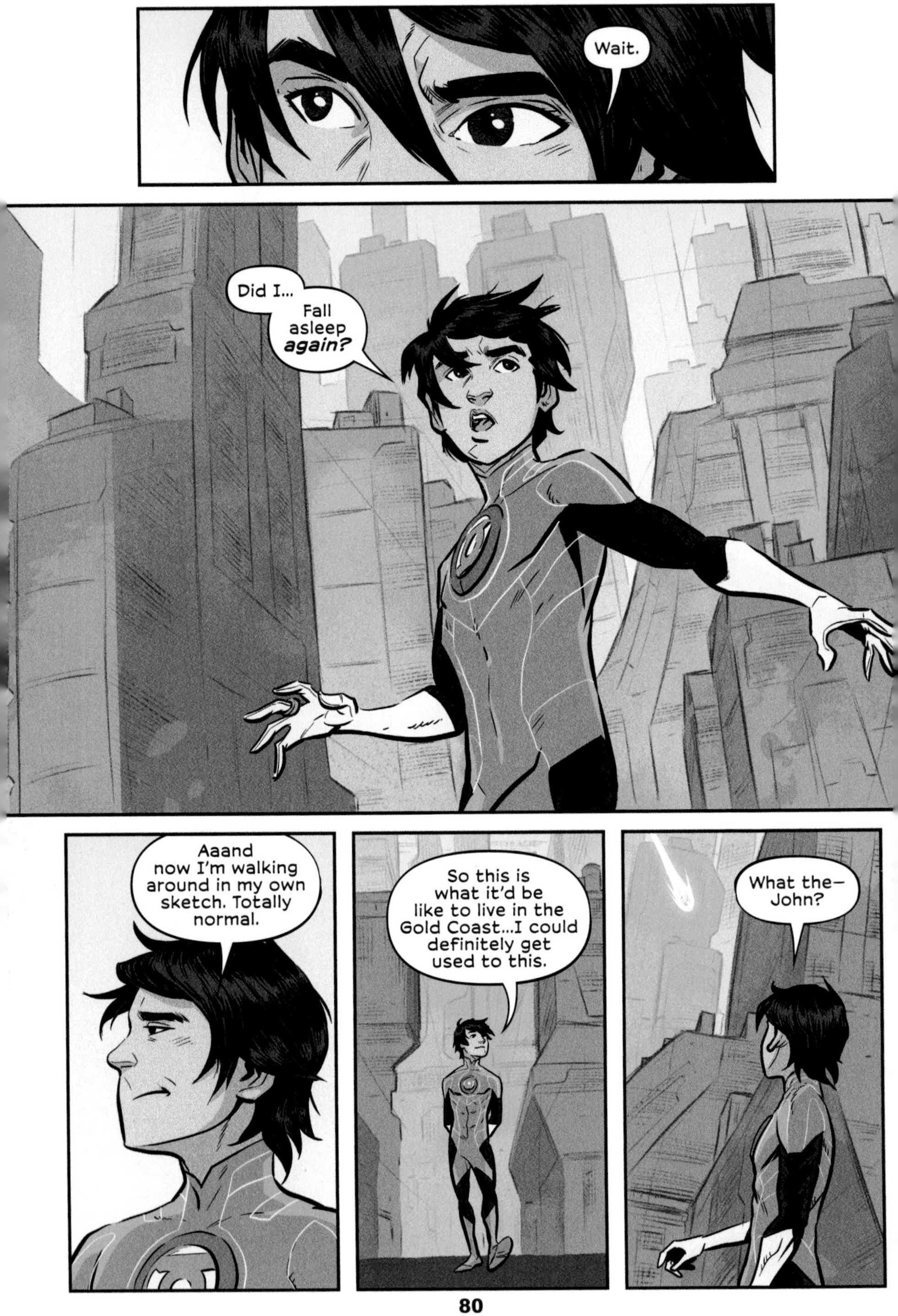
Wait.
Did I... Fall asleep *again?*
Aaand now I'm walking around in my own sketch. Totally normal.
So this is what it'd be like to live in the Gold Coast...I could definitely get used to this.
What the—John?

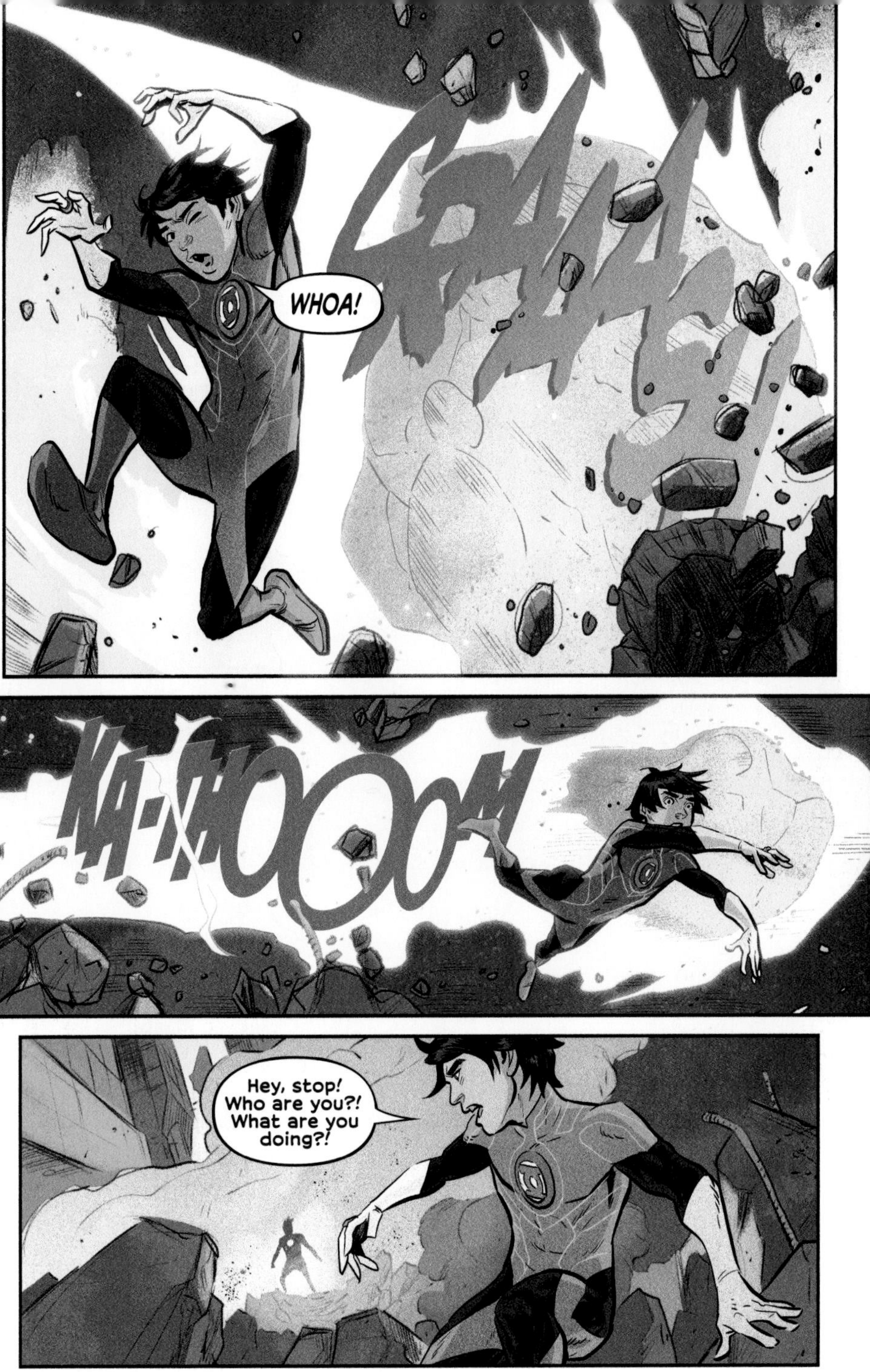
WHOA!
GRAAAGH!
KA-THOOOM
Hey, stop! Who are you?! What are you doing?!

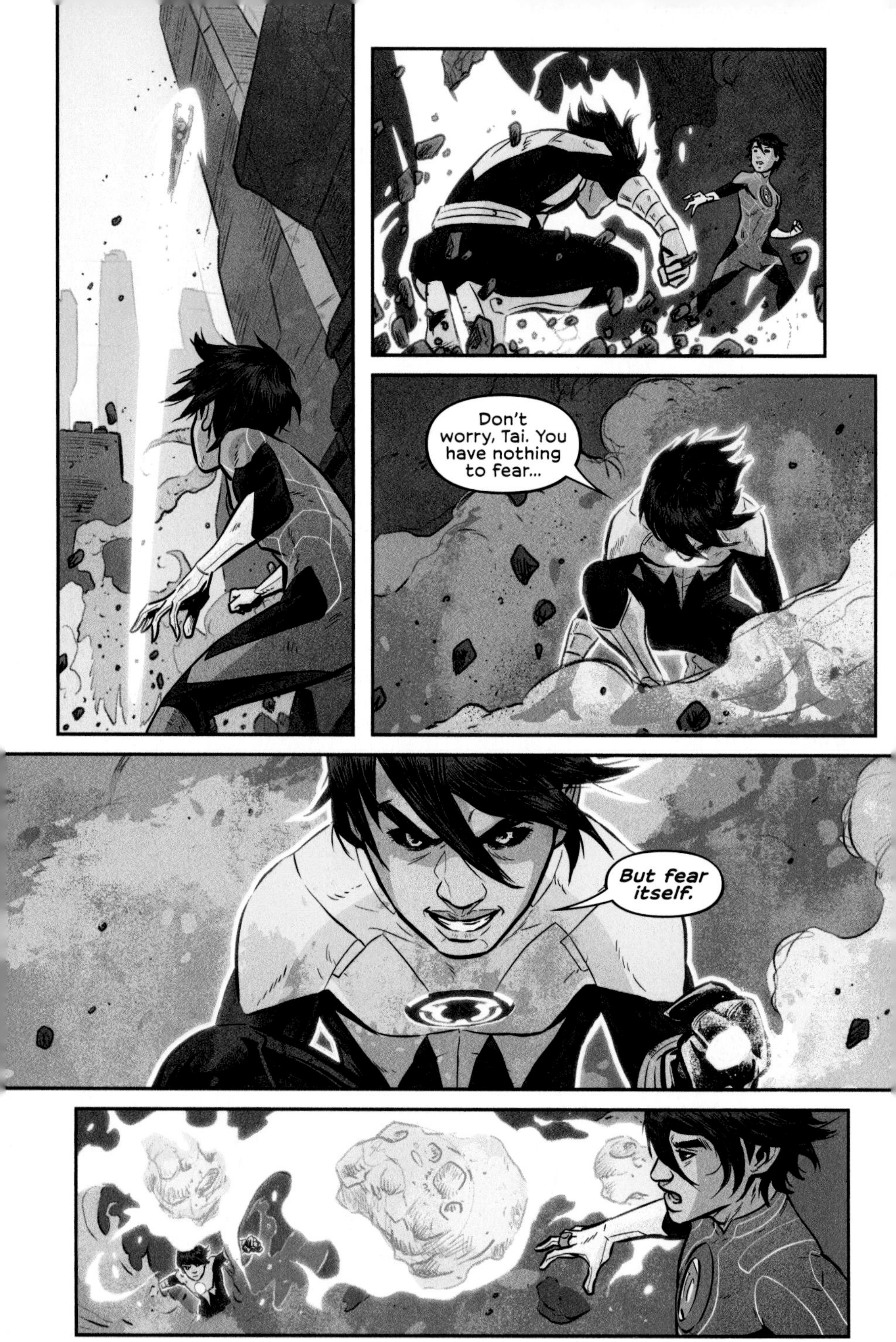
Don't worry, Tai. You have nothing to fear...
But fear itself.

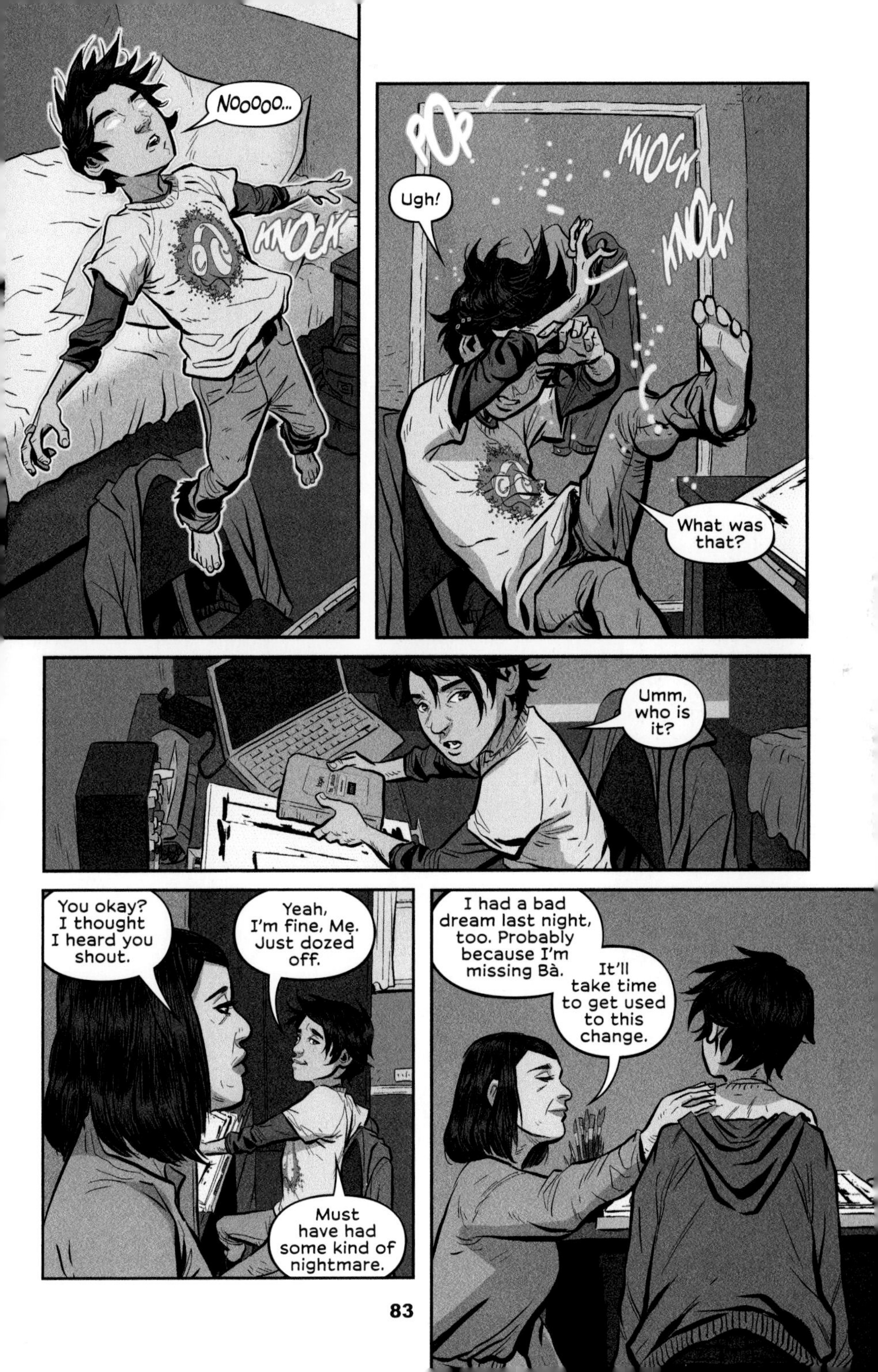
NOOOOO...
KNOCK
POP
Ugh!
KNOCK
KNOCK
What was that?
Umm, who is it?
You okay? I thought I heard you shout.
Yeah, I'm fine, Mẹ. Just dozed off.
Must have had some kind of nightmare.
I had a bad dream last night, too. Probably because I'm missing Bà.
It'll take time to get used to this change.

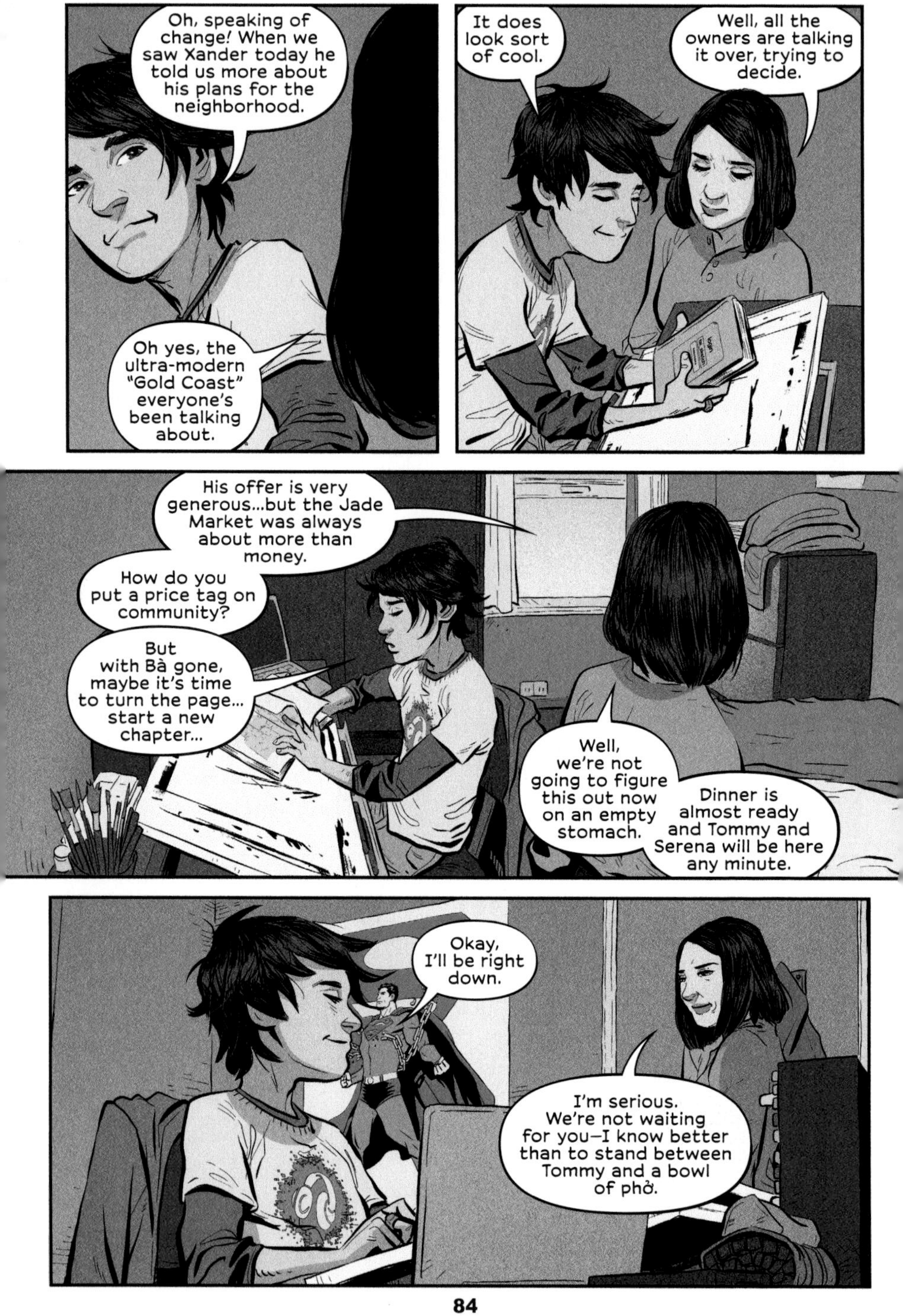
Oh, speaking of change! When we saw Xander today he told us more about his plans for the neighborhood.
Oh yes, the ultra-modern "Gold Coast" everyone's been talking about.
It does look sort of cool.
Well, all the owners are talking it over, trying to decide.
His offer is very generous...but the Jade Market was always about more than money.
How do you put a price tag on community?
But with Bà gone, maybe it's time to turn the page... start a new chapter...
Well, we're not going to figure this out now on an empty stomach.
Dinner is almost ready and Tommy and Serena will be here any minute.
Okay, I'll be right down.
I'm serious. We're not waiting for you—I know better than to stand between Tommy and a bowl of phở.

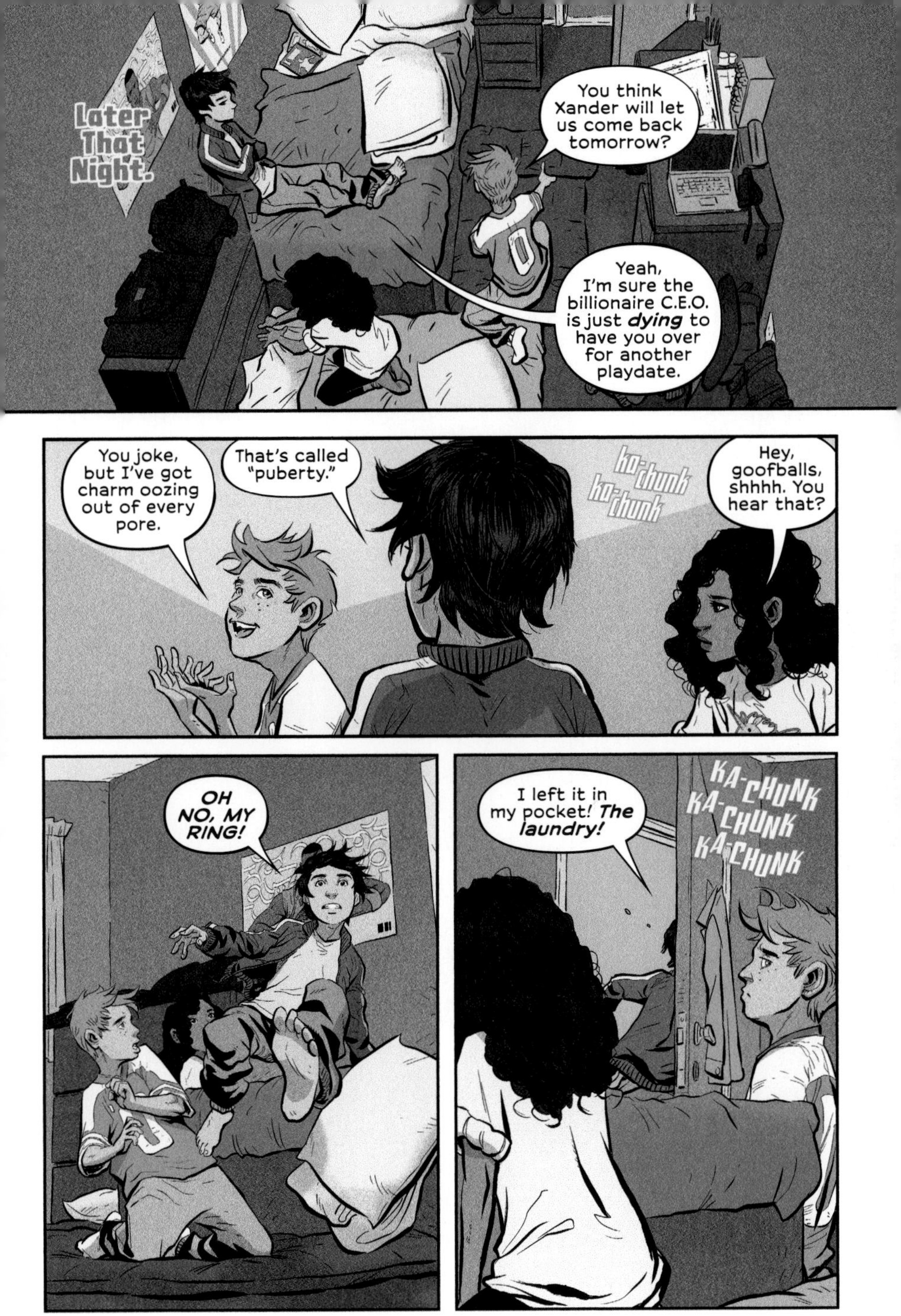

Later That Night.
You think Xander will let us come back tomorrow?
Yeah, I'm sure the billionaire C.E.O. is just *dying* to have you over for another playdate.
You joke, but I've got charm oozing out of every pore.
That's called "puberty."
ka-chunk ka-chunk
Hey, goofballs, shhhh. You hear that?
OH NO, MY RING!
I left it in my pocket! *The laundry!*
KA-CHUNK KA-CHUNK KA-CHUNK

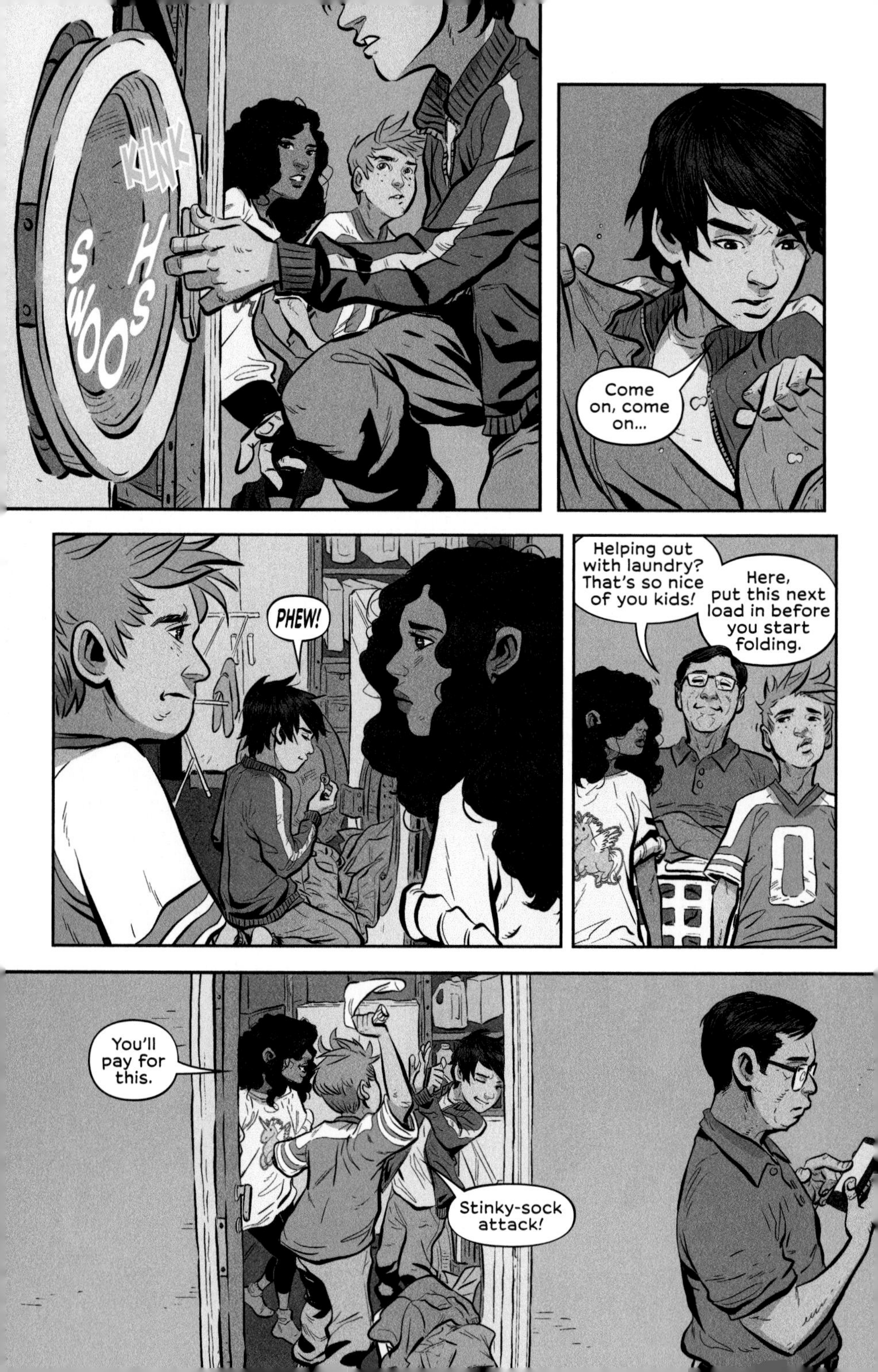
KLINK
SWOOSH
Come on, come on...
PHEW!
Helping out with laundry? That's so nice of you kids!
Here, put this next load in before you start folding.
You'll pay for this.
Stinky-sock attack!

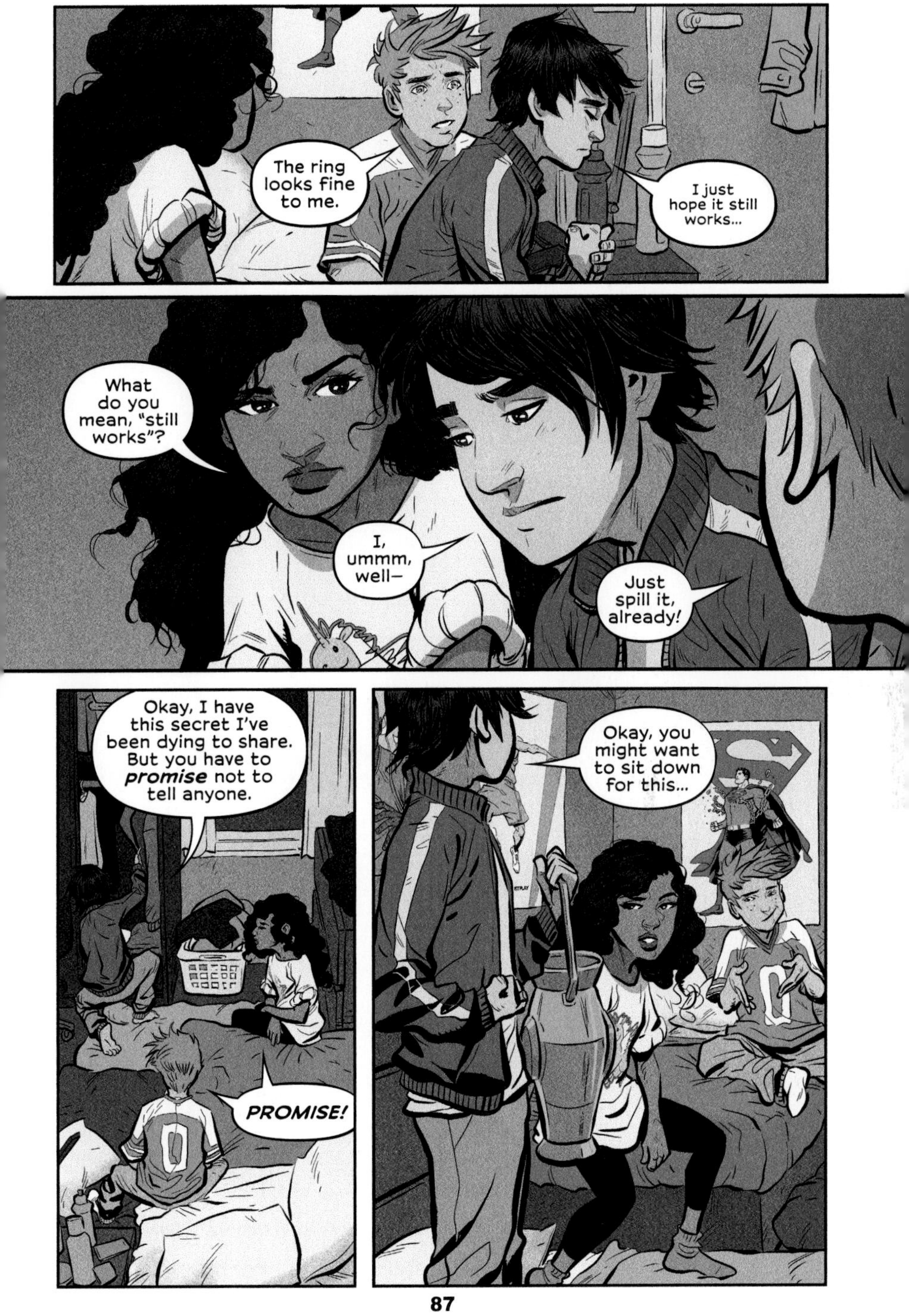

The ring looks fine to me.
I just hope it still works...
What do you mean, "still works"?
I, ummm, well—
Just spill it, already!
Okay, I have this secret I've been dying to share. But you have to *promise* not to tell anyone.
PROMISE!
Okay, you might want to sit down for this...

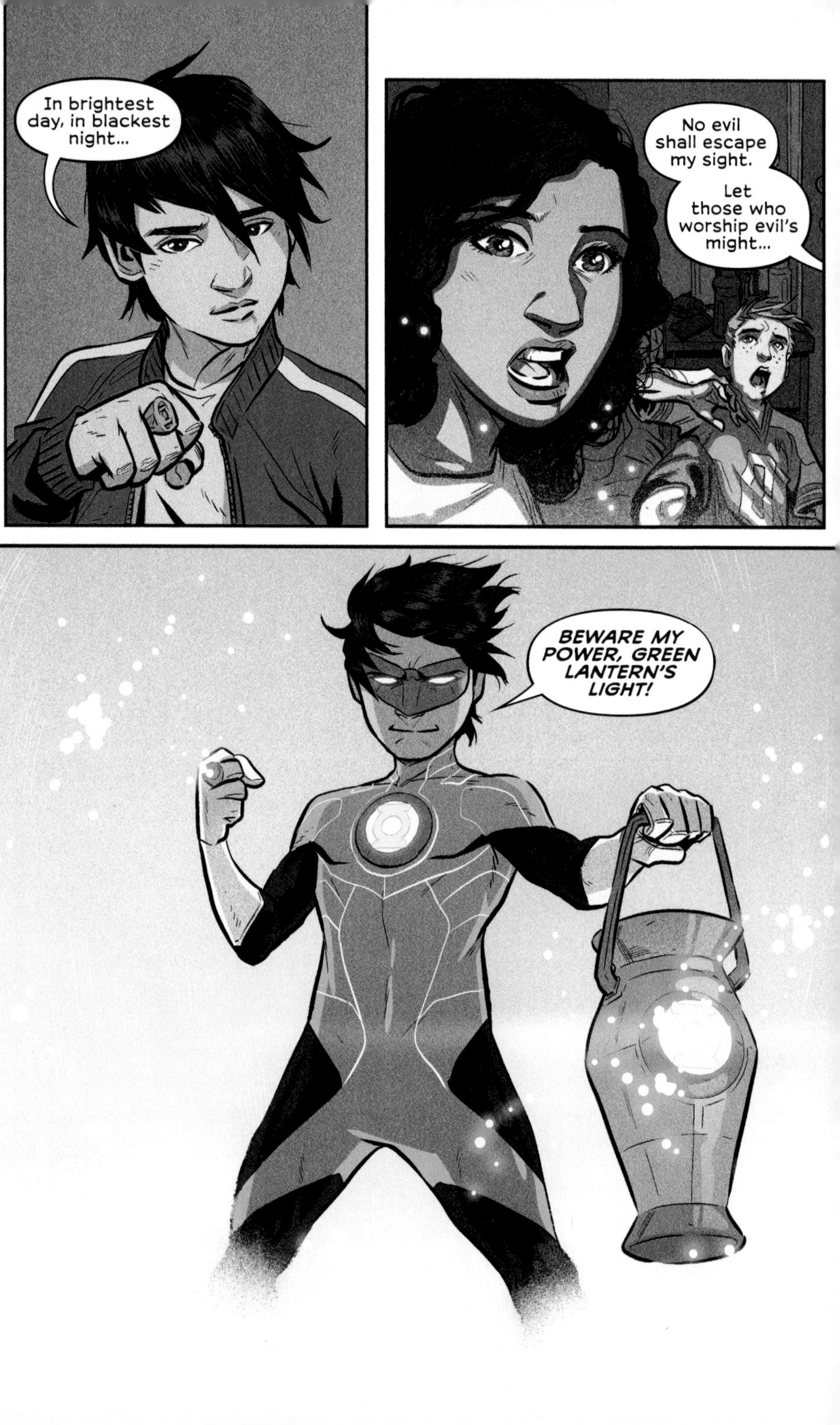
In brightest day, in blackest night...
No evil shall escape my sight.
Let those who worship evil's might...
BEWARE MY POWER, GREEN LANTERN'S LIGHT!

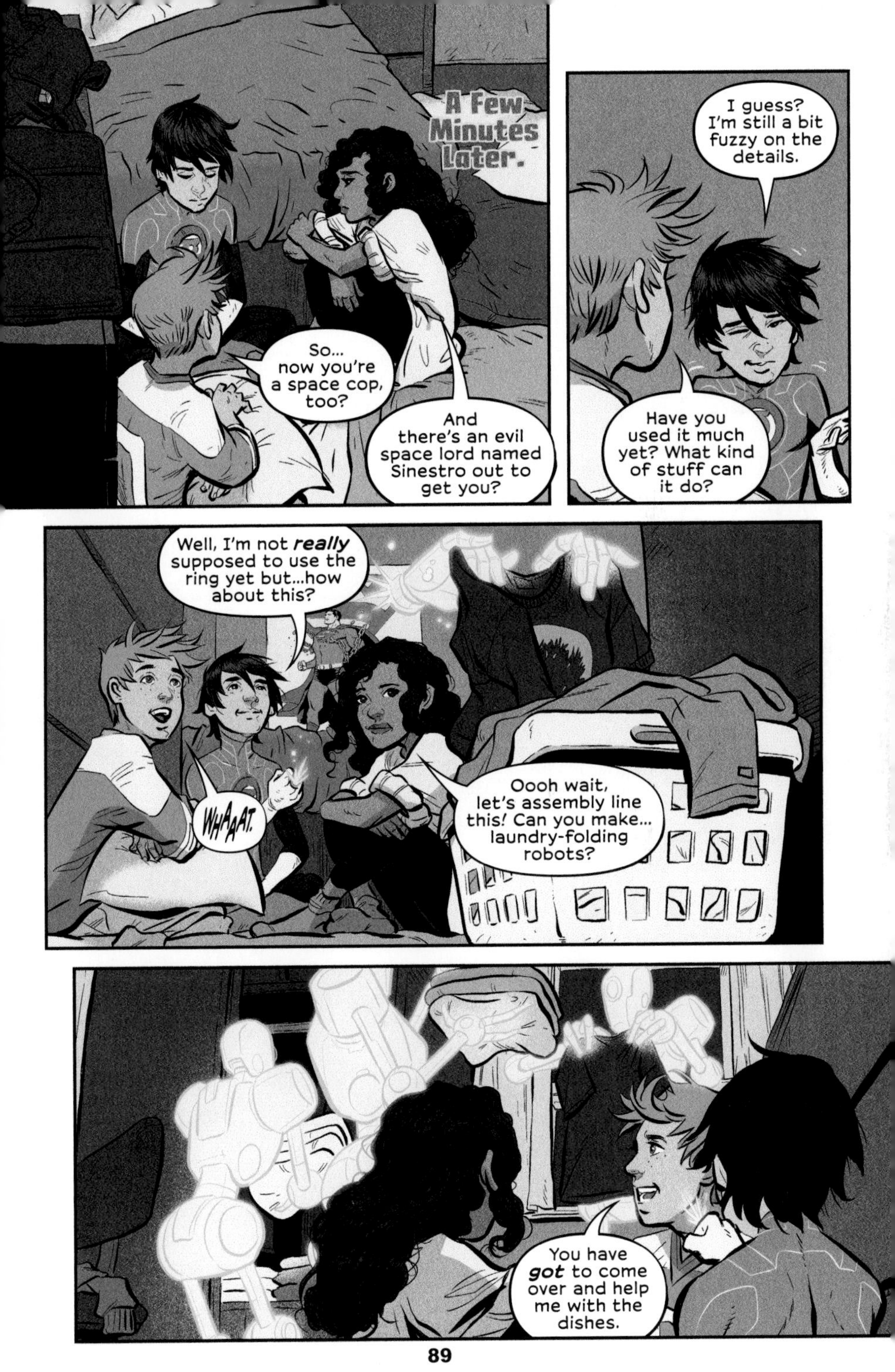
A Few Minutes Later.
So... now you're a space cop, too?
And there's an evil space lord named Sinestro out to get you?
I guess? I'm still a bit fuzzy on the details.
Have you used it much yet? What kind of stuff can it do?
Well, I'm not *really* supposed to use the ring yet but...how about this?
WHAAAT.
Oooh wait, let's assembly line this! Can you make... laundry-folding robots?
You have *got* to come over and help me with the dishes.

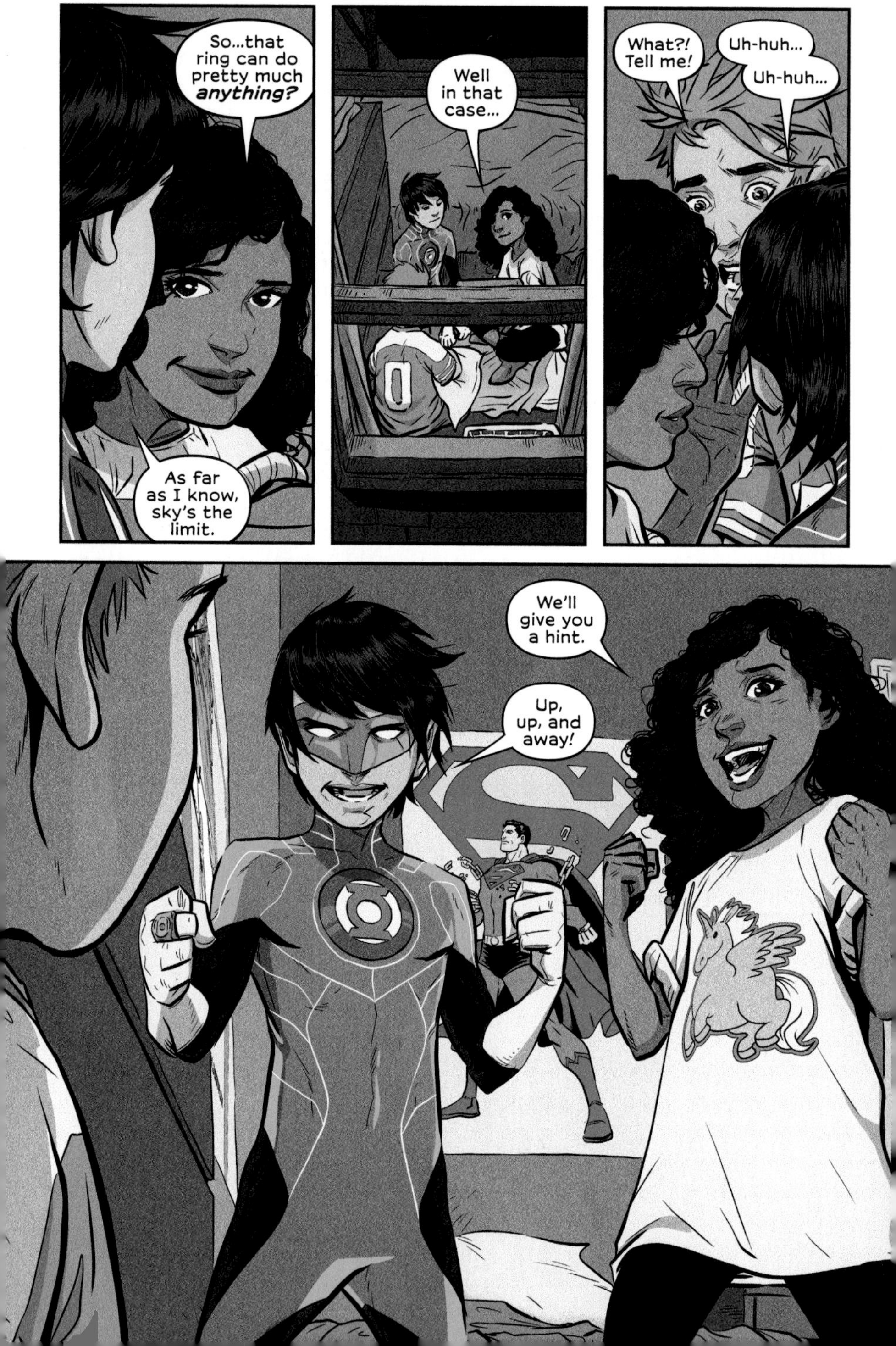
So...that ring can do pretty much *anything?*
As far as I know, sky's the limit.
Well in that case...
What?! Tell me!
Uh-huh...
Uh-huh...
We'll give you a hint.
Up, up, and away!

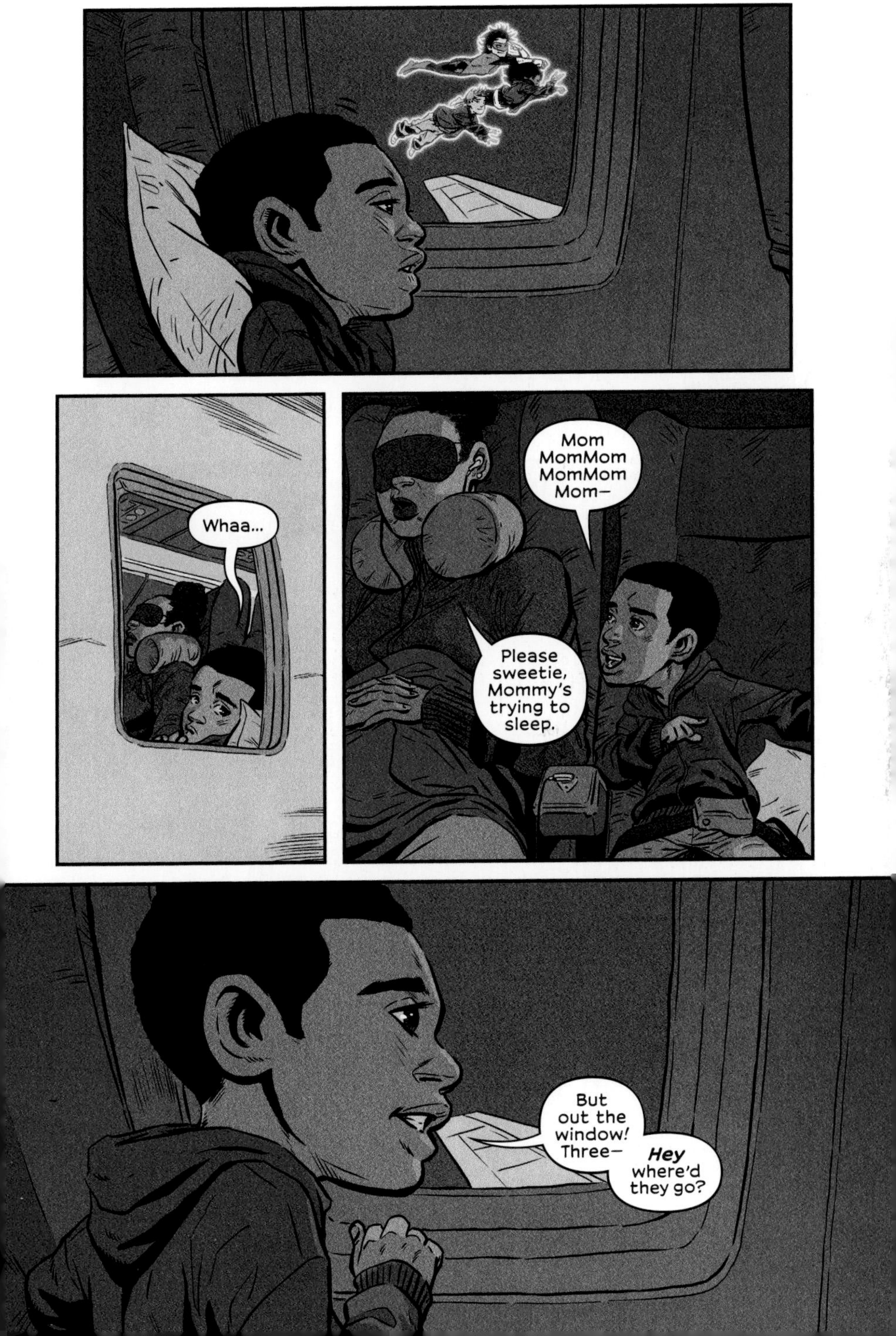
Whaa...
Mom MomMom MomMom Mom—
Please sweetie, Mommy's trying to sleep.
But out the window! Three—
Hey where'd they go?

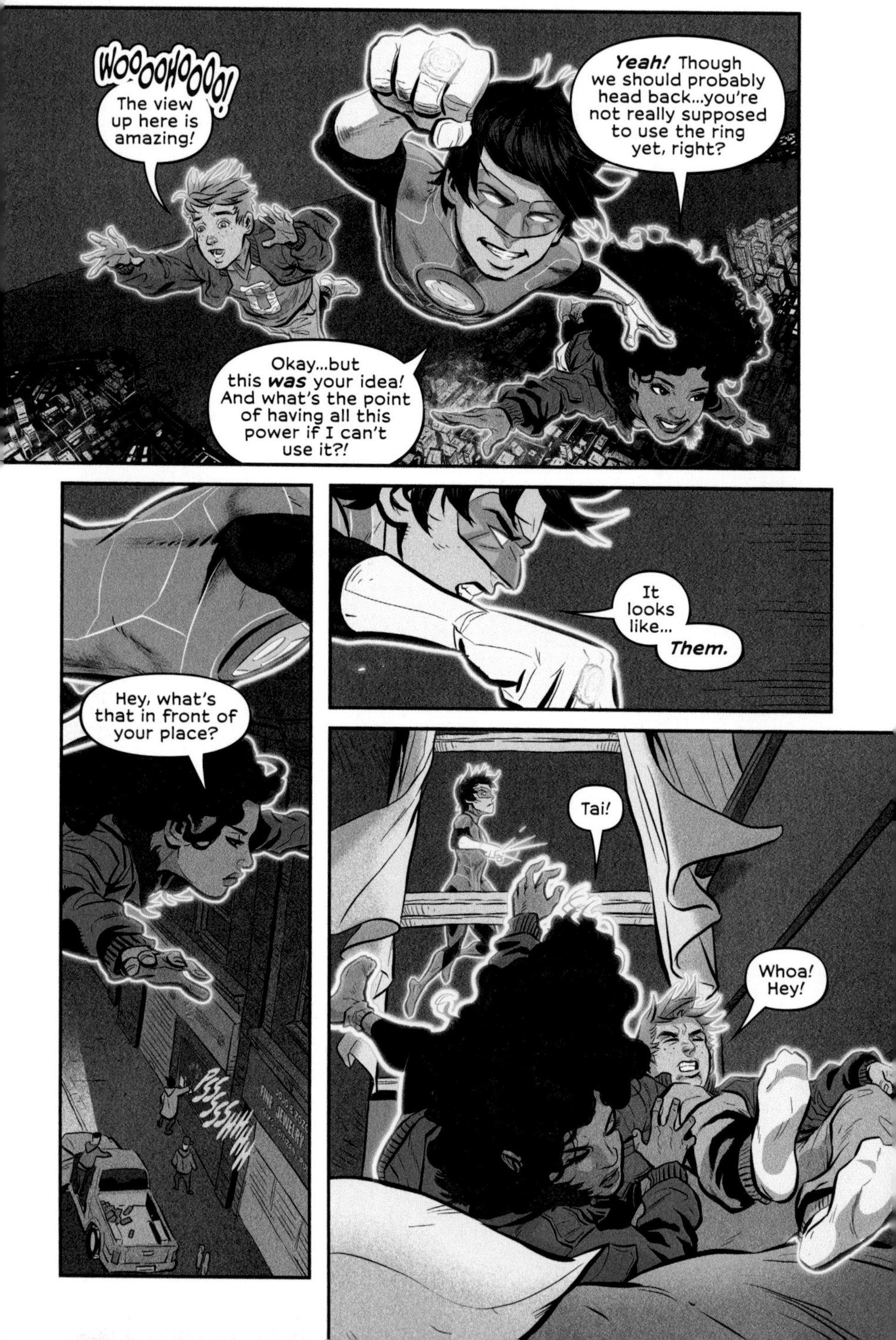
WOOOOHOOOO!
The view up here is amazing!
Yeah! Though we should probably head back...you're not really supposed to use the ring yet, right?
Okay...but this was your idea! And what's the point of having all this power if I can't use it?!
Hey, what's that in front of your place?
It looks like... Them.
PSSSSHHHH
JOJO & ZOZO
FINE JEWELRY
Tai!
Whoa! Hey!

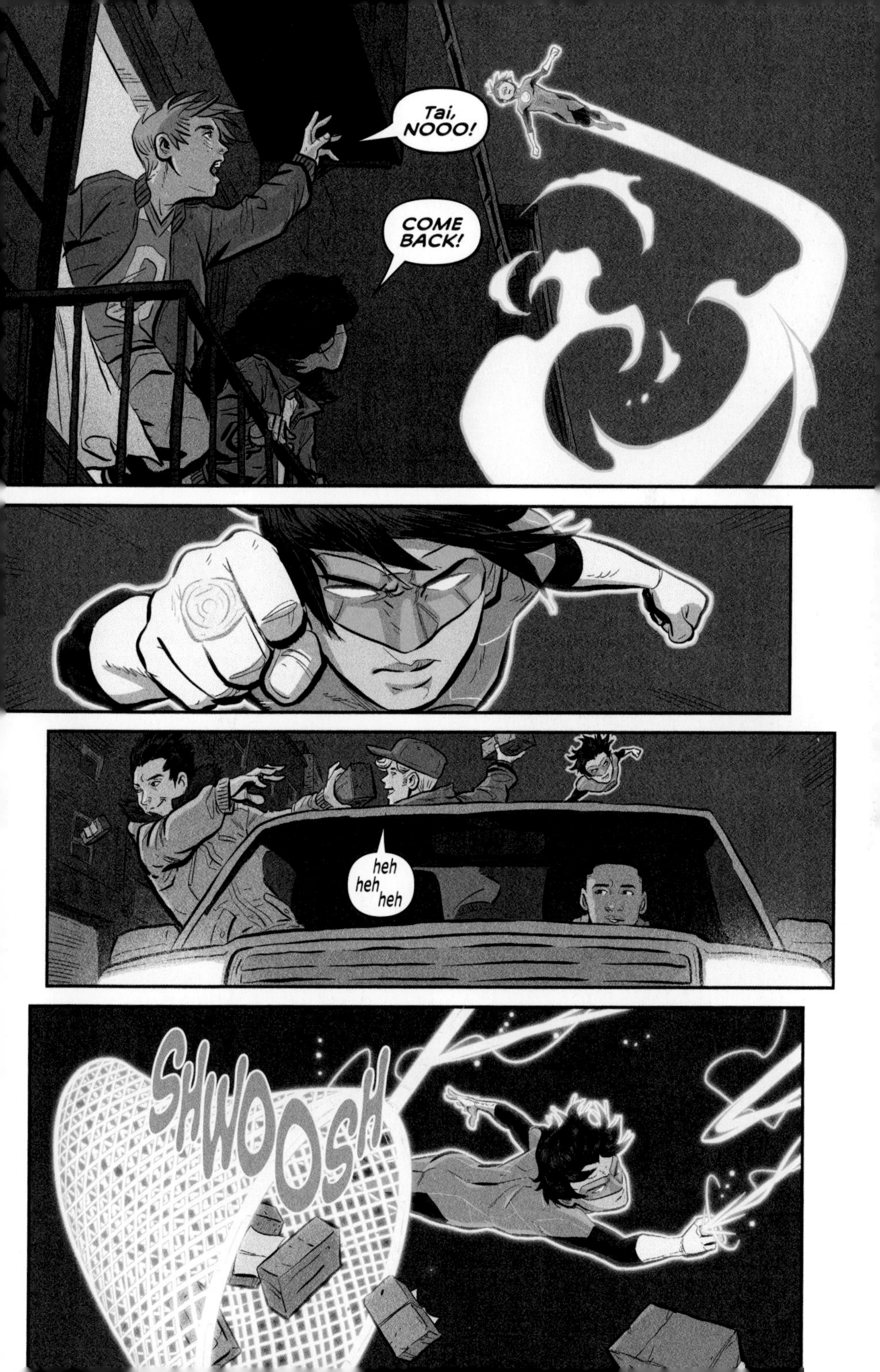
Tai, NOOO!
COME BACK!
heh heh heh
SHWOOSH

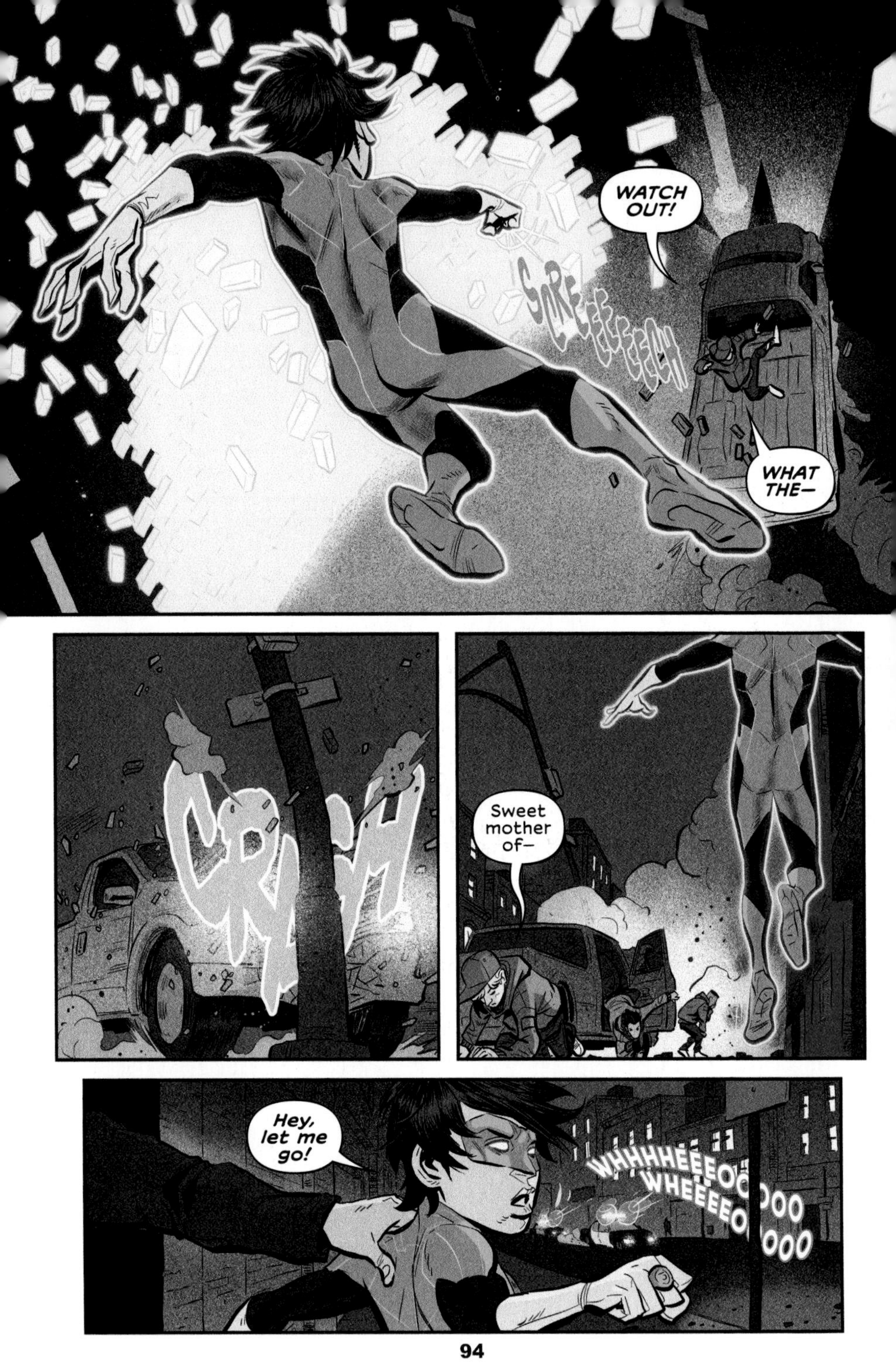
WATCH OUT!
SCREEEEEECH
WHAT THE—
CRASH
Sweet mother of—
Hey, let me go!
WHHHHEEEOOOOO WHEEEEOOOOOO

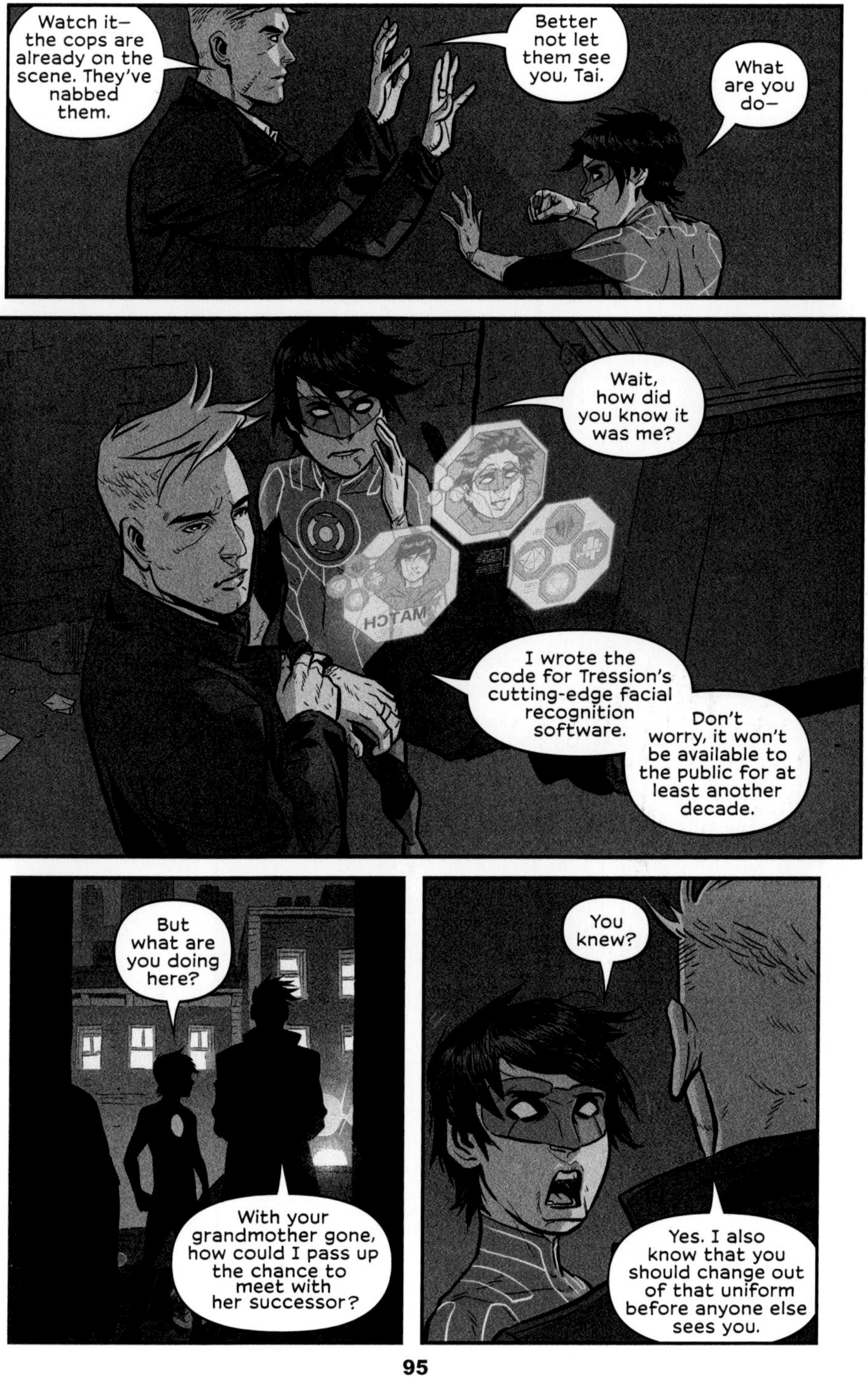
Watch it— the cops are already on the scene. They've nabbed them.
Better not let them see you, Tai.
What are you do—
Wait, how did you know it was me?
I wrote the code for Tression's cutting-edge facial recognition software.
Don't worry, it won't be available to the public for at least another decade.
But what are you doing here?
With your grandmother gone, how could I pass up the chance to meet with her successor?
You knew?
Yes. I also know that you should change out of that uniform before anyone else sees you.

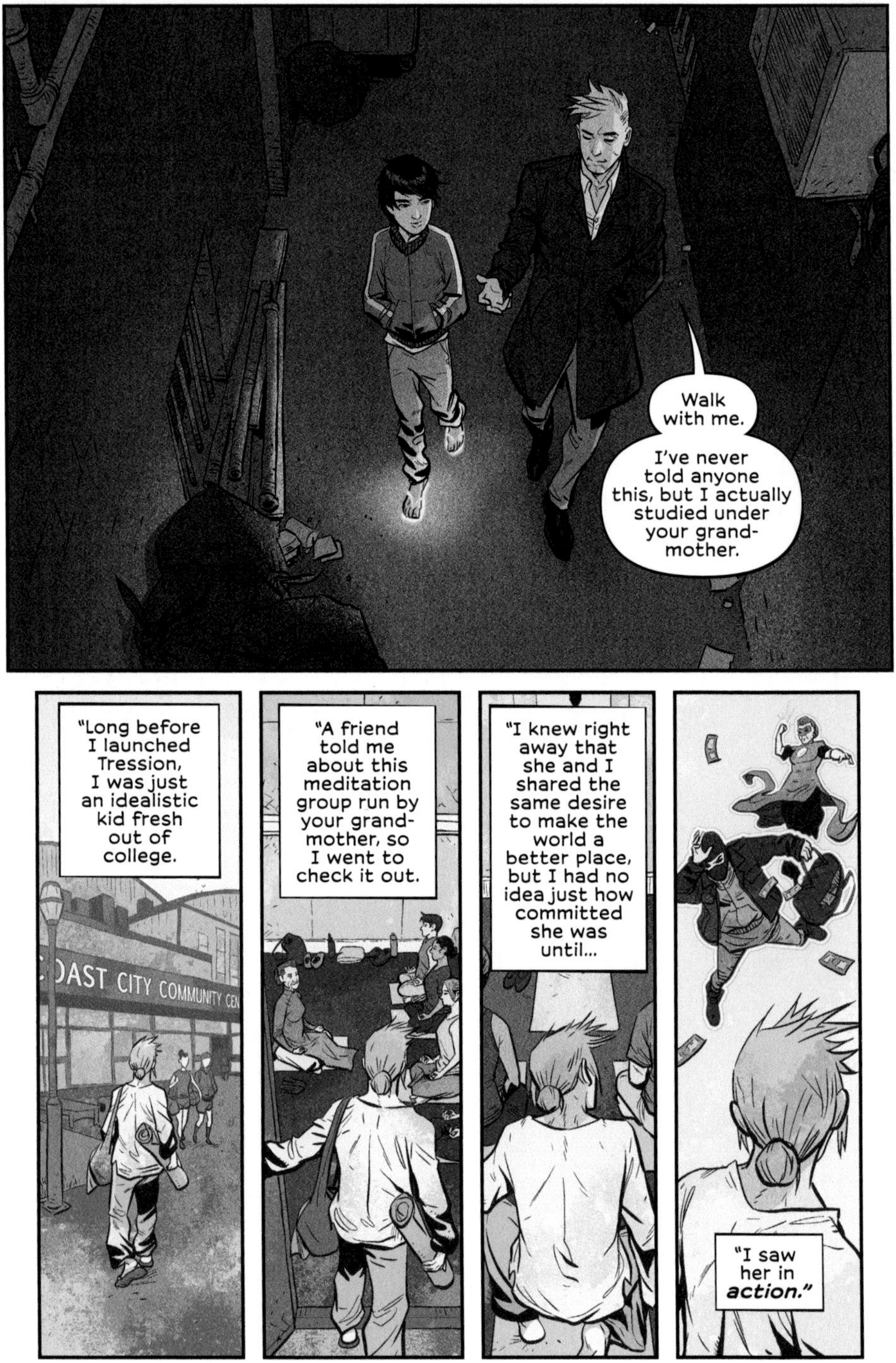
Walk with me.
I've never told anyone this, but I actually studied under your grand-mother.
"Long before I launched Tression, I was just an idealistic kid fresh out of college.
COAST CITY COMMUNITY CEN
"A friend told me about this meditation group run by your grand-mother, so I went to check it out.
"I knew right away that she and I shared the same desire to make the world a better place, but I had no idea just how committed she was until...
"I saw her in *action.*"

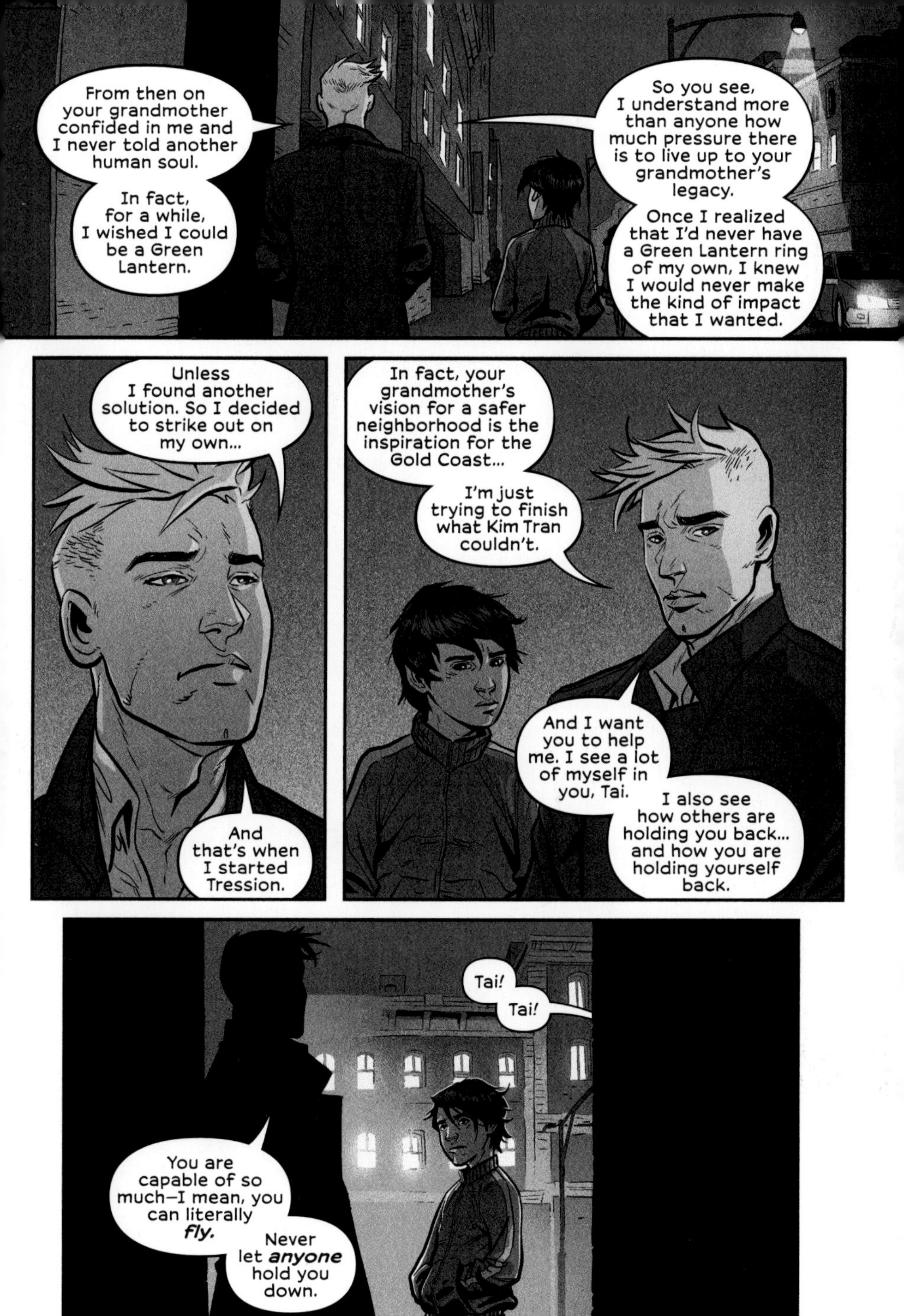
From then on your grandmother confided in me and I never told another human soul.
In fact, for a while, I wished I could be a Green Lantern.
So you see, I understand more than anyone how much pressure there is to live up to your grandmother's legacy.
Once I realized that I'd never have a Green Lantern ring of my own, I knew I would never make the kind of impact that I wanted.
Unless I found another solution. So I decided to strike out on my own...
And that's when I started Tression.
In fact, your grandmother's vision for a safer neighborhood is the inspiration for the Gold Coast...
I'm just trying to finish what Kim Tran couldn't.
And I want you to help me. I see a lot of myself in you, Tai.
I also see how others are holding you back... and how you are holding yourself back.
Tai!
Tai!
You are capable of so much—I mean, you can literally *fly.*
Never let *anyone* hold you down.

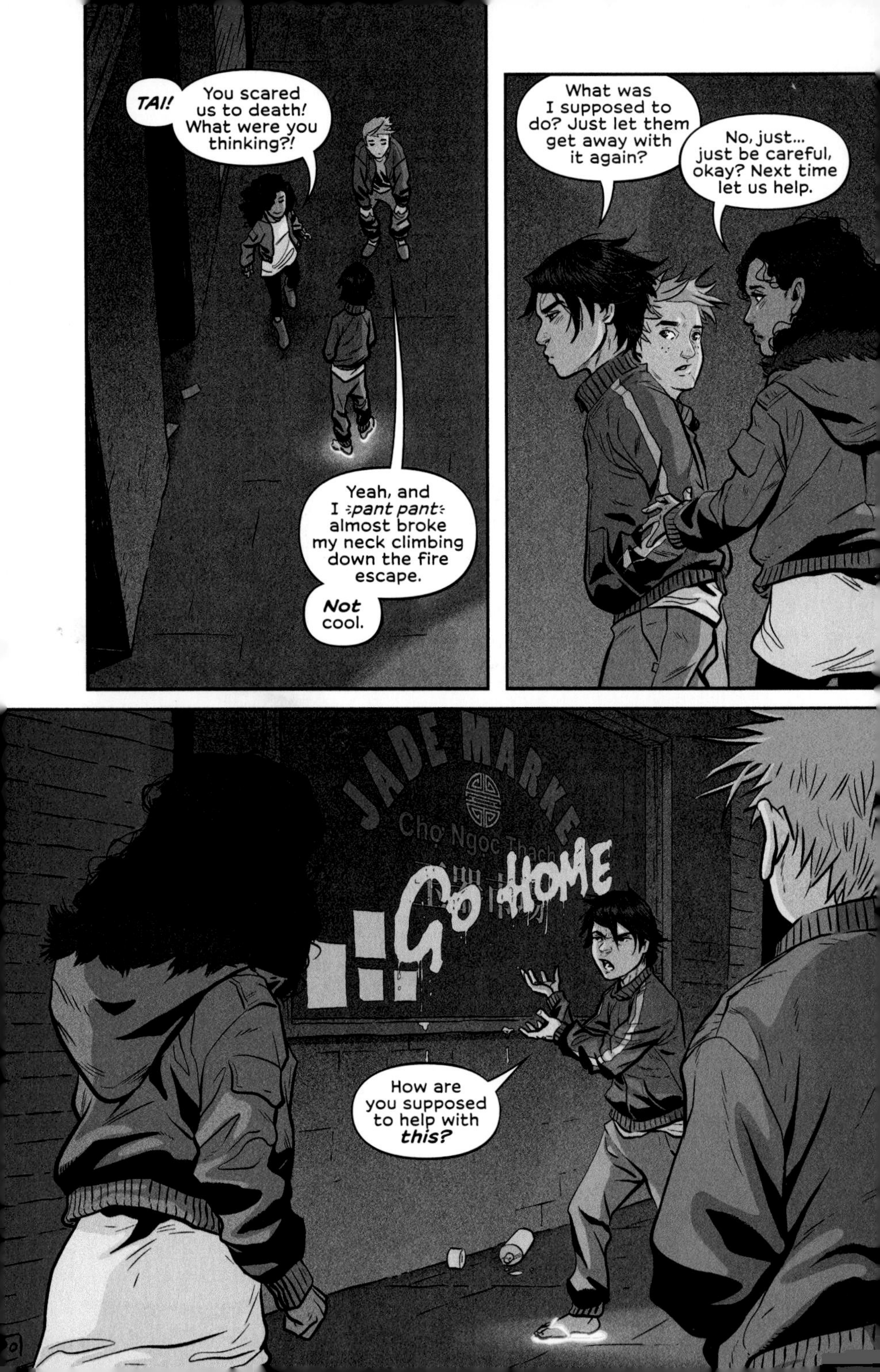
TAI!
You scared us to death! What were you thinking?!
Yeah, and I ≑pant pant≑ almost broke my neck climbing down the fire escape.
Not cool.
What was I supposed to do? Just let them get away with it again?
No, just... just be careful, okay? Next time let us help.
JADE MARKET
Chợ Ngọc Thạch
GO HOME
How are you supposed to help with this?

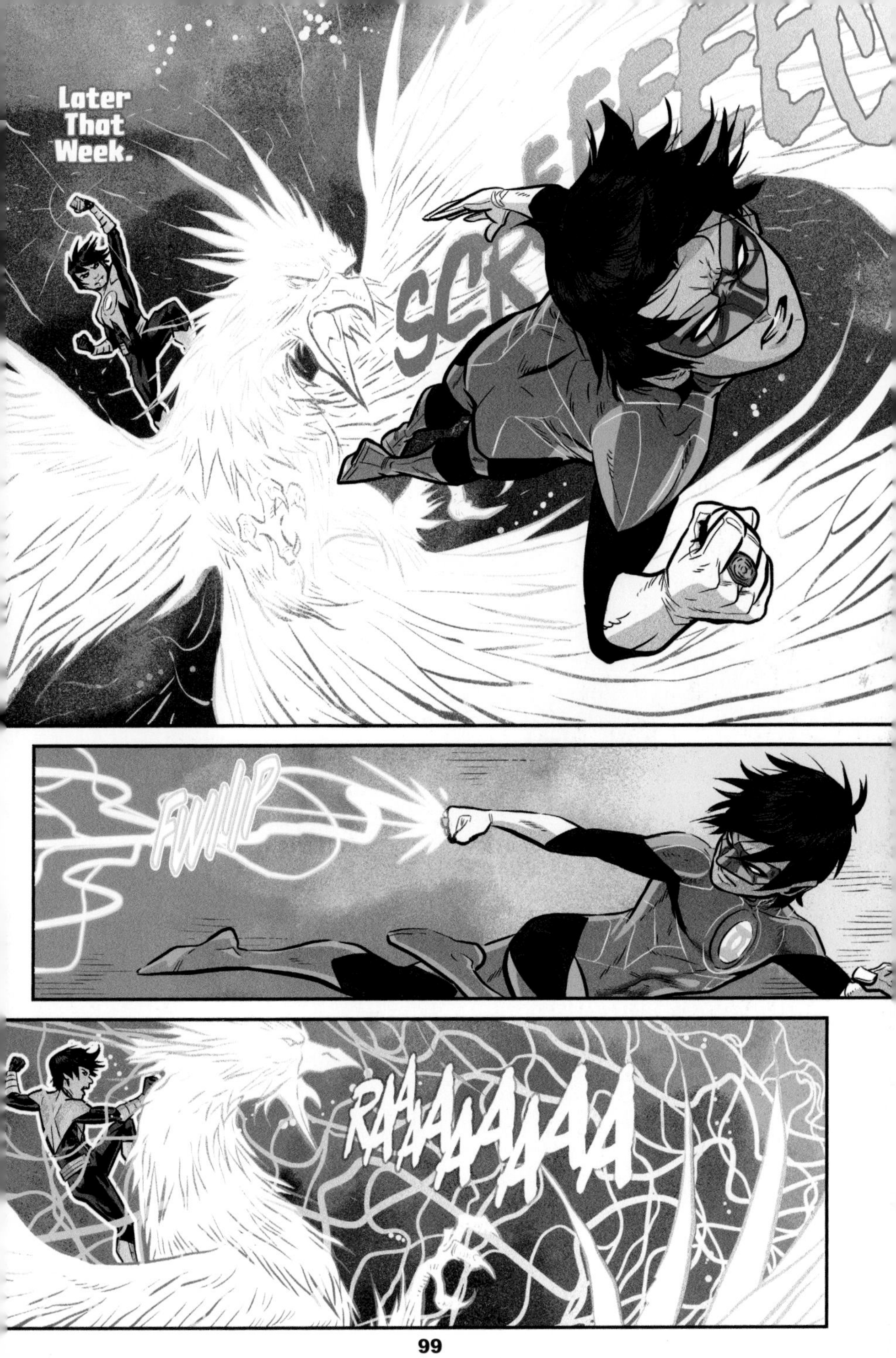
Later That Week.
SCREEEEEECH
FWMP
RAAAAAAAAA

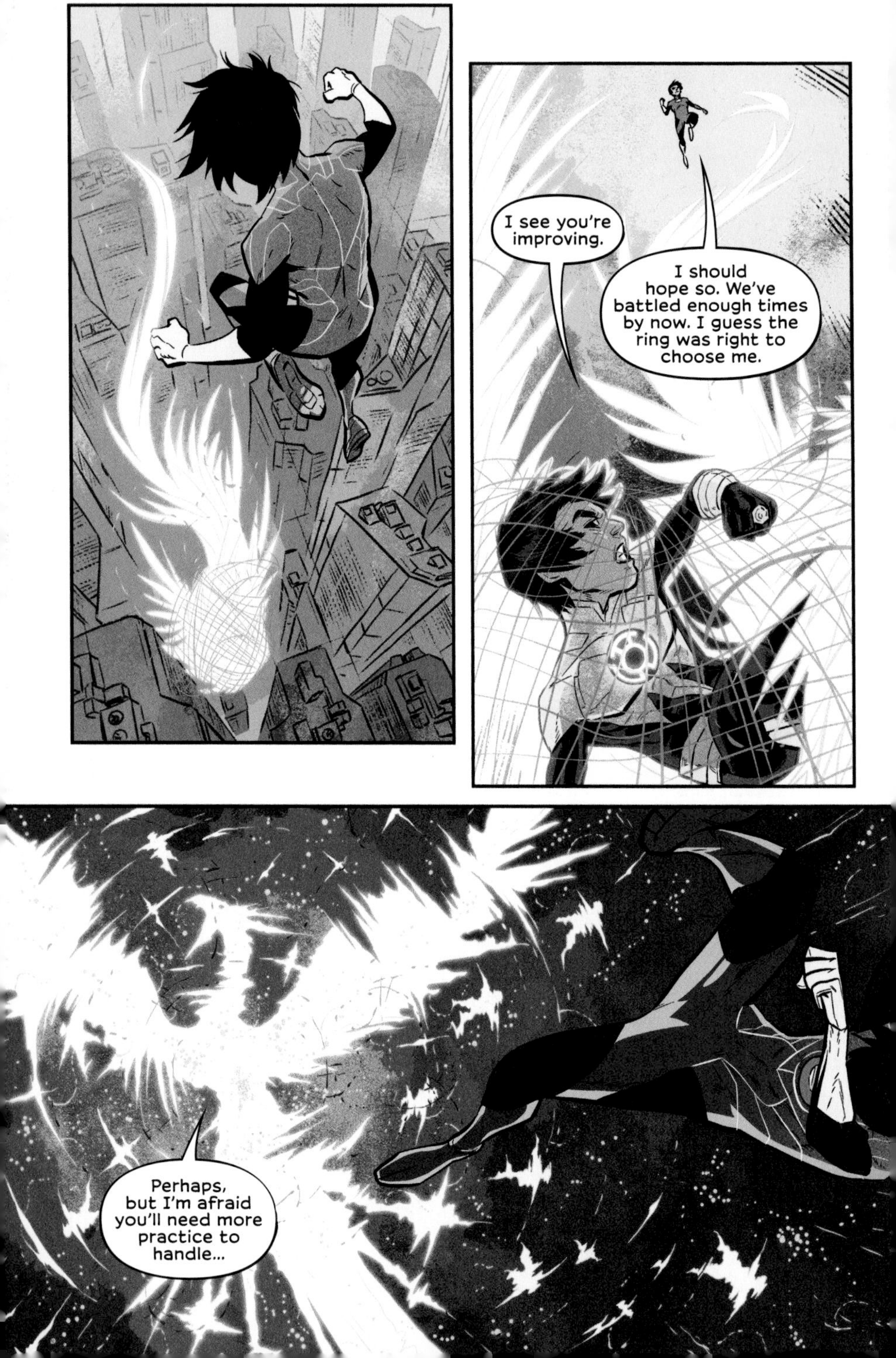
I see you're improving.
I should hope so. We've battled enough times by now. I guess the ring was right to choose me.
Perhaps, but I'm afraid you'll need more practice to handle...

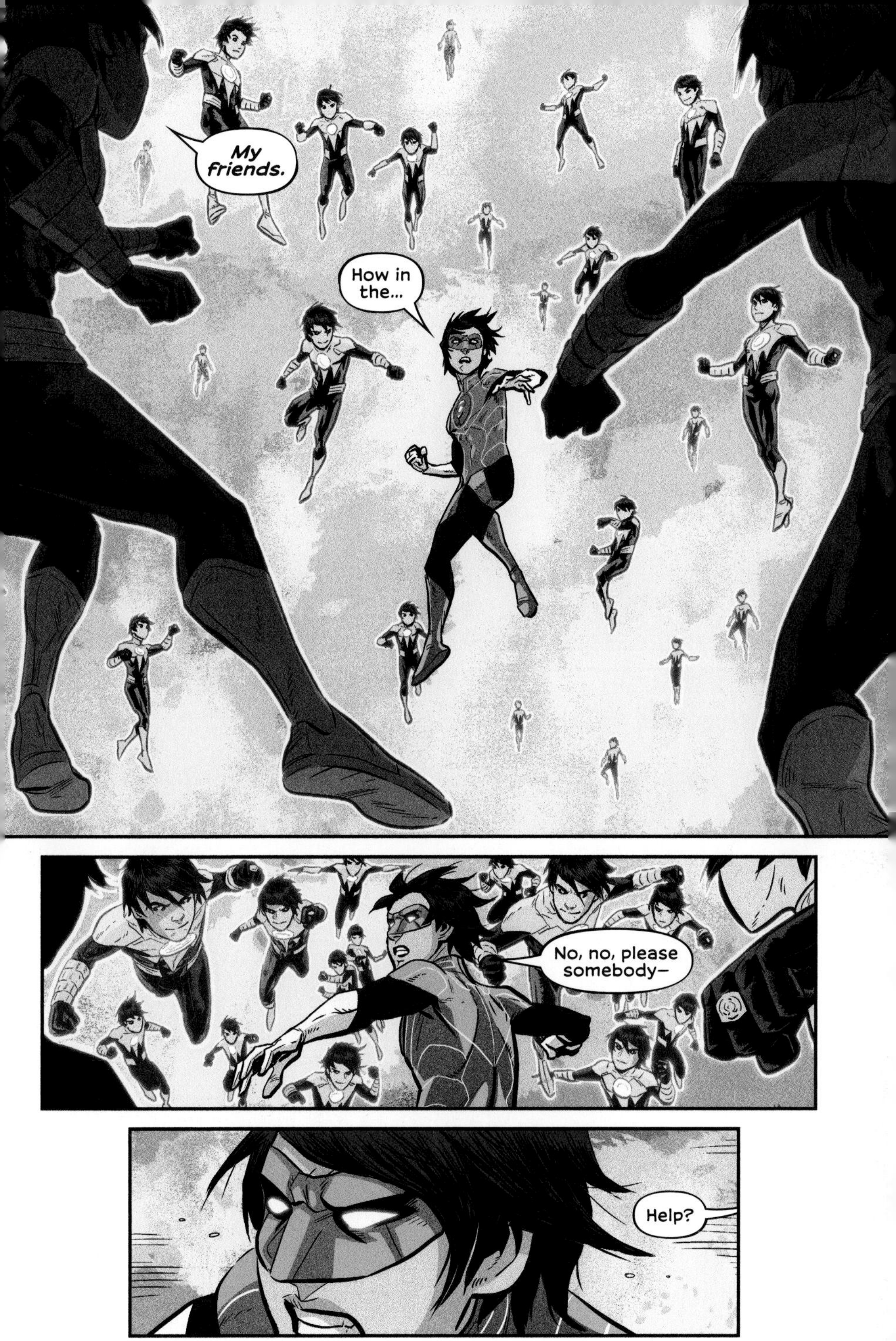
My friends.
How in the...
No, no, please somebody—
Help?

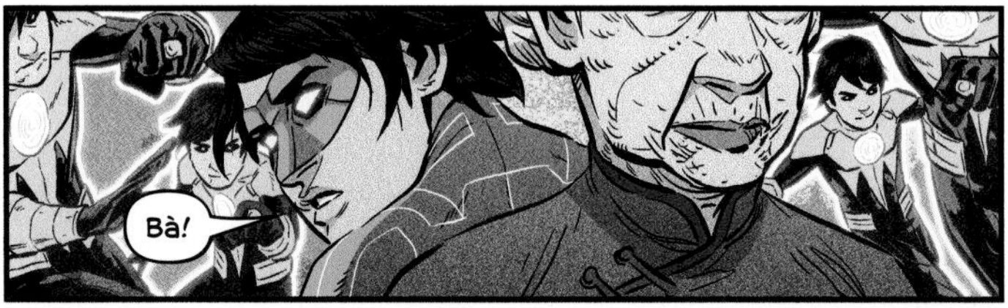
Bà!

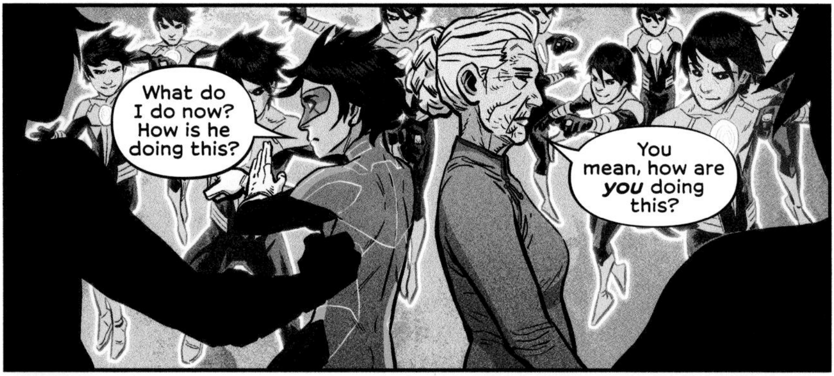
What do I do now? How is he doing this?
You mean, how are *you* doing this?

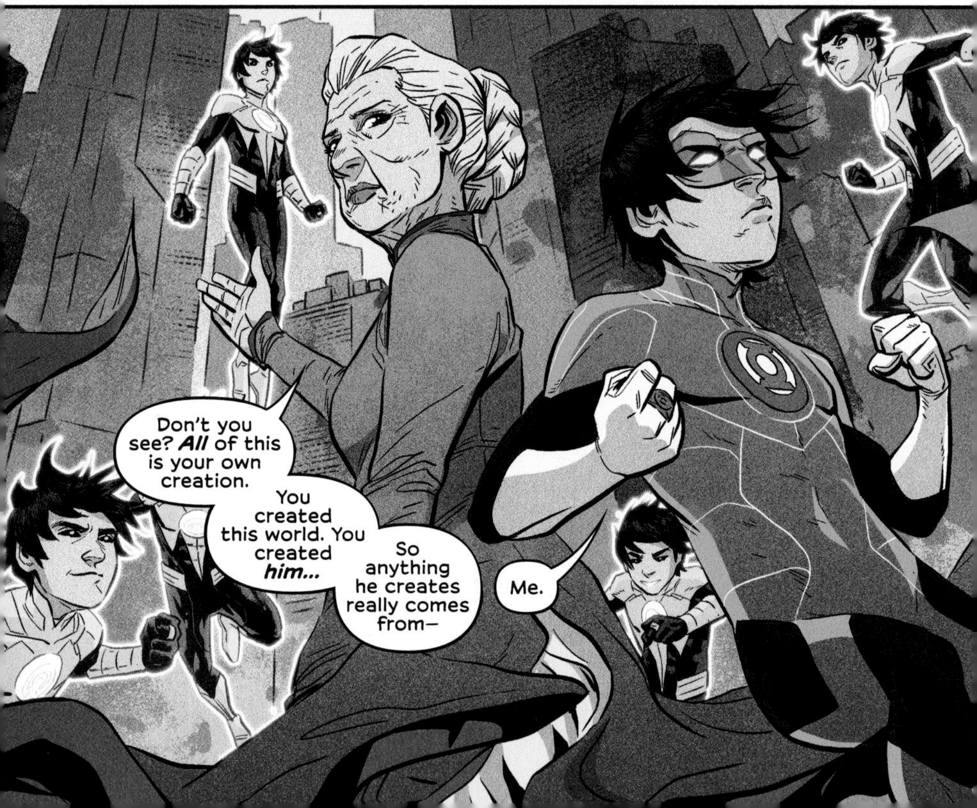
Don't you see? *All* of this is your own creation.
You created this world. You created *him...*
So anything he creates really comes from—
Me.

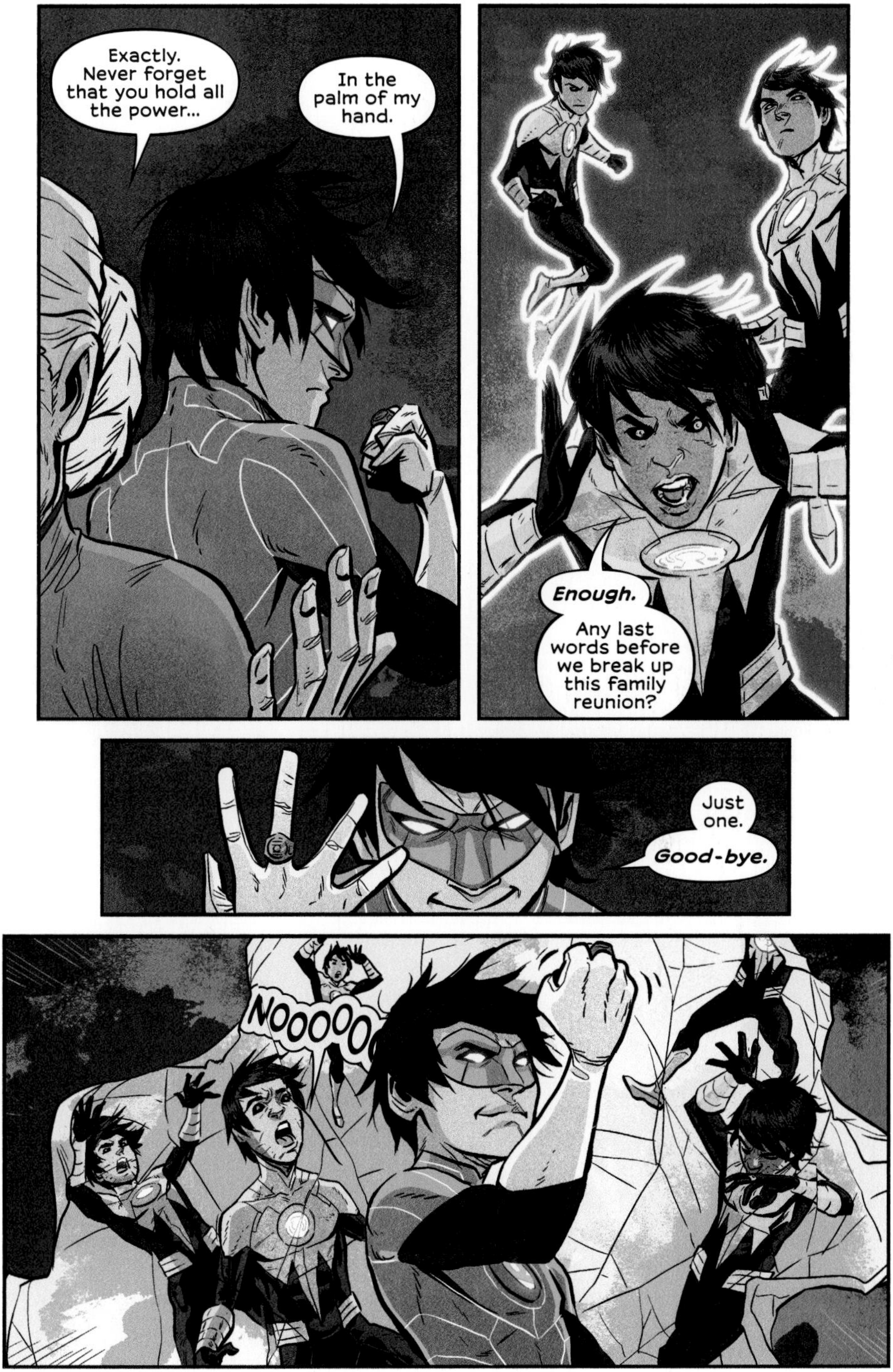
Exactly. Never forget that you hold all the power...
In the palm of my hand.
Enough.
Any last words before we break up this family reunion?
Just one.
Good-bye.
NOOOOO

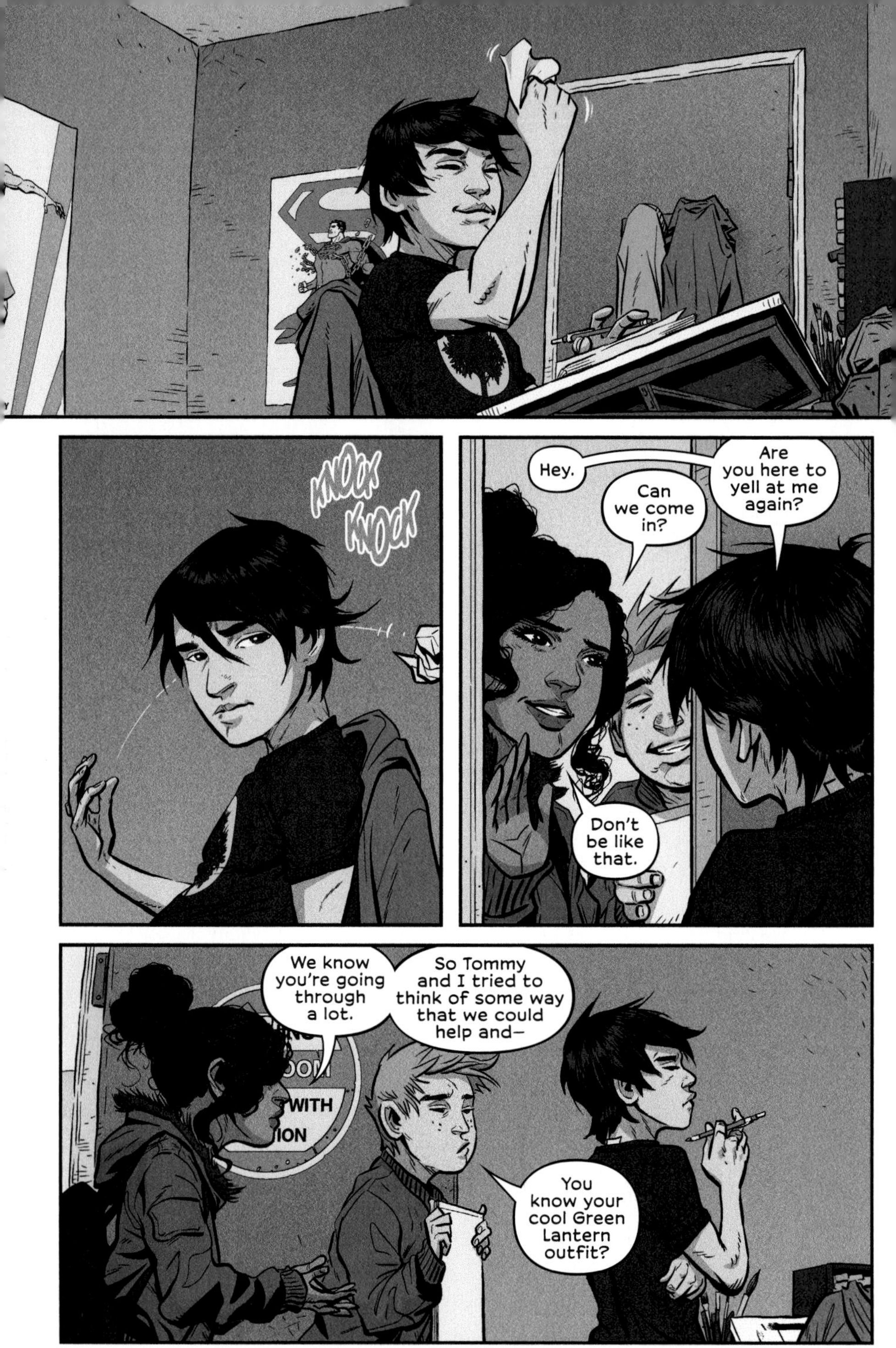
KNOCK KNOCK
Hey.
Are you here to yell at me again?
Can we come in?
Don't be like that.
We know you're going through a lot.
So Tommy and I tried to think of some way that we could help and—
You know your cool Green Lantern outfit?

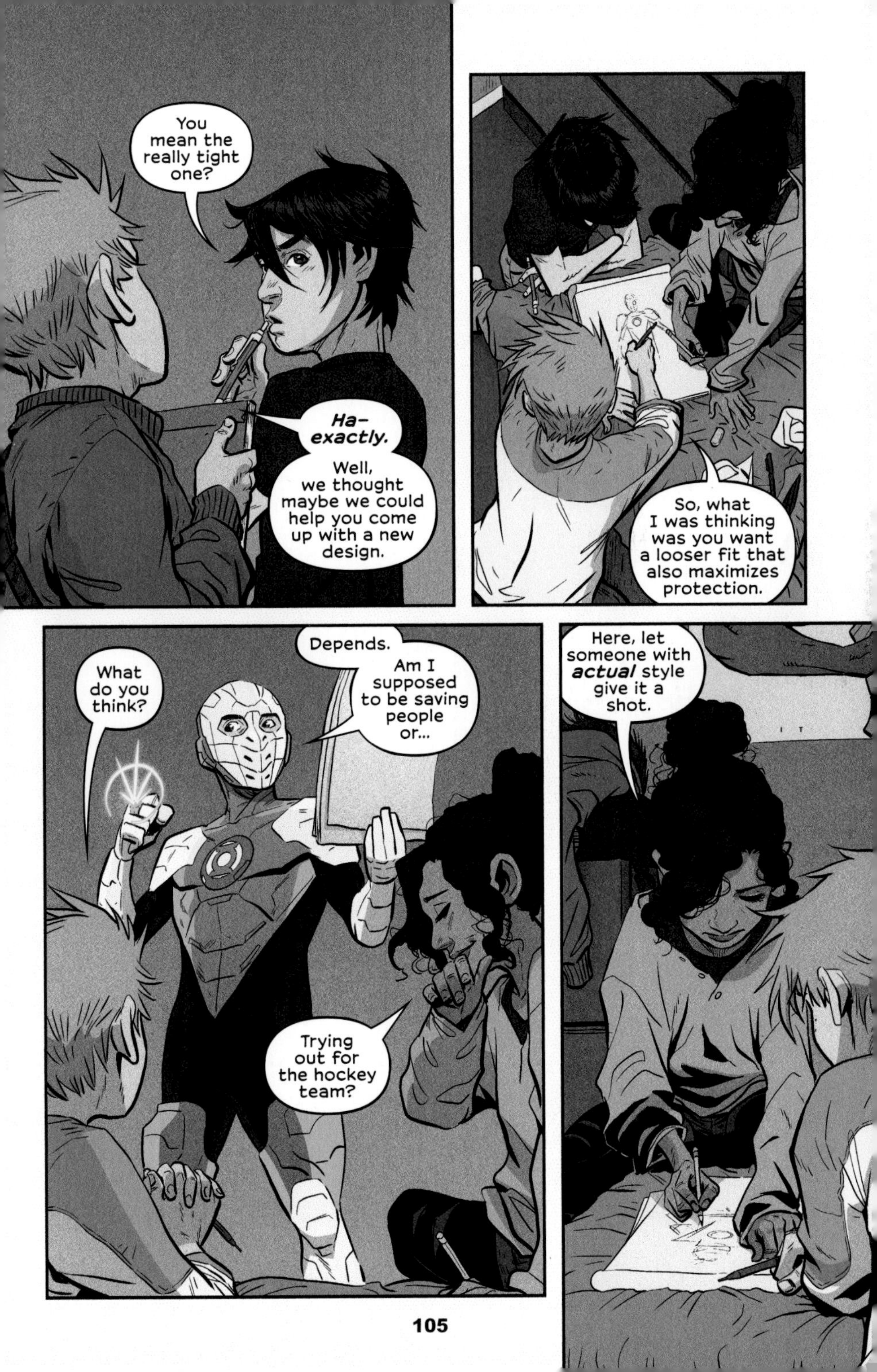
You mean the really tight one?
Ha— exactly.
Well, we thought maybe we could help you come up with a new design.
So, what I was thinking was you want a looser fit that also maximizes protection.
What do you think?
Depends.
Am I supposed to be saving people or...
Trying out for the hockey team?
Here, let someone with *actual* style give it a shot.

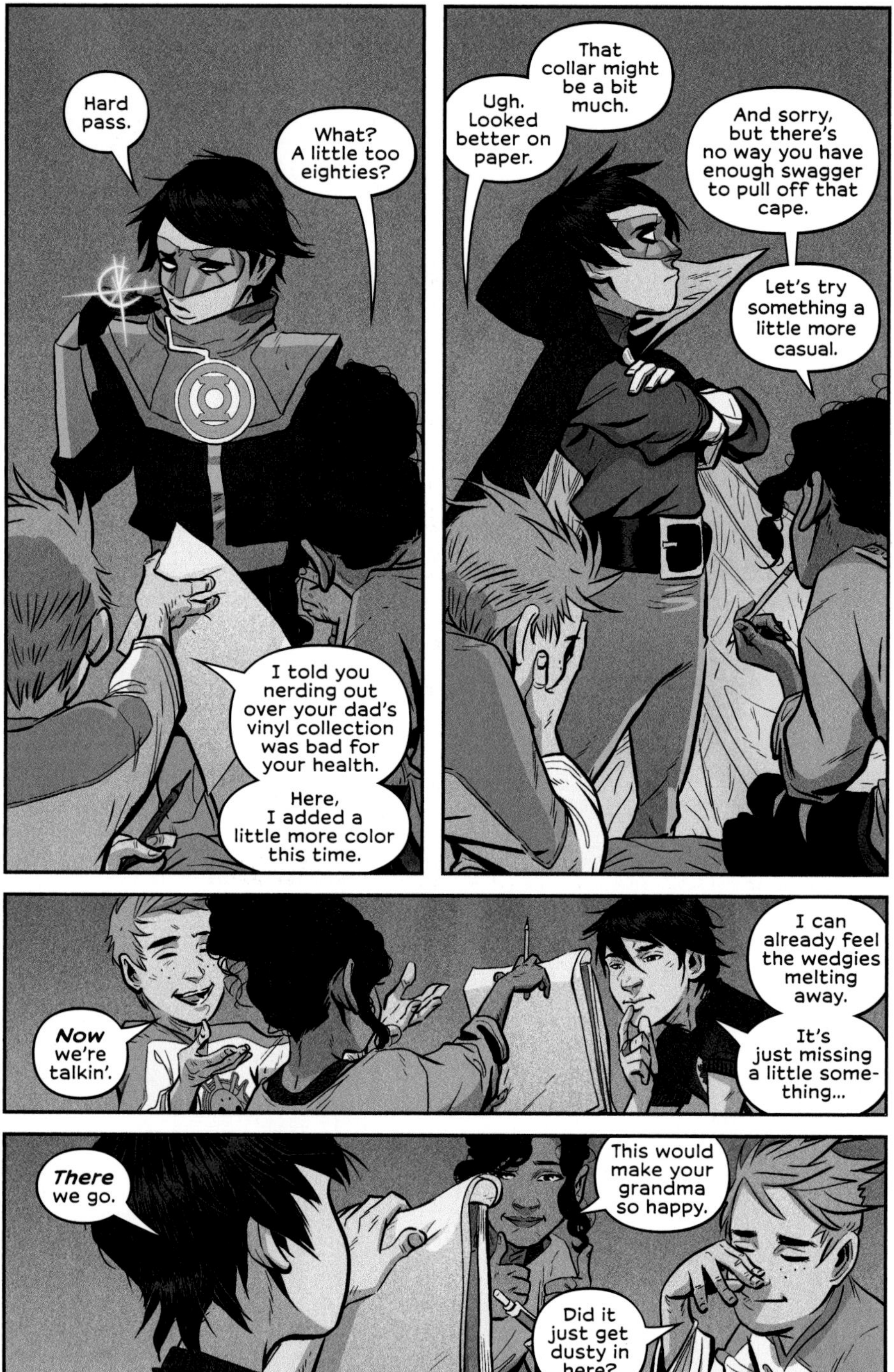
Hard pass.
What? A little too eighties?
I told you nerding out over your dad's vinyl collection was bad for your health.
Here, I added a little more color this time.
That collar might be a bit much.
Ugh. Looked better on paper.
And sorry, but there's no way you have enough swagger to pull off that cape.
Let's try something a little more casual.
Now we're talkin'.
I can already feel the wedgies melting away.
It's just missing a little some-thing...
There we go.
This would make your grandma so happy.
Did it just get dusty in here?

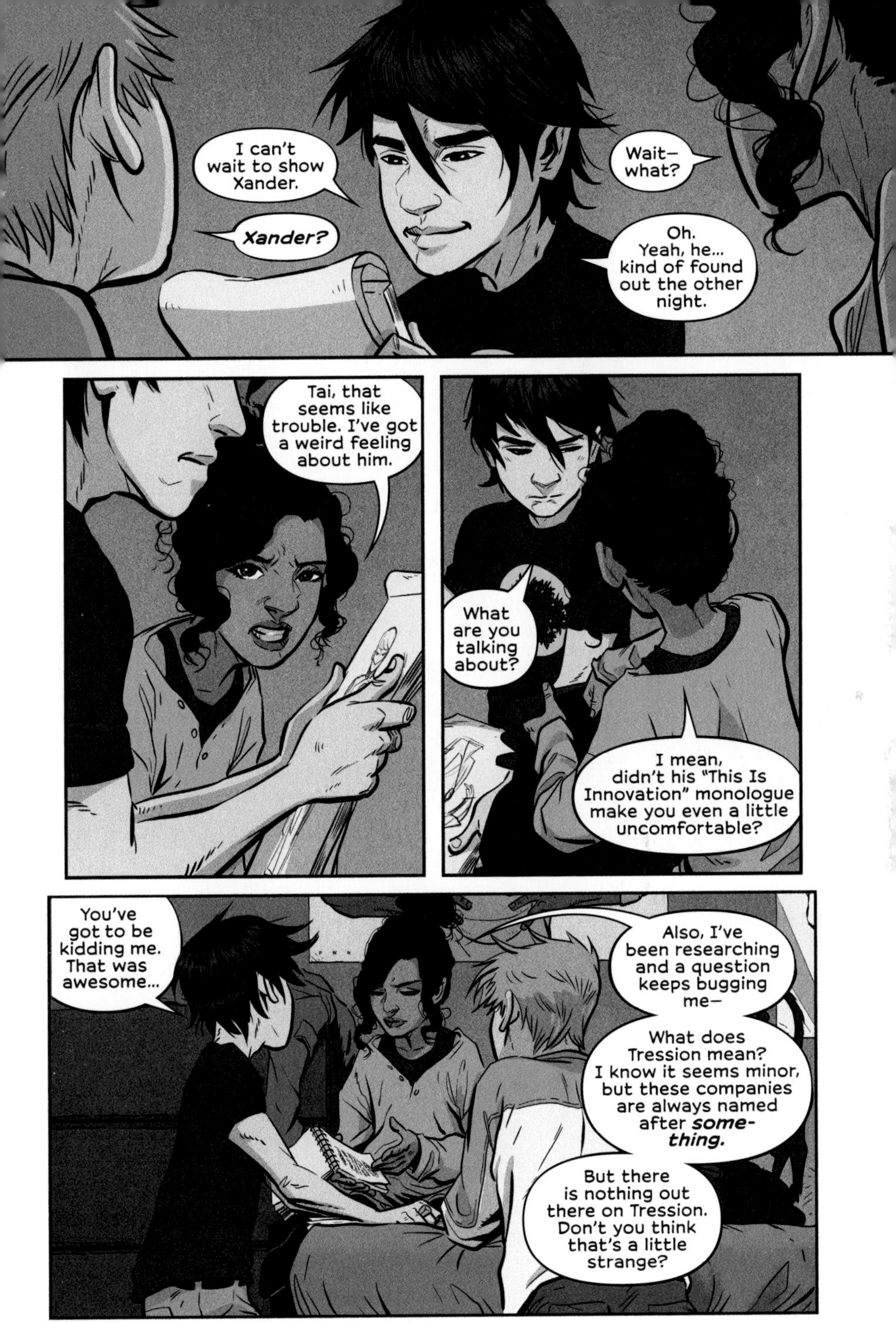
I can't wait to show Xander.
Xander?
Wait— what?
Oh. Yeah, he... kind of found out the other night.
Tai, that seems like trouble. I've got a weird feeling about him.
What are you talking about?
I mean, didn't his "This Is Innovation" monologue make you even a little uncomfortable?
You've got to be kidding me. That was awesome...
Also, I've been researching and a question keeps bugging me—
What does Tression mean? I know it seems minor, but these companies are always named after ***some-thing.***
But there is nothing out there on Tression. Don't you think that's a little strange?

C'mon... Tommy, can you believe this?

I don't know...she's probably right that it's best to play it safe...

Not you, too. You're just jealous, both of you!

You can't stand it that *the* Xander Griffin likes me better than you!

Hey, don't overreact...why don't you take a deep breath and slow down a minute...

Why does everyone keep treating me like a baby?

All of you keep holding me down... Except Xander.

He's the only one who really believes in me.

How can you say that? We—

I don't need this. I'm getting some fresh air.

WARNING
...ARS ROOM
...ROCEED WITH
...UTION

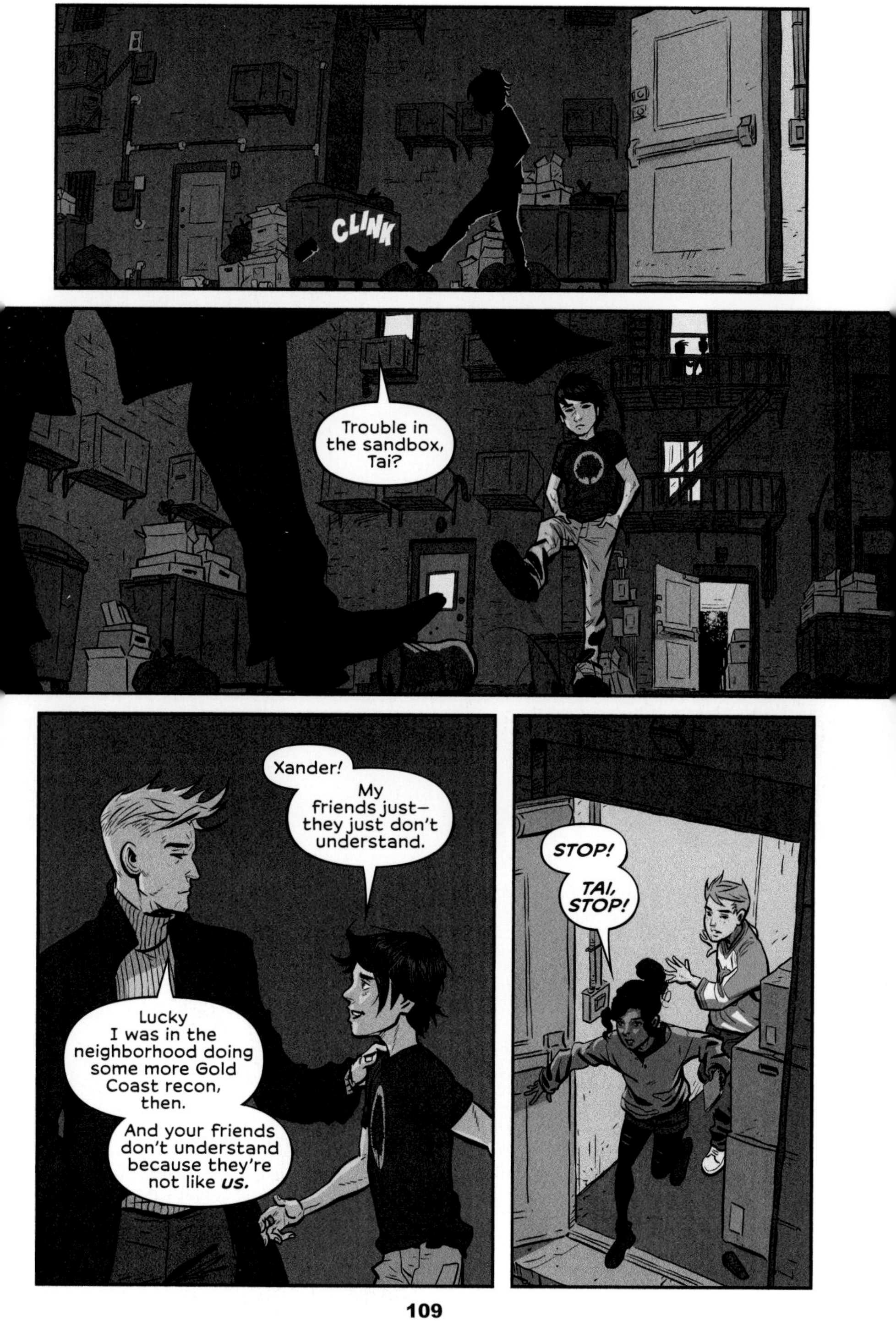
CLINK
Trouble in the sandbox, Tai?
Xander!
My friends just— they just don't understand.
Lucky I was in the neighborhood doing some more Gold Coast recon, then.
And your friends don't understand because they're not like *us.*
STOP!
TAI, STOP!

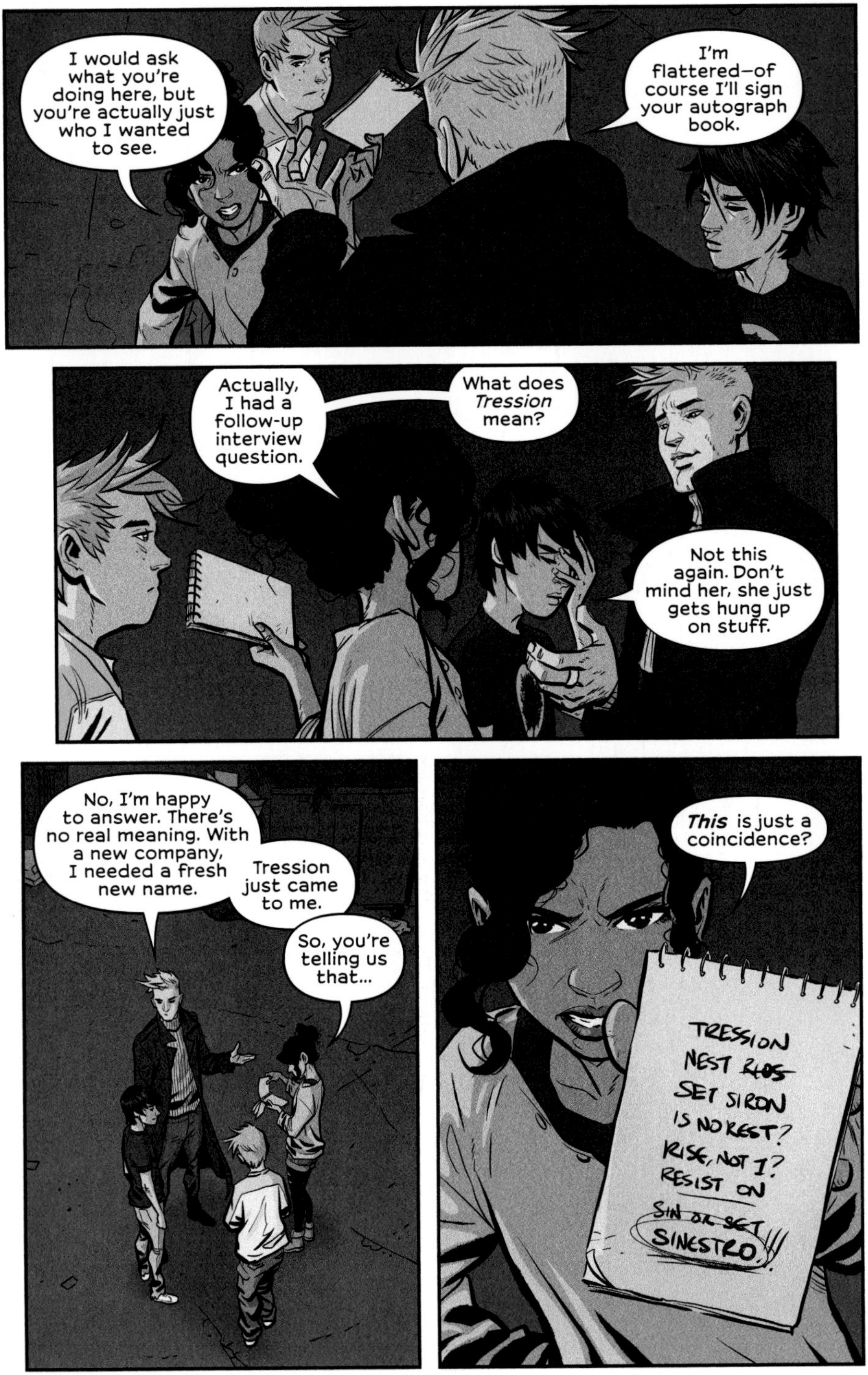
I would ask what you're doing here, but you're actually just who I wanted to see.
I'm flattered—of course I'll sign your autograph book.
Actually, I had a follow-up interview question.
What does *Tression* mean?
Not this again. Don't mind her, she just gets hung up on stuff.
No, I'm happy to answer. There's no real meaning. With a new company, I needed a fresh new name.
Tression just came to me.
So, you're telling us that...
This is just a coincidence?
TRESSION
NEST ~~RIOS~~
SET SIRON
IS NO REST?
RISE, NOT I?
RESIST ON
~~SIN OR SET~~
SINESTRO!!!

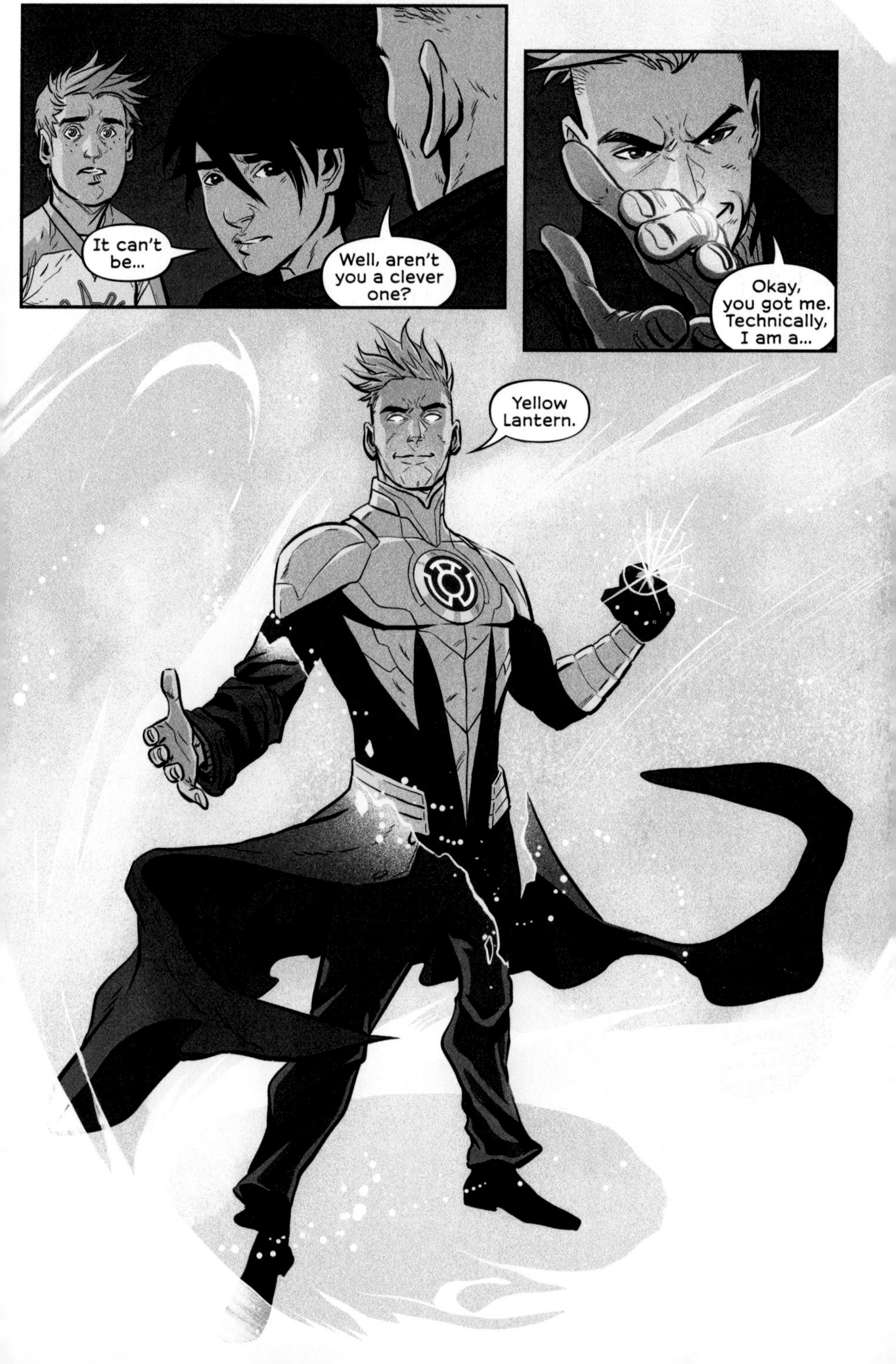
It can't be...
Well, aren't you a clever one?
Okay, you got me. Technically, I am a...
Yellow Lantern.

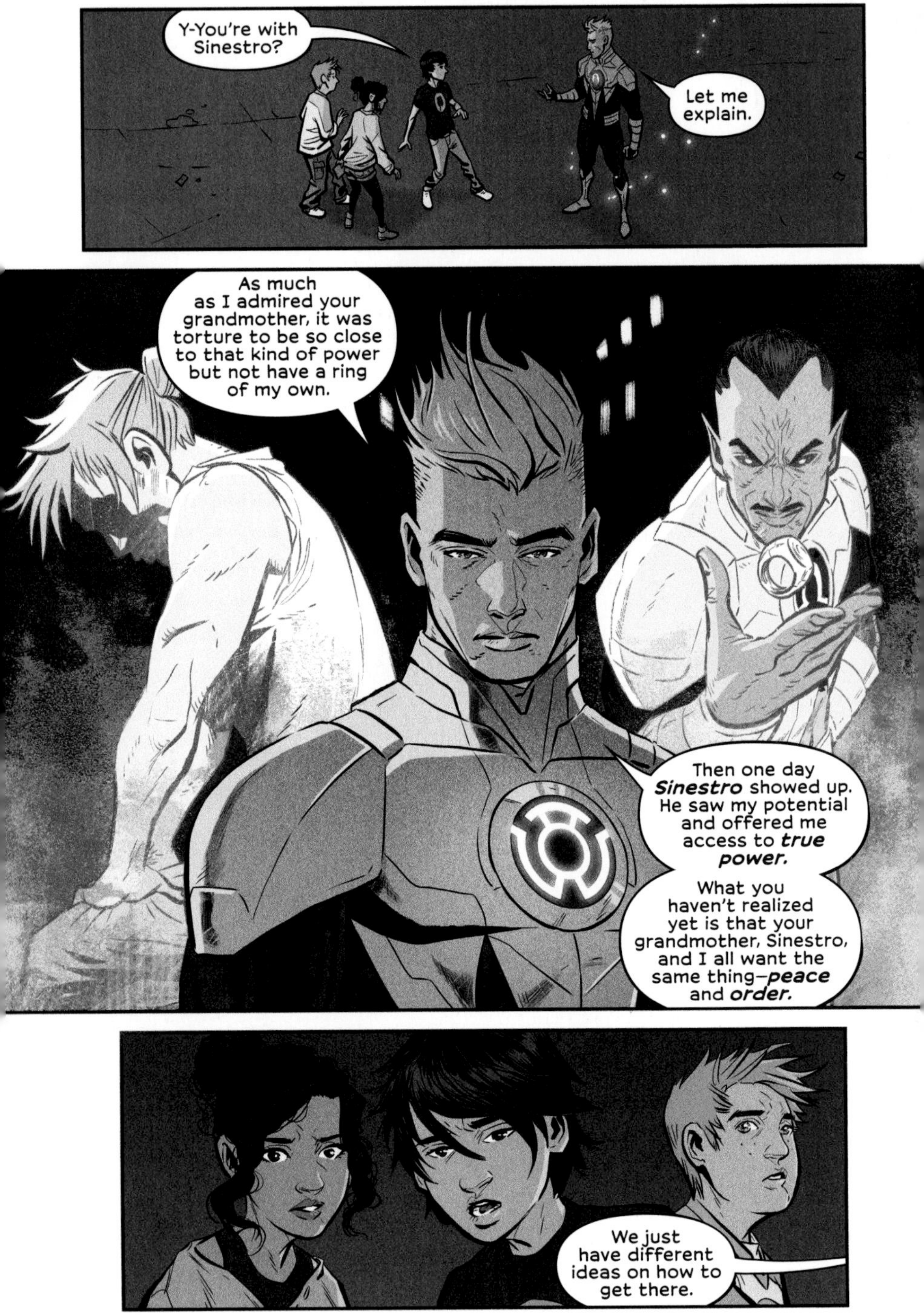
Y-You're with Sinestro?
Let me explain.
As much as I admired your grandmother, it was torture to be so close to that kind of power but not have a ring of my own.
Then one day *Sinestro* showed up. He saw my potential and offered me access to ***true power.***
What you haven't realized yet is that your grandmother, Sinestro, and I all want the same thing—***peace*** and ***order.***
We just have different ideas on how to get there.

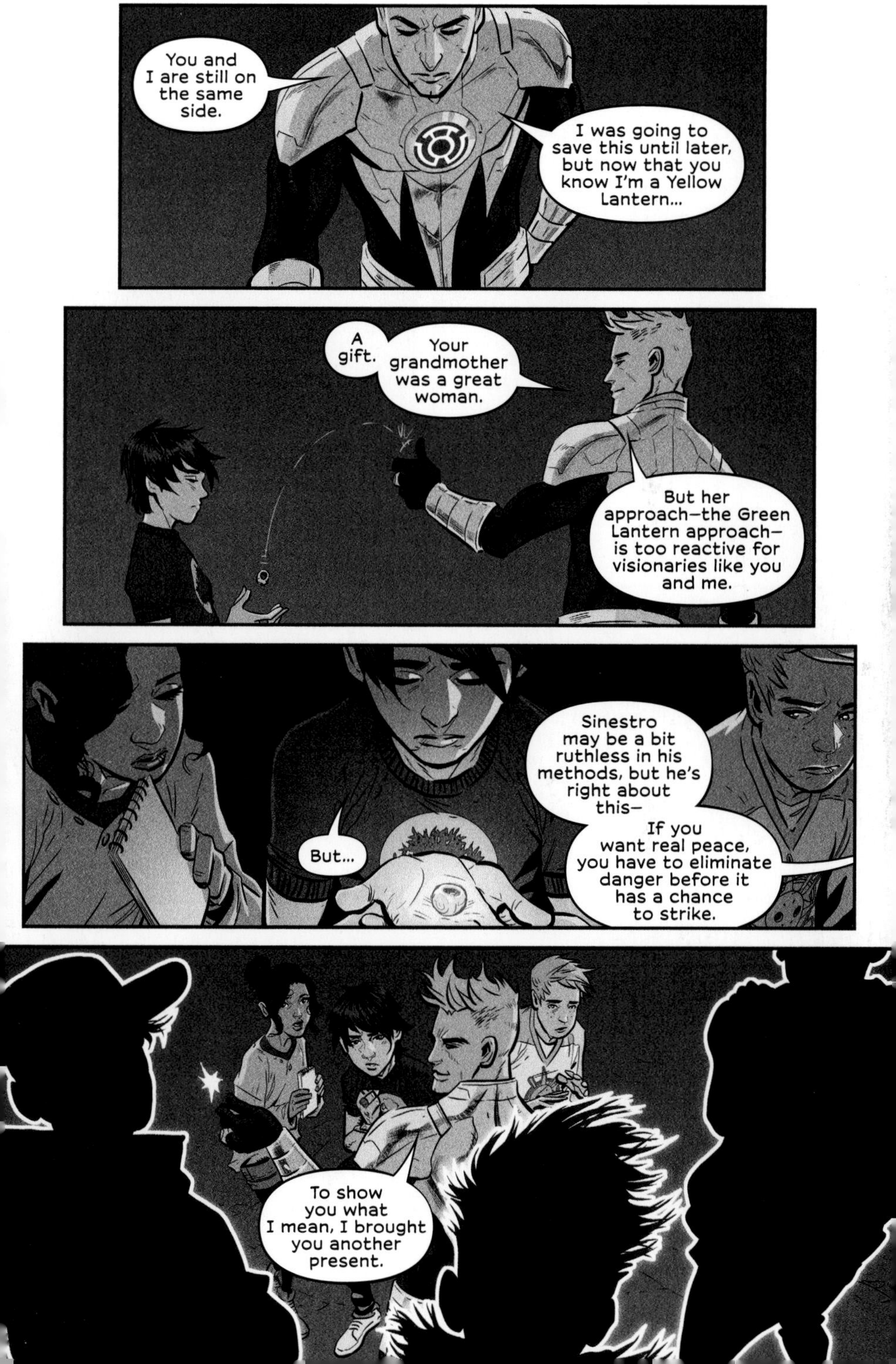
You and I are still on the same side.
I was going to save this until later, but now that you know I'm a Yellow Lantern...
A gift.
Your grandmother was a great woman.
But her approach—the Green Lantern approach—is too reactive for visionaries like you and me.
Sinestro may be a bit ruthless in his methods, but he's right about this—
If you want real peace, you have to eliminate danger before it has a chance to strike.
But...
To show you what I mean, I brought you another present.

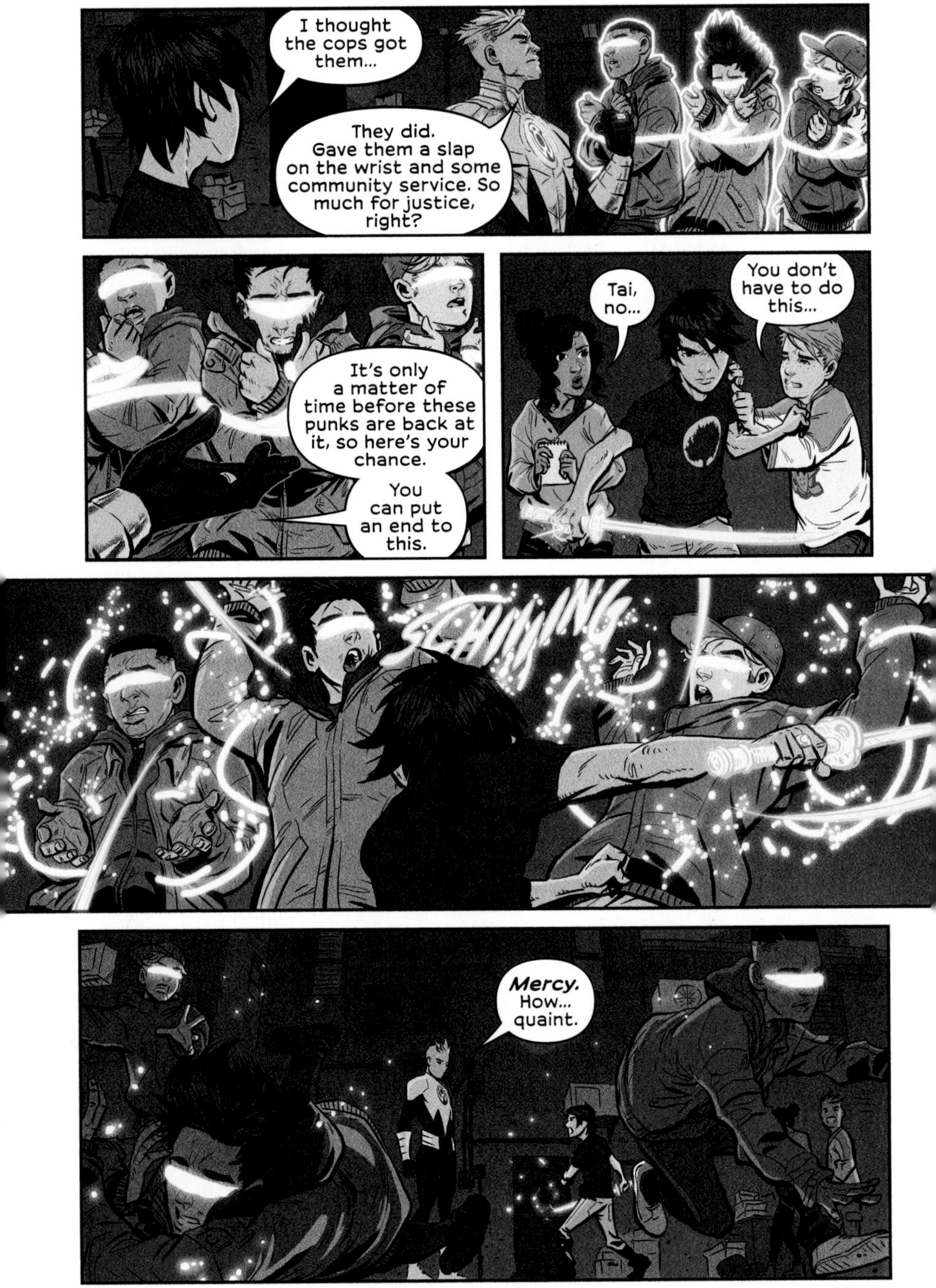
I thought the cops got them...
They did. Gave them a slap on the wrist and some community service. So much for justice, right?
It's only a matter of time before these punks are back at it, so here's your chance.
You can put an end to this.
Tai, no...
You don't have to do this...
SCHWING
Mercy. How... quaint.

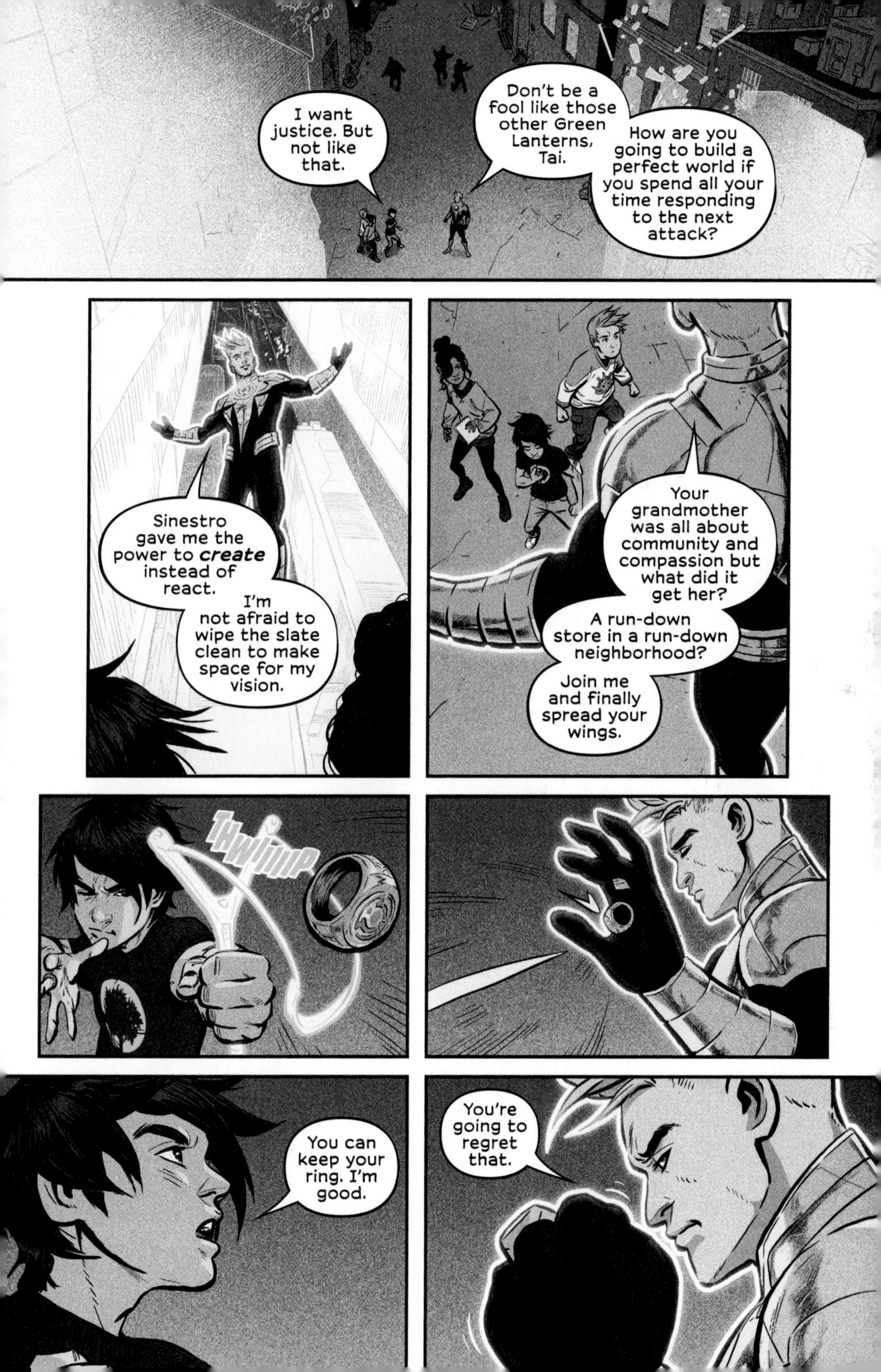
I want justice. But not like that.
Don't be a fool like those other Green Lanterns, Tai.
How are you going to build a perfect world if you spend all your time responding to the next attack?
Sinestro gave me the power to *create* instead of react.
I'm not afraid to wipe the slate clean to make space for my vision.
Your grandmother was all about community and compassion but what did it get her?
A run-down store in a run-down neighborhood?
Join me and finally spread your wings.
THWIIIIP
You can keep your ring. I'm good.
You're going to regret that.

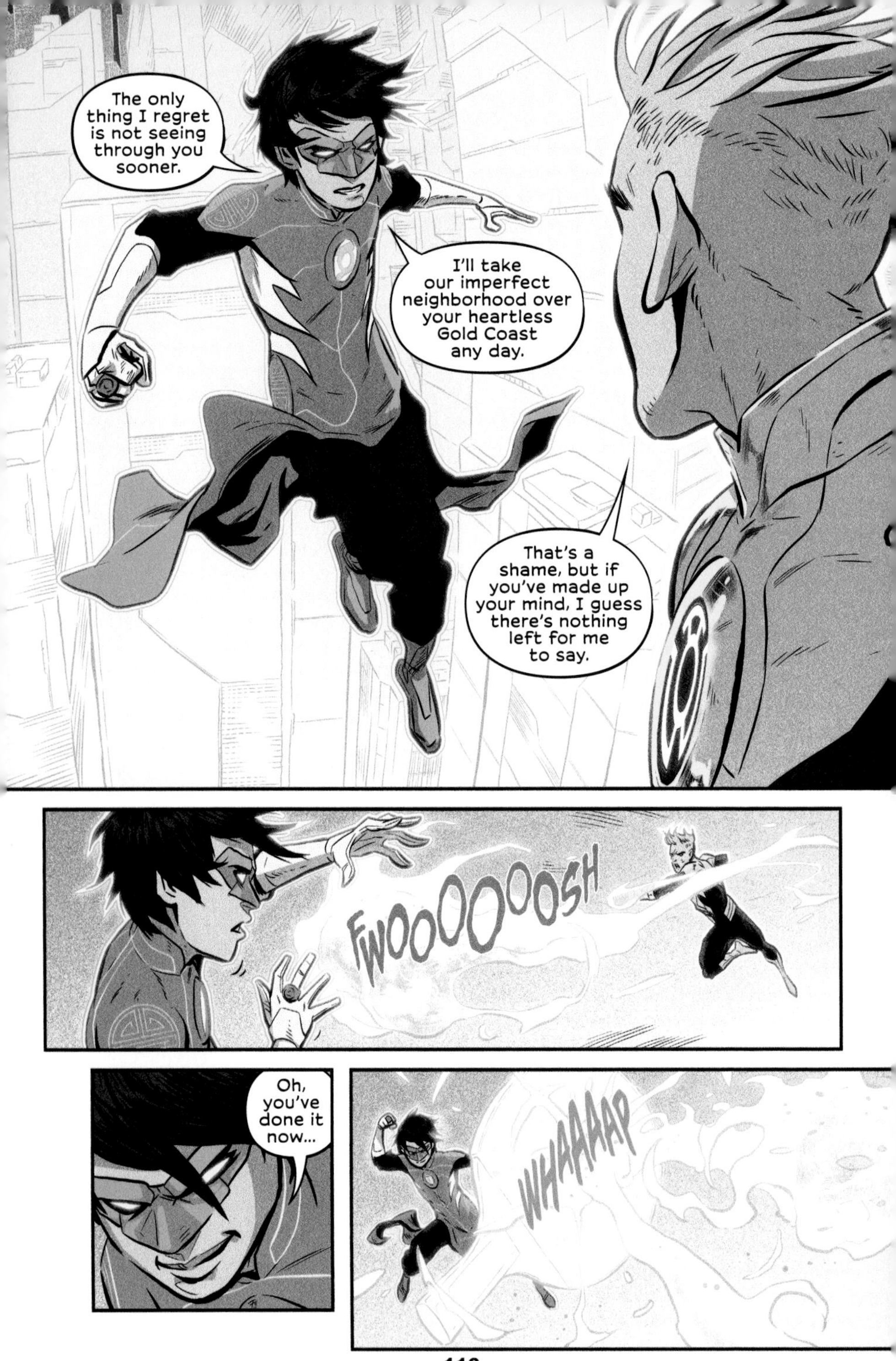
The only thing I regret is not seeing through you sooner.
I'll take our imperfect neighborhood over your heartless Gold Coast any day.
That's a shame, but if you've made up your mind, I guess there's nothing left for me to say.
FWOOOOOOSH
Oh, you've done it now...
WHAAAAP

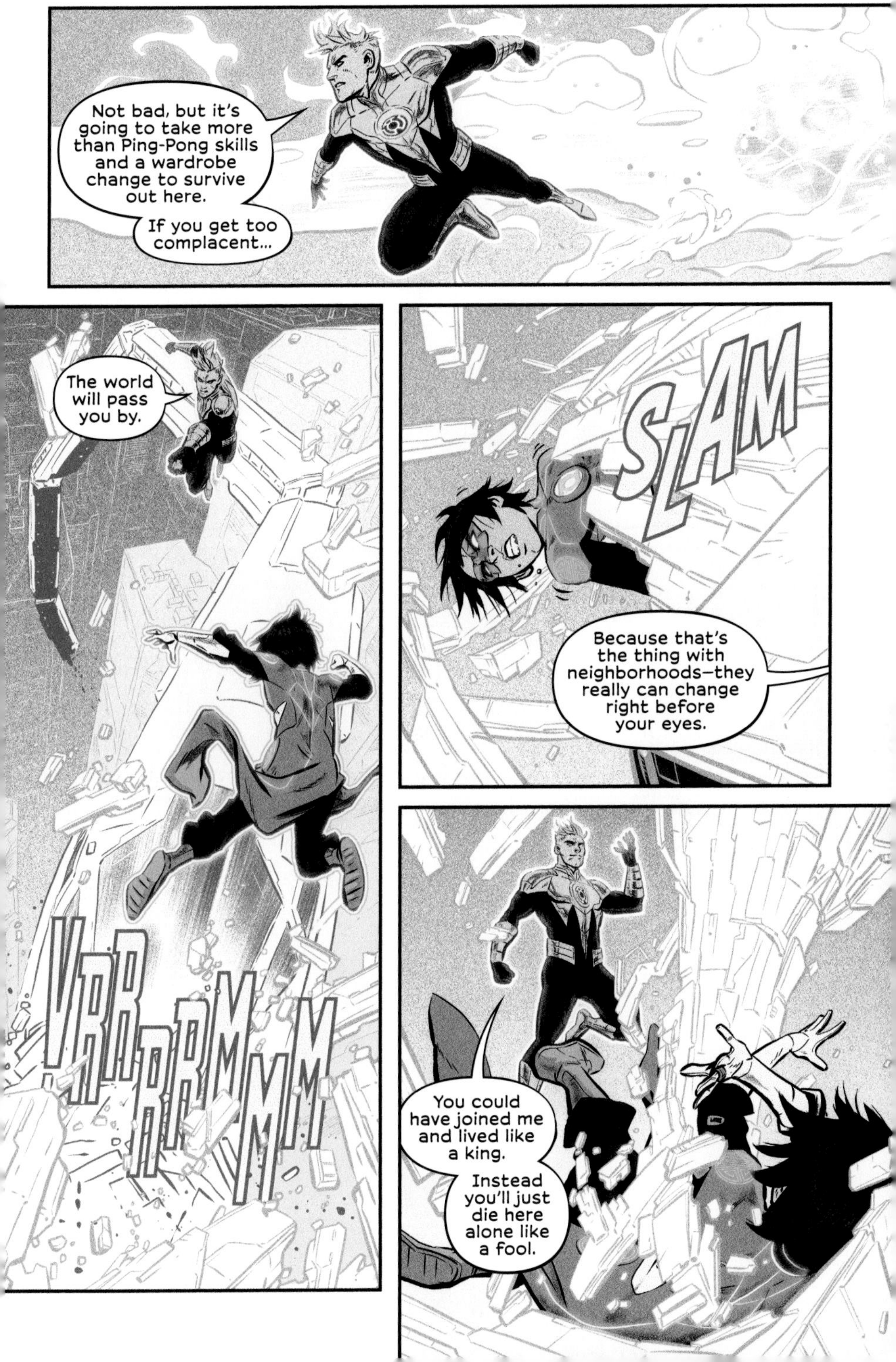
Not bad, but it's going to take more than Ping-Pong skills and a wardrobe change to survive out here.
If you get too complacent...
The world will pass you by.
VRRRRRMMMMM
SLAM
Because that's the thing with neighborhoods—they really can change right before your eyes.
You could have joined me and lived like a king.
Instead you'll just die here alone like a fool.

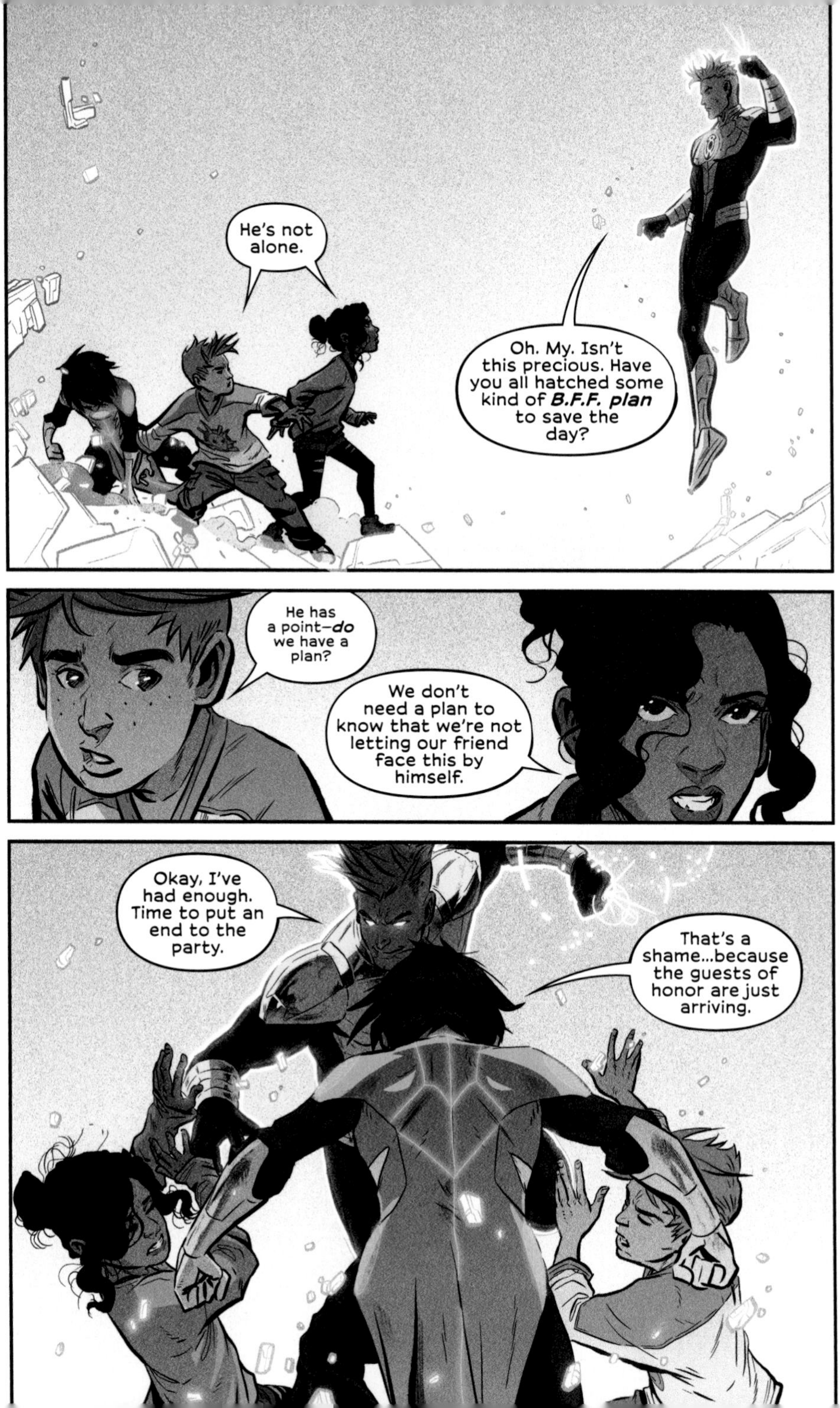
He's not alone.
Oh. My. Isn't this precious. Have you all hatched some kind of ***B.F.F. plan*** to save the day?
He has a point—***do*** we have a plan?
We don't need a plan to know that we're not letting our friend face this by himself.
Okay, I've had enough. Time to put an end to the party.
That's a shame...because the guests of honor are just arriving.

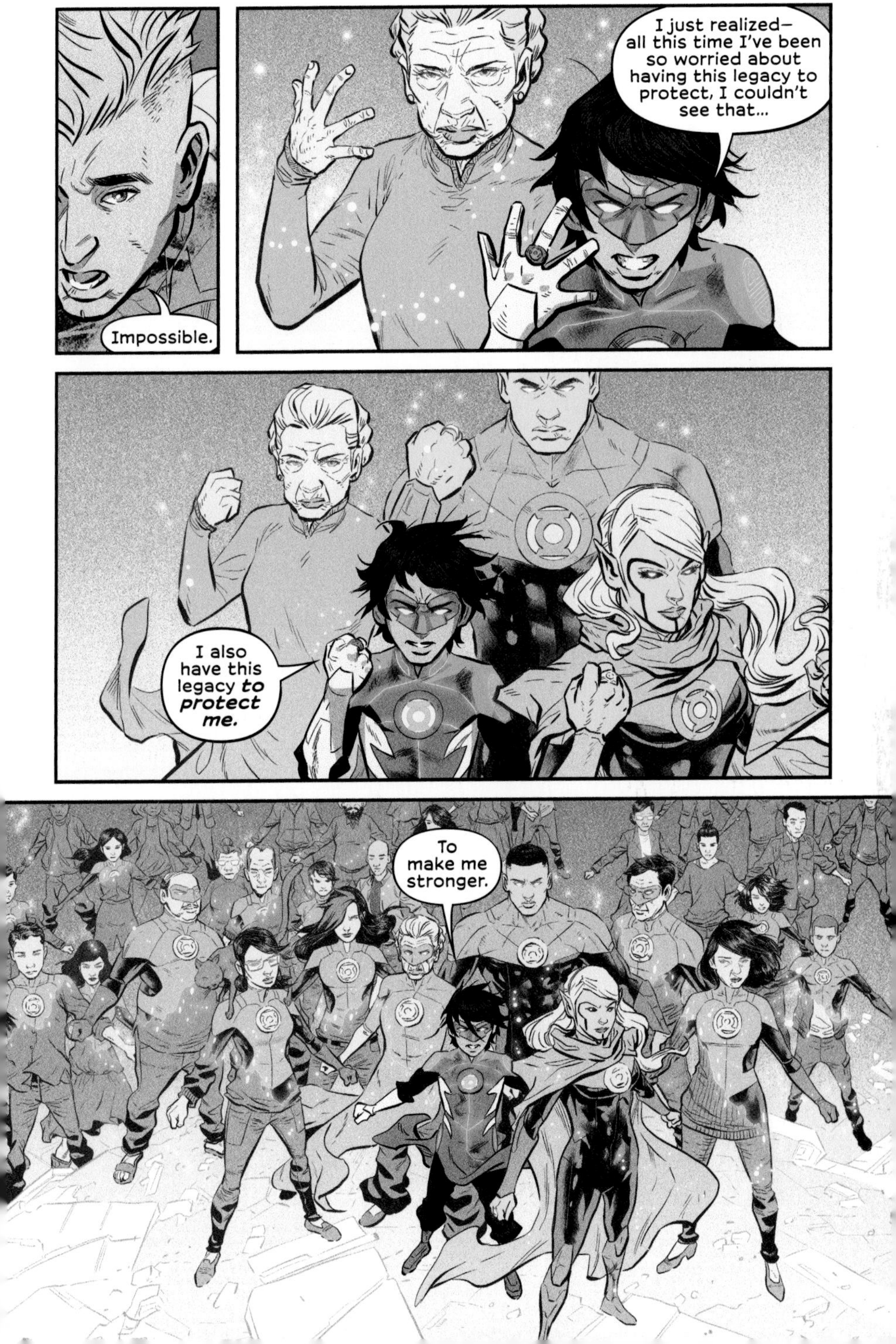
Impossible.
I just realized— all this time I've been so worried about having this legacy to protect, I couldn't see that...
I also have this legacy *to protect me.*
To make me stronger.

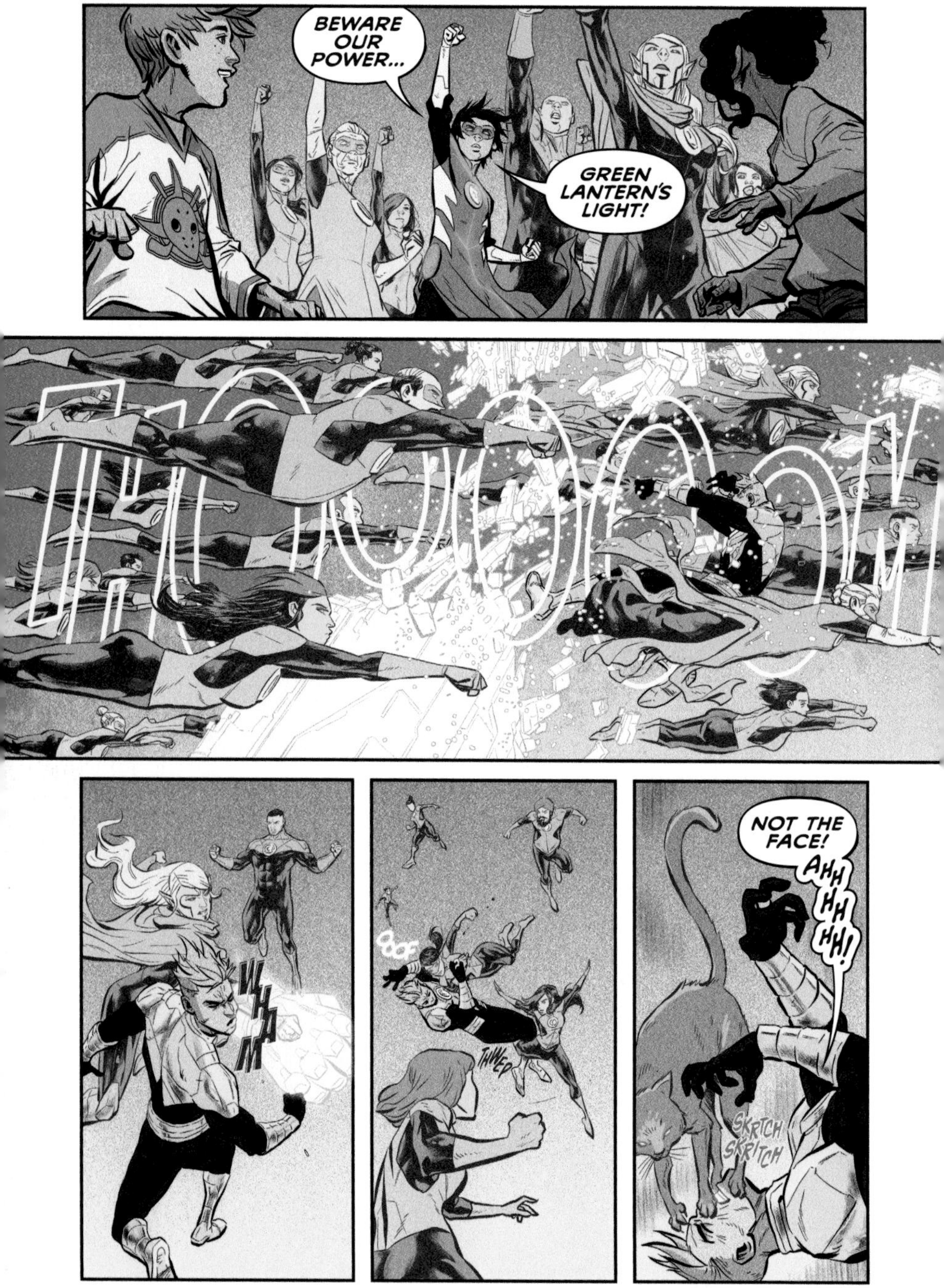
BEWARE OUR POWER...
GREEN LANTERN'S LIGHT!
THOOOOOM
WHAM
OOF
THWED
NOT THE FACE!
AHHHHHH!
SKRTCH SKRTCH

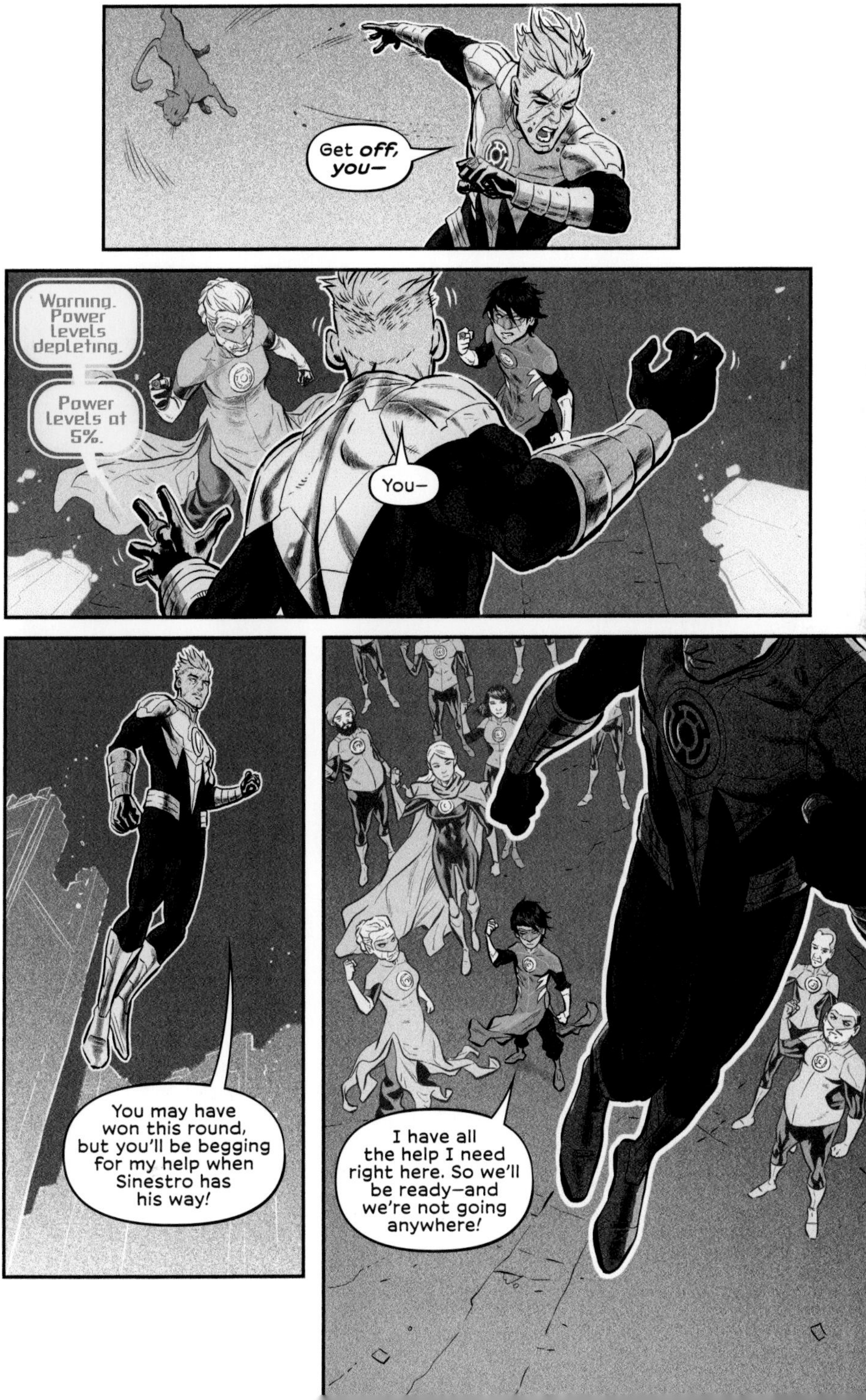
Get off, you—
Warning. Power levels depleting.
Power levels at 5%.
You—
You may have won this round, but you'll be begging for my help when Sinestro has his way!
I have all the help I need right here. So we'll be ready—and we're not going anywhere!

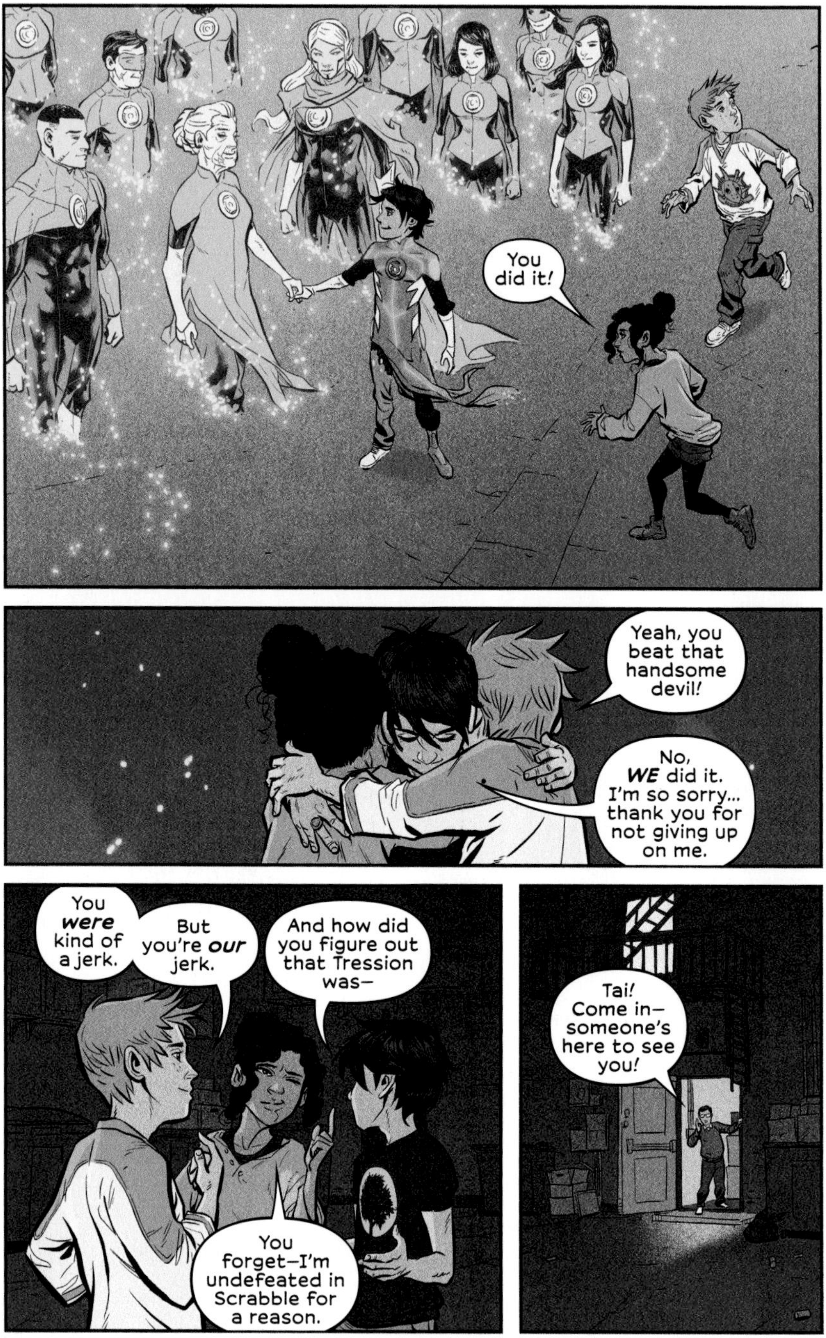
You did it!
Yeah, you beat that handsome devil!
No, WE did it. I'm so sorry... thank you for not giving up on me.
You were kind of a jerk.
But you're our jerk.
And how did you figure out that Tression was—
You forget—I'm undefeated in Scrabble for a reason.
Tai! Come in—someone's here to see you!

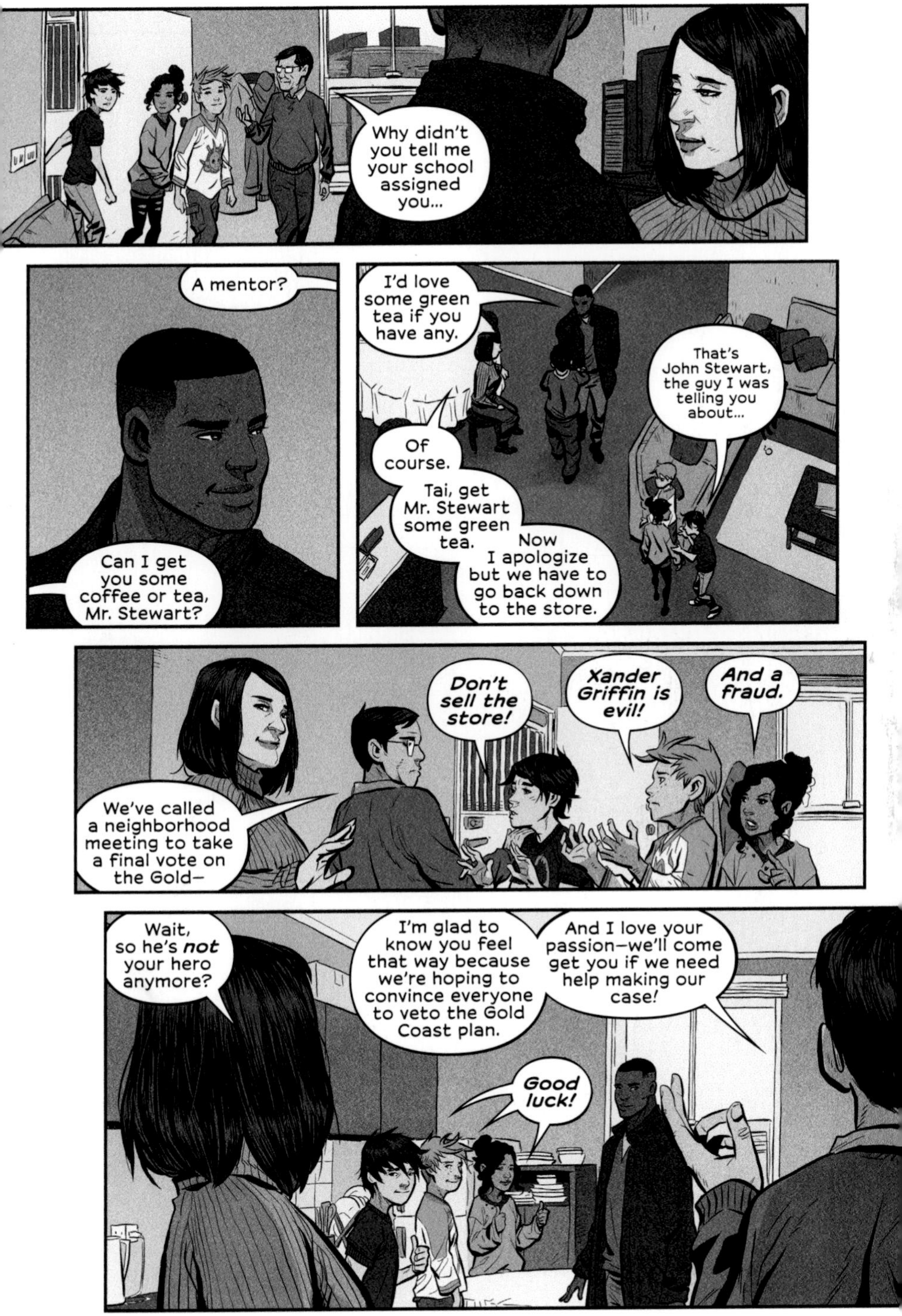
Why didn't you tell me your school assigned you...
A mentor?
Can I get you some coffee or tea, Mr. Stewart?
I'd love some green tea if you have any.
Of course.
Tai, get Mr. Stewart some green tea.
Now I apologize but we have to go back down to the store.
That's John Stewart, the guy I was telling you about...
We've called a neighborhood meeting to take a final vote on the Gold—
Don't sell the store!
Xander Griffin is evil!
And a fraud.
Wait, so he's not your hero anymore?
I'm glad to know you feel that way because we're hoping to convince everyone to veto the Gold Coast plan.
And I love your passion—we'll come get you if we need help making our case!
Good luck!

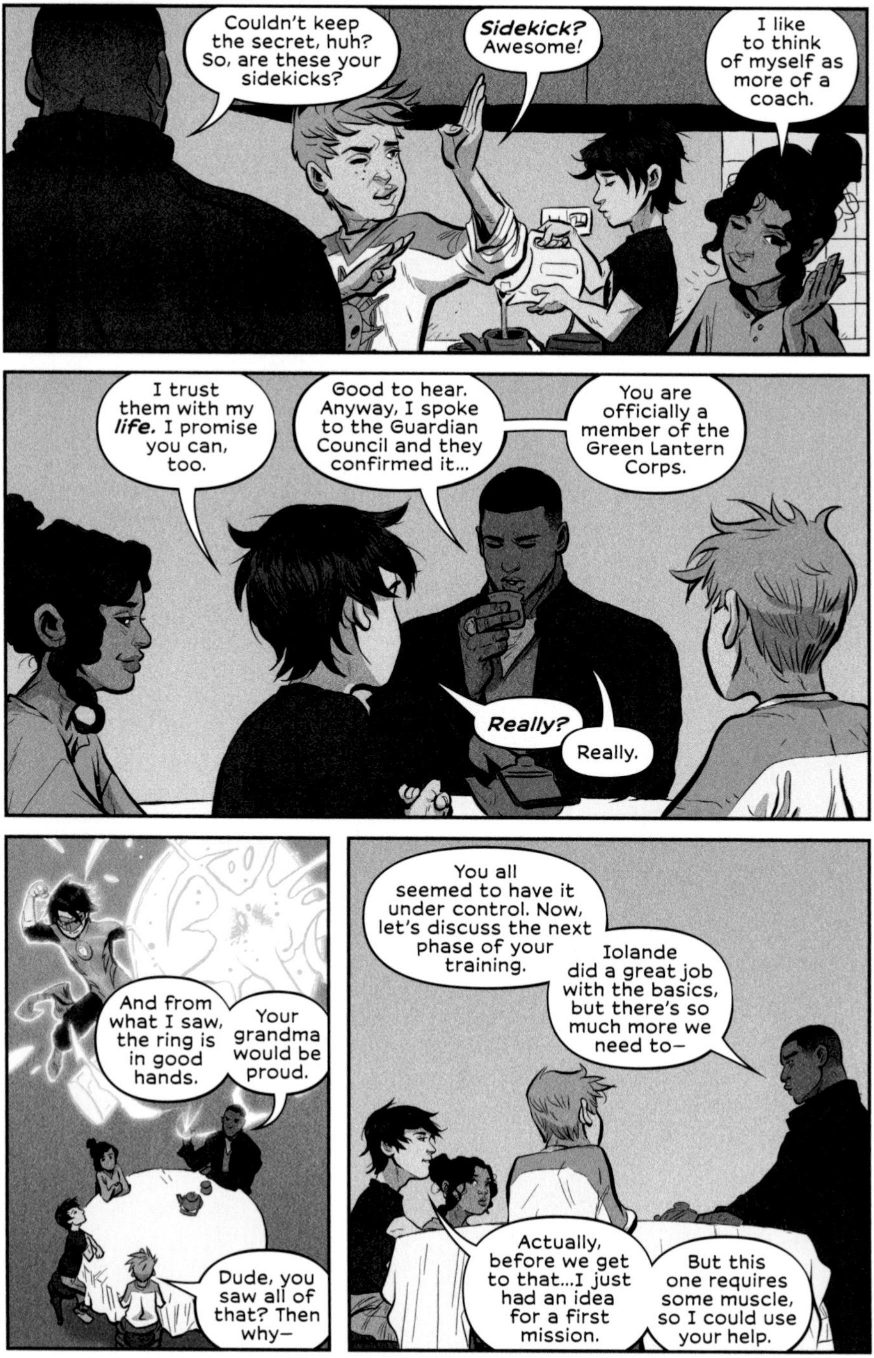
Couldn't keep the secret, huh? So, are these your sidekicks?
Sidekick? Awesome!
I like to think of myself as more of a coach.
I trust them with my life. I promise you can, too.
Good to hear. Anyway, I spoke to the Guardian Council and they confirmed it...
You are officially a member of the Green Lantern Corps.
Really?
Really.
And from what I saw, the ring is in good hands.
Your grandma would be proud.
Dude, you saw all of that? Then why—
You all seemed to have it under control. Now, let's discuss the next phase of your training.
Iolande did a great job with the basics, but there's so much more we need to—
Actually, before we get to that...I just had an idea for a first mission.
But this one requires some muscle, so I could use your help.

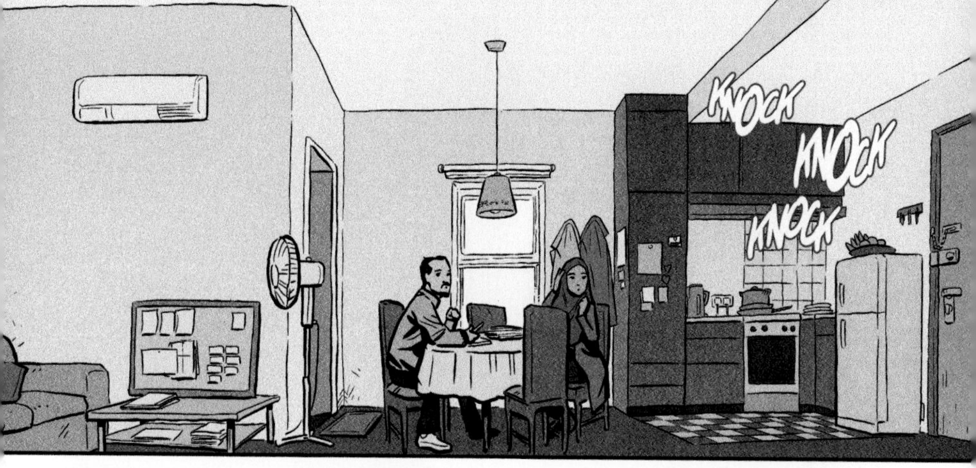
KNOCK
KNOCK
KNOCK

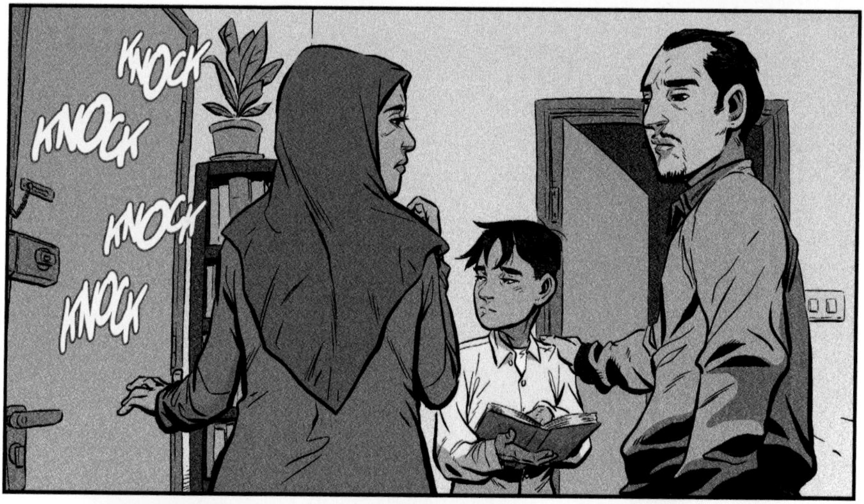
KNOCK
KNOCK
KNOCK
KNOCK

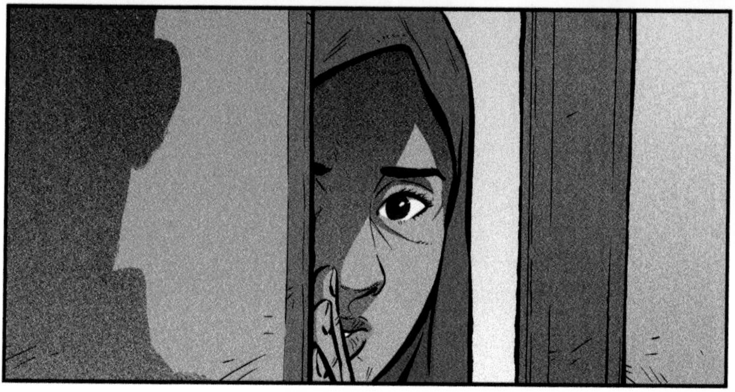

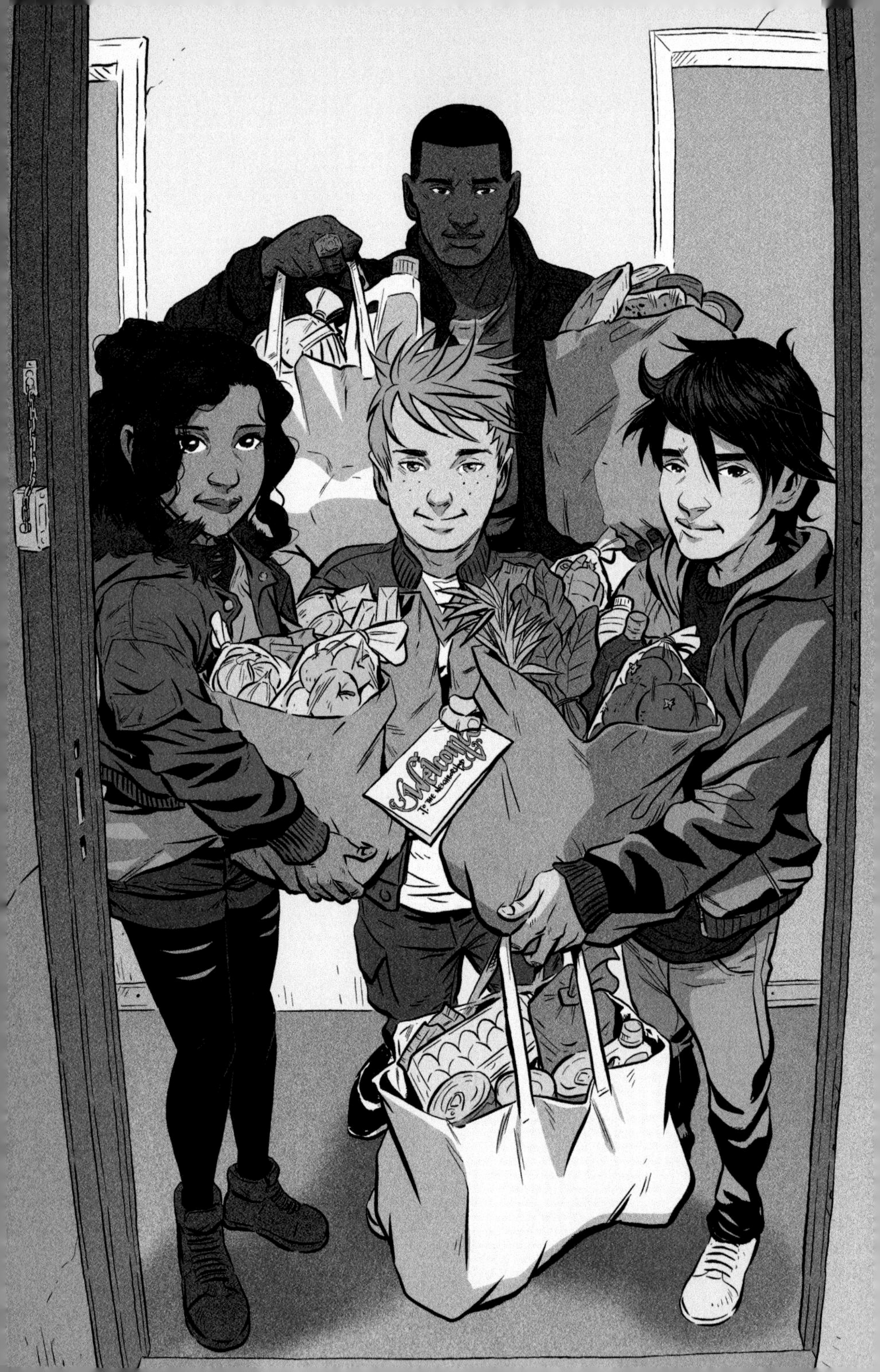
Welcome

Glossary of Vietnamese Words

bà nội [noun]   paternal grandmother
bà ngoại [noun]   maternal grandmother
cha [noun]   father
mẹ [noun]   mother
Chợ Ngọc Thạch [noun]   Jade Market
phở [noun]   a Vietnamese noodle soup
nước mắm   fish sauce
tài [adj]   skilled, talented, excellent [in other words...super]

Minh Lê is the award-winning author of *Drawn Together* (winner of the 2019 Asian/Pacific American Award for Literature, illustrated by Dan Santat), *Let Me Finish!* (illustrated by Isabel Roxas), and *The Perfect Seat* (illustrated by Gus Gordon). He has written about children's literature for the *New York Times*, *NPR*, and the *Huffington Post. Green Lantern: Legacy* is his first graphic novel. A first-generation Vietnamese American, he is also a national early childhood policy expert and went to Dartmouth College before earning a master's in education from Harvard University. Outside of spending time with his amazing wife and sons, Minh's favorite place to be is in the middle of a good book.

Andie Tong's past comic book and illustration experience includes titles such as *Spectacular Spider-Man UK*, *The Batman Strikes!*, *Tron: Betrayal*, *Plants Vs. Zombies*, *Star Wars*, *Tekken*, and Stan Lee's *The Zodiac Legacy*. Andie has also illustrated children's books for HarperCollins for more than ten years and has had the opportunity to work on multiple books with Stan Lee. Malaysian born, Andie migrated to Australia at a young age, and then moved to London in 2005. In 2012 he journeyed back to Asia and currently resides in Singapore with his wife and two children.

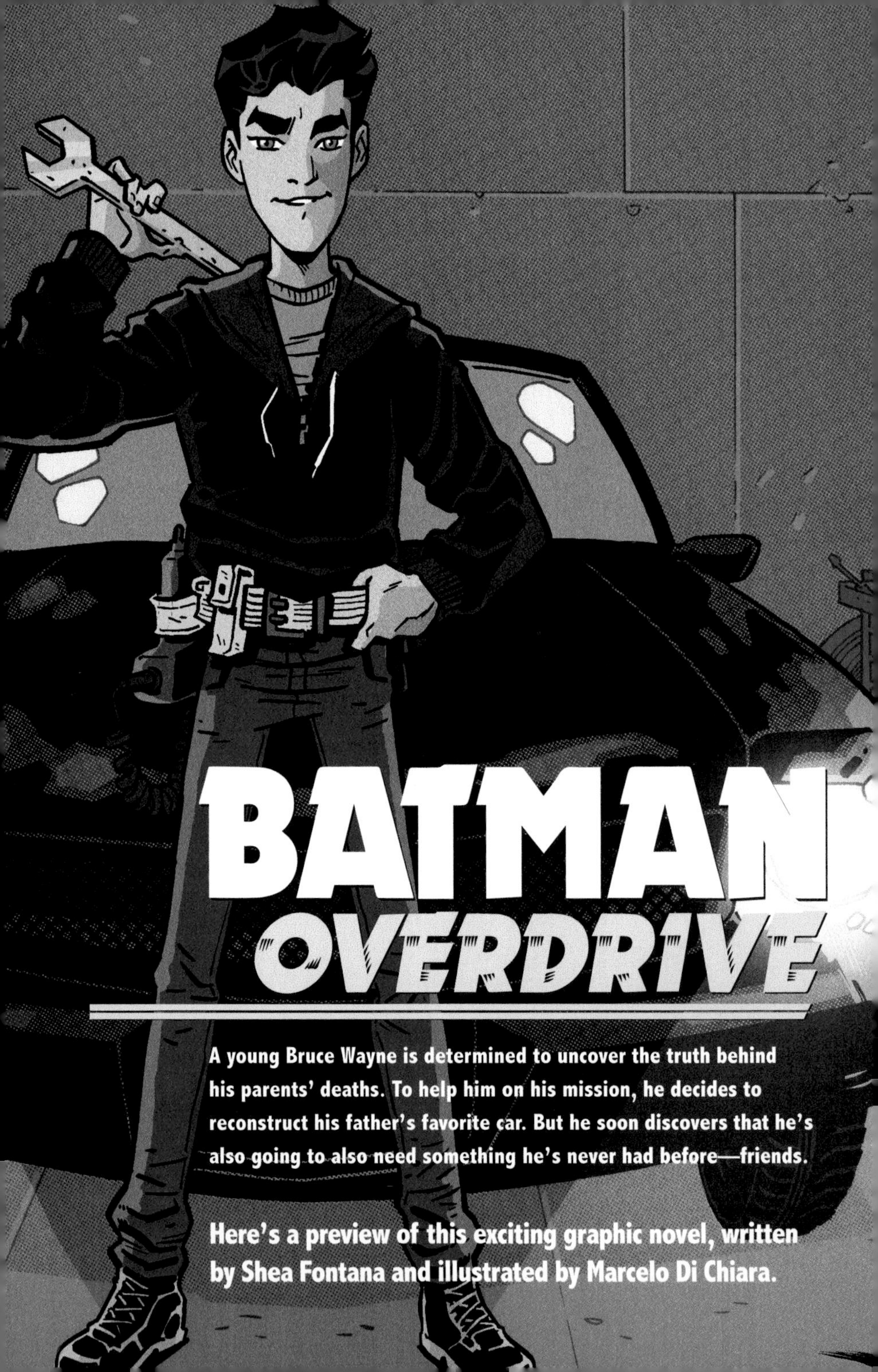

BATMAN OVERDRIVE

A young Bruce Wayne is determined to uncover the truth behind his parents' deaths. To help him on his mission, he decides to reconstruct his father's favorite car. But he soon discovers that he's also going to also need something he's never had before—friends.

Here's a preview of this exciting graphic novel, written by Shea Fontana and illustrated by Marcelo Di Chiara.

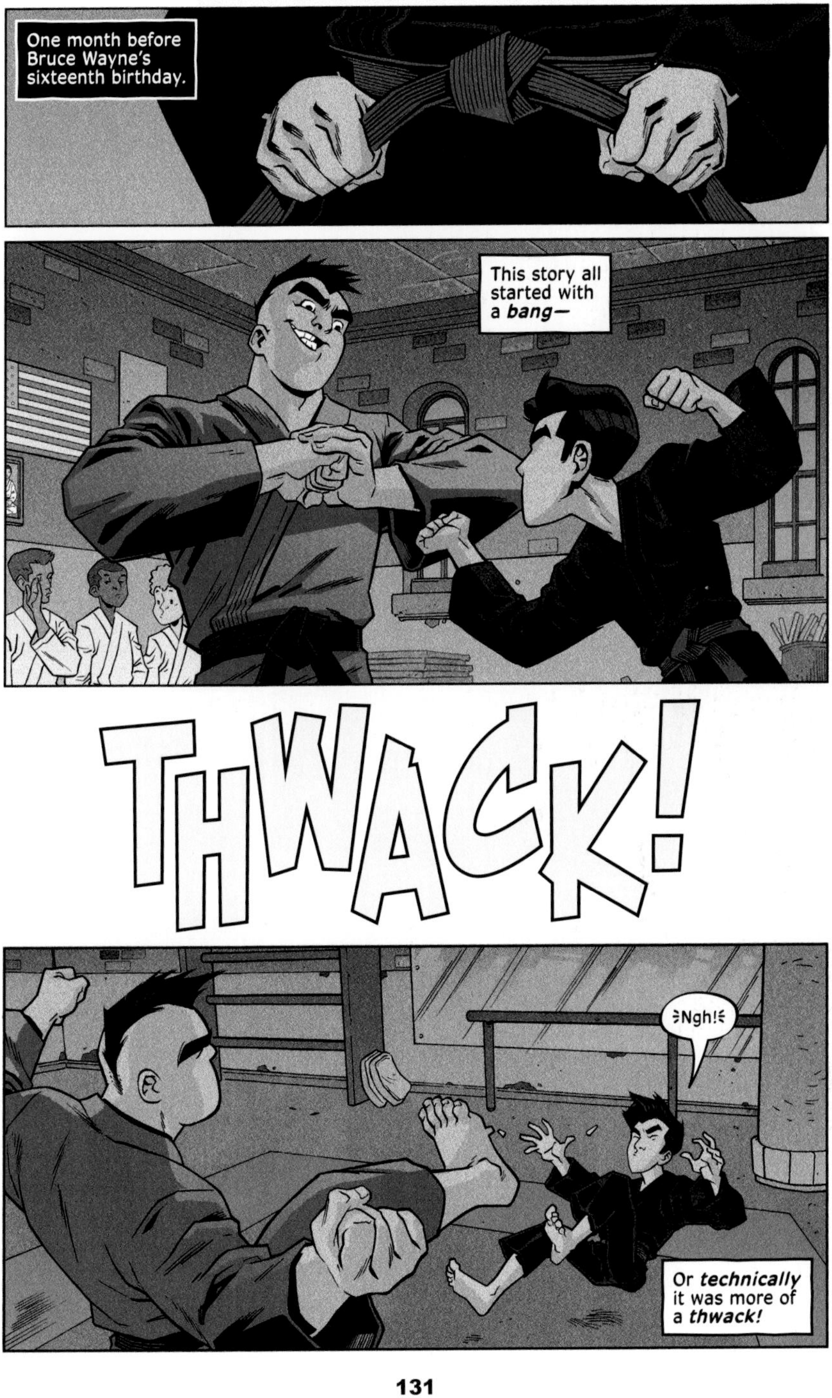
One month before Bruce Wayne's sixteenth birthday.
This story all started with a *bang*—
THWACK!
Ngh!
Or *technically* it was more of a *thwack!*

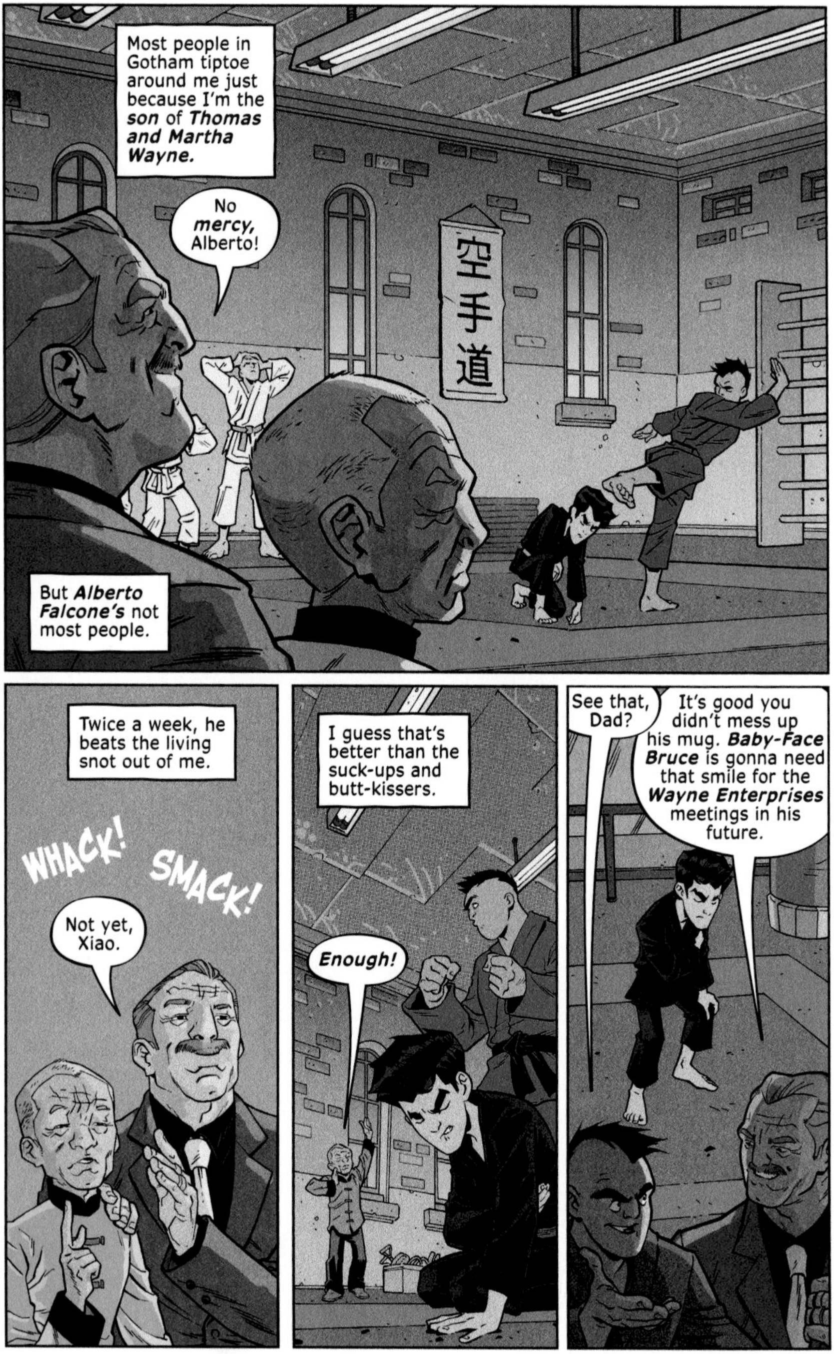
Most people in Gotham tiptoe around me just because I'm the *son* of *Thomas and Martha Wayne.*
No *mercy,* Alberto!
空手道
But *Alberto Falcone's* not most people.
Twice a week, he beats the living snot out of me.
WHACK!
SMACK!
Not yet, Xiao.
I guess that's better than the suck-ups and butt-kissers.
Enough!
See that, Dad?
It's good you didn't mess up his mug. *Baby-Face Bruce* is gonna need that smile for the *Wayne Enterprises* meetings in his future.

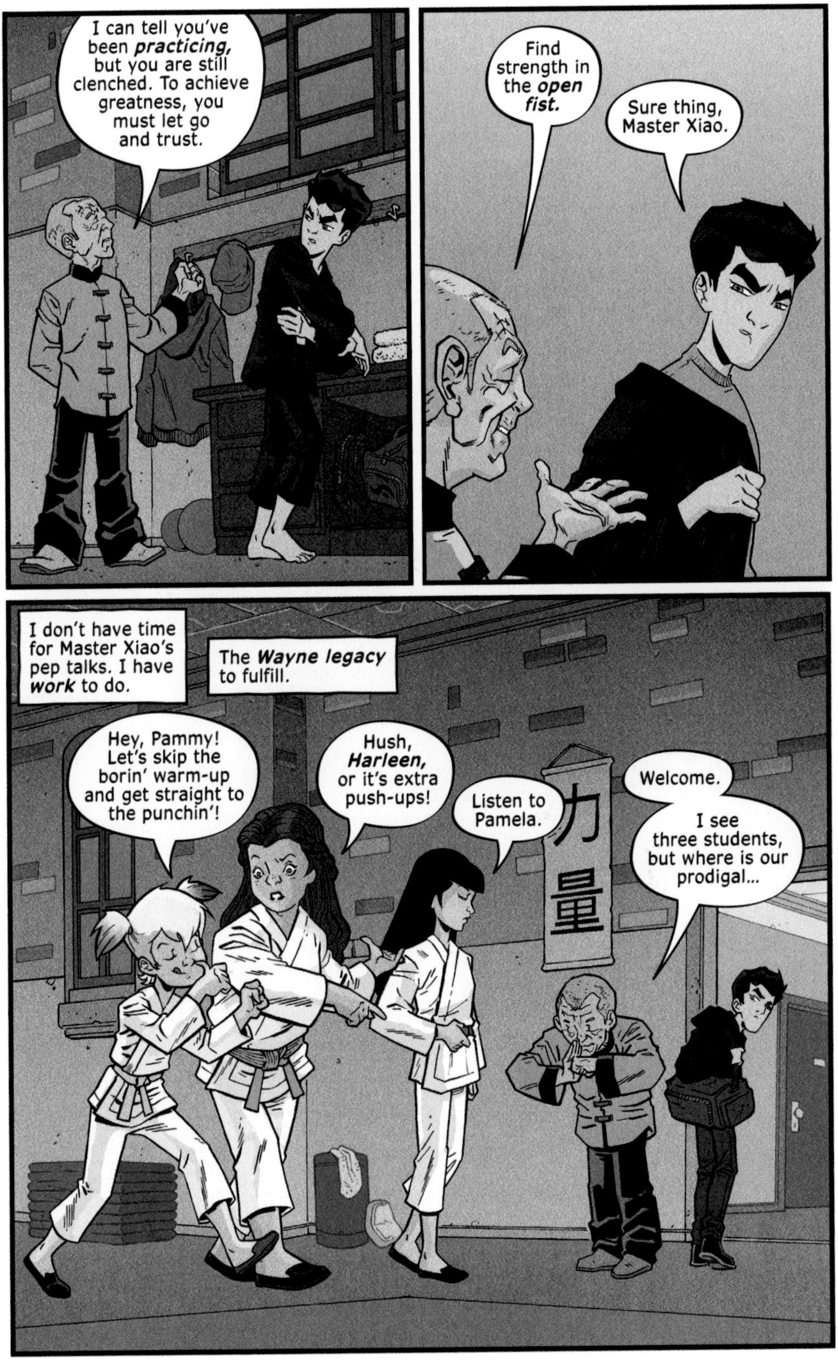
I can tell you've been *practicing,* but you are still clenched. To achieve greatness, you must let go and trust.
Find strength in the *open fist.*
Sure thing, Master Xiao.
I don't have time for Master Xiao's pep talks. I have *work* to do.
The *Wayne legacy* to fulfill.
Hey, Pammy! Let's skip the borin' warm-up and get straight to the punchin'!
Hush, *Harleen,* or it's extra push-ups!
Listen to Pamela.
力量
Welcome.
I see three students, but where is our prodigal...

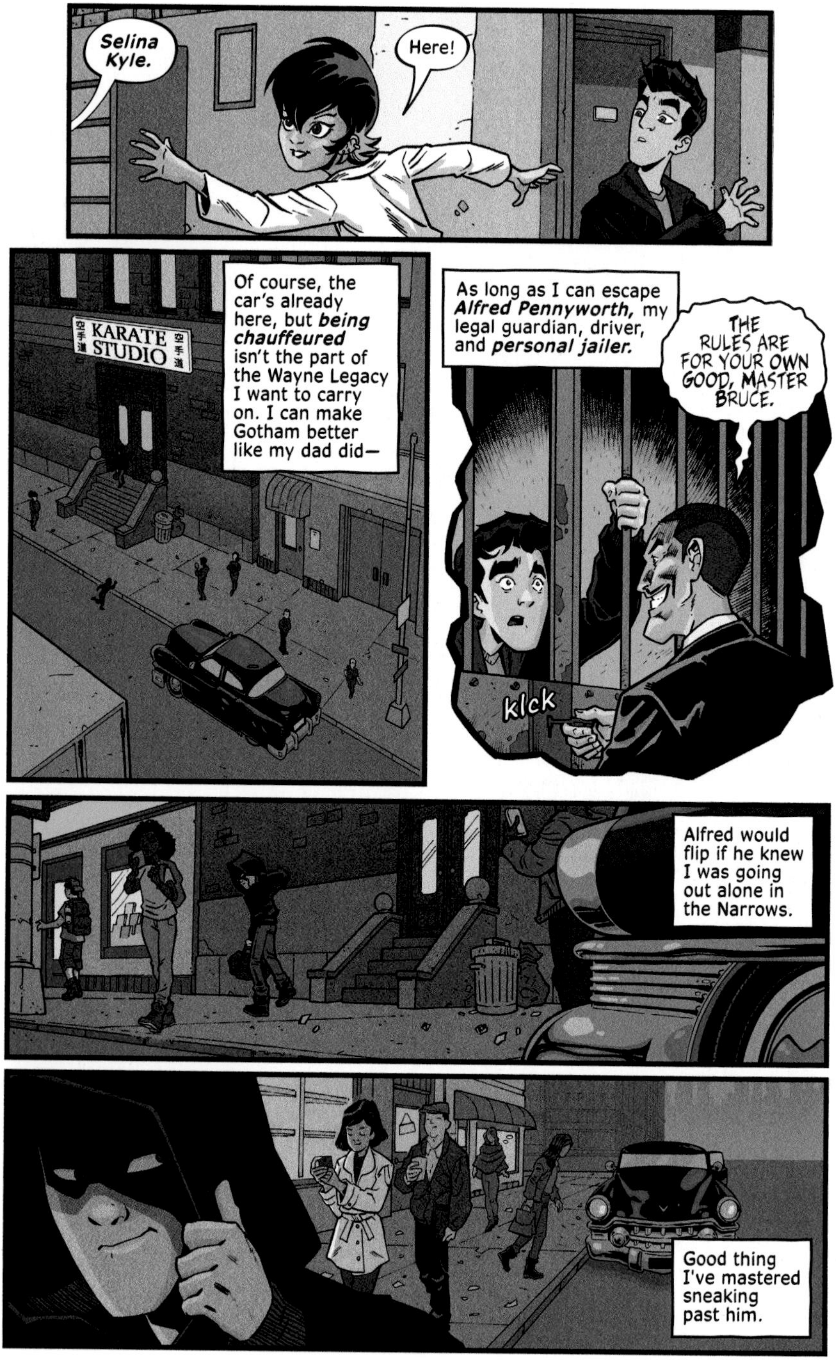
Selina Kyle.
Here!
Of course, the car's already here, but *being chauffeured* isn't the part of the Wayne Legacy I want to carry on. I can make Gotham better like my dad did—
KARATE STUDIO
空手道
As long as I can escape *Alfred Pennyworth,* my legal guardian, driver, and *personal jailer.*
THE RULES ARE FOR YOUR OWN GOOD, MASTER BRUCE.
klck
Alfred would flip if he knew I was going out alone in the Narrows.
Good thing I've mastered sneaking past him.

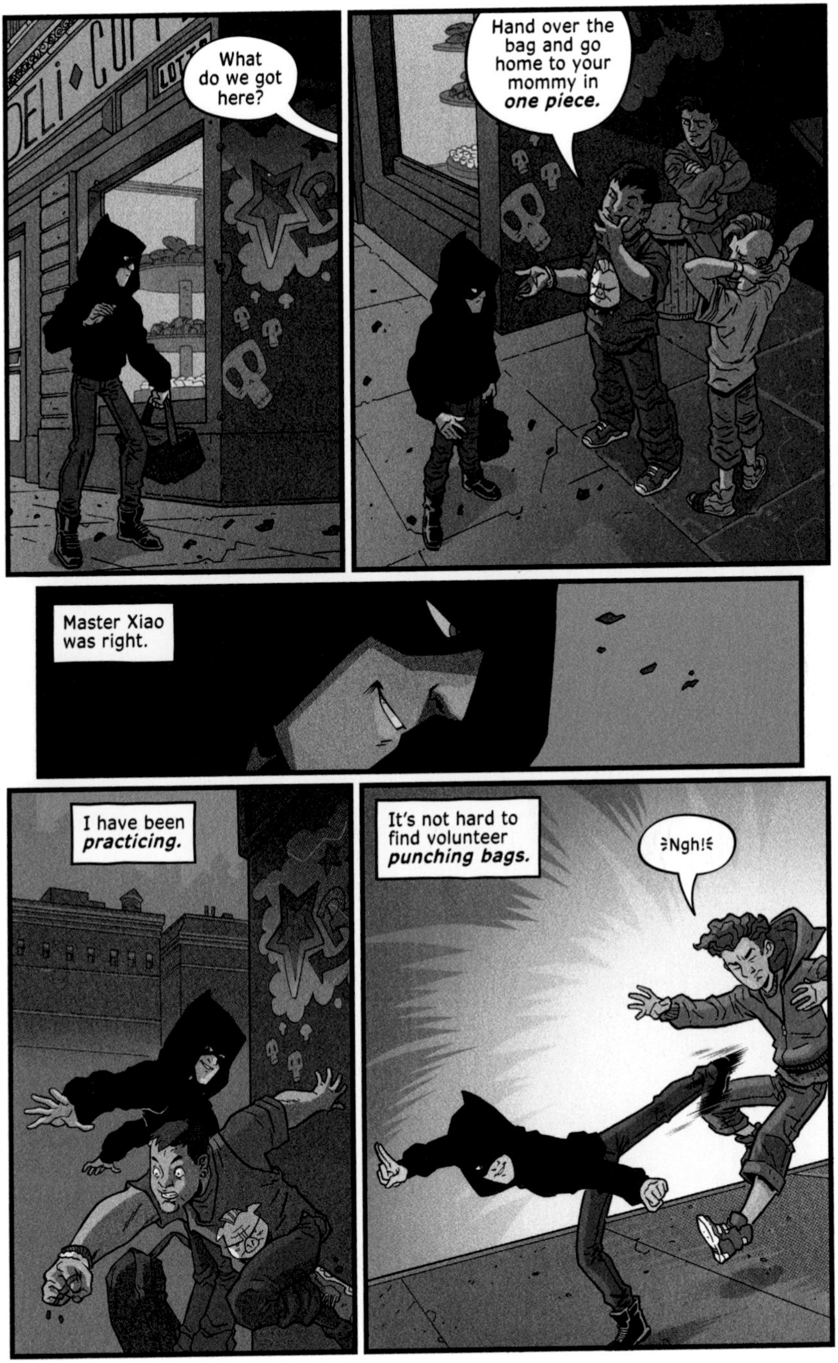
DELI
LOTTO
What do we got here?
Hand over the bag and go home to your mommy in *one piece.*
Master Xiao was right.
I have been *practicing.*
It's not hard to find volunteer *punching bags.*
Ngh!

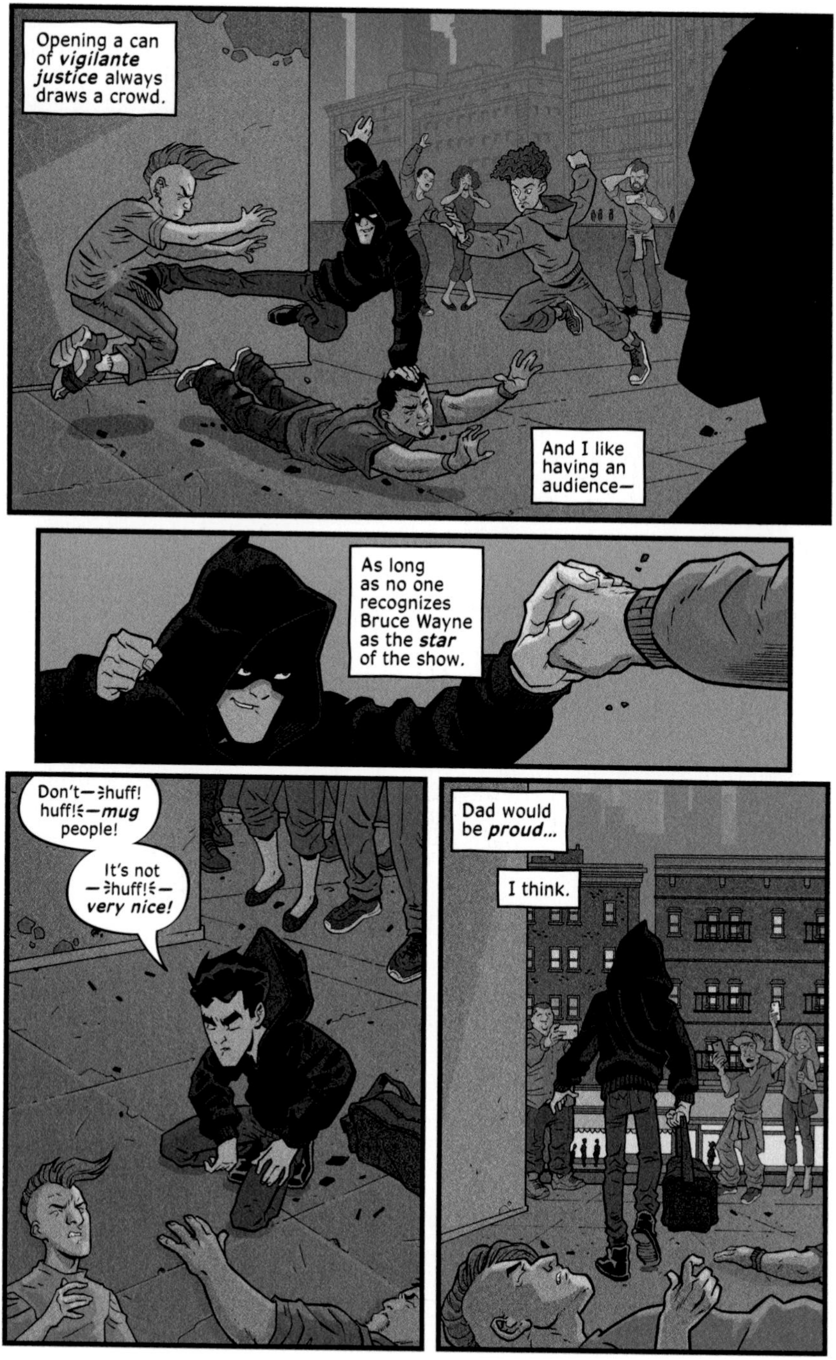

Opening a can of *vigilante justice* always draws a crowd.
And I like having an audience—
As long as no one recognizes Bruce Wayne as the *star* of the show.
Don't—*huff! huff!*—*mug* people!
It's not —*huff!*— *very nice!*
Dad would be *proud...*
I think.

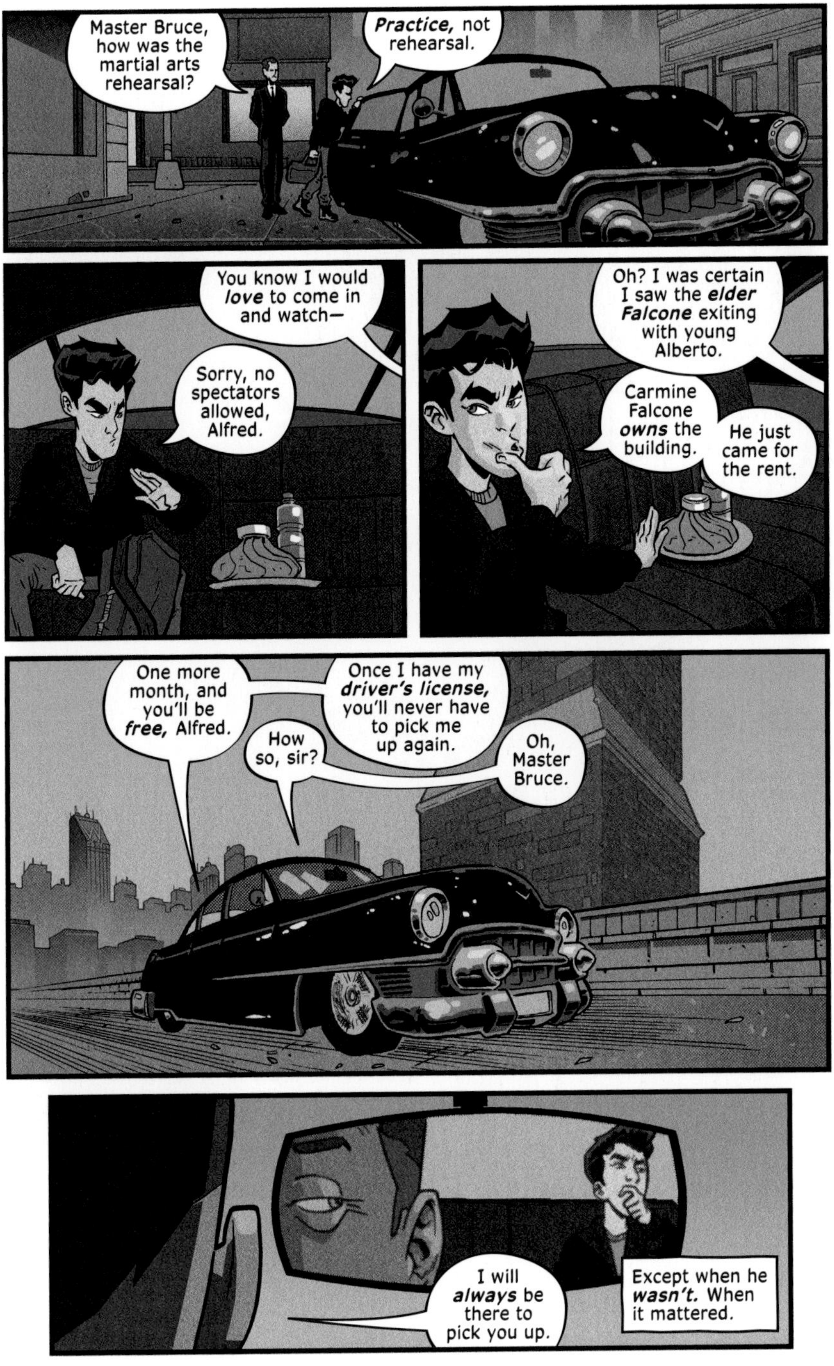
Master Bruce, how was the martial arts rehearsal?
Practice, not rehearsal.
You know I would *love* to come in and watch—
Sorry, no spectators allowed, Alfred.
Oh? I was certain I saw the *elder Falcone* exiting with young Alberto.
Carmine Falcone *owns* the building.
He just came for the rent.
One more month, and you'll be *free,* Alfred.
Once I have my *driver's license,* you'll never have to pick me up again.
How so, sir?
Oh, Master Bruce.
I will *always* be there to pick you up.
Except when he *wasn't.* When it mattered.

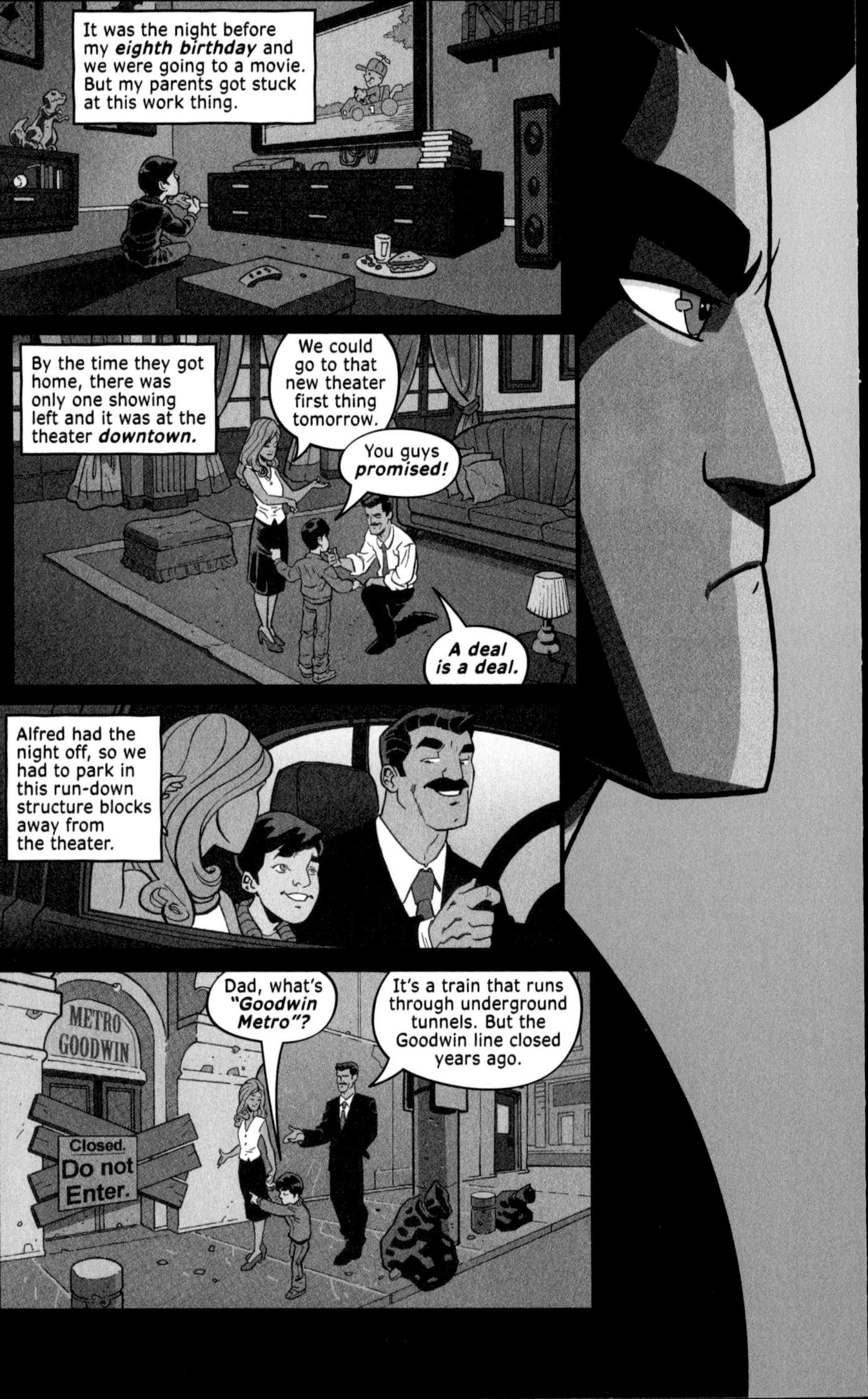
It was the night before my *eighth birthday* and we were going to a movie. But my parents got stuck at this work thing.
By the time they got home, there was only one showing left and it was at the theater *downtown.*
We could go to that new theater first thing tomorrow.
You guys *promised!*
A deal is a deal.
Alfred had the night off, so we had to park in this run-down structure blocks away from the theater.
METRO GOODWIN
Closed. Do not Enter.
Dad, what's *"Goodwin Metro"?*
It's a train that runs through underground tunnels. But the Goodwin line closed years ago.

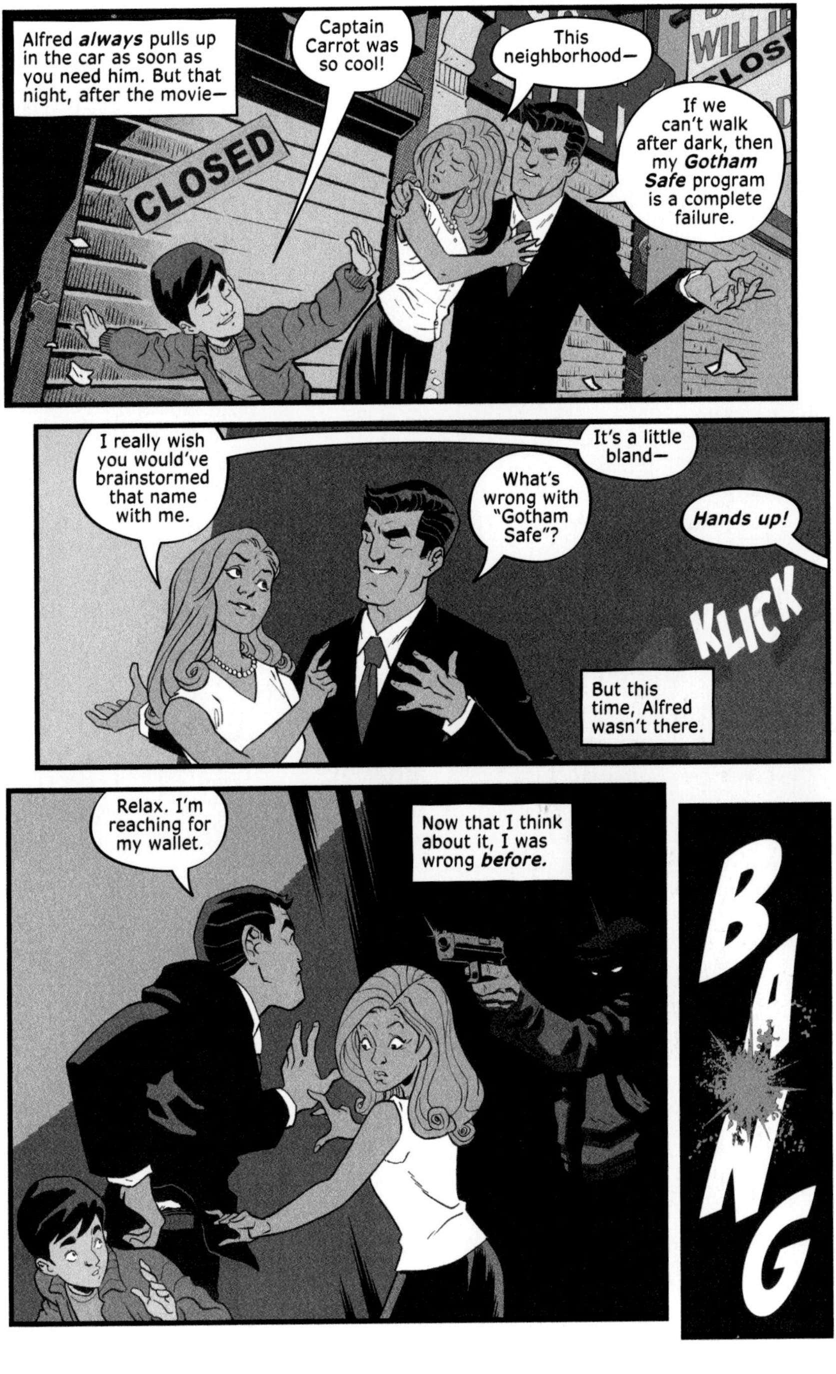
Alfred *always* pulls up in the car as soon as you need him. But that night, after the movie—
Captain Carrot was so cool!
This neighborhood—
CLOSED
If we can't walk after dark, then my *Gotham Safe* program is a complete failure.
I really wish you would've brainstormed that name with me.
It's a little bland—
What's wrong with "Gotham Safe"?
Hands up!
KLICK
But this time, Alfred wasn't there.
Relax. I'm reaching for my wallet.
Now that I think about it, I was wrong *before.*
BANG

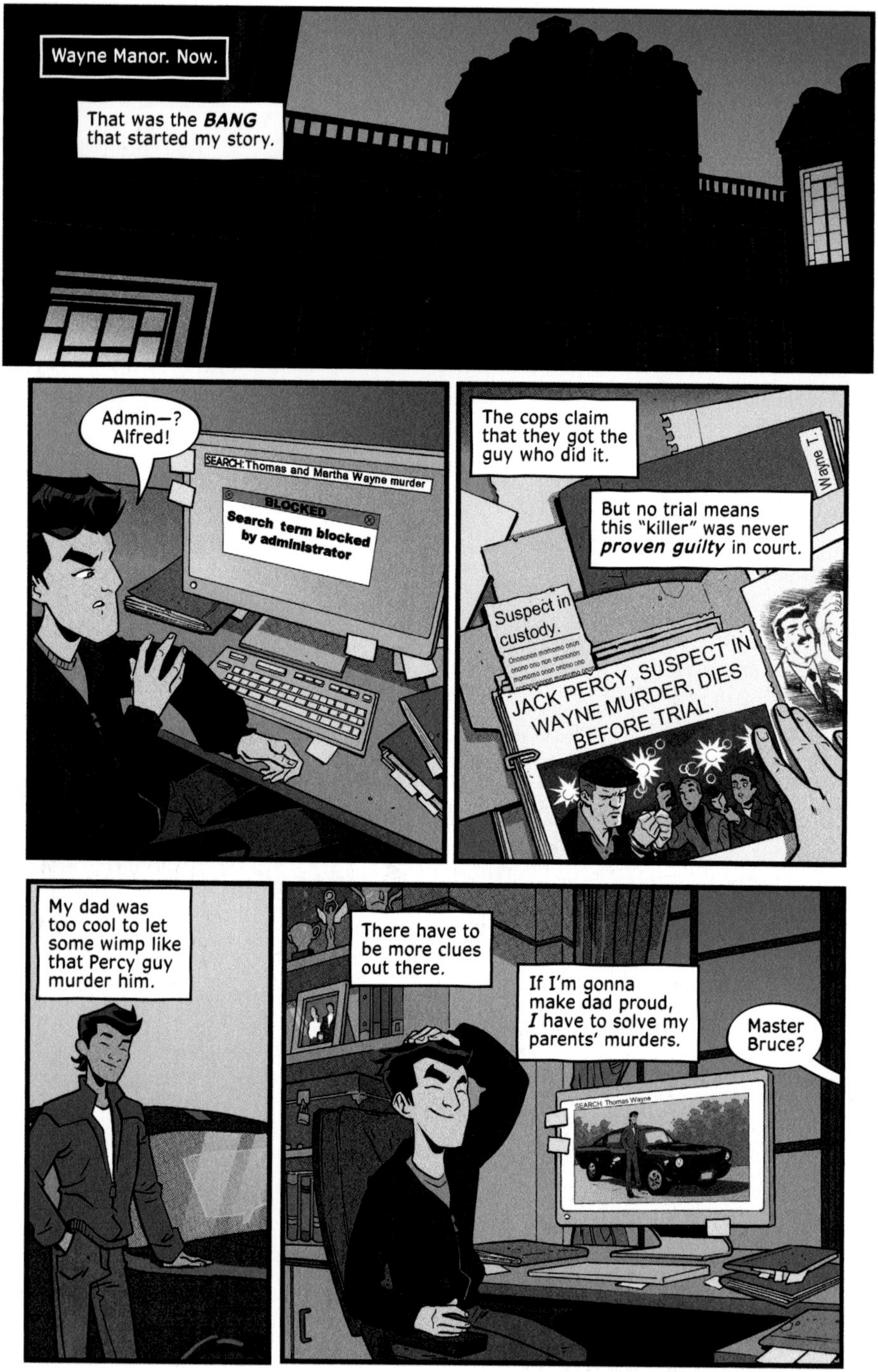
Wayne Manor. Now.
That was the BANG that started my story.
Admin—? Alfred!
SEARCH: Thomas and Martha Wayne murder
BLOCKED
Search term blocked by administrator
The cops claim that they got the guy who did it.
Wayne T.
But no trial means this "killer" was never proven guilty in court.
Suspect in custody.
JACK PERCY, SUSPECT IN WAYNE MURDER, DIES BEFORE TRIAL.
My dad was too cool to let some wimp like that Percy guy murder him.
There have to be more clues out there.
If I'm gonna make dad proud, I have to solve my parents' murders.
Master Bruce?
SEARCH: Thomas Wayne

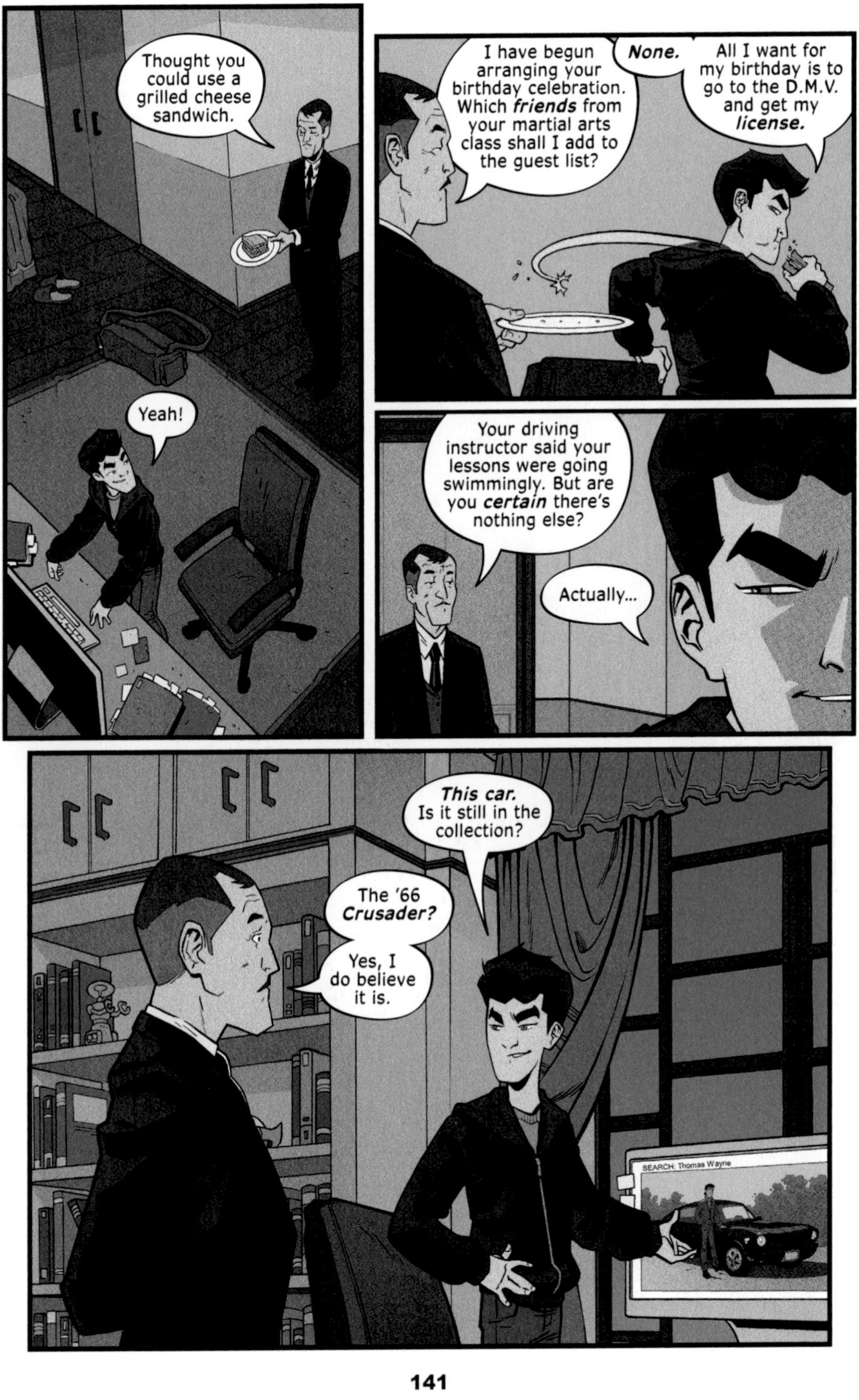
Thought you could use a grilled cheese sandwich.
Yeah!
I have begun arranging your birthday celebration. Which *friends* from your martial arts class shall I add to the guest list?
None.
All I want for my birthday is to go to the D.M.V. and get my *license.*
Your driving instructor said your lessons were going swimmingly. But are you *certain* there's nothing else?
Actually...
This car. Is it still in the collection?
The '66 *Crusader?*
Yes, I do believe it is.
SEARCH: Thomas Wayne

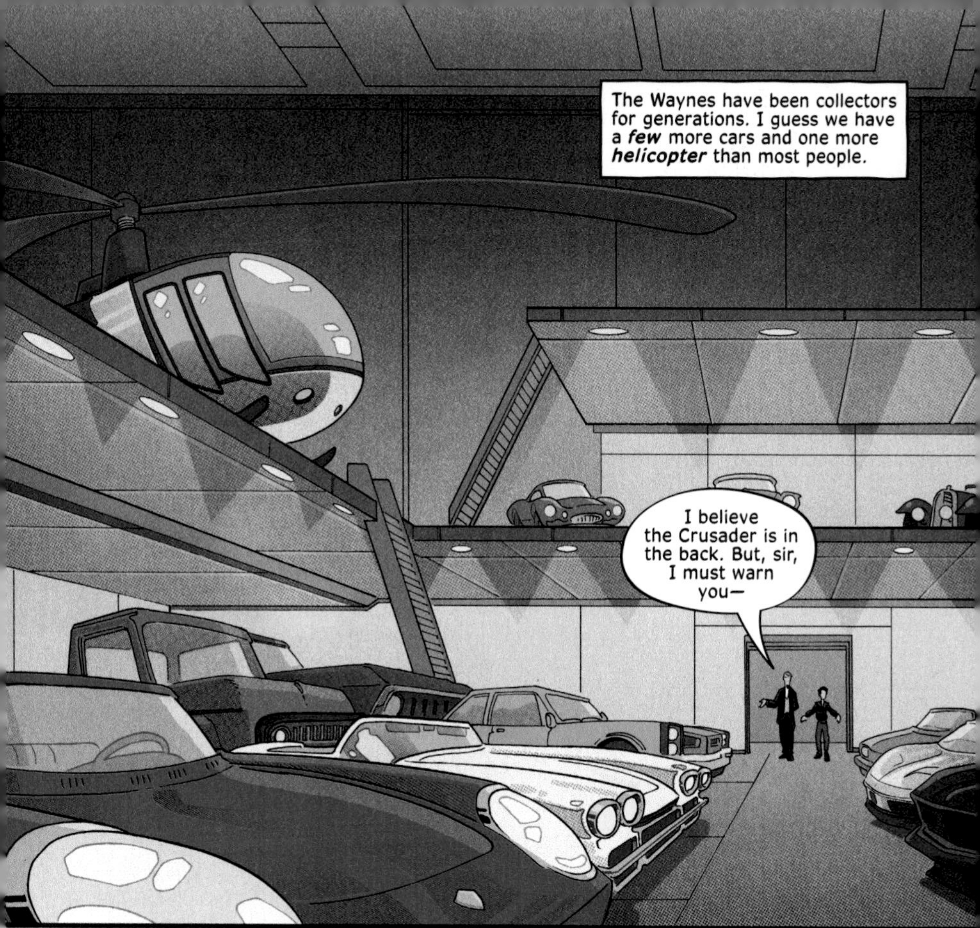
The Waynes have been collectors for generations. I guess we have a *few* more cars and one more *helicopter* than most people.
I believe the Crusader is in the back. But, sir, I must warn you—

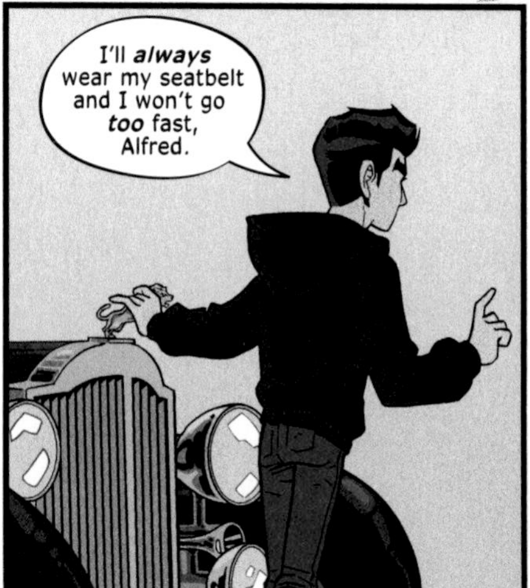
I'll *always* wear my seatbelt and I won't go *too* fast, Alfred.

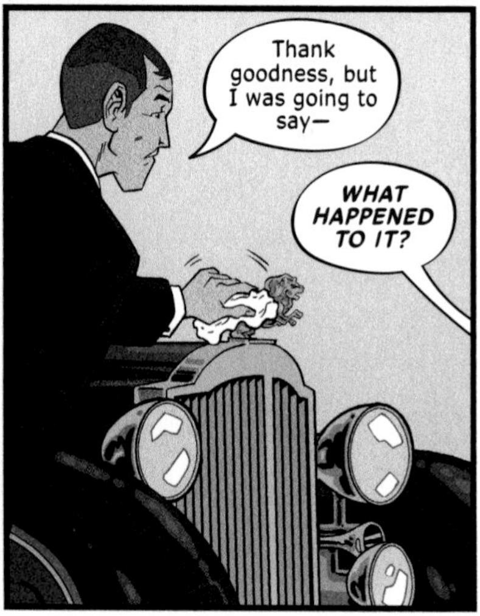
Thank goodness, but I was going to say—
WHAT HAPPENED TO IT?

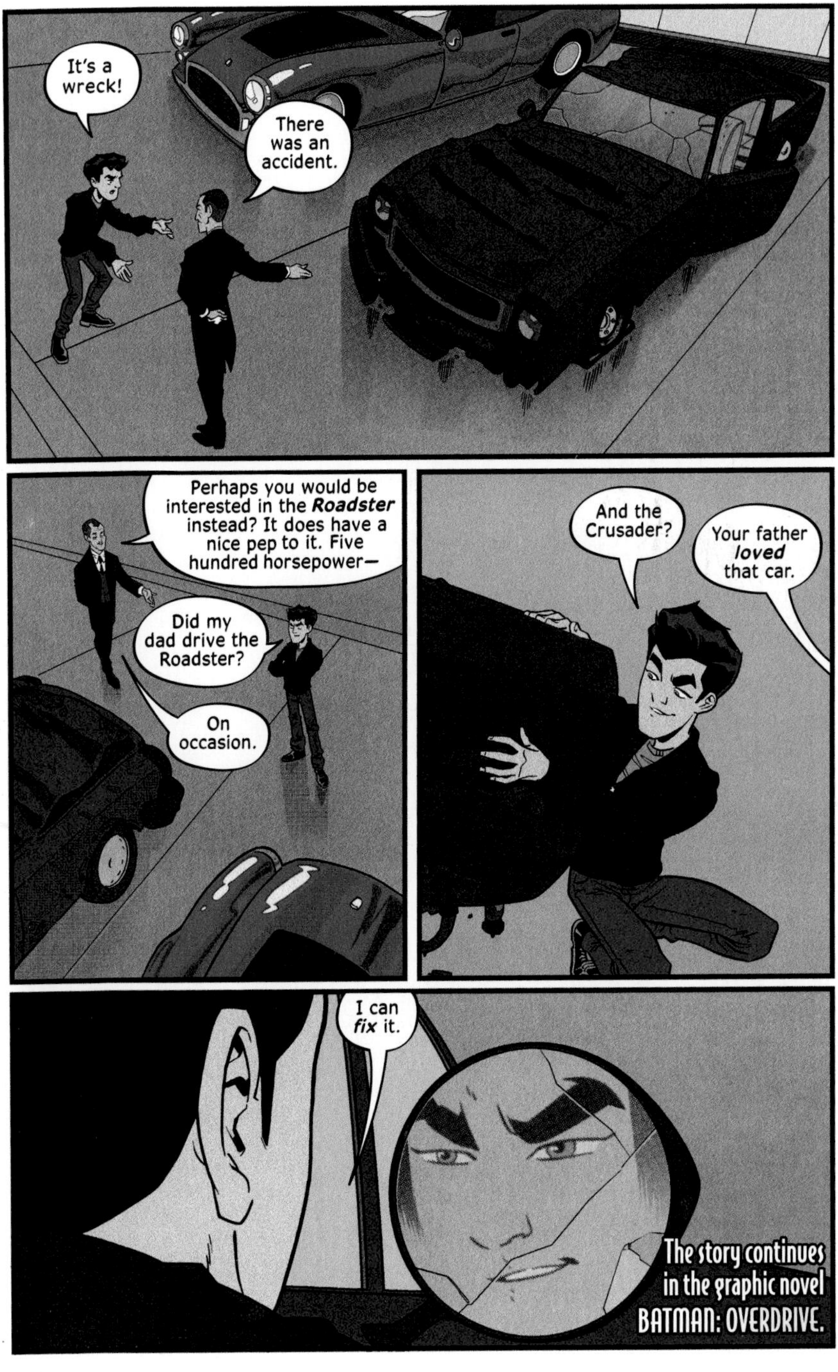
It's a wreck!
There was an accident.
Perhaps you would be interested in the *Roadster* instead? It does have a nice pep to it. Five hundred horsepower—
Did my dad drive the Roadster?
On occasion.
And the Crusader?
Your father *loved* that car.
I can *fix* it.
The story continues in the graphic novel BATMAN: OVERDRIVE.